BLOOD AND STEEL

JOHN STEEL BOOK 4

STUART FIELD

This book is for all the fantastic people who have supported me throughout this journey. To the people who have loved the series and have encouraged me to write more.

This is for you.

Thank you all.

ACKNOWLEDGMENTS

I would like to thank
My Amazing Wife, Ani, and my family and friends for their
constant support.
To my fantastic daughter, who always makes me proud.

CHAPTER ONE

High above the Manhattan skyline, dark clouds clustered. Flashes of light illuminated the blackened mass as the storm brewed. There was a low rumble followed by more eruptions of light within the angry-looking clouds. The wind howled through the city streets like a wraith hunting for its prey. The storm was nearly over, pushed on by the easterly wind. The downpour of rain had left its mark, leaving lakes on the streets and sidewalks. Despite the sparks of electricity in the clouds, there had been no lightning, just a fantastic light show. Bellow in the sodden streets, there was more flashes of light, but these were from a 9mm. The loud cracks were not from the storm, but the bark from the Sig Sauer.

"Stay away from me, you freak," cried a man as he released another volley of hollow points into the dark. Mario, "the Shark" Brunetti, was afraid – scared shitless, someone was hunting him. The man was a mobster, loan shark, a piece of shit who would sell his mother for a profit. He was a short man with a receding hairline and a round figure. Too much of a good life, too much good food from blood money had shaped him and made him slow, vulnerable. Once a man that put fear into people, but now, he was running scared – or rather limping. He'd taken a bullet to the leg; he'd been lucky, his men had been taken out one by one, shot from a distance. All headshots, even the ones that had used walls as cover, however, bricks are no match for a .50 BMG calibre bullet. The M2 Armoured Piercing round was possibly overkill, but the shooter didn't care, he only needed one of them alive – Brunetti. 706.7 grams of full metal death travelled the short distance quickly, and quietly. At 856 meters per second, the bricks were vaporised, and so were the men behind them. One of the men sought refuge behind a steel beam, but the bullet just passed through it like it was made from butter. The hunter had used an AS50 from Accuracy International with a smart sight with multi-imaging, which included thermal and suppressor – no noise, no flash from the barrel. The .50 calibre monster took out the men in a blink of an eye, ten rounds in just less than a minute. Brunetti had run. Smart move – pointless but smart. He had run to his car, only to find a hole in the engine block, and a bloody mess where the driver had been. Brunetti had run back inside the building. It was an old factory in the Bronx built in the twenties and left to rot for years, but he had bought it at a discount, a good place to do business. Brunetti pulled out his Sig Sauer 320XL custom and held it with his chubby fingers. A nice gun, polished steel with rubber combat grips. Fifteen in the mag, one in the pipe. Nice long barrel. Nice if you're a sports shooter or a guy looking for a gun to intimidate. The Desert Eagle used to be the favourite, but gangsters soon learned that more bullets were far better than a few big bangs. If you're in a firefight, you want more bullets. Magnums are good for intimidation – very good, in fact, but it means you must carry lots of heavy magazines. Brunetti was smart, possibly learned the lesson the hard way. Unfortunately, a nice gun is no match against what he knew was coming for him.

He had run inside the building, hoping the deeper he went, the less likely those damned bullets would be able to reach him. A good plan. Brunetti was smart, but the hunter was smarter. Brunetti ran towards the door of his office; he had a secure room there. Three inches of reinforced steel with lead lining, nothing was getting through, not even him. Brunetti smiled as the door came into view. Six more feet, and then he was safe. His eyes widened with eagerness as if willing the room to come to him. His gaze fell to a red LED light on the door. His eyes squinted as he approached. Was it a new alarm system his tech guy had fitted? Brunetti slid to a stop, dropping to the ground as he did so. As the red LED turned green, there was a rush of wind, followed by a blinding flash of light. Brunetti was lifted off the ground and hurled across the open space. A massive explosion rocked the building, but there was no fire, just the blast. Brunetti looked over at the gaping hole where his office had once been, now jus smouldering bricks and twisted metal. The air was thick with smoke and the smell of burnt wood and metal, making his eyes sting and water. Brunetti wiped the tears from his eyes with his sleeve and coughed. He felt the urge to stand, to run, to get the hell out of there. As he stood, he turned towards the way he had come. He looked back at the hole in the wall. Two options, both could mean his death, but for some reason he wasn't, the killer could have taken him out any time, yet he lived. Working on this, Brunetti smiled. The assassin needed him alive. Brunetti laughed and ran towards the hole, confident that the killer was too far away after all the shooter would have to be quicker than an Olympic runner to get from the nest to the other side of the building, no, Brunetti had the advantage. As he ran towards the gap, he froze, there stood a figure in a long coat, the light from a nearby streetlamp showed only the outline of the man, but Brunetti didn't need to see the man's face, he knew exactly who it was – John Steel.

"Brunetti, where is SANTINI?" Steel yelled. Brunetti skidded as he struggled to turn and run. There was a soft sound of metal against metal, followed by a scream from Brunetti. He looked down to see blood streaming from the outer side of his left leg. Brunetti turned and released a volley of rounds at the hole in the wall, only to find an empty space. Steel had gone. Brunetti's eyes darted from side to side, hoping to catch a glimpse of the phantom, but found only darkness. He scrambled to his feet and headed towards the main entrance.

"Where is SANTINI?" Steel yelled out once again. Brunetti released another volley before the clicking sound of an empty gun. Brunetti replaced the magazine with a fresh mag and clicked the bolt release catch on the side, forcing the top slide forward, loading a new round into the chamber.

"Stay away from me, and you freak," Brunetti yelled, firing blindly into the dark.

"I'll only ask one more time Brunetti, where are they?" Steel yelled, his voice echoing around the empty space of the abandoned building.

"Go to Hell, ya freak," Brunetti screamed, then fired off another volley. As he turned to run, he bumped into something. His blood ran cold as he dropped to the floor. He raised the weapon, but Steel grabbed it with a swift movement, ripping it out of the mobster's hand.

"I am in Hell thanks to you and your friends, now, where is SANTINI?" Steel growled. Brunetti looked at Steel. He was a big man, six-two compared to his five-six. Steel's handsome square-jawed face was masked by a pair of military-style sunglasses, which hugged his face like a mask, his black hair styled with a side parting. He was dressed all in black with a long black wool and leather trench coat. Brunetti looked down at Steel's leather military-style gloves with the plastic knuckle guards, but Brunetti's eyes were more fixed on his own gun that Steel was pointing down at his groin area.

"Talk, or you'll never need that vasectomy," Brunetti shook with fear as he noted the emotionless expression on Steel's face as he spoke. "Where are they, talk, or I'll take you one piece at a time, starting with the smallest," Steel said, shoving the 9mm into Brunetti's groan.

"If I tell, I'm dead," Brunetti screamed, waving his arms about. Steel smashed the gun against Brunetti's head to calm him.

"Well, if you don't, I'll keep you alive," Steel said with a deep growl. Brunetti held a puzzled look.

"Don't you mean you'll kill me?" Brunetti laughed, thinking Steel had it backwards.

"No, you'll be alive, but I will make sure that every scumbag in the city knows you like kids – little kids, make sure the word is spread that you couldn't talk enough about every mobster in the city. You'll want SANTINI to kill you, you'll want me to kill you, but I won't, I'll make sure you stay alive – until I get bored of saving your arse," Steel said holding up the gun and releasing the magazine, which fell to the concrete with a clatter of metal. Steel pulled back the top slide enough to make sure to check a round was chambered, then released the slide. "You have three options, one – you say nothing and your life becomes a living Hell, Two – you tell me what I want to know, you live and take your chances, or Three – you tell me, and I leave you with this quick way out?" Steel said, his face half in shadow, half in the light coming from a top window.

"I don't see no incentive, either way, I'm dead," Brunetti moaned, holding his bloody leg.

"You have a choice, more than my family was given, more

than you gave them," Steel said, this time the anger was starting to show.

"But I had nothing to –,"

"You told SANTINI that my family was having a party that day, you told them who was responsible for the raid on the warehouse and who was hunting them, you even provided the weapons used, so do not tell me you had nothing to do with it," Steel screamed and ripped Brunetti from the floor as though he was a rag doll. Brunetti gasped at the display of power. "I grow weary of your excuses, and I'll give you one more chance to answer, use it wisely." Brunetti stared into those damned sunglasses and his scared reflection. The question wasn't whether he was going to live or die; it was how he was going to die, horribly, or by his own hand? Steel had given him that choice, SANTINI wouldn't.

"What do you want to know?" Brunetti sighed, his body going limp, the fight, and fear had drained out of him. Steel smiled and placed the man onto the floor.

"You help me – I'll help you," Steel said, dragging Brunetti out of the hole in the wall and to a waiting vehicle. As the blacked-out Yukon drove off, the old factory was ripped to pieces by several explosions, leaving nothing but rubble.

———

Several miles away, deep under the city, in the depths of the Manhattan subway, Tara Burke looked out of the subway trains window. Raindrops had pooled onto the rubber corners of the safety glass, droplets of water rolled together like globules of mercury. They had collected from when the train had gone above ground. Her thoughts were a million miles away. Dreams of a different life, a better life. The cold glass felt good against her warm skin. The first time she had felt cool all day. The diner where she worked had been busy from breakfast up to the end of her shift. *Thank God for nine o'clock,* she had thought as she clocked out. The nights were getting warmer, but the season was bringing the rain. Sometimes she hated spring, sure it was getting darker later, and if she never saw another snowflake, it wouldn't be too soon, but the nights were still cold. Tara had one of those 'girl next door' pretty faces, which was framed with shorter hair. Weeks before it had hung along the length of her back, but she needed a change. Now her red locks hung on her shoulders. *New spring, new you,* she had promised herself the year before. A New York summer is not the best time to have long hair, especially if you work in a Diner.

She looked at her reflection in the nearby window. A sad face stared back at her from the black background of the unlit subway line. Tara stared into her large blue eyes, noting the sadness within them. That was going to change. She had plans that would make her dreams come true. Tara took a deep sigh as she thought about her life. She had just celebrated her twenty-fifth birthday and had nothing to show for her life. She had been nowhere, nor had she done anything special. Straight after school, she had gotten that stupid job in the Diner just so she could live. Her mother had skipped out as soon as she could, leaving Tara with the two-bedroomed apartment while she disappeared to God knows where not that Tara cared.

Good riddance, Tara thought as she remembered reading the note telling her she was on her own. That was the only thing her mother had ever given her apart from the beatings. Now, she was on her own, apart from the new roommate, who was only there to help pay the rent.

The screech from the train's brakes signalled that they were approaching the station on 50th Street. Tara took her face away from the glass. She felt the tingle in her cheek as the skin began to warm up. As the train came to a stop, the doors opened with a hiss from the hydraulics. She stood up and headed out into the chill of the night. It was almost quarter to ten at night as she reached Main Street. The walk home would take her five minutes—she knew this for certain after walking it for so many years. Down West 50th, then onto Ninth Avenue until she got to 48th Street. Tara took out her cell phone and checked her messages. She had forgotten about the vibration the phone had given off on the train. But then, late at night is not the time to pull out your cell phone on the subway.

Where the hell are you, we must talk...

She stared at the message for a moment, and her blood froze at the tone. Something was wrong. Tara put the phone back into her pocket and walked home. Her pace had quickened. Her heels tapped the concrete. The sound echoed through the streets like tiny horses' hooves on cobbled roads. The night appeared darker than usual, even though there were plenty of street lamps and lights from the houses as families stayed up to watch television, but it was a different dark. A fearful darkness that no one could see unless you were terrified by it.

To her left, there was a dark spot, a gap in the light, Clinton Community Garden, a nice place in the day, but it was bathed in darkness. She shivered again, and her imagination began to run away with her as she began to see and hear things, she was sure weren't there, or hoped. Tara looked at her watch. The digital display read twenty-one-forty.

She had worked overtime to help pay the rent until her new roommate moved in properly. Tara smiled as she thought about the fresh-faced girl who had answered agreed to move in. An old friend who needed digs, she had a good job so money wouldn't be a problem. The friend was a pretty woman in her late twenties, but hey, who was Tara to judge why a woman like that was single? All Tara knew was she had been in a bad relationship but was now single...of sorts. Tara turned on to her road; the apartment wasn't much further. A cold breeze met her as she started down the final stretch, making her shiver as though someone had just danced over her grave. She had that feeling again.

Something was wrong.

Tara walked up to the door at the front of the building. Stopping, she looked around to see if there was anyone lurking in the shadows. She shook her head as if to shake the silly idea from her mind; she was letting a simple text spook her. It was probably nothing. She smiled at her foolishness. The bad thing about texts is they don't convey emotion unless you want to lighten the tone, and you put the standard *LOL* at the end. Tara took out the phone again and re-read the text.

Where the hell are you, we must talk...

She had to admit that at first, it had looked bad, but then she looked at it again. She had pulled a double shift and not told him, plus he could get a little jealous what with her flirting for tips and all. Once, she had gotten a twenty for giving some guy a peck on the cheek because it was his birthday. A little harmless fun, she thought, plus it paid the bills. Tara smiled as she walked up the stairs to her apartment on the fourth floor, her *exercise for the day* as she called it. The sound of televisions filled the tight corridors, some people watching games shows, others watching police dramas. Music blared through the thin flooring above. There was a baby's cry from number 4.

She stopped outside number 42 and slipped the key into the lock. Tara pushed the door open and stepped inside the dimly lit room. An orange glow from the streetlights outside broke up the blackness. All she wanted now was her bed after a long day. Tara listened to the couple next door: loud moans of

9

passion came through as if there was no wall between them at all. She smiled as she shook her head and shut the door behind her. A scream filled the building—a scream like no other. Then there was only the sound of the neighbours' televisions filling the corridors once more.

CHAPTER TWO

DETECTIVE JOSHUA TOOMS WAS WOKEN BY THE SOUND OF banging. He sat up quickly and listened more carefully, just in case it was coming from inside the building. His wife was about to speak, but he raised his finger to his lips as a signal for silence. At first, he thought the banging was from a neighbour's house, reasoning that the noise had travelled through the open bedroom window. He listened harder. The hammering was coming from downstairs. Someone was at his front door. His wife Barbara held on to his muscular arm for comfort. He patted her hand for reassurance. Tooms looked over at his clock: the display was blank, signifying a lack of power. Had someone cut the power to his house? Tooms rolled out of bed and stretched off his muscles, unwittingly showing off his large frame. Even though he was in his late forties, he was still in good shape. Years in the Marines had taught him to look after himself.

"Don't worry, it will be OK," he told his wife. "Just lock the door behind me and get ready to call 911."

Barbara nodded and watched as he turned to his bedside

drawer and pulled out his service 9mm Glock 17 pistol. He didn't need to check it; he always had a full magazine of fifteen rounds and one in the chamber. The bullets were called *critical duty*—quite appropriate, he always thought. The 135-grain bullets were meant to put someone down, not just tickle them. He never turned as he heard the door close behind him; he just stopped and listened for the lock to be put on. Moving to the staircase, he saw his two daughters holding each other in fear as they looked down the stairwell, almost hypnotised by the banging. They looked up to see their father, who was now padding towards their rooms. Quickly they hurried away and locked themselves in, tears of fear running down their faces.

The downstairs was bathed in a vale of blue. Streams of moonlight flooded through the sitting-room window like the sun on a summer's day. Tooms was thankful for the illumination, realising he'd left the flashlight in his car. He stood there in his sleeping shorts, the moonlight glistening off his large muscular form, making him look almost like a black gladiator. The banging became more violent, but there were no voices to let him know who was there. Cautiously he headed for the door, the Glock raised up in his right hand, leaving his left free. Again, the person hammered on the door, always in blocks of three knocks interrupted by a brief pause. He put his back against the wall next to the door, then breathed in a lungful of air to steady his heart rate.

"Who the fuck is there?" he yelled, expecting the door to be shredded by gunfire. "I'm warnin your ass. I'm a cop. I'm armed, and I'm pissed, so you better answer up or get the fuck away from my house," Tooms's voice bellowed like a brown bear that had gargled a shot of whiskey.

"Tooms, it's Tony. Open the door, man!" came a voice from the other side of the door. Tooms opened the door to reveal a white guy with short brown hair, wearing jeans, and a black three-quarter-length leather jacket.

"Tony, what the fuck, man? Why didn't you call first? I could have shot your ass," Tooms said, exhaling the air he had been holding. Tony walked in through the open door and saw the three women coming down the stairs to see who was making all the noise.

"I tried calling, but some idiot who was higher than Armstrong ran into a transformer. Looks like the whole block has lost power. It must have affected the cell tower as well as the power lines, which means no phones," Tony explained. He looked past Tooms's large frame and, giving an embarrassed smile, waved at the now angry women who stood at the bottom of the stairs. Tooms reached over and tried the light switch near the door. He had tried the switch several times, to the point of not knowing whether it was in the on or off mode. The *clicks* filled the air, but no lights broke the darkness.

"You've come to check on me, man, now that's touching, bro, you know I can take care of myself?" Tooms joked as he shut the door, and Tony made his way into the sitting room.

"Yeah, you got Barbara to hold ya hand, just in case it's too dark," Tony laughed. Suddenly the television and the lights came on, making them all jump. Tooms and Tony laughed at their cowardly display in front of the women.

"So, what you doin' here, at...?" Tooms remembered that he didn't know what time it was.

"Eleven o'clock. Sorry, man, but we picked up a fresh one," Tony apologised. The two detectives were on call. The one thing Tooms hated about the job was that most people died at night or early in the morning. A social job this was not; however, compared to the army, it was a dream occupation. Being shipped off to God-knows-where at the drop of a hat wasn't great for family life either. Joshua Tooms left Tony to make some coffee while he showered and got dressed. The girls had gone back to bed after saying their goodnights, leaving Barbara Tooms to look after their unexpected guest. Tony looked around the house, feeling a touch of jealousy. Tooms had the package: a great family and a nice house in a nice part of town.

"So, Tony, what you been you to?" she asked with a warm but weary smile. "Apart from dragging my husband out of bed in the middle of the night."

"Not much, I am sort of seeing someone now ... Sort of," Tony replied nervously. He knew she would be firing a million questions at him, just because of that gossipy interest she had. He saw her eyes light up at the thought of meeting his girlfriend, and Tony could tell that she was planning a cosy dinner party to engineer it.

"So, what's her name? Where does she work?" Barbara was suddenly awake as if she had had too much coffee.

Tony looked up thankfully at the staircase as Tooms came down the stairs, pulling his jacket on as he walked. It hadn't taken him long, five minutes tops, but then he had had a lot of practice. Tooms crossed the room and gave his wife a kiss before heading for the door.

"OK, partner, you're drivin'." Tooms smiled as he opened the front door, and the two men stepped through into the fresh night air. Tooms looked around. He hadn't even noticed it had been raining. Tony had parked in the driveway next to Tooms's blue Honda Odyssey. As they got into Tony's red Challenger, Tooms smiled as he looked over towards his house. It wasn't a mansion or anything. It was comprised of just three bedrooms with a bit of a garden to make barbecues in the summer, plus a front porch where he could sit outside and watch the world go by, but most of all, it was home.

His parents had left it to them when they moved away.

They had won on the lottery and decided to get that house in the Hamptons that they had seen once on holiday. It hadn't been' a big win, but it was enough for a couple of pensioners to live on.

"So, where we off to?" Tooms asked, taking a sip from his travel mug.

"Midtown, we got a woman found dead in her apartment." Tony stuck the car in reverse and powered out of the driveway. Tooms blew down the small hole in the mug's lid to cool down the coffee a little. His face held a saddened look, and he realised that this was going to be a long night.

CHAPTER THREE

THE TRIP TO THE CRIME SCENE WAS MORE LIKE AN interrogation. Tony had regretted telling Barbara Tooms anything about his new girlfriend because he knew that even if she couldn't ask the questions, Joshua would. Tony loved her like a sister, but she was too much into the 'need to know' group. She was a gossip, and her husband were worse because he fuelled her addiction. Tooms checked a message on his phone. It was from Barbara, Tooms smiled before replying to the message and tucked his phone away into his pocket. Tony felt nervous as Tooms adjusted his seating position to face his partner.

"So, who is she, and where did you meet?" Tooms asked as they passed another coffee shop.

"You're kiddin' me, right? Can't it wait until after we have solved the case?" Tony asked, knowing full well that Tooms would be badgered with the same questions when he got home. Tooms just shrugged and gave a little noise of disapproval.

"What?" Tony asked in response to the little 'Huh' that his partner let out. He knew what it meant—his mother did it every time she wanted to show her disapproval of a choice he had made—normally a girl he was dating.

"Nothing," Joshua Tooms replied. "Just you never mentioned her before, that's all. We have been partners for how long? And you keep this from me, man, I thought I knew you?" Tooms looked away in a childish manner as if turning his back on Tony.

"Barbara's gonna nag the shit outa ya if you don't bring back some gossip, ain't she?" Tony said, realising the real pain his friend was going through.

"You got that right. And it's all on you, brother, it's all on you," laughed Tooms, after he gave up trying to keep a serious face. Tony parked as close as he could to the building. Black-and-whites cordoned off the area, as well as the police barriers that were blocking off the building to people who just wanted to get a view of the crime scene. Tooms and Tony approached the building and showed their shields to one of the uniforms at the cordon. Even though it was late, 'rubberneckers' had gathered there, eager to feed their morbid fascination.

Inside the building, the two detectives spoke to another uniformed officer, who directed them upstairs to the fourth floor. To their dismay, they had to take the stairs as the elevator was in use, with the CSU – or Crime Scene Unit offloading in their equipment. The stairwell was only just wide enough for two. The walls were painted a sickly yellow, probably to hide the dirt, so that the owner didn't have to clean them too often. However, in general, the building was clean, with no apparent cracks or peeling wallpaper. This was a 'cheap rent' place, but the landlord had some sense of pride about his property, that much was obvious.

"So, this girl of yours, where did you meet?" Tooms smiled as Tony shot him a look.

"Seriously? We're on the way to a crime scene, and you're

bringing this up now?" Tony asked, even though he wasn't surprised. Tooms shrugged and smiled as they reached the first floor.

"We met at a flower store, OK?" Tony said, feeling he had to give his inquisitive friend some information or the trip to the fourth floor would be unbearable. Tooms stopped and turned, placing a hand on Tony's chest to halt him.

"Wait a minute," the Tooms asked him. "you pick up a chick while you were getting flowers for another girl?" Tooms shook his head in disappointment. "That's ... cold, man. I don't know whether to be proud or disgusted, man, No wonder you're single!" Tooms turned and started towards the stairwell. Despite his words, he was impressed, but he didn't want to let Tony know.

"The flowers were.... for my mother. It was her birthday." Tony felt almost embarrassed to admit how it had happened. The sound of Tooms's laughter echoed up to the second floor.

"OK," Tooms stopped, his face cringed with disappointment. "I preferred to be disgusted and proud, now I just feel.... never mind," Tooms said, shaking his head as he walked, all manner of being impressed had crumbed.

"So, where does she live? What does she do?" Tooms grilled Tony once more.

"She has just moved actually. Moved in with an old college friend, she said. Better on the bills as her other roommate bailed on her," Tony explained. Tooms shook his head, for he could understand that kind of situation. It had happened to him once or twice before he joined the service. As they rounded the corner of the fourth floor, Tooms and Tony saw the circus getting ready. CSU were putting on their coveralls and opening aluminium cases that had their gear neatly packed inside. A young blonde CSU woman was getting her camera gear ready and attaching the special lens lamp onto the Canon 1d. As far as they could see, each member of the team of six had a task: fingerprint lifting, fibre collection, or laying evidence markers.

Tooms led the way into the room, which was empty apart from the ME (Medical Examiner), Tina Franks. The dark-skinned woman was crouched over the body, blocking the two detectives' view.

"What we got, Doc?" Tooms greeted her as he pulled on his surgical gloves.

"White female in her late twenties, I would say," Tina said as if she was reading off a menu. "Cause of death undetermined as she has multiple injuries." The police's medical examiner wasn't being callous or unfeeling, and she was simply being focused on the job.

"Do we have a name?" Tooms asked as Tony walked around the ME to look at the body. Something about the corpse looked horribly familiar to him. He thought he recognised her clothes and the small silver pendant necklace that had a small dragon on it.

"Her name was Amber ... Amber Taylor," Tony announced, deathly calm. Both Tooms and Tina looked up at their pale-looking colleague. Tooms's stomach turned over as he had a horrible feeling.

"Don't tell me that she was—," Tooms began hesitantly.

"—My girlfriend. Yes, she," Tony's voice was a choking whisper, "was."

Joshua grabbed Tony by the arm and walked him out. Tony's face betrayed a jumble of confused emotions. Should he cry? Yell? Break something?

"Make a hole!" Tooms yelled, forcing people out of the way with his roar. Uniforms and techs parted like the red sea, allowing the two detectives through. They headed for the elevator, and Tooms barged past a couple of techs who were waiting to go in.

"Get the next one," Tooms ordered the two shocked men, letting the doors close in front of them.

Outside, the cold wind stung the two friends like a swarm of wasps. It was cold enough to see the smoky breath of passers-by. Tony was uneasy on his feet, his legs unable to support him. But his powerful partner held him long enough for them to make it to the wall next door. Suddenly Tony vomited in the bushes next to the building. Tooms stood watch over his partner as he hung onto the wall and screamed out in emotional pain. Tooms's massive hand hovered above his partner's back, ready to give him a sympathetic pat, but somehow it felt not so much wrong as not enough.

"No point tellin' you to go home, because I know you won't," Tooms said. "So, get your ass to the precinct, man. I will fill you in there." Tooms rested a gentle hand on his partner's shoulder. Tony stood up. His pain had turned to anger, and it showed in his eyes. Tooms looked over towards the crime scene as Tony sat down on the doorstep of the adjacent building. Joshua pulled out his cell phone.

"Yeah, McCall? It's Joshua. We got a bad situation here."

———

It only took fifteen minutes for McCall to turn up. Her arrival was signalled by the roar of her GT 500 Mustang. Tooms looked over from his spot next to Tony on the neighbour's front step. He stood up and looked down at his partner.

"Back in a bit, man," he told him. Tony, unable to talk, just nodded in response. Tooms smiled and walked over to the beast of a car. The motor purred as she let the engine idle before switching it off. Detective Samantha McCall swung her long legs out of her car and stood up, showing her catwalk model height. Her gaze was on Tony as she slipped on her black leather jacket.

"Hey, Joshua, how's he doing?" she asked as the large black cop approached her.

"Pretty much as you would expect," Tooms replied as they hugged as if they were close relatives. They made their way towards Tony, who was staring down at the pavement while his thoughts were elsewhere. The sound of the clacking heels of Sam's high leather boots caused him to look up at them. Samantha McCall gave him a comforting smile, then moved closer. She had shoulder-length brown hair and had an athletic form that was currently hidden beneath a pair of jeans that hugged her perfect behind and a black baggy T-shirt under a black leather jacket. In another life, she should have been walking catwalks or photoshoots in faraway places, but her father's death by gunshot had made a model's life impossible for her. Indeed, McCall had the looks and the body of a supermodel, but she also had the brains and the instincts of a first-rate cop, something she had always wanted to be after coming from a long line of police officers, detectives, and one lawyer. Detective Samantha McCall walked up to Tony and gave him a hug. She knew what he was going through, and if anyone did, it was her.

"Where's Steel?" Tooms asked, looking around and paying attention to the rooftops. "I figured he would have come with you?"

"Who knows?" She shrugged as she spoke. McCall didn't really care about Steel's whereabouts; she was too preoccupied with Tony's pain.

"You OK, partner?" Tooms asked as he watched Tony nod, then shrug with mixed emotion. He knew the answer, but he just wanted to hear it from him.

"No, not really. I just saw my girlfriend dead on the floor

with bits cut out of her," Tony growled. He wasn't mad at Tooms. He was angry at whoever was responsible for the killing.

"You know the captain ain't gonna let you work this?" Tooms told him. "In fact, he probably won't let me be on the team either." Tony looked up at Tooms, confused.

"I am your partner, man," Tooms explained. "He ain't gonna let us work this." Tony knew he was right, but he wanted blood.

"I'll talk to the captain and make sure Steel, and I get the case," Sam said. Tony looked up and gave her a smile of gratitude. Sam simply nodded with that same sympathetic smile.

"Head back to the precinct and start digging up what you can about her," McCall ordered. Tony was confused.

"I thought we weren't on the case?" Tony stood up. He suddenly looked different, less angry, and more driven.

"You're not on the case, Tony, but you are the only one who knew her. For that reason, we are using you as our best source of information until someone better comes along. Is that a problem, Detective?" she asked in a stern voice. But Tony saw through her plan to keep him in the loop, despite the regulations.

"No, ma'am," Tony replied, trying to keep a straight face. However, the quick lift of the corner of his mouth gave him away. As Tooms and Tony headed back to their blue Challenger, McCall looked up at the building, towards the fourth floor. She took a deep breath to get herself in the right frame of mind.

———

McCall had ended up taking the elevator, having rejected the prospect of the long walk up the stairs. She felt a little lazy for doing so, but then it was far too early for a Stairmaster workout —besides, she hadn't had her coffee yet. The steel box elevator was small, and she wondered how the designated 'twenty people allowed' was even possible.

With a shudder and an alarming flicker from the lights, the elevator stopped on the fourth floor. The doors slid open to reveal the crime scene technicians getting to work on evidence collection. McCall could see through the open door her friend Tina, kneeling over the body, taking the liver temperature of the young woman.

As she approached, McCall tried to repress a sudden expression of disgust at the way the woman had been brutalised. Amber Taylor had been tall with long brown hair. Her blue eyes were open, and still registered the terror she must have felt. The rest of her face had been badly cut, and the jaw was broken. If she had once been a pretty woman, someone had clearly gone out of their way to hide it.

"Hey, Tina," McCall greeted the ME as she walked round to the side of her friend.

"Are we sure it's her?" McCall asked, almost daring to hope there might have been a mistake.

"Tony identified the clothing," Tina replied. "They had met up that morning, and she had worn the same outfit then, in fact, poor Tony showed me a photograph he had taken on his cell." Tina picked up a small evidence bag, inside which was a necklace. "The photograph also shows that this was around her neck." The doctor pointed to a purse next to a large beige handbag, which lay on the breakfast bar. McCall picked up the purse and found Amber's ID inside.

"I will still run tests, but I think we've got enough for an identification for the time being." Tina sounded as sad as she looked. McCall nodded as she placed the purse back onto the breakfast bar.

"Hey. How's our boy doin'?" Tina still couldn't forget the look on Tony's face when he had identified her.

"Too soon to tell, I guess," Sam said as she pulled on her surgical gloves. "I sent him back to the precinct to do a check on our vic."

"Are you sure that's the right thing to do? Why not send him home?" Tina's question made McCall give her one of those 'really' looks.

"If I send him home, then he goes stir crazy and does God knows what. Besides, you're a fine one to talk, lady. Did you stay at home after that trouble in the morgue?" Tina shot McCall a guilty look, knowing that her friend was right.

"So, what killed her?" Sam asked, taking out her small notebook to note down any facts the ME had.

"Well, I don't know for sure until I get her back to the office, but I'd say she was tortured. Possibly for hours," Tina said, jotting down another point on her report form.

McCall took a small camera from her jacket pocket and started to take her own photographs. This was something she had learnt some time ago, and it made sense because she didn't have time to wait for the CSU to produce their shots. Besides, she figured that she might pick up on something that they missed.

"By the look of things, they started at the feet and worked up. Some of the injuries I won't find till later, but others are obvious." Tina pointed to a hole in Amber's upper leg. "Someone took a corkscrew to this poor woman's femur. By the look of things, it went in deep." Tina pointed to the metal corkscrew that lay next to the body.

"They removed the skin from her fingers using a potato peeler. Sammy, I tell you we are lookin' for one sick individual."

As Tina finished her sentence, she could see the look of horror in McCall's face.

"Could it be him – could he back?" McCall mumbled. A shiver ran down Tina's spine as she realised who McCall was talking about, a sadistic killer they had all encountered almost a year ago, a man who now called himself Mr Williams.

"But he has been gone for over a year now. In fact, I thought he was dead," Tina said, standing up. The two women looked at each other, terror in their eyes. A sudden noise from above made the pair jump, breaking McCall from her trance of concentration. Someone was in the room above. McCall turned to one of the two uniforms who were guarding the door.

"Officer!" she yelled to get their attention. The young cop immediately turned to face her.

"Yes, Detective?" he answered, but he did not enter the room for fear of contamination of the crime scene.

"Has anyone spoken to the neighbour's upstairs?" Sam asked as she looked up at the sound of heavy footsteps on the flooring above.

"I don't know, but I will find out," the cop replied and was about to head off to check.

"Never mind." She raised a hand to signal for him to stop before he disappeared to find someone.

"Go upstairs and talk to whoever is above us. They may have heard something. If they say they didn't, ask again, because we can hear everything that's happening up there," Sam said with a smile. The officer nodded then rushed away to go and find out what he could.

McCall turned back around to face her friend. Dr Tina Franks was busy watching two men in blue overalls with the words 'Coroner's Office' on the back in white lettering. The men were carefully placing the body into a black plastic body bag ready for transport back to the morgue.

Tina looked up and met McCall's gaze, which reflected her own look of concern. Previously they had known a man, an evil man, who had killed three women in the most horrible way. Now their thoughts went back to that person and hoped it was him because it was terrifying to think that there could be another who was as depraved as he was.

"So, where's your shadow?" Tina asked, looking around for the tall detective. McCall shrugged as if it was no big deal he wasn't there.

"He's probably off saving the world or something," McCall's words were uncaring. She had work to do, and he knew the address and the circumstances. She figured that if he wanted to be there, he would be.

But he wasn't.

The sound of the uniformed officer knocking on the door's frame caused both McCall and Tina to turn to face him.

"Detective, the couple above said they didn't hear anything until around ten o'clock. That's when they heard a woman scream." The officer almost sounded apologetic that he didn't have more. McCall smiled and thanked him before turning to Tina.

"That doesn't make sense," Tina said, shaking her head. "There was no way that she could have endured that much pain and not screamed out."

Sam had to agree. Amber must have wanted to scream out, if only as a way of attracting the attention of neighbours.

"Where's the roommate?" asked a voice that came from behind the young officer. McCall tried to hide her smile at the sight of the uniform, who had nearly leapt out of his skin at the sudden appearance of the man behind him. Detective Steel was standing close enough to the man to be his shadow.

"Where have you been, Steel? I texted you ages ago." McCall's words sounded hurt and angry.

"I met Tony and Tooms on the way. I was making sure Tony was OK." His British accent had a calm and gentle tone. The officer turned to face the tall detective; whose unorthodox appearance had made him nearly soil himself. At six foot two, Steel was taller than the officer by about two inches. Enough to make the young cop rethink the scornful look he was about to give him. Steel wore a black suit with a high-collared black shirt. Black Bugatti boots shone from being highly polished, but the uniformed cop only noticed two things: the strange leather-and-wool trench coat that stretched from Steel's broad shoulders to his calves, and the sunglasses. It was eleven at night, and he was wearing sunglasses!

"Good evening, doctor. Always a pleasure to see you, despite the circumstances in which we have to meet." Steel's words sang with an innocent flirtation, which made the attractive ME blush. Steel watched as one of the orderlies closed the body bag. He noticed the victim's face had been pretty before someone had gone to work on her. He wondered how Tony could have been so sure of her identity after such injuries. As the zipper closed, there was a silence from everyone, as if they had all lost a friend. In a way, they had, for she had been Tony's girlfriend, which made her family. Steel headed towards McCall, who was still taking photographs of everything she felt was important.

"Any idea where the roommate is?" he asked.

McCall stopped shooting and shook her head.

"We don't even know who she is or what she looks like. And in case you hadn't noticed, this place isn't exactly bustling with photographs," McCall said, waving a gloved hand around the room, pointing out the unusual lack of pictures of anything on the walls. "No pictures of boyfriends, family, or even of a pet. Nothing."

"Maybe she's camera shy?" Steel joked as he looked around

the room, then headed for a stack of boxes that sat neatly in the middle of the floor near the breakfast bar. The boxes were full of Amber's stuff. Each one was neatly labelled, showing its contents like an inventory list. Steel found it strange that there were only around seven large boxes but then figured that the rest were in storage or en route.

"She had just moved in by the look of things," Steel pointed out.

McCall nodded, but he figured that she had already noticed that.

"Surely the building super should know what her name is, a neighbour even?" Steel said, shocked that there was nothing to show there was a roommate apart from a bedroom full of clothes and some personal items.

"We will speak to the super in the morning. Unfortunately, he picked tonight to see his kid in New Jersey," McCall added. "We called him, but he doesn't have a car, but he'll be on the first train tomorrow." Steel shot McCall a strange look, which she disregarded, turning away from him.

It was too late at night for stupid conspiracy theories.

"Do we suspect the invisible friend to be part of this?" Steel asked as he continued to browse through the boxes. McCall shrugged at Steel's question.

"Who knows? But you can be sure I will ask her as soon as we find her." Her voice was angry, but the fury was not directed at Steel. She was angry that one of their own had been hurt. Tony had not been physically hurt but emotionally harmed.

Tina Franks picked up the metal suitcase, which contained her examination kit, and turned to the two detectives.

"I am heading back to get her ready for the autopsy," she told the pair of detectives. "If you want to be there, I will be starting around eight o'clock."

McCall shook her head, although she was pleased to be invited.

"No, it's fine, you can just let us know when you're done," McCall replied.

"Sure. It looks like your vic died between eight and ten o'clock, but I will have more for you once I get her back to the lab," Tina said, pulling off her blue surgical gloves.

McCall nodded. Tina waited for the orderlies to finish strapping the body onto the medical gurney then followed them out. Samantha McCall looked back around the room, hoping to get some sort of clue as to why the girl had been tortured. The room was still immaculate. She could have understood if the apartment had been trashed, indicating a frenzied uncontrolled attack.

But everything looked as if nothing unusual had happened there.

CHAPTER FOUR

BACK AT THE IITH PRECINCT, A DISTRAUGHT DETECTIVE Tony Marinelli sat in the quiet of one of the briefing rooms. The room was long—around twelve feet by ten—with a large window at the back, the walls were painted a putrid yellow, possibly to cover the day-to-day stains. In the centre was a large wooden table, which could comfortably accommodate twelve people sitting around it whilst being briefed on a case. Surrounding the heavy looking table sat twelve blue plastic chairs, six on each side. A large corkboard stretched the breadth of the short right-hand wall. This was placed to allow a perfect view for the twelve seated around the table so that visual exhibits could accompany the verbal briefings.

Tooms walked in, holding two coffee mugs. Using his heel, he closes the door behind him before handing over the mug of fresh coffee to Tony. The two men had been through a lot in the seven years they had worked homicide together. But nothing like this had happened before. Tooms looked at his partner as he struggled to make a list of anything which may help the investigation. He was listing everything he knew about his girlfriend – their murder victim. Where she worked, where she used to live. Family, her other friends. Her life was suddenly under a microscope, and he didn't like it, because now, so was his.

"You sure you want to do this now, man?" Tooms asked. "It's OK if you want a bit of time first?"

Tony gave Tooms a scowl, but Tooms knew it wasn't for him. Tony was hurting, and nothing mattered to him more than catching the bastard who did this.

Tony's expression changed suddenly as he realised his partner's meaning.

"Sorry, man, I know you didn't mean it like that. It's just—"

"—Hey, I get it, man. Don't worry. We are gonna get whoever did this," Tooms interrupted.

At that moment, Tony's words were as broken as his soul was. As far as he was concerned, no one knew what he was feeling.

No one could.

"So, where did she work?" Tooms asked, sitting in the chair across from Tony.

Tony tapped his pen onto the A4 legal pad. He had written as much as he could before realising; he didn't know that much about her. They had been together for a long time, but the fact was that he was privy to very few of the details of her life. The sound of Tooms clearing his throat made Tony look up from what he was doing. Tony tossed the pen down and sat back in the chair. He smiled at his partner, who waited patiently for an answer.

"Sorry, man, I was miles away." Tony laughed.

Tooms smiled and placed down his coffee mug onto the scratched surface of the table.

"I was just wondering where she worked. It might be an idea to go there tomorrow ..." Tooms looked at his watch to check which side of midnight it was. "Better make that later today," Tooms corrected himself. Tony blew onto the hot coffee before taking a small sip. The smell of freshly brewed coffee wafted up to his sinuses. It was good coffee.

"She worked at some large shipping firm." Tony smiled and shook his head. "Which I found funny because it turns out they're just a delivery company. Sure, they use ships, but they haul the goods mainly by truck."

Tooms was glad to see his partner smile. He had gone through something no cop should have to go through losing a loved one. Joshua noticed the name of the firm on the yellow legal pad in front of Tony: 'Trent Shipping' stood out on the paper. It was written in big, bold letters and circled. The list also contained several names. Tooms wondered if they were the names of her family and friends.

"Did she talk about her family?" Tooms asked, almost hoping there was a family member so that Tony didn't have to grieve alone. "her parents, brothers or sisters?"

Tony nodded and pointed to a name that Tooms couldn't quite decipher properly.

"Her name is Brooke, Brooke Taylor. She lives in Washington." Tony's gaze drifted into nowhere. Tooms figured he was remembering some happy day shared with his girlfriend, and he wasn't contemplating the crime scene. A quick smile from the corner of Tony's mouth confirmed it, and Tooms was glad.

"Did you meet her mom and dad? Maybe some of her friends?" Tooms asked.

But there was no reply. Tony was still somewhere else in his head.

"Hey, Tony. Are you with us, man?" Tooms's voice raised its volume slightly. He wasn't shouting but had sharpened his tone just enough to bring his partner back to the present.

"Sorry, man. Just remembering ... never mind." The smile had fallen away from Tony's mouth.

"Did you meet any other family or friends? Perhaps, someone she worked with?" Tooms asked. Tony began to shake his head, but a quick recollection stopped him.

"Her parents are dead. They were killed in a car accident years ago. But I did meet one friend of hers. Tara, I think her name was." Tony looked worn out as he answered. Tooms wished he could let him go home, but he was afraid he would get some bad ideas if he was left by himself.

"OK, nice," Tooms went on. "So, have you got any ideas where this Tara chick lives?" His face had lit up at the prospect of a lead.

"We think she was the girl Amber moved in with," said McCall, who was standing in the doorway. Steel stood behind her like a looming shadow. They walked in and sat down, hoping to share in the findings.

"We found some bills in the kitchen addressed to Tara Burke. The question is, where is Tara now?" McCall said.

"Maybe she came home and found the body, then she bolted just in case the killer was still there," Tooms added. His voice almost sounded hopeful that might be the case, and that they weren't looking at two homicides.

"It's possible," Steel said, leaning back in the chair. "She may have come back and seen the body. The neighbours did say they heard a scream at around ten o'clock."

Samantha McCall saw the expression on Steel's face turn to stone. She knew that hardened look meant that he felt something was wrong.

"What's wrong?" she asked. Steel turned to face her. Her eyes sparkled with the reflection of the overhead lights. He smiled and shook his head.

"Nothing. Just a passing thought about something else,

that's all," Steel replied. She could see through his white lie but said nothing.

"OK, you guys. Find out where Tara works, and we will go to where Amber worked," McCall suggested as she stood up. She had noticed the name on the yellow legal pad and figured that was first the place they had to go. Steel stood up as McCall approached the door.

"Road trip?" he asked with a smile.

"Road trip," she replied, rattling her car keys.

———

Tooms and Tony went back to the crime scene to see if there was anything that would help with finding the roommate. Before, they had only concentrated on the victim—Amber. But now, they might have a missing person or worse, another body.

Tooms didn't really want Tony in the apartment. He would have preferred to have gone alone and left him at the precinct, but his friend made out he was OK. Tooms didn't believe a word of it, but that was Tony Marinelli all over—putting his job first and his personal life second.

As they reached the front door to the apartment, a uniformed officer stood watch. The two detectives showed their shields. The young uniformed cop nodded, then watched as they went to enter. Tony froze as Tooms reached for the handle. Joshua sensed something was wrong and turned.

"Damn it!" Tooms cursed, patting down his jacket. "Hey, Tony, you couldn't go back to the car, could you? I forgot my friggin' camera." Joshua saw the relieved look on Tony's face.

"Yeah, no problem. Besides, it gives me time to check on that other thing," Tony bluffed. Tooms watched his partner walk away towards the staircase. Then his gaze fell to the young cop, who was trying to look as if he hadn't been taking it all in.

Tooms turned the door handle and walked in. CSU had removed the yellow evidence markers, but back smudges remained from the fingerprint powder. The clean-up crew hadn't been in yet: it was still a crime scene. Tooms stood for a moment and looked down on the large red stain on the carpet. He was glad Tony was downstairs, for he didn't need to see this. Joshua pulled on a pair of blue sterile gloves as he moved towards the second bedroom. He stood back as he entered the missing girl's room. The walls were painted bright pink. The light from the small window reflected on the right-hand wall and seemed to turn it neon. A double bed rested against the left-hand wall next to which was a large cheap-looking closet. The room was small—ten feet by eight if that. Purple shelves were attached to the walls fixed with metallic right-angled supports. Books and stuffed toy animals sat neatly as if they were on display. A nightstand separated the bed from the wall. Its glossy white paint was broken up by pink swirls that Tooms figured she had done herself. A tall bedside lamp with a pink plastic shade sat next to a 'pink cat' alarm clock: the digital display was held in the smiling mouth of a pink-and-purple striped cat.

The detective looked around the room. Initially, it had reminded him of his girls' rooms, and they were considerably younger than Amber—thirteen and fifteen. Tooms made his way to the bedside cabinet, hoping to find something in its four drawers. He quickly closed the third one. He had no intention of prying in a woman's 'naughty' drawer. The top one was full of odd bits of junk and bracelets. The others contained mostly magazines and holiday brochures. He stood up and made for the closet. Joshua found it odd there were no photographs anywhere. No pictorial evidence of family, friends, snapshots from holidays, nothing personal like that. To look at the apartment, you would think it was a show house.

The curious officer then opened the closet door and there before him was a rail of neatly pressed clothes, on hangers: blouses, jeans and so on. He stopped and smiled as he reached in and pulled out a red-and-white uniform. The name 'Bob's Diner' was stitched into the white top in red lettering.

"Time to get some breakfast," Tooms said with a grin. He placed the uniform back in the closet and left the apartment.

CHAPTER FIVE

STEEL AND MCCALL ARRIVED AT THE TRENT SHIPPING yard. The whole place was in a massive fenced off area. Several large warehouses stood in rows, each of which had six trucks of different sizes parked with their trailers backed up to the loading bays.

A tall five-storey building sat in the centre of the industrial estate, with two large warehouses either side of it. Large billboards crowned their upper levels, advertising the company. The large building was the main office, the central hub. Its windows were blackened by the glare of the morning sun. McCall pulled up to the front gate, where a tall security guard waited. She had seen him get out of his booth as she approached. As she stopped, he smiled pleasantly. She noticed that the man was in his late fifties, but he looked as if he was in good physical shape.

Steel wasn't sure if his welcome was just natural courtesy, the fact an attractive woman like McCall was there, or if he was just happy to see someone new.

"Good morning, how can I help you folks?" the guard asked. His eye contacts never left McCall, even when Steel showed his shield at the same time as she did.

"We are with NYPD, and we would like to speak to whoever is in charge here," McCall said with a smile and a bat of the eyelids. The guard directed them to a parking lot next to the main building. McCall thanked him and left the guard with a broad smile that Steel suspected he wouldn't lose for quite a while.

She pulled up to the parking space the guard had instructed her to use. There were several other visitors' parking spaces, all of them empty. The front entrance was just around the corner from where she had parked her beloved Mustang. Steel got out and immediately looked up at the five-storey building. Cream coloured walls and smoked windows made the structure look more like a Manhattan office than a shipping headquarters.

The two detectives entered the lobby through automatic doors. The room was huge, with white tiled floors and cream painted walls. Small potted ferns and palms were dotted strategically around the place, breaking up the sterile colour. Steel and McCall stood for a moment taking in the layout of the place. Steel smiled as he gazed over at the front desk and the two attractive ladies at the reception. McCall gave him a quick look and shook her head in disbelief.

"Unbelievable," she groaned and headed for the two women who were sitting behind a long wooden information desk. On the front of the light wooden frontage was the company name in brass lettering. Steel reckoned it was more likely to be imitation 'stay bright' rather than metal. This would be more practical since brass needs to be cleaned regularly, what's more, it picked up every fingerprint and scratch. As they approached the desk, a tall woman met them halfway along the floor. She wore a light blue skirt suit and white blouse that was open at the neck, and she had a broad smile to match. She tossed her head, flirtatiously. Her long, wavy, fiery red hair brushed past her shoulders. McCall had wondered if she had popped a couple of buttons after seeing Steel: enticing his interest more as a distraction tactic than a 'come-on.'

"You must be the detectives," she began. "I am Helen Adler, Mr Adams's personnel assistant." Her voice was husky as if she had just had a glass of Jim Beam to gargle with.

"Of course, you are," Steel replied, raising an eyebrow. McCall rolled her eyes then smiled before shaking the woman's hand.

"This is Detective John Steel, and I am Detective Samantha McCall," she said.

The woman smiled back at McCall, but there was a different kind of smile on her face for Steel.

"If you follow me, I will take you to see Mr Adams," Helen Adler said in a sultry voice. They followed her to the brass-coloured elevator doors, whose surfaces had a strange texture. Small indents covered the bright metal, almost as if it had been attacked with a pin hammer. Steel walked behind the two women. His concentration was on checking the security and cameras. There were two large men at the main entrance and two more at the elevator. Each was dressed in a black suit with white shirt, black tie, and the bulge in their jackets indicated that they were 'packing.' He nodded to one of the men as they waited for the doors to open. The man nodded back after eyeing up Steel and McCall. The doors slid open, and Steel let the ladies enter first. As they closed, Steel saw the man he had greeted touch his ear, after which he shot Steel a glance before saying something into his wrist microphone. Suddenly, Steel had an uneasy feeling. The ride up was quiet. The only interaction was Helen checking Steel out in the walled mirrors. He smiled at her failed attempt to be discreet.

As the doors slid, open Helen walked out first with McCall and Steel following not far behind. Steel noted two more men at the elevator doors. A long corridor led them to another desk by a large window, next to which was a wooden double door. To the right was a corner couch, which Steel figured was in the waiting area. Helen smiled and nodded to another woman who sat behind the desk: this was Adams's secretary. The woman was in her thirties with black hair and a black skirt suit. Helen knocked on the door, then entered. McCall and Steel followed her into a large office. The whole of the right wall was made of glass and showed a fantastic view of the parking lot and the warehouse with the billboards. The only greenery in view were the trees that had been planted in the parking lot. To the left, there was a long cabinet that housed awards for industry and a couple of sport trophies. At the end of the large room sat a large metal and oak desk, behind which sat a man. He was a large built man with broad shoulders and a square head. His neatly cut grey hair was gelled and styled, and he wore a suit that probably cost enough to pay for McCall's rent for the next three months. As he rose to meet them, Steel noted that the shipping giant was all of five foot eight. But what he lacked in height he made up for with self-confidence.

"Mr Adams, may I present Detectives Samantha McCall and John Steel?" Helen's gravelly voice almost purred Steel's name. David Adams looked frantic and annoyed as he gathered up some papers and stuck them into a leather case.

"What's up, detectives? Has my chauffeur forgotten to pay her parking tickets again?" He growled the question whilst shaking his head.

"What?" McCall said, almost shocked at his abrupt manner. "No, we are homicide detectives, and we would like to ask you some questions about one of your employees."

"Well, it had better be about my overseas financial adviser. At least then she might have an excuse for not being here five minutes before a major deal!" Adams yelled, standing up and heading for the door.

"And who is that exactly, if I may ask?" Steel said, hoping his gut was wrong.

"Amber Taylor. The funny thing is, she has never missed a day's work until now," Helen Adler said. Her tone was filled with confusion, as well as a hint of worry.

"Look, can't this wait?" Adams barked as if the thought of two homicide detectives asking about his people didn't bother him. "I'm a very busy man."

"Actually, no, it can't," McCall said. "We're investigating the murder of one of your employees. Amber Taylor, to be precise." Samantha McCall's eyes were fixed on Adams's face, to try to gauge his reaction.

"What? Amber's dead? How? When?" Adams said, looking alarmed and shocked as he walked back to his chair and collapsed into it.

"Last night, someone attacked her in her apartment." McCall watched the businessman's face as she delivered the news. She could tell if someone was genuine or not, and he seemed to pass the test.

"What exactly was it that she did here?" Steel asked as he put back a glass award that was in the shape of an eagle that he had been examining. Steel turned slowly to face Adams, making sure he gave Helen a quick smile as he did so.

"She was one of my top financial managers, she handled a lot of overseas business, export and import, that sort of thing,"

Adams replied, but his gaze never left his large monitor that was on the right corner of his desk. Anyone else might have considered this as evidence that he was avoiding eye contact, but Steel knew that the man could see himself in the reflection.

"Do you know of any reason anyone would want to kill her? Any rivalry in the office, an ex-boyfriend perhaps?" McCall asked, knowing sometimes it was people the victims knew who were the most likely to be their murderers. Money, jealousy, and love were all good motives to kill.

"No. Everyone loved her. She got on great with all of us. As for a boyfriend, I'm afraid I couldn't say. She liked to keep her private life private," Adams said, shrugging his shoulders and raising his hands.

"I guess you could speak to Rebecca Miles, she worked closely with Amber," Helen said. Her gaze was on Adams as he just sat there staring at his monitor. "Maybe she knows something."

McCall nodded after jotting down the woman's name. Adams looked up at the two detectives then shot out of his seat.

"Miss Adler will help you with anything you need." Adams's voice trembled as he spoke. He grabbed his leather pouch bag and left the room, leaving Steel and McCall looking at each other in surprise at the man's strange behaviour.

"Please follow me, I'll take you to see Rebecca," Helen said, leading them out of the room.

"So, it's Miss Adler, is it?" Steel said with a playful tone. McCall rolled her eyes and wished she had come alone.

Rebecca Miles, or 'Becca' as her friends called her, was busy getting some files together. Steel could see by her demeanour she had not yet been told of her friend's fate. She was around five foot six with short hazelnut-coloured hair and was young and attractive – Steel reckoned she was in her late twenties. Becca was clearly a 'fresh catch' from one of the many prestigious universities – probably Stanford or Columbia. Steel smiled as they approached, seeing that she was singing away to herself. He noticed the earplug headphone in her ear as she danced around, sorting out the paperwork.

"Becca?" Helen shouted just as Becca reached a high note, or at least tried to. "BECCA!" Helen shouted louder, causing the young woman to jump. Paper was tossed into the air like confetti. Becca pulled out her headphone and switch off her music wired from her phone.

"Sorry, Miss Adler, I didn't hear you," she explained. "I've been trying to get all this paperwork sorted for the meeting." She knelt to retrieve the scattered documents, and Steel crouched down, joining her on the floor. She looked up at the gallant man dressed in black and smiled. He returned the smile as he gave her a handful of papers.

"Becca, these people are with the police. Something has happened to Amber." Helen's words were soft and full of compassion, almost like a mother giving a child some bad news.

"What? No! Is she OK?" Becca asked, her voice sounding dry as if all the moisture in her mouth had dried up. McCall always hated this part; the part of the interview when she could see the person grasping the hope that whatever had happened, it didn't involve death, at worst that it was just a bad accident. She hated the part where she had to crush that one hope.

"I am afraid she was found dead in her apartment last night," McCall explained. Becca stumbled back towards the office chair. Steel rushed forward and caught her as she dropped just short of her target. Sam McCall rushed forward and pushed the chair closer so that Steel could place her down comfortably. Becca's face was pale, her eyes were wide, and her mouth was moving but failed to produce words. Helen grabbed one of the bottles of water that was on a side table. She handed it to Steel, who cracked the top and placed the mouth of the bottle to Becca's lips. She took a small sip then her eyes looked directly at Steel. She saw her own reflection in his dark sunglasses. Becca smiled and thanked him. Steel stood up straight and moved back, giving the shocked woman some space.

"Are you alright now?" he asked. She nodded and took another sip before wiping her eyes with the sleeve of her blue blouse.

"So, what happened? Was it an accident?" she asked.

Steel shook his head and passed Becca a cotton handkerchief he had gotten from the inside breast pocket of his jacket.

"I am afraid not. Someone broke into her apartment and attacked her," he explained. He could see that Amber and Becca had been close. Hopefully, they'd been close enough to have shared some secrets.

"Who did this to her?" Becca's tone changed as she began to get over the initial shock.

"That's what we are trying to find out. I can see you two were good friends. Can you tell us anything? Did she have any problems with anyone? Work colleagues, old boyfriends, maybe? Is there anything you can think of?" Steel asked, his voice soft.

Becca shook her head after thinking for a moment.

"She was seeing some guy for a while. I think he was a cop or a security guard, I can't remember. That ended kinda bad. He used to call her up all the time, saying how she had used him." Becca looked away as if she was straining to remember details.

"This ex, did he have a name?" asked McCall with pad and pen at the ready.

"Tony, I think ... Yeah, that was it. Tony. Medium build with dark hair. Had an Italian look about him."

McCall looked at Steel, who had the same unhappy expression on his face as she had.

"Oh bollocks," Steel said, knowing what they had to do next.

CHAPTER SIX

McCall drove back to the precinct as fast as the midday traffic would allow. The sun was now hidden behind massive billows of white clouds. The thick traffic gave her time to reflect about what had been said back at the shipping company. Her thoughts were all heading in one direction.

And it wasn't a good direction.

Steel could see the frustration in her face. Samantha McCall and Tony Marinelli had worked together for a long time and been through a lot during that period. She was angry at what Becca had said: that Amber had a boyfriend called Tony.

Had as in past tense.

Had Tony lied about being with Amber? Had they broken up and he had taken it badly? Steel had not known the detective as McCall had done, but Steel normally had a pretty good take on people, and for him, Tony was one of the good guys. Someone you wanted watching your back.

"Maybe there is another guy called Tony?" Steel said, hoping to dilute the trail Sam's thinking. He held on to the seat belt as she put her foot to the gas after seeing a space to charge into. He shot her a look of disapproval as she raced through the traffic as though she was in the Indy 500.

"Yeah, right. And this other Tony just happens to look like him as well?" she growled, and her knuckles whitened as she gripped the leather-bound steering wheel.

John Steel had to admit to himself that the whole thing did sound all too much of a coincidence. The ex-boyfriend, whose name was Tony and the guy had the same build and hair colour as their friend!

"Maybe she has a type she goes for. It can happen." Steel kept his eyes on the road but tried to hide the need to jump out of the car in fear of his life.

Soon they would be back at the precinct, and he hoped that she wouldn't jump in with both feet by tackling Tony without asking him first. She was mad and wounded. Suddenly Steel realised they were heading back to the crime scene. He didn't question it. In fact, it was probably a better idea than going back to the office and her jumping all over Tony.

She pulled in next to the kerb, stopping near the junction and killed the engine. Steel turned to her slowly. She just sat there for a moment as if gathering her thoughts.

"Sam," he began, "when we get back, take it easy on Tony, just in case what Becca told us happens to be a coincidence. Don't forget he just lost his girlfriend."

McCall shot him an angry look as if he had said something to insult her.

"All I am saying is be careful. You can't 'un-say' something. If you're wrong, he may not forgive you."

McCall's face calmed as she took in the words. He was right. She was angry because of something that could be, not something which had been proven.

"OK, we let him know what was said. If he is hiding

something, I will know." McCall smiled at Steel. He had saved her from making what might probably be a massive mistake that could have changed everything. Tony was a friend, and she didn't want to lose his friendship. Steel went to say something to McCall, but his mouth remained open as if dumbstruck by a thought. McCall looked at him curiously until she saw the reflection in his glasses. She turned to see a tall man standing outside on the sidewalk. He was wearing a white shirt, blue jeans, and was covered in blood.

They both jumped out of the car and rushed over to the man, who appeared to be in a daze.

"Sir, are you OK? Are you hurt?" Samantha asked. The man looked up as she finished her sentence. He looked at her with a confused expression.

"Sir, what's your name? Can you tell me if this is your blood?"

He looked around at his surroundings then back at McCall. He now had a panicked look on his face.

"I don't know," he muttered. "Oh, God, I don't know anything!" The man screamed out the words and then fell to the ground, unconscious.

"Well, this could complicate things," Steel said. McCall just shot Steel a look that said it all as she pulled out her cell to call for an ambulance.

Steel sat back in the comfort of the leather and cloth seats of the muscle car, while McCall followed the ambulance to the hospital. In a way, McCall hoped that this injured man was somehow connected to the Amber case, but then life was never that simple. The trip over was silent. Steel was thinking about a million other things; McCall's thoughts went back to Tony. The route to county hospital was anything but straight forward due to construction. Another new building was taking shape; for the moment, it was just the bare skeleton of the steel framework. John Steel was born and had lived in the country on his family's estate for most of his life. After that, he had travelled with the Army. In truth, this last year had been the longest he had stayed put in one place for most of his adult life, so the pleasant chaos of Manhattan was somewhat alien for him, the city of constant change. McCall found a parking spot near the hospital, placing the plastic-covered NYPD parking pass in the window she looked over at Steel.

"You check with the nurses, we need his clothes, I'll speak to the doctors," she said, Steel smiled as her request seemed to be more an order. She was a strong woman, tough as nails, he liked that, but he didn't take been ordered too well.

"Not a problem, but only because you asked so nicely," Steel said with a smile, his words rang with sarcasm. McCall scowled at him, and she didn't have time for his pride, antics, or him just been – well, him.

They got out of the car into a bitter wind. McCall pulled her coat tightly around her, Steel just stood with his head high, and his eyes closed, feeling the crisp wind against his warm skin before walking over to the hospital entrance. Inside had a mixture of smelts, the strongest of which was sterilising chemicals. Steel didn't care much for hospitals or doctors; he had uttermost respect for them but had no great desire to be near them.

While McCall chased after the doctors, Steel perched himself at the nurse's station and talked to the nurses behind the counter. At the station was two large black women in their mid-forties. Both had eyeglasses that hung from beaded chains around their necks, both held a dreamy look, and shoed away anyone that sought to interrupt their conversation with the British detective. Steel eased the request for the man's clothes into the conversation, hoping sugar would get more of a quicker response than an order. It took less than a minute to get the clothes along with several phone numbers. Steel just hoped that CSU could find something on the mystery man's clothes, knowing that they would be able to tell if it was Amber's blood he was covered in, or someone else's. While Steel continued to flirt, McCall waited for the doctors examined the mystery man. On the way to the hospital, McCall had phoned ahead to CSU, requesting a tech. She knew that they would need pristine samples. As McCall paced up and down the corridor outside the man's room, she chanced several glances inside the room. Inside, the doctors examined while a CSU tech took nail scrapings and brushed the man's hair for trace materials. If he wasn't their killer, they needed to find out where he had been to get himself so messed up, also whose blood it was that he was covered in.

McCall waited impatiently on the other side of the curtain. She needed to get in there to find out what the guy knew. McCall looked over to see Steel return from the CSU guys, who were walking around with several paper evidence bags containing the man's clothes.

"Is that all of his stuff?" her words sounded almost disappointed.

"Yeah, unfortunately, there's no wallet or cell phone," Steel told her. "I figure he had a jacket that he put all his other items in," Steel answered, he could tell she was anxious, this was the last thing she needed while there was a possibility that Tony could be incriminated in his girlfriend's murder.

"Are you still thinking about Tony?" Steel asked, almost knowing the answer. She looked over at him, her face filled with mixed emotion.

"Go, do what you have to do," he suggested. "I will take care of this, and you can sort it out with Tony." Sam knew that

Steel was right. Besides, she realised that in her frame of mind, she wouldn't be much use now. She smiled and thanked him.

As Steel watched McCall disappear through the ward doors, his smile faded. He looked over to the curtains as they drew back. The guy was sitting on the side of the bed wearing a medical gown, his legs hanging over the side while the doctor looked at his eyes, searching for signs of concussion. Steel turned to the tech, who was busy packing away his CSU sample jars and swab containers.

"Did you get everything?" Steel asked quietly. The tech nodded as he closed the metalwork case and headed off back to the lab. Steel turned to the doctor and the man on the bed.

"Any ideas, doctor?" Steel asked, hoping for a simple answer. The doctor was in his mid-fifties with thick grey hair and a trimmed beard to match. His white coat covered a striped shirt and a stocky build.

"There was a nasty gash at the side of his head," the medical man told him. "It was bad, but not bad enough to explain his memory loss. If you want my opinion, he has probably suffered a great emotional shock." The doctor smiled and shrugged. Steel looked over to the 'John Doe'—the name police and the legal profession traditionally assign to an unidentified person. The man was in his late twenties, tall with a medium build. His thick strawberry-blond hair was all messed up from the recent medical examinations, giving him that *just got up* look. His blue eyes were bright but held a sadness. Someone had to get into this guy's head, and Steel knew just the guy.

CHAPTER SEVEN

DOCTOR COLBY DAVIDSON WALKED INTO THE 11TH Precinct feeling full of mixed emotions. The last time he had worked with the Homicide division, it had nearly cost him a lot. His six-foot, thin frame was draped in a two-thousand-dollar blue pinstriped Armani. The tap of his black Christian Louboutin shoes was dulled by the noise of the precinct's lobby. The sound of the bustle made his body tingle. Uniformed cops yelled at criminals who refused to do as they were instructed, crying women who had been mugged or lost their kids, ringing cell phones just added to the chaotic melody. The desk sergeant's phone was ringing off the hook, while he gave 'directs' to a woman trying to give a missing person's report.

Davidson smiled as he revelled in the chaos. He believed that most of these problems could have been stopped if the wrongdoers had seen a good shrink. He stood in front of the elevator and pressed the call button. He caught a glimpse of his reflection in the dull aluminium fittings on the elevator's exterior. He combed a long-fingered hand through his greased back brown hair and smiled at what he saw. His face was long with a thin roman nose and pale skin, his deep-set large eyes were pale blue, with a menacing touch to them. He wasn't a handsome man, but he held a strange allure.

The elevator opened, and he stepped inside and turned to face the heavy steel doors just as they were closing he sported the kind of wicked grin you would expect to find on a Cheshire cat.

As he rode the elevator, he noted the pungent mix of smells, most of which he decided not to try and think about what they could be. It stank of cleaning fluid, vomit, piss, body odour, not to mention the unknown ones. The box came to a stop with a shudder, and the doors slid open. Davidson lost the grin as he stepped out on to the department floor. Familiar faces looked up from their desks, watching him as he stepped off the elevator and stopped to look around the room. The other detectives remembered him.

He wasn't welcome.

Davidson headed for McCall, whom he had spied from the elevator. Steel was with her in a small conference room, along with another man he did not recognise. As he walked across the busy floor of the bullpen, people stopped and stared, remembering what had taken place the last time he had worked a case, what his brother had done – the man that was now known as Mr Williams. The doctor knocked on the door and then stood in the doorway, almost as if he was waiting for a friendly invitation to step inside.

"Doctor Davidson, good to see you again," McCall said with a smile. They shook hands while Steel stood behind her with his arms crossed.

"Hello there, doctor, good to see you again," Steel said, then paused and moved closer for a better look. "It is you – isn't it?" he added jokingly.

"And if it wasn't, do you think I would say so?" Davidson replied with a smile. Steel laughed and shrugged as if to agree with the statement. Davidson turned towards John Doe and smiled a greeting. "Don't worry, it's a private joke," he explained to the amnesiac man. "Someone once impersonated me."

"Yeah, your twin brother did," McCall pointed out. "A guy who was, let's face it, a little *off*," McCall said diplomatically.

"A little *off*? Really the guy was a bloody psychopath," Steel butted in.

John Doe just sat there with a bewildered look on his face, up until the point when the doctor approached to shake his hand.

"Sorry for ignoring you, sir. I am Doctor Colby Davidson," he said, stretching out a pale palm. John Doe just stared up at this strange-looking man, noting his tall thin body, his long fingers, and *that face*. But it was the large blue eyes and the mouth that wore the most terrifying smile he had ever seen. Naturally, red lips curled up at the sides in a menacing grin, exposing rows of pearly white teeth. John Doe just stared, hypnotized by the doctor's unnatural smile. He imagined a shark having the same expression just before devouring someone.

"Doctor Davison is a psychiatrist," McCall explained. "He is here to hopefully help you with your memory."

John Doe's face looked almost shocked at the revelation that this guy was here to help him, and not to kill Batman.

"Don't worry, he is good at what he does," Steel said, trying to sound convincing. "We worked together before, a long time ago."

The man with no name seemed calmer at Steel's

reassurance, but there was still something about the newcomer that he didn't like.

"Right then, shall we get started?" Davidson said, placing an aluminium briefcase onto the desk. He stood in front of a chair as he unpacked a block of plain pieces of paper, a large yellow jotter pad, and a tape recorder. He took out of his pocket a gold pocket watch and placed it onto the table. Steel stared at the watch. Memories of that first case came flooding back.

"What's with the watch, doc?" Steel asked, slipping his hand under his jacket to the small of his back.

Davidson picked up the watch and dangled it brieflyso that it swung back and forth in a pendulum motion.

"It's so that I can hypnotise him and take him back through his thoughts," Davidson said with a straight face.

"Really? You can do that?" John Doe said, seeming uncomfortable at the idea.

"No, I am only joking. My watch is in the shop getting serviced. I bought this because ... You know, I don't really know why. I just liked it." Davidson grinned and placed the watch back down. Steel saw the fear in John Doe's eyes, and he felt sympathy for him: being stuck in a room with this guy was enough to drive anyone nuts.

"You know I don't know what is worse. Having amnesia or having to see the good doctor," Steel joked as they walked out, leaving the two men alone. McCall slapped Steel on the shoulder then shook her hand in pain.

"You've been working out again, haven't you?" she joked, but all the while, she undressed him in her mind's eye. Suddenly she shook her head to stop the unclean thoughts before they started. They headed for Tony and Tooms, who were in the break room, draining the last of the coffee from one of the machines. McCall had a lot of questions, and Steel could sense her eagerness to ask them. As they entered the room, Steel walked in front of McCall and headed for Tony.

"So, Tony, we spoke to a work colleague of your girlfriend, or should I say your ex-girlfriend," Steel said bluntly. Tony looked blankly at him at first, then the look of confusion was replaced with one of clarity.

"I tracked down her sister, Brooke," Tony replied. "The captain asked me if I would break the bad news to her, thought it might be better coming from someone who knew her." Tony sighed deeply and closed his eyes tightly for a second, thinking back to the conversation, remembering how she had cried down the phone at the news. Tony didn't want to admit he had asked Brant if he could do it, feeling it was his responsibility to do so as her boyfriend. Tony had found Brooke's number on Amber's cell phone, which she never locked. "She cried for a while. Then she asked me how I knew her sister, asked me all sorts of questions about us, probably trying to avoid the inevitable conversation, I guess. We talked for a while, about her Amber's past, her friends from before, her boyfriends. It seemed kinda weird; it showed me how much we didn't know about each other," Tony shook his head in dismay.

"Tony, you were only going out for a short while, it takes time to really know someone, and sometimes, even then you don't know them as much as you thought," Steel said, his face was emotionless, but his words were bitter. Everyone looked over at Steel, wondering who he had been talking about.

"Did you learn anything new?" McCall asked, her gaze glancing back towards Steel who stood motionless with his arms crossed.

"She was seeing a guy before me, they had dated for about a year, Brooke said the guy was a real dooshbag, used to smack her around, treated her like garbage, they broke up about six months ago," Tony explained, massaging his knuckles as though he had thoughts about doing to this ex-boyfriend what the asshole had done to Amber.

"Did we get a name on this charmer?" Tooms asked.

"His name was Tony – Tony Russo," Tony said, leaning back in his chair. After hearing Tony Russo's name and getting his description, Tony knew that the coincidence was going to come back on him, from how Brooke had described him, Tony and the asshole could have been twins. Amber had a type, which didn't make Tony feel any better. "Brooke lives and worked in D.C. However, she said she'd be on the first flight out," There was a sadness in Tony's eyes as he explained what he had found out. McCall smiled and touched him on the shoulder.

"You OK?" McCall asked, sensing something new was gnawing at him.

"I have made that phone call so many times, but that was the hardest," Tony said, looking up at McCall. She nodded, then smiled at him and turned to Steel, who was staring at the murder board next to her desk.

"Any luck with the roommate?" she asked, looking at Steel for a moment before turning to face Tony and Tooms. The British detective's thoughts were a million miles away from the rest of them. His imagination was conjuring up images of what may have befallen the missing woman.

"The roommate was Tara Burke, as we thought. She is twenty-six, five-seven with red hair," Tooms read from his pad. Steel stood still staring at the board, unmoving and not uttering a word, but Tooms knew that he had taken everything in.

"Do we know where she worked?" Steel asked after a short while.

"Bob's Diner. It's in Harlem," Tooms explained, handing McCall a yellow post-it notes with the address on. McCall looked at the piece of paper for a couple of seconds as if to memorise the address. Then she opened her leather folio case and placed it onto the blank A4 pad inside.

"OK, you two take the ex-boyfriend, and we'll take the diner," McCall said, suddenly looking at her watch. It was nearly half-three, and she knew they were going to hit traffic on the way back. She shrugged. It wasn't as if she had anything better to do.

"Shall we go, Detective?" Steel said, raising an arm towards the elevator.

"Yes, we shall, and 'WE' are probably driving again," she growled as if to make a point. "Seriously, are you saying you don't have a car? Or does it have to come with a chauffeur?" she joked.

John Steel smiled and shook his head. "Oh, don't worry, Detective, I have a car, and I can assure you, you will want to play," John quipped.

Sam McCall walked off towards the elevator, shaking her head.

"No thanks, I got my pony." Her voice almost purred, and Steel laughed to himself. McCall and Steel stood at the elevator. Behind them, the boys were busy trying to locate the ex-boyfriend. As they stood in front of the heavy steel doors, Steel looked up at the LED display that showed that the elevator box was one floor above them.

"I hope this isn't going to take long. I have dinner plans," Steel said, giving a quick smile from the corner of his mouth as he bounced off his heels.

"Sorry if work is getting in the way of your personal life," she growled. "You could always quit, then you would have plenty of time for your bimbos." Although she was joking, she was still somewhat jealous that he had a personal life that didn't include her. The doors slid open, and he stepped inside and leaned against the back wall.

"And you're doing what tonight?" His words were playful, but they left a bitter sting. McCall stepped in after him but said nothing. She had to wonder though, what was he going off to do tonight? Dinner and dancing? Or chasing down the people responsible for his family's murder. Whatever it was, he would be having more fun than she would be having tonight.

CHAPTER EIGHT

THE DINER WAS ON A BUSY CORNER OF ADAM CLAYTON Powell Jr. Boulevard and West 148th Street. Above the white-walled exterior of the building began the red-brick apartments. Steel noticed a 'For Rent' sign on one of the walls. Its green writing was bold, designed to catch the eye. The dinner was in the corner building. A double-door entrance was situated directly in view of the pedestrian crossing, giving good easy access for all customer needs. The place itself was clean, with PU leather upholstery in the booths and dark wood tables. The black-and-white checkerboard tiled floor glistened from the overhead lighting.

To the back of the diner was a long counter with glass showcases full of doughnuts and cheesecakes. Behind that was the delivery counter, where the waitresses collected the orders from a large angry looking man who was wearing a white T-shirt and a small chef's 'skull' hat. Steel was convinced that he looked more like a bulldog chewing a wasp, the hanging jowls and beady eyes just added to the picture. On a far wall, a small twenty-inch television set was tuned to the news. The customers just looked through the two cops as if they weren't even there. Steel sat at one of the padded seats that was in front of the counter. The stainless-steel pinion was bolted firmly to the ground a little too close to the counter for Steel, causing him to sit with spread legs. McCall shot him a look of disapproval, then did the same. McCall didn't want to stay and have lunch, they were there to deliver bad news and get information, something she hated to mix, but it was necessary given the fact it was a homicide investigation. Two waitresses rushed about frantically, like catchers in a ball game. Steel picked up one of the menu cards and checked the vast array of artery-blocking dishes on offer.

"I don't think they have caviar here," McCall joked, just as a pretty black-haired woman in a red-and-white uniform appeared behind them, her pad and pencil at the ready.

"Hey there. Welcome to Bob's Diner. So, what can I get you folks?" the waitress asked, sporting a bright smile.

"We are with the NYPD," Sam said, flashing her shield. "We are here about one of your waitresses. Tara?"

The woman's mouth fell open as if to say something.

"That bitch better be in hospital or dead!" yelled the man who wore a grease-stained T-shirt and jeans. "I am down three waitresses, and she decide to not come in!" A dirty white chef's cap covered most of his large fat head.

"I take it you're Bob, the owner?" McCall said. Her tone had changed, her voice now sterner and more authoritative as she spoke to him. He stayed behind the wall and just blew hot air and waved his spatula about.

"Yeah, I'm Bob, what's it to you, lady? Look, I am busy here, so what do you want?" he yelled. Sam McCall could feel her blood boil at his apparent lack of manners or respect. It wasn't so much that she was a cop; she felt his disregard was more because she was a female cop.

"So, what's happened to her?" asked the waitress, her voice full of genuine concern.

"She's gone missing," Sam said softly. "Her roommate was found murdered, and we are worried about her safety."

The waitress looked shocked, and her face blanched as she stumbled backwards. Steel was already up and had caught her before she fell any further. He led her to a booth, where they all sat down.

"Hey! No sitting down on the job, you hear me?" came Bob's angry voice from behind the counter, but everyone just ignored him.

"My name is Detective Samantha McCall, and this is Detective Steel." McCall smiled as she spoke.

"I am Kim, Kim Washington. She was ... She *is* my best friend." Kim's eyes shone with fresh tears.

"You don't think she could have done this murder, do you?" Kim asked, her voice sounding dry and scared at the possibility.

"We don't know. She isn't in any trouble, we just want to talk to her," Steel said reassuringly. Kim looked up at him and smiled.

"When did you see her last?" McCall asked. Kim looked up at the clock above the door as if she was trying to remember.

"It was around half-eight, nine, I guess. She had pulled a double and was heading home. It had been a long day for everyone," Kim explained.

"Are you open all night?" Steel asked, looking around the room, but paying special attention to Bob, who was sneaking brief, worried looks from his area beside the grill.

"No, four until midnight. Unless we know something special is on, then we are open twenty-four-seven," Kim told them. Steel sat back and continued his unobserved scan of the place. There were around twenty people sitting in various places. Most of them appeared to be drivers who were just passing through. He looked out of the window at the traffic that was beginning to build up outside.

"Did she have any problems with anyone that you know of?" McCall asked—she was almost hoping that Kim would say that her boss was causing problems. The thought of getting him in the box was making her salivate.

"No, not really. Everyone liked her. She didn't have time for a boyfriend or anything," Kim added, expecting the usual question about personal relationships.

"What about Bob? Any problems there?" Steel asked. He noticed Bob look up suddenly at the mention of his name. Kim shook her head but said nothing.

"How did she seem when she left?" the British detective asked.

Kim looked puzzled at this strange cop's question. "She was distracted, but then she was tired. Why?" Kim said, still wondering about Steel's question.

"We are just trying to piece everything together," Steel said with a smile.

McCall passed across her business card. "If you do see her, can you get her to contact me, please?"

Kim looked at the card and placed it in a breast pocket of her uniform. Steel looked up angrily towards Bob, as he hammered a brass call bell. Kim stood up. She knew that was her signal to get back to work.

"Are you OK?" Steel asked as he noticed the strange eye contact Bob was giving Kim.

The young waitress turned towards Steel and smiled quickly before nodding. "Sure, I'm fine. Look I've got to get back to work. If I see her, I will let her know."

Sam nodded in appreciation. "Thanks for your time," she said, shaking Kim's still trembling hand. As they watched Kim return to her station, the two detectives became uneasy.

Something was wrong, and whatever it was had nothing to do with their case.

Bob dragged Kim into the kitchen so no one could see, and then he slapped her hard.

"What did they want to know about that silly bitch?" Bob growled; his voice toned down so as to not to not draw any attention.

"Nothing. She has disappeared and they—"

Bob slapped her again, hard. So hard that his finger marks were visible on her face.

"You don't say anything, you hear me?" he screamed, his voice breaking its strained tone. He raised his hand again to give her another shot just in case she didn't understand. Then he looked around suddenly, shocked to feel the firm grip around his wrist. He turned to find Steel holding him back.

Bob swung with his other fist at the British man, but he failed to connect. Steel wrenched down Bob's arm and pulled it behind his back. As he did so, Steel added a bit of force, bouncing Bob's shaven head off the stainless-steel preparation table. There was a metallic thud as skull met metal, making Steel feel a little better.

"Bad move, jackass," McCall said, almost with a hint of pleasure as she slapped the cuffs on the bruised Bob's wrists.

"OK, you're both coming with us," McCall growled as they dragged Bob to the door. Kim followed sheepishly. As they left the place, the second waitress stood watching the scene, open-mouthed. There was a helpless look across her long face as the double doors swung closed. She was alone with twenty customers, all of whom had just ordered food.

———

Steel and McCall headed back to the station. McCall had collared a passing black-and-white to take the dazed Bob to lock-up, whilst they escorted Kim Washington. The journey to the 11th was quiet. They had to take the FDR back to East Village where the 11th Precinct was based. It took nearly an hour and a half due to a three-car pileup, but Steel didn't mind, McCall's Mustang was more comfortable than a squad car. He had never asked her why she was banned from using police vehicles; a mystery he thought he would leave for his imagination. That said, the way she had treated her own car – namely the car before they one they were enjoying the comforts of, had led to many questions for him. Sure, she had sacrificed her beloved car to save him from a situation, but he was sure they could have been another way to have done it? Of course, his gratitude for saving his arse came in the form of a new car, and what a car.

Warm sunbeams broke past the gaps in the towering buildings filling the car like strobe lights. The only sound came from the police radio, and the daily commotion as everyone headed home. The local radio station was on low and was more background noise than anything. McCall looked in her rear Kim Washington, who was doing something on her cell phone to pass the time.

"I hope you ain't putting this on social media!" McCall said, looking around at Kim; who shot her an angry look.

"Yeah, I can see it now "Having a fun day stuck in a police car on the FDR," that will get loads of likes," Steel laughed turning to McCall, Kim giggled, and McCall shot him a burning gaze.

"You're such an ass," McCall said with almost a whisper.

"No, just bored, and hungry," Steel said, looking over at the street food vendors. McCall looked back at Kim, who was sitting in the back with her earbuds in, listening to music or watching a film on her phone. McCall had questions for her, but they could wait until they reached the station. Steel had plans for later, plans that could not wait.

On the way to the precinct, they had taken Kim Washington to New York-Presbyterian Hospital to get her checked out. She had taken quite a beating from Bob and McCall wondered what other wounds she had sustained since she had worked there. McCall had gotten a female uniformed officer to stay with her to make sure she was safe. When Kim was finished, the uniform would bring her to the precinct. McCall didn't want to wait; she was afraid what the doctor might find and give McCall to lose control and beat the shit out of the owner. Steel convinced McCall to go back to the station, for her good and Bob's.

The 11th Precinct was busier than usual. Hordes of people filled the entranceway, yelling and screaming – mostly abuse. Steel smiled as they entered, think that the last time he had seen this kind of chaos, he was waiting for a flight out of Germany. As Steel and McCall stepped off the elevator onto the department floor, they saw John Doe still in the room with Doctor Davidson. Steel opened the door to the small briefing room slowly and entered almost unnoticed. Steel felt that John Doe looked nervous and uncomfortable, but then, how else would anyone look after losing track of everything they ever knew, their entire life gone in a moment. In a way, Steel envied him, wished he had no memories, especially of that day he lost everything, and everyone. Unfortunately, he couldn't change being inquisitive, and Steel knew that if he had lost his memory, he would do everything to find out who he was and what had happened. Surely that would be worse, to find out that way rather than having the memories – or rather, nightmares?

"How's he doing, Doc?" Steel asked, his gaze firmly resting

on John Doe. Steel heard the door open behind him. But he didn't turn as McCall entered the room and stood next to him.

"Well he has his muscle memory," Davidson replied. The two detectives shot him a blank look. Davidson smiled and nodded as he realised what pleasure he would take when he explained.

"Muscle memory is something you do every day, for instance, signing your name, tying your shoelaces," the doctor explained. "This man's memory for those actions is intact. However, his long-term memory is gone, or at least hindered." Davidson directed his lecture to Steel in particular, behaving almost like a teacher explaining something simple to a stupid child. Steel prodded the bridge of his sunglasses with his middle finger to adjust them and smiled, knowing full well what the doc was doing.

"So, what could cause this?" McCall asked. "A bump on the head?" She took a seat opposite John Doe.

"There are many possibilities. Head injury or a stroke, substance abuse, or the most likely thing, since we haven't found any relevant injuries, is a massive emotional event. You know? Something like a serious car accident—that sort of thing." Davidson smiled as he answered McCall's question.

"Will he get his memory back?" Steel asked, his tone dry and distracted.

"Nobody knows. He could get it back in an hour, five days, a year, or never. It is a waiting game," Colby Davidson said, shrugging. John Doe suddenly looked alarmed at the last part. *Never getting his memory back.* It was a lot to take in.

Steel nodded as if he understood, but his mind was elsewhere. He had questions of his own, such as: who was this man, and why was he covered in blood? Not forgetting, who the hell's blood was it?

"OK. So, is there —" McCall froze in mid-sentence. She

was about to ask if there was someone they could call, or if he needed dropping off somewhere. Her mouth slammed shut, and she gave John Doe an embarrassed smile.

"Don't worry, Detective, this is a first for me as well," John Doe said to her, smiling. Steel had left the room and was on his cell whilst they spoke.

"OK. So, we need to find you somewhere to stay. I will speak to my captain and try and arrange something." McCall knew there was no budget for dealing with lost people who had amnesia but decided she could spin it as a 'protective custody for a potential witness'.

"Don't worry, I got it covered. I think he has been through enough, so I have got him a hotel room," Steel said, with a broad grin on his face.

"OK, so where is the hotel?" McCall asked, suspicious of Steel's intentions.

———

McCall's mouth dropped open as they walked into the suite at the five-star Manhattan Hotel. There were panoramic views and marble bathrooms. The two-bedroom suite even had a small dining table. Sam shook her head at the sight of a hotel room that was bigger than her apartment and probably cost more to build.

"So – uhm, John, I hope you will be comfortable. There will be two policemen outside for your protection, so there is no reason to worry." Steel smiled.

John Doe shot him a confused look. "Do I need protection?" he asked. His tone sounded almost angry at the thought of being watched. Steel smiled reassuringly.

"Sir, you were covered in blood, and you were not hurt,"

Steel explained. "Which means that you either saw something you shouldn't have—"

"—Or I did something I shouldn't have done. In which case, this is my prison." John Doe scowled at Steel, who nevertheless kept his smile. The British detective reached into the inside pocket of his jacket as his cell phone began to vibrate. He checked the message and smiled at the text from the desk sergeant.

The babysitters should be there now.

Steel sent a 'thank you' reply, then placed the phone back into his pocket.

"So, sleep well, and we will see you in the morning," Sam McCall said reassuringly "Hopefully you may have remembered something by then."

"I will come around tomorrow to check on him, detectives," Dr Davidson, who had come with them, butted in. "I am sure you have other things to attend to," Davidson said as he opened the refrigerator to check its contents.

"You take it, you buy it doc," Steel said with a smile, as he saw Davidson take out a small bottle of sparkling wine. Davidson reached into his pocket and pulled out a wad of bills. "It's OK, first one is on me," Steel smirked before walking off. McCall rolled her eyes at the show of testosterone. McCall headed for the front door, where Steel was already waiting. Outside in the hallway stood two officers, who were dressed in plain clothes. Steel smiled as he recognised the two men. His previous encounters had left the guys unnerved, to say the least. One was tall and thin, the other shorter with greying hair and had a 'veteran cop' look about him. As the two officers saw Steel their mouths dropped open. They, too, had recognised him and instantly had a bad feeling.

"Gentlemen, the task is simple," John Steel told them. "One man is to be on shift out here, while the other acts as back-up inside the room behind you. You work out the shift change between you, but someone is always out here. Nobody is to come in or out of that room except us and the good doctor there." Steel opened the door so that they could see the tall strange-looking doctor in the grey suit. The two men nodded.

"Any questions?" Steel asked, almost trying not to grin at the confused look they both wore. The two officers shook their heads. Steel smiled and turned for the elevator.

"Right then, see you all tomorrow." Steel said with a smile then checked his watch. McCall followed, leaving the two men to argue about who was going to take the first shift.

As Steel pressed the call button, he heard McCall approach. He could feel her almost agonizing need to get the millions of questions off her chest. The doors slid open, and they stepped inside. He just looked forward at the doors and towards the two cops in the distance. He looked contented as McCall stood patiently for the doors to close before she opened on him.

"Steel, just what the hell is going on?" she screamed as the doors closed, and the box began to move. He just smiled and took in the rant. She was pissed and had every reason to be. McCall regarded amnesiac John Doe as a victim, perhaps even a witness. But Steel saw something else. There was something about the man that set off every alarm bell in Steel's head.

CHAPTER NINE

After Kim Washington had been released from hospital, she was taken to see McCall at the 11th. Kim didn't like police stations at the best of times. In fact, the only times she had been in one was to pick up her mom, something that happened too often.

McCall had spoken to the doctor's and found she was in perfect health considering a slight case of malnutrition. If the chef had beaten her, he had hidden it well, or it had been some time since the last one.

Kim Washington stepped off the elevator at the third floor – the Homicide Division of the 11th precinct. She stood for a moment and looked around as if hoping to find a familiar face in the sea of people. Detectives were either on their phones or darting around after getting that "hot lead." She felt alone as eyes stared at her, judging her. Kim could feel their questions, "why was this woman there, what had she done, was she a criminal or a witness?" Kim felt like turning around, getting back on the elevator and going. Did she really need to be there? She went to leave, but a familiar voice called her name, "Kim, over here," said the voice. It was detective Samantha McCall. Kim looked back towards the voice, McCall was stood next to a room – a briefing room, or so she thought. Kim walked over slowly, dragging her heels, feeling the eyes on her once more.

"Thanks for taking the time to talk to us," McCall said, ushering Kim into the room. The room was small – ten by ten with a large window, a square table and two chairs. The room – despite being scares of furnishings, was friendly, or more so than an interrogation room. On the white plastic covered top of the table was two mugs of coffee. There were no recording devices, no cameras. Defiantly not an interrogation room. Kim sat and looked around the room. No double mirror, just a mug of coffee.

"Did I have a choice?" Kim replied as she took her seat.

"Sure, but then we would have had to talk to you again, at home or at your work, I just thought this would be easier," McCall said with a comforting smile. In truth, McCall wanted to get Kim out of her comfort zone, away from distractions or intimidations.

"What do you want to know?" Kim finally asked. McCall smiled inside.

"Tell me about Tara, what kind of person was she?" McCall asked, picking up her mug of coffee.

"She's nice, the kinda gal that would give you her last dollar if you were in trouble, which is weird considerin," Kim said before blowing on her hot beverage.

"Considering what?"

"Considerin her past, her poppa died when she was young, her momma was a real piece of work," Kim explained, her Southern Georgia accent broke through her Brooklyn. "Her Momma took off when she was in her late teens, poor thang had to survive by herself since she was a littlun, not right, not right at all," Kim shook her head.

"Did she have a temper?" McCall asked, taking note of Kim's reaction.

"You mean, could she have killed her roommate, her best friend?" Kim scowled. "No ma'am, Tara was the sweetest thang, sure, don't get me wrong, the gal stood up for herself, took no shit from nobody, includin that piece of shit boss of ours," Kim smiled, a distant memory slipped into her mind. "One time the bastard tried somethang with one of the new girls, Tara wasn't havin none of that, put him in his place she did," Kim's expression changed as if she had just said something she shouldn't have. McCall saw it and leapt on it.

"How did she – handle it?" McCall asked, leaning forward. Kim swallowed hard.

"She... she, look you gotta understand, she was just savin the girl from a beatin," Kim spurted the words, trying to un-ring that bell, but it was too late, it had been well and truly rung.

"How did she handle it?" McCall repeated the question.

"She put a knife to his balls and told him next time he'd lose them," Kim explained, her head tilted with shame of giving up her friend. "She looked after us, protected us, I guess the only reason the boss did what he did today was because he knew she wasn't there," Kim's voice trembled, the sudden realization that Tara wasn't going to be there to look after them hit home. McCall saw the panic in her eyes, and she knew in that instance how big a roll Tara played in their lives. Tara had been their bodyguard against an abusive boss; now, she was gone.

"If you are worried about your boss, you could press assault charges?" McCall said, but her words were met by a frightened, tearful gaze.

"Yeah, and then what, he gets out after, what, a month. Then he'll really do some beatin. And what about my job, he goes away, I got no work, whose gonna pay my way, you?" Kim growled. She was bitter and terrified.

"I have no answer, I wish I did, but I don't, all I can do is promise to keep an eye out for you and the other girls," McCall's voice was soft but held a power to it. Kim smiled and nodded.

"Maybe, you gonna cook as well, we ain't got no chef no more?" Kim laughed. McCall smiled and shrugged.

"Sorry, I can't help you on that one, I mostly get takeout," the two women laughed. McCall's smile faded. She knew that they had lost the momentum. "About Tara, did she have any boyfriends?"

"No, she didn't have much time for those, not the hours we were pullin," Kim shrugged. "She had a couple of casual pick-ups, but nothin serious." McCall nodded and made a note on the yellow pad.

"Did she have any problems with customers, anything like that?" McCall asked, trying to get a picture of the missing woman.

"Nah, she was friendly to everyone – well, everyone except that asshole, but he wouldn't do nothin," Kim explained. The picture that McCall was getting was of a bright, friendly, caring woman, who by all accounts could hold her own. So, did this make her and victim or the killer? The questions continued for a short while longer. While McCall was busy with Kim Washington Steel decided to make some calls. He knew a man in the room would just make Kim clam up, mostly through embarrassment, besides, McCall had told him to stay the hell out.

It wasn't long before the door opened, and McCall and Kim stood at the entrance. Steel looked over at the two women and smiled. They looked calm in each other's company, and that was what McCall was good at, getting through to people.

"Thanks again for speaking to me Kim, I will do everything to make sure your boss stays away for a while," McCall said handing over her business card. "if there is anything you ever need, call me." Kim smiled and held the card in both hands before tucking it away in her pocket. "I'll get uniforms to bring you home," McCall offered.

"No, that's OK detective. Unfortunately, I don't need the neighbours seein me gettin out of a police car. In my part of town, only two kinds of people get out of a police car, snitches, drunks and the cops themselves. Unless of course, you're the lady from number seven, this old gal always got a lift because she was always too drunk to drive herself home," Kim shrugged. "I'll be fine detective, thank you." Kim turned and faced Steel who was sat at McCall's desk with his feet up on the desk talking on his cell phone. Kim smiled and nodded to him. Steel returned the gesture and watched her walk to the elevator.

As Kim headed for the elevator, she smiled to herself. Bob was in lockup as a result of the assault on her and the attempted assault on a police officer. Kim had smiled when she saw her pig of a boss take a swing at the big cop. Kim was shocked at how fast the cop had moved and remembered that he'd been dressed completely in black clothes. She could still hear Bob's head impacting with the metal table. He had swung at a cop, and that would cost him a good couple of years. As Kim waited for the elevator, she hatched a plan, and she would keep the diner running, after all, she had done all the accounts and orders because Bob couldn't. She was already running it anyway, not that he had paid her any more for all those extra duties. In a way, it was her diner now, or at least it was until he got out of prison, by which time she would be long gone. While the place was running, she and the other waitresses had cash coming in.

. . .

Two subway rides later; she was nearly home. Kim had checked up on the diner before leaving. Fran's cousin, Carl, had taken on the cooking after she and Bob had left with the police, and Fran had done a hell of a job after they had gone. The night shift had come in, and so had Stan, Carl's boyfriend. He had offered to be the night shift chef. The place would run OK; indeed, it would probably run better now that Bob was out of the picture.

It was late, and her watch said it was half-past nine. She cursed the time, as she had missed her favourite TV show. Her street was at least two blocks from the station, but she began to hurry. Kim would be on early shift tomorrow and needed some sleep. The night air had a bite to it, and dark clouds covered the heavens from view. She turned onto her road and hurried towards her home. The sound of her heels echoed through the avenue of buildings.

She saw nothing around her, only the screen from her cell as she searched for missed messages. Even as she made her way up the stairs to the third floor, her vision never left the mass of messages from her social media pages. Her corridor was poorly lit, as though some of the bulbs had blown, but she was chatting to some guy on Twitter. Even as she opened the door with her key and nudged it open with her foot, she was away in another place. She never saw the hand cup her mouth or the person who thrust her into the apartment and slammed the door behind them. The corridor was silent apart from the sounds of the television sets behind closed doors.

No one had seen it happen. No one knew what had happened.

Inside Kim Washington's apartment, the darkness made the situation seem a thousand times worse. She had seen the movies: the ones where a girl gets attacked in a dark apartment, and they never ended well. Then she remembered what the cops had said about Tara's roommate, found dead in her apartment. Was she next, she wondered?

Suddenly the lights came on, and Kim shielded her eyes from the sudden brightness. This suddenly made it worse. With the lights off she could say she hadn't seen anything but now! She kept her hand over her eyes, but this time it was to shield her view of her attacker. She didn't want to see them; she didn't want to die.

"Kim put your hand down. I am not gonna hurt you," said a familiar voice. Kim ripped her arm down to her side.

There before her stood Tara Burke.

Kim's terror subsided as she saw the look of utter panic in Tara's eyes. Tara was scared, alone and hungry.

The scared waitress sat down on her brown fabric-covered couch and hoped that Tara would do the same. Slowly, Tara sat. The dazed look in her eyes made them seem larger than normal. This was a woman running scared. But from what, Kim wondered. Of the killer? Or of the cops?

"Where have you been, Tara?" Kim's voice was soft and soothing, but the tone rang with a hint of weariness. "The cops have been lookin' for ya."

"Amber ... Amber ... is—" Tara raced to the bathroom and threw up. The shock of what she had found still burned in her memory. As Kim walked into the bathroom, she found Tara on the tiled floor, holding her legs against her body for comfort. Tears ran freely down her pale cheeks. Tara looked up at her friend with large scared blue eyes.

"They butchered her, cut her up. Why, Kim? Why?"

Kim didn't have any more answers than Tara did. Kim helped her friend to her feet then led her back to the couch. As Tara crashed down onto the cushioned couch, Kim headed for the kitchen. She needed a drink—hell, they both did.

She passed Tara a glass with two fingers of scotch in it, then sat down next to her friend. Kim sipped the golden liquid whilst Tara just cradled the glass and stared into nowhere.

"Hey, it's OK. You're safe now."

Tara looked over towards her friend and smiled. She was hoping that Kim was right. She hoped she was safe here.

"Why didn't you go to the cops?" Kim asked, before taking another hit from the glass.

"Don't know, I was scared, I guess."

Kim nodded as though she understood, but then the sight of Tara's pink suitcase made her wonder. If she was so scared, why had she packed a suitcase to leave?

"You leavin' the city?" Kim asked, her eyes now fixed on Tara, who just shrugged and took a sip of the golden liquid.

Tara coughed as the whisky hit the back of her throat. Kim smiled to herself as she watched her friend wave a hand in front of her mouth.

"Not a whisky gal then." Kim laughed, and Tara joined in, almost forgetting her troubles for a moment.

"The police came around the diner looking for you," Kim said.

Tara just nodded as if it was expected.

"What did you tell them?" Tara asked before trying another sip from the glass.

Kim shrugged. "What could I tell 'em? I didn't know anything." She smiled wickedly. "One good thing happened, though. Bob took a swing at a cop." She explained what had happened, and Tara's mouth fell open.

"Did he get him?"

Kim shook her head to the question. "Nah, the cop was too

fast, the man moved like lightning, put Bob right down on his fat ass!"

The two women laughed, but Tara's laughter died, and she stared into her glass.

"I keep seeing her lying there in all that blood. I keep thinking that should have been me!"

Kim gave Tara a puzzled looked. "What do you mean?" She suddenly had a bad feeling about what the answer might be.

"Kim, she wasn't supposed to have moved in for another two days. She shouldn't have been there!" Kim shuddered at the revelation. Was her friend being stalked? And if so, would they come here?

———

Steel entered his park view loft apartment and was greeted by the orange glow of the city. The large three-bedroom apartment's trio of huge windows allowed a panoramic view over the skyline. A huge sitting area gave way to a kitchenette and two staircases. One of these went to the gallery, which was also his bedroom, and the other led to the spare rooms. A long corridor next to the kitchen was home to the bathroom and two other rooms: an office and another which was at the end. The door to this room looked heavier than normal and could only be opened by using a security pad.

John Steel walked to a small drinks cabinet that was next to the breakfast bar and poured himself a glass of Johnny Walker Blue Label. He took off his jacket and tossed it gently onto the large L-shaped brushed-leather couch. Steel signed, at last, he had quiet. Even though he liked working with the cops, he found it too noisy. Steel looked over to his answering machine which was blinking with a red glow. He had messages, the last thing he needed. He walked over to the machine and noticed that seven missed calls showed up on the LED display.

He pressed the 'play' button and walked slowly towards the window to take in the view. Two messages were from the CEO of his father's company, Steel Industries, or Kyoi Industries as his father had named it. The other one was from some woman from a charity who was wondering if he was attending an event in September. More people after money for a good cause that they possibly didn't give a shit about, but it made them feel better every time they did their taxes.

Steel smiled and shook his head. September was a long way off, and he never planned anything further than two weeks ahead. The rest of the messages were from people who were wanting to talk to 'Lord Steel' rather than 'Detective Steel'. He liked it like that, gave him a little sense of home.

As a beep sounded, the machine told of the time and date of the next call. It was from a man called Laurence. Steel turned his head slightly to hear better. The message was simply to tell him of his resupply. Steel smiled and walked towards the locked door at the end of the corridor.

Stopping at the door, he punched in the code and placed his hand of the scanner that slid out of the wall. A red light turned to green on the keypad, and he entered. As the door closed, the machine's voice told him: 'No more messages.'

Steel returned to the sitting room wearing a new watch. He topped up his glass and headed for the leather chaise longue that was in front of the windows, with their spectacular view. He liked it there: the view, the silence. He sat down and stretched out along its full length. John took a mouth full of the whisky and let it warm in his mouth before allowing it to trickle down his throat rather than swallowing it in one go.

He closed his eyes and hoped for a peaceful sleep, but he

knew that would never happen. His memories haunted him, but strangely enough, he found strength in the pain.

Images of a bright summer's day broke through the darkness of his thoughts. His return home from nearly a year overseas with his SAS Regiment. He had done his tour and was returning home. With the war still in his head, he needed rest, quiet and most of all his beloved wife.

Steel's eyes creased together in mental anguish as the memories unfolded in his head. The memory of his homecoming. The bright summer's day, the marquee on the back lawn. The people lying dead: all of them had been family and friends murdered by gunmen—the mercenaries he had taken out. He could almost smell the cordite, feel the heat from the explosions. His body tensed up as in his mind he was back in the attic. The dimly lit place of his death and rebirth.

The sound of laughter, the six shots, the image of his poor dear love in his arms and her lifeless eyes.

The darkness.

The plastic glass fell from his hand and bounced on the wooden floor. Steel sat up and screamed. He looked around, confused and disorientated. His cold emerald-green eyes appeared almost black in the dull light. Cascades of sweat flowed down his forehead. He swung his legs around as he sat facing the room. Tilting his head back, he sucked in the conditioned air.

Standing up, he headed for the bathroom. He had at least an hour before his car would arrive. He stripped the shirt off his back and tossed it onto the couch. On the underside of each step of the staircase to his bedroom, there was a metal bar. This created the perfect facilities for a workout, and they were almost like monkey bars that led upwards. Steel moved up and down the twenty-bar construction at least five times. He could feel his muscles tighten. Sweat poured down his chiselled form as he moved quicker and quicker. Steel felt the pain in his shoulders and arms. His forearms burnt from the grip.

Finally, he just stood, his hands on his knees, sucking in the air. He stood up straight and leant back as far as he could, feeling his midsection stiffen. Steel grabbed the whisky glass from the breakfast bar and headed for the shower. In less than twenty minutes, the car would be there. He stripped off the rest of his clothes and stuck them into the hamper, before turning on the shower. There was a whoosh of water that sounded like rain on the glass divider. Steel looked at himself in the mirror. His large dead green eyes stared back at him. He tested his stubble growth with his left hand, weighing up whether to shave or not. His stubble was rough; it felt like he was stroking sandpaper. He couldn't really be bothered to shave, but then he realised that he had an appearance to maintain. Tonight, he would be attending as Lord Steel, not as Detective Steel.

The warm water cascaded over his muscular form, soaking every inch of his powerful body, washing the soap lather from his overworked muscles. After shaving in the shower, he just let the water run over him. He placed his hands on the side and let the shower pound his tight flesh. The alarm on his phone alerted him that he had ten minutes in which to change into his clothes. He grunted in disapproval of leaving the soothing waters, then got out.

After drying off, he slipped into his all-black tuxedo and Bugatti shoes. He checked his reflection: he had to admit that he looked good, just did not look happy about where he was going.

He looked at the hands-on his new Military style smartwatch. The carbon-fibre face was illuminated by the luminous dials. It was nearly eight o'clock. There was a benefit on at The Museum of Modern Art, and the Mayor and the Governor had insisted that he attend.

Steel stood in front of a long Elizabethan mirror and checked his attire. He had put his blue contact lenses in and set his phone to vibrate instead of ring.

He was ready to go but not willing. He looked around at the comfort of his sanctuary. Suddenly his house phone rang. Steel picked it up and listened to the concierge, informing him that his car had arrived. John opened the drawer and looked at his Barretta Storm bulldog 9MM sub-compact pistol, then closed it. He feared that if he took it out, he might end up using it on himself.

"Oh well, for Queen and country," he said, opening the front door.

It would be a long night of rubbing shoulders. A night he could do without. With people, he could do without too.

CHAPTER TEN

At Four in the morning, the garbage men and cops doing their own kind of patrol. Sirens wailed as fire engines, and ambulances travelled to emergencies around the city. The city that never sleeps was right; there was always something going on. Yellow cabs made their way with tourists fresh from JFK or businesspeople heading for that early meeting. The city was bathed in a mix of bright multi-coloured lights from stores, delis and restaurants. It would be hours yet until the sun would brake over the horizon. Soon the dullness would be replaced by bright ochre, and the city would come alive. The day before the weather girl had predicted: "Sunny spells and highs in the fifties." Joggers got an early start, and so did the paper delivery service.

McCall's alarm let out its usual loud serenade of *BEEP, BEEP, BEEP.* Her arm snaked from under the covers like a mythical beast, then slammed down on the off button before disappearing back under the covers. There was a three-minute pause before the second alarm went off. She groaned disapprovingly, then crawled out of her warm bed. She needed coffee and a shower. Sometimes she wished someone would invent a showerhead that would give out coffee instead of water for those early mornings. But soon changed her mind as she smelt the aroma coming from the kitchen as her coffee machine switched on, using the timer.

She poured the first cup of coffee and headed for the bathroom. McCall leaned in and switched on the shower before slipping out of her shorts and T-shirt. She stood there looking at her slightly tanned firm figure. She had the body of a supermodel from *Sports Illustrated*. She kept fit by training with her kickboxing instructor every Tuesday and Thursday.

Men dreamt about her, and so they should—that was her power over them. But she was a damn good cop, and she would never let her looks take precedence over her abilities as a detective. She had worked hard for her position and then she worked even harder and got the due respect for it. Sure, she had been passed over by others she had joined with because they were men, but she didn't mind because they ended up riding a desk and doing what they were good at kissing ass.

Sam reached up to her left shoulder and touched the scar she had got a year ago. A mercenary had shot her, for him to draw out Steel. McCall could still hear the screams of the man after Steel had gotten hold of him. It had been their first case together and what a ride that was.

McCall stepped into the shower and let the warm water cascade over her athletic body. She closed her eyes and leant against the tiled wall with outstretched arms. The water was relaxing to the point where she wanted to stay there all day. But she had work to do, and she owed it to Tony to find his girlfriend's killer.

She dried off and dressed in a grey trouser suit with a blue blouse. Her Gabor boots were almost flat-bottomed with a slight heel, which enabled her to run. She had tried heels, but they just slowed her down.

Pulling on the suit jacket, McCall headed for the front door and the dresser next to it. Opening the right-hand drawer, she pulled out her custom Glock 17 and her shield. Tucking the brushed steel pistol into the holster under her jacket, she grabbed her keys and headed out.

———

Walter T. Hobbs walked out of his apartment building. He was a small man with a large balding head that had tufts of black hair clinging to the sides. A pair of gold-rimmed glasses perched on a fat nose, giving him the appearance of a school physics teacher. He wore a black suit with a green tie and brown brogue shoes.

Behind him, he dragged the wheeled suitcase towards the curb. The doorman raised a gloved hand to flag down an approaching cab. Walter pulled out a ten-dollar note for the man's trouble, which was snapped up and tucked away before anyone else saw it.

"Where you goin, buddy?" asked the cabby as Walter sat on the long back seat. The doorman shut the door behind Walter and doffed his hat as the cab sped away. At that moment Walter noticed two large men in black suits enter his building, and he knew they were there for him.

"JFK if you would, please hurry," Walter said, taking note of the man's credentials that were on the dashboard. His eyes scanned the driver for a moment. Walter noted the man's lumberjack shirt and blue padded vest, which resembled a life preserver.

He smiled happily to himself then let his gaze fall to the

outside, the passing streets and pedestrians, his thoughts a million miles away.

"So, you are going anywhere nice?" the black cabby asked, his dreadlocks dangling from under his multi-coloured woollen cap.

"What – sorry, I was miles away, I'm off to see my aunt in Portugal. She is very ill, poor dear," Walter said convincingly, almost as if he had rehearsed it a thousand times just in case the line was needed.

"Wow, Portugal," the cabbie replied, shouting back through the plated dividing screen. "Never been there myself but I have heard it is very beautiful."

Walter took a handkerchief from his inside pocket and removed his glasses to clean them. Beads of perspiration were beginning to form on his forehead.

The cab's passenger used the white cotton handkerchief on his moist forehead, then put his small spectacles back on. He took a deep breath, exhaled and sat back in the seat. He glanced out through the window again. He knew the turn-off for the airport would soon be coming up and then he would be home free. A panic ran through his body as he noticed they had gone past the exit. Walter leaned forward and tapped on the safely glass that separated them.

"Hey, you missed the exit!" Walter screamed.

The driver shook his head and smiled. "No, man, I saw it. It's just that Mr Williams said he wanted to say goodbye before you left."

Walter's head began to spin. He tried the door handles, but the deadbolt was on.

He was trapped, and he was on the way to see a madman.

The worried man knew at that moment that he would be going on a trip, just not the one he wanted. The cab's interior began to spin, and he fell into darkness as he lost consciousness. The cabbie mumbled curses to himself as he tossed his Taser to one side. He had been waiting all through the trip to use it and then that loser of an accountant had gone and fainted. He picked the Taser back up and Tasered Walter anyway, just out of spite.

He smiled and drove on into Brooklyn. Walter had an appointment, and Mr Williams didn't like to be kept waiting.

———

Walter T. Hobbs awoke to the sound of voices. Voices that seemed to be muffled, as if they were far away, or on the other side of a door. Everything seemed blurred and distorted, and everything seemed dark.

He tried to lift his hand to check his glasses but found that he could not move. He was being held down by something. His senses had been shot as a result of an electric shock. He tried to struggle but gave up after a few minutes. He was strapped to a table, a cold metal table.

Walter's heart began to race as he realised where he was. He stopped moving and listened. The room was silent, but he knew he wasn't alone. Heavy impacts struck the floor as someone large entered the room.

"Mr Hobbs, our employer, would like to know where it is," said a deep angry voice.

"I don't know what you mean. Where is what?" Walter screamed, tears of fear running down his face. He was glad of the darkness, for he didn't want to see anything.

"Some merchandise came in a couple of days ago, very important merchandise. Now it's missing, and unfortunately, only a few people knew about it. So, you see my problem ... Well actually, your problem right now," said the voice.

"I don't know! Really, I don't. If you mean Tuesday's shipment, I made sure it was secure," Walter answered.

"So why were you in such a rush to get out of the country, Mr Hobbs?" The mystery voice sounded calm but authoritative.

"My aunt, she's sick. I was—"

"—Blah, blah, blah," the voice interrupted. "You really expect me to believe the coincidence that your aunt is sick the same week that information goes missing?" The man was now yelling loudly, and Walter knew that his time was up.

"Look, tell us what we want to know, or else Mr Williams is coming in, and believe me you don't want that." The man's voice almost sounded cheerful at the prospect.

Walter had heard things about Mr Williams: bad things. He would perform unspeakable acts on people that weren't even worth thinking about. He wasn't a butcher. He was a surgeon, an artist some said. Either way, if you ended up on his table, your experience would be long and painful.

"Please! I don't know anything," Walter cried out.

The footsteps walked away, and Walter began to shake.

He heard a door open, and then after a time, it closed again. Then he heard something. A sound that chilled him to the bone. Music, soft music from a music box or ... a pocket watch.

Mr Williams was there.

Walter began to shake uncontrollably. The music grew near, and the sound of metal-tipped shoes on a tiled floor echoed around the room.

Both sounds were moving around him, as though he was being circled. He wanted to cry out to ask who was there, but in another part of his mind, he didn't want to know. The tapping grew slower until finally, it stopped, and so did the music. There was a silent click as the watch was closed and put away.

Then came a voice that made Walter nearly soil himself: it was a voice like knives on violin strings:

"Hello, Mr Hobbs. My name is ... Well, they call me Mr Williams. I don't know why, but for what they pay me they can call me Susan and stick me in a leather corset for all I care."

Walter felt puzzled at the man's apparent joviality. Mr Williams was softly spoken, but his tone raised and lowered with each word. However, his voice ground like nails on a chalkboard.

"I don't know anything!" Walter pleaded. "I did what I was asked, and then I locked it away."

The footsteps tapped slowly, as though Williams was thinking as he walked.

"My colleague said you were fleeing the country," Williams spoke softly.

The sound of metal sliding against metal filled Walter's ears.

"My aunt is sick, she has cancer. I was off to see her." Walter's voice was filled with fear and defeat. He knew whatever he said they would not believe.

"Oh, I am sorry. I had no idea. There must have been a terrible mistake, I do apologise," Williams said, and the tone of sincerity rang in Walter's ears. But he felt more afraid than ever. He felt the sudden weight of someone on top of him, but the darkness revealed nothing.

"OK, so can I go now?" Walter said, taking a chance in that moment.

A long thin pale face emerged from the blackness and loomed over Walter. Williams had high cheekbones and large maddening eyes, and a long Roman nose under which was a smile. Pearly white teeth behind ruby red lips. His blond hair was brushed back to reveal a large forehead.

Williams leered down at Walter like a tiger looking at its prey.

"Well, Walter ... I can call you Walter, can't I?"

Walter nodded quickly to the question so as not to antagonise his captor.

"It seems the powers that be feel that you're a bit of a fibber and a thief, which is good. I mean, that's what we do, isn't that right?" Then Williams's tone changed; his voice went deeper. "But we don't appreciate it when we get this treatment from one of our own. It's kind of takes you off the Christmas card list," Williams growled.

Their eyes met. Walter wanted to look away, but Williams's eyes were strangely hypnotic. Williams drew closer so that his nose rested on Walter's.

"I have been asked to come down here and find out if you're lying or not. So far—"

Walter held his breath. He waited for the words: 'No you're not lying' or 'I believe you'.

But Williams said nothing more. He just sunk his teeth into Walter's nose and bit down hard.

Walter screamed in pain. Williams jumped down from the table and spat the bitten off chunk of flesh back at Walter. There was a small burst of light which illuminated the operating table from above, then a scrape of metal. Suddenly Walter found himself moving as the table was being repositioned. To the side of him was a large mirror.

"This is for you, Walter, because I don't want you to miss anything," Williams rambled. "It is very rare that I get an audience so I can't wait to share my performance with you. That is until you either die or blackout. Whichever comes first, I guess."

Walter felt the warm urine flow down his leg, making Williams smile.

"Oops a little accident, oh well, never mind," Williams joked as he moved back into the darkness.

"OK, Walter, last chance. Where's the goodies?" Williams asked again as he pulled on some long surgical gloves, then pulled at a metal stand covered with various bottles of fluids. Williams clearly had enough chemicals and drugs to keep Walter alive and conscious. Tapping the side of Walter's neck, Williams found an artery and stuck in a needle.

"Normally we would use an arm but ... Well, you get the picture." Williams laughed as he began to walk off to fetch more equipment.

"Please don't—"

The torturer turned and slammed a gloved hand over Walter's mouth.

"Dear Walter. Here's the thing. If you say that sentence once more, I will rip out your teeth. You'll need your tongue to tell me the truth later. So, tell me the truth or don't say anything, OK?"

Walter nodded frantically.

"Smashing!" Williams said, clapping like a child who had won a prize. He moved to a small table that contained some bottles of water. He wiped his forehead then cracked open a bottle. As he moved the opened drink to his lips, he stopped and turned towards the bleeding Walter.

"Oh, dear me, where are my manners? Walter, you must be parched. Do forgive me, won't you?" Williams walked over to Walter, who opened his mouth to receive the cool liquid, his mouth feeling drier than a sandstorm. Williams took care to pour a bit at a time into his victim's mouth, so as not to choke him.

Walter nodded a 'thank you', careful not to speak after the last instruction. Williams smiled, pleased that he understood.

"You see, Walter, I am not such a bad guy. All I want is the truth, that's all." Williams smiled again and pulled up a chair that was at the far side of the room. He placed it next to Walter's head and sat down.

"I got the information from the courier and proved it was the real thing," Walter explained for what he thought must be the thousandth time. "It was then sealed in the safe, and then I gave the keys to the night watchman—Donald, I think his name was. Anyway, after that, I left. That's it. That's all I know."

Williams sat and tapped an index finger on his lips. "So, your aunt is ill, you say? Sorry to hear about that."

Walter looked at his captor in some confusion.

"What?" the powerless man answered, surprised to see the compassionate look on the other man's face. "Yeah, I got the call this morning. The hospital called to let me know."

"I believe you, Walter, really I do. In fact, the hospital confirmed your story just a while ago," Williams explained.

Walter exhaled a lungful of air in relief.

"So, am I free to go?" Walter felt a huge surge of relief at the thought of his ordeal being over.

However, Williams's sympathetic expression changed to a callous grin.

"I believe your story about your aunt, my dear Walter. But I never mentioned anything about the other matter."

Walter's face fell, and his fear returned with a vengeance.

"You said you sealed it in the safe, but the safe was empty. You said you gave the keys to the watchman Donald. Tell me, who the fuck is Donald? WE DON'T HAVE A DONALD; YOU ARE LYING PIECE OF CRAP!" Williams yelled.

He lost control, and in one swift movement he turned, picked up a meat cleaver from the instrument table and smashed it down onto Walter's right wrist. Blood erupted from the wound as his hand was separated from the wrist.

Walter screamed in shock and pain as he looked in the

mirror. Williams stood back in disgust at the screaming Walter. He had been a trusted member of the organisation. Suddenly the door opened, and a guard rushed in, holding a cell phone. Williams looked over at the guard with a disapproving look.

"What is it?" Williams simply said, not in the mood for chit chat on the phone. The guard sheepishly held up the phone.

"It's the warehouse, sir," the guard said, sweating.

"What do they want? Oh, never mind, give it here before you give yourself a friggin' heart attack." Williams took the phone and held it to his ear. The guard's eyes were transfixed by the sight of the meat cleaver that Williams was playing with as he listened. Williams nodded to the guard, indicating that he should silence the still-screaming Walter. The scared guard put his hand over Walter's mouth to dull the screams.

"Yes ... Uh ... Yep ... R-right. OK then, thanks." Williams pressed disconnect on the phone and smiled at the guard.

"Oh dear, this is s-so embarrassing. Really it is," Williams said, laughing and passing the phone back to the guard, who reached for it.

Quick as a flash, Williams grabbed the man's hand and swung the cleaver, neatly slicing through his wrist, severing the hand entirely. A cascade of blood-drenched the poor confused Walter.

Williams threw the freshly amputated hand at the guard, who was cradling his wound, the shock so fresh he hardly realised what had happened.

"So, tell me. How long did you wait outside before you gave me the phone?" Williams said calmly.

The guard turned to face the madman, still dazed. But as he began to reply, Williams's fury peaked once more. He threw the cleaver so hard that it embedded itself deep into the man's skull.

"Well, you know what they say. Don't shoot the messenger.

Thankfully they didn't mention decapitation or the severing of limbs," Williams joked. He looked down at the still-bleeding Walter. Williams grabbed the clothes iron that he had been saving for later and slapped its red-hot soleplate directly onto his gaping wrist, thus cauterising the wound. Walter screamed even more, and Williams rolled his eyes and stuck a rag into his mouth to silence him.

"I am sorry, Walter, it appears there was a bit of a mistake. They found that apparently there *was* a guy called Donald working there that night. A Donald Soap. Apparently, he was a sick relief for the regular man. Anyway, it looks like we were all duped and now I have egg on my face."

Williams headed for the door and called for a guard. A large man walked into the room. He seemed to have virtually no neck, and his bull-like appearance probably matched his IQ.

"Mr Hobbs has been, erm ... injured. Make sure you take good care of him, OK?" Williams said, keeping his voice level down. The guard nodded and smiled, revealing bad teeth, a sight that made Williams jump backwards in repulsion.

Williams left the room and started marching down a long corridor. Suddenly he heard a gunshot. Williams stopped and stood still. He looked at the ground and shook his head.

"How can I soar like an eagle, whilst working with turkeys?" he wondered.

CHAPTER ELEVEN

McCALL MET STEEL OUTSIDE THE PRECINCT. SHE noticed he wasn't wearing his usual suit. Today he was in black jeans, T-shirt, a pair of Bugatti boots and a pea coat. The body of it was made of wool, but the sleeves and collar were padded leather.

"Going for the sporty look today?" she joked. Steel shook his head and smiled.

"I've got to go to the range, apparently I have to qualify," he said, shrugging.

"Oh, you qualify for lots of things, Steel, believe me," she answered with a large grin. She didn't have to drive him, but she wanted to see what he could do. In all their time together, she had never really seen him shoot. McCall was itching to see 'Supercop' mess it up, or at least miss the target a few times. In fact, it so happened that McCall was the department's 'best shot'. Her dad had taught her to shoot when she was in her teens, and her natural aptitude had caused her to improve over the years.

They arrived at the outdoor range. It was a wooden

construction, arranged into individual 'pens' that denoted each shooter's firing point. Several staff were on standby to assist and to monitor the firers. Before heading to his position, Steel was briefed on the conditions of the shoot and the safety protocols. John nodded to the veteran cop and put on his ear defenders and headed for his given lane. McCall sat at the back next to the rear wall and opened the box of popcorn she had gotten from the vending machine. She was going to enjoy this.

———

The pair's drive back to the precinct was silent, as was their elevator ride to the department's floor. McCall was pale and felt ill. As the doors opened, they found Tooms and Tony ready with some toy pistols and a large target, their joke in order to shame Steel for when he failed the shooting test.

Steel marched into the captain's office and handed him the folded target and the 'pass confirmation' paperwork. Tooms and Tony looked at McCall who was sitting at her desk, a strange haunted look on her face. Then they crept over to the captain's door, just in time to see the captain unfold the target. The 'ten ring' in the centre was completely gone, the hole in the target being around twenty millimetres in diameter.

"Holy shit!" yelped an excited Tooms, causing his boss, Captain Brant, to look up at him.

"Quiet!" Brant said, folding the target back up and filing the paperwork.

"So now you are qualified you can get your ass back to work, Detective," Brant said to John Steel. "And that goes for you two jokers as well," he yelled after Tooms and Tony, who quickly hurried back to their desks.

As Steel approached his office, he said nothing, nor did he

smile. He could see that Sam McCall was pissed at him: he had beaten her previously unmatched score.

"Is there anything you're not good at?" she yelled after him.

He stopped and gave a small uncomfortable smile.

"Yes," he replied grimly. "Not letting the people, I care about get hurt or killed." His face was pained. Then he disappeared into his office.

McCall sat there with her mouth open, suddenly feeling shitty. She stood up and followed him into his office, via the break room.

Steel's office was an old storeroom he had commandeered and made his own. During a Christmas break, he had arranged for workmen to come in and turn it into something fantastic. The walls were covered with wooden panelling and burgundy velvet wallpaper. The same shade of oak that was on the wall panels was also that of the timber floorboards. Victorian furnishings filled the floor space, along with a large carved oak desk that was near the back of the room.

Two brown leather chesterfield armchairs were in front of the desk, and a red leather ship's 'captain's chair' sat proudly next to the footwell and the back of the desk. On the left-hand wall, a sixty-five-inch monitor acted as Steel's murder 'smartboard'.

McCall entered the room, brandishing two mugs of fresh coffee. Steel looked over at her and quickly tucked something away in a drawer.

"I thought you could use a coffee," she said apologetically.

He smiled and took the mug from her. Funnels of fresh steam drifted up from the fresh brew. McCall sat in one of the armchairs, and the creak of heavy leather filled the room as it took her weight. The smell of the room was intoxicating old wood and leather filled the senses. McCall was sure that if he could have done, he would have had a fireplace installed as well.

McCall liked it there, for it was almost like stepping back into time. The only thing missing was the Sherlock Holmes-style deerstalker cap and the briar pipe. It had a very Victorian feel to it all.

"Sorry about before," McCall said, swinging her legs over one of the arms of the huge armchair, with her head resting of the other.

"I was ... Well, I guess I was shocked, really, to be honest." She smiled at her own confession.

Steel sat back in his chair and cradled the cup into his hands.

"I have always been good at that sort of thing." His voice was soft, but there was a strange bitterness to it. "I don't know. Maybe it's a genetic thing. I joined the tactical combat engineer Regiment when I was seventeen," he explained, smiling as he thought back. "By the age of nineteen I was being poached by the SAS Regiment—they saw potential in me. Somehow I passed the entrance course first time—a lot of good men didn't." Steel's words almost sounded regretful of his past and the friends he had lost.

"I was with them for several years until ... Well, until something happened."

Sam McCall could not see Steel's eyes, but she knew if he could cry, he would be weeping right now.

"You mean your family?" she coaxed. "The massacre at your home?"

He looked shocked. But then smiled and nodded as if it was a relief that she knew already.

"After that, it was not safe for me to be in the SAS, so my father-in-law got me into the training for the SEAL teams. He is a senator with connections to the defence department, so all I had to do was pass." Steel smiled again as if remembering.

"I passed the training first time. Of course, when they learned of my past employment, they couldn't wait to give me a hard time because of it. I joined Team Five. A good unit with good men. In the first Iraq War, one of the helicopters carrying another team went down. Operations knew where they were, and they just needed a nod to get them out. We knew by dawn they would either be moved, or they would be dead before the extraction plan could be approved."

McCall stared at him; her eyes wide, almost afraid to hear the rest. But she felt a strange compulsion to know what happened too.

"The problem was they were being held in a small town, a well-fortified town that had been there for a couple of thousand years at least. It had high walls to see off invaders. The powers-that-be could have ordered heavy armour and a couple of squads, but that meant collateral damage. The town was historic, so they had to come up with some other idea. That night I went for a walk and found myself getting captured." Steel frowned as he remembered the details.

McCall's eyes were still fixed on him, her hands shaking with a mixture of excitement and fear.

"They tortured me for what seemed like hours. They had their fun until the commander came. I knew he would come eventually; that was why I waited." Steel took a sip from the coffee.

"I was hung upside down, like an animal ready for the slaughter. The commander laughed when I explained what was going to happen. About how I was going to kill them all. He seemed confused when I never mentioned killing him." Steel took another sip from the mug, and the hot steam fogged up his sunglasses for a few seconds before clearing.

"I have no idea how many men died that day, but I do know that twelve of my brothers walked out, including fifteen others from different nations. The commander realised at that moment why he had been spared: so that he could warn others of the 'green-eyed demon'. But rather than face the humiliation of losing all his men he shot himself." Steel shrugged as though it was nothing.

"After that, I got picked for LOAN WOLF missions."

Sam McCall lifted her cup with shaky hands, the dark liquid almost spilling over the sides.

"So ... W-why did you leave?" she asked, her voice as unstable as the rest of her.

Steel smiled. "Something happened, and I lost a lot of friends. You could say that my past had found me. Later I was recruited by an agency to do ... Well, *things*, shall we say."

McCall suddenly had an uneasy feeling. She knew he had a past but not one that was as colourful as this.

"So, then you left the agency and became a cop?" McCall asked, hoping that was the end of his résumé.

"You could say that." Steel spoke with an almost playful tone, which spooked McCall even more.

"Anyway, that doesn't matter. What matters is finding Amber's killer and finding out how our John Doe fits in, or if he indeed does fit into all this."

"Sure." McCall nodded and sipped her coffee. "So, what's the plan?" she asked.

"We break Bob. We find out what he knows."

McCall looked sceptical of Steel's idea. She wanted to watch the bastard squirm, and she wanted to be the one who made him talk.

CHAPTER TWELVE

OWEN LEVITT WAS HIS REAL NAME. HE TOLD EVERYONE IT was Bob Gablonski just for the image. He was a large no-neck man with a bald head, and even shorter temper and a large bruise on his head above his right eye.

"Bob Gablonski, or should I call you Owen Levitt?" McCall said smugly.

The large man just folded his arms and looked away.

"You have been informed of your rights and your right to counsel," McCall said calmly. Bob just sat there and grunted whilst avoiding eye contact.

"I'll take that as a yes," McCall said, laying down an open yellow legal pad and placing a thick brown file next to that. She took a pen from her jacket and clicked the end revealing the ballpoint and then placed it gently onto the pad.

"So, when did you see Tara Burke last, Bob?" McCall asked, her voice calm but authoritative.

Bob smiled and shook his head.

"It wasn't me," he growled, a smug grin crossing his large face.

McCall shot him a puzzled look. "What wasn't you? It wasn't you who killed or kidnapped her?"

Bob suddenly looked panicked at McCall's accusation. "What do you mean, lady? Tara's dead? What do ya mean she's dead? Nah, nah, nah. You ain't pinnin' that on me!"

The detective saw genuine concern in the big man's eyes. "So, what do you think you're in here for? Apart from being an idiot and swinging at a cop of course," McCall asked as she leaned back. Behind the two-way mirror, Captain Brant stood with Steel, both taking in the show. Brant looked at Steel, who just shrugged at the statement McCall had just made.

"He took a swing at you?" asked Brant. Steel just shrugged and smiled broadly. Brant shook his head, thinking what a bad move that had been on the part of their interviewee.

"Here's the thing, Bob," Sam growled, whilst leaning on the edge of the table. "I am going to get a warrant, and we are going to search your home and your diner. And if I find anything to say you had anything to do with her disappearance, you're going down." McCall's tone left him cold. "So, what happened that night?" she continued. "Did you two get into a situation and she bolted?" McCall went on, bluffing as a ploy to make him talk.

"No, it wasn't like that. Some guy came in lookin for Tara. Didn't think much of it, just thought it was some guy hopin' she did 'after-work' stuff. They met up and took a seat in one of the corners, out of the way, like. Anyway, they start gettin' into it, so I kicked the guy out. Tara left soon after, 'cause her shift had ended," Bob was talking fast, leaving little time for a breath, he was nervous, and had the right to be, he was looking at a murder charge. McCall sat back, feeling a sense of fulfilment because she had brought this bully down.

"Do you think you can talk to a sketch artist to get a description?" she said, with an arm hanging over the backrest of her chair. Bob shrugged and nodded, hoping his cooperation would get him off the charges, unaware that McCall wasn't feeling that generous.

"So, what did he look like—this mystery, man?" she asked.

"Gee, I don't know. Average height, ginger hair, blue eyes. Kinda plain lookin'," As Bob described the man, Steel and McCall both had the same thought.

Bob had just possibly described their John Doe.

———

Tony and Tooms had tracked down Tony Russo, Amber's previous boyfriend, and sat him down in one of the interrogation rooms with a cup of coffee. The two detectives watched him through the two-way mirror. He was around five foot seven and weighed about two hundred pounds. He was broad-shouldered, and the muscles of his ripped body showed under his tight T-shirt. He was a security guard in the local mall but acted as if he was a top detective.

Russo's brown hair was styled and held together with enough grooming products to be a fire hazard. His pearly white teeth glinted in the bright lights of the small room as he checked himself out in the large mirror.

Tony shook his head. "What the hell did Amber see in this dork?" he said as he watched this player start to pat his hair in case one strand had fallen out of place.

"Beats me, man. Sure, as hell wasn't for his personality," Tooms noted as he bit into a snack bar, he had gotten from the vending machine. "I think I know who ended it though," Tooms added after swallowing down his snack.

Around half an hour had passed before they went into the small grey-walled room. They had checked up on their vain and preening friend, ensuring they knew everything about him before they went at him with questions. Nothing kicks off an interrogation more than a big fat surprise.

They found Tony Russo asleep on the table, his jacket nestled comfortably between his head and the cold metal surface. The two detectives looked at each other in a mix of surprise and anger, because to their way of thinking, this was an interrogation room, not a hostel. Tooms purposely slammed the door, causing Russo to stir and wipe the drool from the corner of his mouth.

"Get your ass off of my integration table!" Tooms growled like a hungry bear with a taste for dirtbags. Russo slid off the table and onto the chair. He yawned as he picked up the empty coffee cup and stared at its brown-stained bottom. He looked up at Tony and raised the cup.

"Don't even think about askin' for another one," Tony said angrily, beating Russo to the mark. Russo shrugged and placed the cup back onto the table.

"Mr Russo, do you know this woman?" Tony asked, sliding a photograph of Amber over to their sleepy interviewee. It was an old photograph that he had found in an album Amber had stored in one of her boxes. Russo looked at the picture but never picked it up. He sat back and smiled smugly.

"Yeah, I knew her, we went out for a while, but she broke it off." Tony could sense the bitterness in his voice, and that suited Tony just fine. Anger was always a good motive for murder.

"When was the last time you saw her?" Tooms asked. Russo shrugged and tilted his head as if this whole thing was a waste of his time.

"I am sorry, are we boring you?" Tony growled at Russo, feeling the blood boil in his veins. Russo shrugged again and sucked his teeth as if he was removing the remnants of his breakfast. Tooms slammed a fist onto the table and leant forward. "Look, Russo, this woman is dead and so far, you're the only suspect. So, unless you give us something, I am gonna lock your ass up. Have I got your attention now?" Tooms's eyes became wide with anger. The other man suddenly sat up in his chair, and a look of utter panic contorted his face.

"Wow now hang on, fellas! Look, I haven't seen her in, like, months. She found out I was trying to hook up with her sister, and she got a little mad and threw me to the kerb." Russo held his hands up as if to show that was all he had to say.

Tony shot Tooms a confused look.

"So, you were trying to hook up with Brooke?" Tony asked, drawing a big question mark on the yellow legal pad. Russo shook his head and gave the two cops a disgusted look. "Brooke? Nah, she's way too old for me. No, I am talkin' about Sharney, Amber's twin." Russo had a look of surprise on his face as though he was astonished that he was the only one who knew of the existence of this twin.

Problem being, of course, that he was the only one. Tooms leant forward with interest.

"Her twin? Are you sure?" Tooms looked into Russo's eyes to try to detect any hint of a lie.

"Amber had just got this job at some shipping place, International Removals or something. Anyway, she was always working and had no time for me. So, one day I am just walking down Park Avenue when I bump into Amber, leastways that's who I thought she was. She explained that she was Amber's sister and that she worked in Philadelphia."

Tony stood and picked up Russo's coffee cup, thinking that he had earned a refill. He opened the door and passed the stained cup to a uniform and asked him to fetch another.

"Go on," Tony said, closing the door and heading back to his seat.

"Apparently she had worked in one of the hotels there and

was just back to get her stuff before heading off." Russo's eyes darted between the two detectives, hoping this was pulling him out of the grave he had dug earlier.

"So, you tried hitting on Sharney?" Tooms asked, already having guessed the answer. "So, what happened? Did she call Amber or something?"

"Yeah, the bitch called her sister, totally sold me out, Next day Amber kicks me to the kerb."

Tony detected the merest hint of remorse on Russo's face as he talked.

"Strange girl!" Tooms added sarcastically.

Russo's face lit up as if he had finally found someone who understood his pain.

"Yeah, right, she sure was," Russo said, his hands held out in surprise.

"So, what happened then? Let me guess. You got pissed and tracked her down. Thought you would make her pay, did you?" Tony's voice was gravelly from lack of moisture. His anger with this guy had made his mouth dry.

"Nah, sorry, cop. You got the wrong guy," Russo sat back and waved his palms at them as though to say "wow, stop." When did this all go down?" Russo asked, almost hoping he wasn't home alone at that point.

"Tuesday night, around ten," Tony answered, hoping that this scumbag had no alibi. He felt his soul die a little as Russo thought for a moment before a big smile came over his face.

"I was with some buddies. We had gone to Eddie's Bar on 3rd. We were there until closing time." Russo sat back, exuding an air of relieved smugness.

"OK, Mr Russo, we will need to know the names of your buddies, just so we can check your story out," Tooms said, almost as disappointed as Tony was.

As Russo got up to head out, Tooms saw the look on Tony's face. It was a lost, faraway expression.

"You OK, man?" Tooms asked his partner. Tony shook his head, then looked up at his friend.

"Tooms, if our victim wasn't Amber, then, where is she? And is she still alive, or are we going to be looking at a second body?"

Tooms felt a chill at his friend's words.

Because he was right.

CHAPTER THIRTEEN

McCall had put a request into Traffic for any CCTV footage around the diner. The description they had gotten from Bob made no sense. If their John Doe had something to do with the murder of Amber, why was he walking around half a day later covered in blood?

This whole case was making no sense. She stared up at the murder board to see if there was something that they had overlooked. From the corner of her eye, something moved, causing her to look over. Steel approached with two steaming coffee cups. She smiled as he placed them down on the comical coasters that sat happily on her desk. Steel pausing slightly before covering the coasters, the yellow 'smilies' all had different expressions. There was a stack of them next to a photograph of her with her mom and dad. It appeared to be an old photo, judging by the age she seemed to be. The British detective stared at the photograph for a couple of seconds. McCall looked up at him with a curious stare.

"Anything wrong?" she asked.

He turned and smiled before sitting in the chair next to her desk. "You must miss your father a lot." Steel's voice had a soothing tone to it. She looked at the small eight-by-five photo and nodded.

"It's been eleven years this September. Eleven years since we got the call about his shooting in that hotel." A small tear had gathered in the corner of her eye, but she forced back the emotion. *Time enough to cry later*, she thought. McCall picked up her coffee mug and blew on the pale-coloured coffee before taking a sip.

Steel looked across towards the murder board. The collage of photographs and scribbles were all held together in their own little headings: SUSPECTS, VICTIM, PERSONS OF INTEREST.

At the bottom, a think black line denoted the timeline. A thick red bar reached from seven in the evening until ten o'clock in the evening, when she was found. McCall was aware that the ME had put 'Time of Death' at around eight to nine o'clock that night, but McCall liked to be more thorough and accurate than that generality.

The only picture in the 'Suspect' column was that of Tony Russo, and the likelihood of his guilt was looking shaky. Amber had been liked by everyone as far as they could see. But then who would stick their hand up and say otherwise during a murder investigation?

The door to the interrogation room opened, and Tooms and an angry Tony stepped out. Steel looked over to see the smug Russo sitting comfortably on his chair, waiting to be told to go home.

"So, what did you get from laughing boy?" McCall asked, not feeling hopeful when she saw Tony's burning eyes.

"He has an alibi which we are about to check out," Tooms told her. "But one thing he did say was that Amber had a twin." The Tooms sat at the desk next to McCall's.

Sam's jaw dropped open in surprise.

"So, what you are saying," Steel said grimly, "is that we have no clear idea who is in the morgue?" His expression was extremely serious.

McCall shot him a look of disappointment. "John Steel, did anyone ever tell you that you're a very 'glass half empty' kind of person? I was going for the hope of Amber being still alive, but of course, you're right," she said, keeping the scowl.

"What else did you get from him?" McCall asked, this time looking over to Tony.

"Not much," Tony spoke with a hint of disappointment in his voice. "He said he hadn't seen her for months. Apparently, he hit on the sister, and Amber found out and told him to hit the bricks. I will contact Brooke and see what she can tell me. Hopefully, she has an address for this sister."

McCall nodded at Tony in agreement.

"And what did you guys get from the meathead?" Tooms asked, hoping they had gotten more than they had.

"Well it appears that Mr Handy saw our runaway with a man a couple of days ago," McCall said with a hopeful tone in her voice.

"Did you get a description?" Tony asked with a newfound vigour.

Steel smiled and nodded.

"Sam has gotten Traffic to send footage from around the time, but from what Bob told us we may have a match." Steel pointed to the board with his thumb.

Tooms and Tony looked up at the general direction towards the 'Persons of Interest' section. They looked at each other, then in unison spoke loudly: "John Doe?"

Tooms shook his head in confusion. "So, your suspect is the guy with no memory?"

Steel nodded in answer to Tooms's question. "Convenient,

don't you think?" Steel said with an almost evil grin, like the cat that got the cream.

"Well I hope it is him, I want to go home this weekend to see my mom," McCall said, looking at the photograph once more. "In the meantime, CSU have his clothes and are testing the blood, once they finish the backlog that is." She stuck out her bottom lip in disappointment at the situation. She looked up at the board for a second then stood up and grabbed her jacket.

"Where you are going?" asked Tooms, suspicious at the sudden movement.

"Off to the crime scene, see if we missed something." McCall watched Steel get up from his chair to get ready to go with her.

"Let me know when the footage comes in and if I don't see you guys, don't stay too long, and I'll see you in the morning," she ordered as she headed for the elevator with Steel.

"Come on, let's find that sister," Tooms said, patting Tony on the shoulder.

———

As McCall turned onto 48th Street, she groaned at the sight of the mass of parked cars. Then as she drove up to the crime scene, McCall saw the red-and-white hazard tape and orange cones as city officials marked their spots for making repairs to the pavement.

The sun was high, considering it was late in the afternoon, but the heat had burnt off hours before, leaving a cool breeze. McCall found a parking spot near to the junction. The narrow street was made more difficult to negotiate because of badly parked, or as McCall called them, 'abandoned' vehicles.

The two detectives walked the forty or so feet to the

building. Steel welcomed the walk, it gave him time to think, or as he called it "walk the walk." A fresh gust carried Sam's hair upwards, and she closed her eyes for a second to enjoy the 'natural air conditioner'. Steel smiled at the sight and shook his head. If anyone had witnessed, her expression, they would have thought she was doing an advert for hair products or perfume.

"Come on, supermodel." He laughed.

She shot him a friendly scowl and pretended to walk the catwalk to the apartment building. McCall stopped suddenly. She looked over at the taped off area to see the workmen wolf-whistling and applauding her performance. She bowed and headed inside, leaving Steel to look to the heavens and shake his head in disbelief.

McCall had used Amber's keys to gain entry. The key chain was full of different sets of keys plus a small teddy bear. McCall had wondered if Tony had given her the bear as a present: perhaps a reminder from a date at a fair or just a simple gesture of kindness. The tiny panda looked worn, as though it had seen a lot of use or alternatively had been there awhile.

They ventured up to the fourth floor and stood in front of the yellow police tape. Using another of her keys, they opened the door and entered.

The afternoon sun acted as a spotlight. The sitting room was almost aglow with the natural illumination. CSU had taken what they needed, including the rug where Amber had bled out. On first impression, no one would have even consider there had been a murder in the room. Everything seemed as normal as could be. All perfectly straightforward, apart from the faint bloodstains on the carpet. The rug had soaked most of it up, but not all of it.

Steel stood in the middle of the room and stared into nothing. His body was solid, like one of the statues at the Metropolitan

Museum. McCall watched him for a moment, a look of concern on her face. She knew what he was doing, for she had seen him do it before. He was re-enacting the movements of that night in his head. She also did the same when she got to a crime scene but seeing the way that he did it somehow scared her, and it was almost as if he could actually see the events taking place.

She had a good imagination for these things, but the imagination needed for this kind of work could only be gotten from experience. She dreaded to know what experiences John Steel had gone through in order to conjure up such nightmares. Steel moved his head slowly as if he was watching someone come through the door. He moved back as if to give them space to move uninterrupted.

John suddenly stopped and looked around the room. He had a confused look on his face as though something was wrong. Suddenly he dropped to the floor and searched the carpet, his hands gliding across the short fibres.

"Lost your contacts?" McCall asked jokingly. However, her smile faded as she realised, he was either ignoring her, or he had simply blocked out her existence. Steel stopped at one point before moving across the coarse brown flooring. His fingers swept another area. Then he stopped and stood up before turning towards her.

"Did CSU move anything?" he asked, his tone almost sounding excited.

McCall opened the report file and scanned the pages. She shook her head. "They only moved things in order to retrieve the rug, but they put everything back as they found it. Why?" she asked curiously.

"The couch and these tables have been moved." He pointed out the large blue fabric couch and the two nesting tables on either side. McCall knelt to find the set of indentations from where the couch's round feet had stood. Their shape and depth were consistent with how long the piece have furniture must have stood in that spot. By their look, McCall estimated it to be years—a lot of years.

"Someone moved the furniture!" she said, almost as puzzled as when she had watched him pat down the carpet. "Why the hell did they move the furniture?"

Steel looked around the room, then shook his head.

"I don't know. But one thing is clear," he said, helping McCall to her feet. "They were looking for something."

She shot him a confused look as she straightened her clothes out.

"They?" Her tone was as if she was unconvinced. She wondered how he had come to such a 'so exact' assumption that there had been more than one person present. Sure, they were waiting for toxicology to come back, but she was sure that Amber had been knocked out by something. Chloroform was a possibility.

"How do you know there was more than one person, just from seeing that the furniture has been moved?" She sounded unconvinced.

John raised a hand and pointed to the furnishings. "There are no drag marks for one thing. If you move something that has been there a long while it's going to leave a trail. Then there is Amber herself. How did 'they' or 'he' subdue her?" Steel could see the glint in her eye, as if to say that she had a theory, possibly a good one.

"Before you say chloroform, just ask yourself how they would have got it to her," he went on. "She has a peephole in the door. If the killer was a stranger, she wouldn't have opened it, which means she knew him or them. And if so, why would they do all this?"

McCall folded her arms in disappointment at his deduction. He had been right, and she hated to admit that.

"OK, Sherlock, what's your theory?" she said, waiting for some elaborate deduction, some grand scheme revealed.

But Steel just shook his head and shrugged. "Elementary," Steel started mockingly, causing McCall to scowl at him, "You see I don't think they were after Amber. I think they were after the roommate."

His statement shocked Sam McCall.

"In fact, I don't think Amber had just moved in. I don't think whoever did this expected her to be here. She shouldn't have been here." Steel pointed to the mountain of removal company packing boxes that were just visible through the open spare bedroom door.

"So, she surprised someone in here and paid for it with her life?" McCall suggested, looking around the room for more clues, but finding nothing but more questions.

"Yes, but she surprised them when they were doing what? They weren't searching for something; the place is spotless. They could have thought Amber was the roommate, but then if so, why did they torture her?" Steel shook his head. Something didn't feel right. In fact, something felt very familiar, and that scared him.

"Perhaps whoever did this didn't know the face of the person they had to kill, only their address? They figured that there was only one person living here, so poor Amber just happened to be in the wrong place at the wrong time." McCall voiced her theory as she was opening one of the removal company packing boxes and sorting through its contents.

"Which would lead us to another question," Steel continued. "Who sent them and why?" Steel caught a brutal look from his partner. "Hey, sorry, but it was your theory," he concluded, before turning and heading for Tara's room. Of all the rooms, this was the only one with photographs, making it seem almost as if she didn't want to share them with anyone else.

He stopped as he noticed a blank space where a photograph had obviously once hung. The lonely nail looked out of place, but the paint had not faded, meaning it hadn't been there long. The remaining photos were of Tara in the park, in which she seemed very happy. This suggested that she had been with someone special to her.

Sam McCall noticed that Steel was standing there at the wall, studying it as she closed the box.

"Is something wrong?" she asked, almost hoping that he might give her a clue.

"There is a photograph missing. And it looks like these were taken recently too." He said, his thoughts lost in theories.

"Maybe the killer took it?" she suggested.

He nodded and looked closer at the area in the picture, hoping to get an idea of where it had been taken.

"Maybe the killer was in the missing picture?" he said, taking one of the pictures down and showing it to McCall, who was making her way over to him.

The glossy six-by-four was of the fountain at Bethesda Terrace. McCall smiled. She knew that place had cameras all over it.

"If we can find out when it was taken, we might get lucky," he said, thinking the same thing as McCall. She opened the file again and looked at the crime scene photographs, observing the way that the body was positioned, the brutality. However, there did appear to be care taken in the undertaking of the deed. This wasn't just a brutal killing: this was a torture. She looked at the photographs again. A shiver ran down her spine, one of such intensity that she nearly buckled. McCall looked over at Steel, who just stood there with a solemn look on his face.

"You think he's back, don't you?" she said, the dreaded words almost creeping out of her mouth. He nodded slowly. She felt an anger towards him. She wanted to scream at him.

"How long have you known that it might be him?" she demanded.

He shook his head slowly. "I suspected more than anything really. It was ever since I first saw the crime scene photographs. I didn't want to say anything until I was sure." His words were soft and calming, but she maintained her pained expression.

"And are you?" she said, almost hoping he wasn't.

Steel shook his head again. "No, I am not."

He could see that this was not what she wanted to hear. He felt her sudden fear of that monster's return. The man who had unknowingly brought them together.

The man most knew only as ... Mr Williams.

CHAPTER FOURTEEN

TARA BURKE AWOKE TO THE SOUND OF A POLICE SIREN wailing. She jumped up, confused at first at seeing her strange surroundings. Tara sat up, holding her beating chest through the T-shirt. As her breathing shallowed, her memory began to return. The frightened young woman reached for the bottled water and cracked the cap. Beads of sweat cascaded down her back, and her forehead looked as though she had just made good time running the hundred.

She heard a noise from the kitchen and knew that Kim was up and getting ready for work. Tara stood up and carried the water with her to the door.

She found Kim's ginger cat prowling the worktop for leftovers. It was seven in the evening, and Tara knew that her friend was heading off for the night shift at the diner. Tara sat on one of the tall stools at the counter to the kitchenette—not quite a breakfast bar, but it made up for a dining table. She smiled at the post-it that was stuck to a large mug with a smiley on it. *Fresh coffee in the machine, frozen lasagne in the freezer. don't leave the apartment, don't open the door to anyone.*

Tara stood up and walked round to the large coffee machine. She switched it on and waited for the sound and the aroma. The ginger tomcat came up and purred loudly as Tara picked him up.

"Don't worry, Mr Jinx, we're not going anywhere," she crooned. The cat let out a quick meow as if to answer. Tara smiled and placed him back down, then poured him some milk from the fridge into a small saucer. The coffee machine would take a while, so she decided to shower.

Tara stripped off her sweat-drenched clothes and wrapped the large red towel around her slimly built body. In the bathroom, she pulled the shower curtain, so it covered the cast-iron bath, then reached in and turned on the water. The bathroom was a comfortable size for one person. It had plenty of wooden shelving that housed folded towels and cosmetics. The walls were beige with white tiles in a half-and-half match, the pattern repeated on the floor, which had matching coverings.

She looked at herself in the mirror. She had that girl-next-door prettiness about her. Her pale skin showed disturbing echoes of her past. Thick, angry scars covered her back, evidence of her mother's abuse: a reminder of how worthless she was to her. But she had survived. She had outlived her drunken abuser.

Tara stepped under the hard torrent of water which came out of the large shower head like a bad storm shower. Tara leant against the cool tiles and just let the water run over her. She felt the hard-warm spray beat down on her skin, and it felt good. So good that she didn't want to leave.

The attractive woman had dried herself off and put on her blue pyjamas. She figured she wasn't going anywhere, so why change? She had poured herself a coffee and put the suggested meal into the microwave. Dinner in five minutes, he'd said, but she made it ten, just to be sure.

She picked up her phone and checked it for any new messages. She tossed it down onto the small coffee table which sat in front of the blue couch. She hadn't heard from him for a long time, too long in fact.

Tara didn't just think she was in trouble. She knew she was.

And they were coming.

———

Mr Williams sat in a large office that looked as if it had fallen out of the 1800s. Oak and brass covered the walls and furnishings. Even the computer's monitor had been dressed up to fit in with the antiquated surroundings. The oak panelling with brass touches and the stand looked as if it had once belonged to ancient lamp.

A large fireplace with a dark marble surround was to the left of a large ebony desk. Carvings of snakes and beasts were cut into the desk's heavy wooden panelling. The large windows to the right were in the original Elizabethan style.

On the wall opposite the desk was a large painting of a battle scene from the Vlad, the Impaler campaign of the 1400s. But the ink was false, and the image itself was in fact a high definition screensaver. The immense eighty-inch monitor blended into the room seamlessly. Suits of armour and swords guarded the corners and the walls.

Williams held a brandy bowl of cut crystal in one hand while he sat back in a thick padded, red leather chesterfield office chair. His feet rested upon the antique desk as he listened to a loud rendition of *Vesti La Giubba*—otherwise known as 'The tears of a clown'. His eyes closed as he held the glass under his nose. He inhaled the scent of the eighty-year-old brandy whilst the music grew to a crescendo. The psychopathic torturer waved his free hand as if he were conducting the masterpiece. He was in heaven: a good brandy, loud opera and his plans were going well.

Suddenly his desk phone began to ring. He opened one eye and stared at the wood and brass 1904 replica. He didn't want to answer it, for he knew it would be trouble. If someone was ringing him direct, it was a problem, and he didn't like problems. He reached over whilst trying not to lose his comfortable position. He kept the brandy glass held by the hand with an outstretched arm, using the other to reach for the receiver.

"This better be good. I am in the mood for giving someone a spinal tap," he growled as he used a remote to turn off the music, after finally putting his glass down. He listened to the voice at the other end. His eyes rolled with disappointment as the voice gave the report.

"So, did you find this Douglas fellow? OK, so – that's a no then. I take it you found the woman?" As Williams listened a wide grin crossed his face, his pearly white teeth on display, looking like a shark spying his next meal.

"When you get hold of her bring her to me UNSPOILT, do you understand?" he instructed. The voice on the other end confirmed the order and quickly hung up. Williams stretched over and replaced the handset onto the brass cradle. He was suddenly in a good mood again. Sure, two pieces of good news would have been great, but he could settle for just one.

He sat back in the chair and picked up the glass. He raised it to the large fake picture to salute it. He took a mouthful of the brandy to celebrate. Then he sat for a moment whilst a wicked thought crossed his mind. Williams reached for the small intercom next to the phone and pressed the button.

"Crystal," he said whilst swilling the brown liquid around

in his glass. He stopped and looked at the intercom, on which he was trying to reach his secretary.

There was no response.

"Oh, Crystal," he said a bit louder this time.

But there was no answer.

"CRYSTAL!" he yelled down the intercom, almost losing his footing and the brandy from the glass.

"Yes ... Yes, sir," a squeaky mouse-like voice came at last. Williams rolled his eyes again, knowing full well what was probably happening in the room next door.

"Be a dear and arrange for the operating room to be set up, will you?" he said, then took another hit from the glass.

"Yes, Mr Williams," she answered, her voice sounding breathless.

"Thank you, Crystal. Oh, and tell the young man with you that if he makes you late answering my call again, I will make lampshades from his skin, and he will watch me do it."

Williams smiled at the thought of the young guard suddenly soiling himself at the thought. The torturer reached over and turned the music back on, then returned the glass to its former position under his nose.

CHAPTER FIFTEEN

TOOMS AND TONY DECIDED TO CHECK OUT THE HOTELS ON West 59th Central Park South. They had been told about a hotel with a park view, of which there were many. They had tossed a coin as to where to start north or south. Heads had won the toss, so south it was.

As they entered the lobby of one of the hotels, they were met by a tall man with a broad smile wearing a blazer with the hotel's name on it. He was thin, with a pencil moustache, his black hair brushed back as though it should reveal a large forehead, but in the event all there was to see was a receding hairline. His whole demeanour was that of a snake—even his face had a serpent's aspect to it.

"Hello, gentlemen, may I help you?" asked the snake man, who was obviously the floor manager. Tony and Tooms showed him their shields and his smile quickly disappeared.

"I am Detective Tooms, and this is Detective Marinelli," Tooms said, tucking his ID back into his jacket pocket. He pulled out a photograph of Amber, and it was obvious that the man immediately recognised her.

"Has something happened to Sharney?" the man asked, almost panicking. Tooms and Tony looked at one another in surprise.

"Her sister was found murdered on the night before last. Sir, is there somewhere private we can speak?" Tony asked as he looked around the lobby at the other guests.

"Yes, of course. Please follow me." The man nodded and led them to a back office near the reception.

"Sorry, but who are you, sir?" Tony asked, taking out his notebook to jot down any details. The man was sitting on the edge of a small desk in a decent-sized office.

"I am Mr Tate, and I am the daytime floor manager," Tate said, still looking badly shocked.

"We are trying to track her down," Tooms said, with a stern look on his face. "To let her know about her sister."

"I didn't know she had a sister. I'm sorry," Tate said, sincerely.

"How well did you know Sharney?" Tooms asked, letting Tony take notes. Tate shrugged and smiled as he considered the question.

"She used to work here, part-time of course. She had a kid, so she could only work half days. But unfortunately, she had to go." Tony looked up from his notebook, his pen poised over the paper. He was shocked to hear about Sharney having a child.

"So why did she leave?" Tooms asked, folding his massive arms.

"She had a new job in Phoenix, or was its Philadelphia? I can't remember, sorry," Tate said and shot them a quick embarrassed smile.

"How long did she work here?" Tony asked, curious about the manager's strange demeanour.

"Oh, around six months, I believe. She was a cleaner here." Tooms noticed Tate's hand move a photograph in a stand-up frame, as though he was trying to hide the picture from them or from himself. Tate was obviously hiding something: he clearly had a little skeleton in the closet.

"Did you know her well?" Tooms asked, suddenly getting a bad vibe from the floor manager.

"No, not really. It was a manager/employee relationship. I told her what to do, and she did it." Tate's smile almost made Tony want to push his head in the fish tank that stood on the far wall.

"So, do you have this kind of formal relationship with all of your staff, sir?" Tooms asked, almost seeming to be polite. Tate's mind seemed to wander off, and his grin returned as if he was thinking about past employees.

"Yes, we have good working relationships here at the hotel." Tate's eyes began to sparkle. Tooms smiled before he spoke. "Thank you, sir, for your time. Would it be OK to speak to any of your staff?" He watched the smile disappear from Tate's face, to be replaced by a wary, nervous expression.

"Uhm, what for?" Tate's voice began to tremble, and he started to fidget with his hands.

"Because they may know Sharney better than you do," Tooms said, trying his best to sound reassuring. "After all, they were all work colleagues. It may give us a better picture, that's all." Tate smiled again; this time, it appeared to be more relieved, more like a friendly gesture. The two detectives turned to leave the office. Tate got up from his spot on the desk to look outside to make sure they were heading out of the building. Tooms said nothing as he opened the office door and stepped back into the lobby. As he did so, the guests all seemed to either hide their faces in magazines or suddenly start gazing out of the window. Tony smiled at their poor attempts to look casual. He wondered what stories would arise from this investigation. The pair headed for the door and stepped out into the street. It was three o'clock, and they were beat. It had been a long day. They both knew they wouldn't get any information from the other staff members. In fact, Tooms was certain that they wouldn't even remember Sharney. They climbed back into their car and headed back. But first Tooms needed to make a stop-off. He felt another chilli dog coming on.

———

McCall stood in front of her murder board with a marker in her hand. Tooms had called her with news of the sister. How people remembered her and that she had supposedly moved to Philadelphia or somewhere with else with a 'P' in its name.

Sam had contacted Philly P.D. to see if they could track her down. She didn't seem hopeful, though. Her gut told her that Sharney had never left New York. The truth was they didn't know a hell of a lot about either of the sisters. Financials had come back, and nothing had popped. Amber's records were clean. From what McCall could gather, she was well-liked and hard working.

Feeling frustrated, McCall sat on the edge of her desk and just looked at the board, hoping something would pop out at her. This was one of those cases she hated. The sort of homicide that would be investigated for a short while and then become a 'cold' case. She looked up at the clock. Tooms and Tony would be back soon, but from what Tooms had said on the phone, they had very little information to share.

McCall looked up at the picture of Tara Burke. She was now missing; the chances were she was scared and running. A sane person would go to the cops for help. But McCall had seen the body, and she could understand how scared that might make anyone. *Run before they come back for you,* would have certainly been the first idea on Tara's mind.

This was a puzzle with far too many pieces that were missing or lodged in the wrong spaces.

Captain Brant walked out of his office and just stood staring at McCall. He could almost feel her brain sorting through the evidence on the board. He could also feel the tension emanating from her.

"Trouble with the case?" he asked. She didn't turn around, just nodded slowly.

"There is something wrong here, Captain, and I don't know what it is." Her words sounded bitter, as though she was angry with herself for not having been smart enough to see the truth.

"What have Tooms and Tony found?" Brant asked, hoping to break her concentration.

"Not much. Apparently, there was a sister, but she moved away, possibly to Philly," she said, then shrugged as if to say she didn't believe it either.

"*Possibly?*" Brant said, almost surprised at the lack of uncertainty.

"Her old boss apparently didn't know her that well, but the boys think otherwise." McCall frowned at the thought of Tooms's description of the manager: *a snake-like weasel,* or something along those lines.

"They should be back soon," she announced, finally turning to face Brant.

"Any news on our missing waitress?" Brant asked, taking a seat in the chair of the desk next to hers. McCall shook her head as she bit her bottom lip.

"No, she's in the wind. Not that I blame her. Seeing that body made me gag, so God knows how she felt," McCall said, remembering her first case. It had been a mugging gone wrong. The perp had gone for the woman's purse. She must have struggled to give it up. She was shot point-blank with a .38. McCall had been a rookie back then, and she had been first on the scene. Someone had reported shots in the park. On seeing the scene, McCall had been frozen to the spot. Her training officer wasn't far behind, but it was unfortunate that he hadn't arrived first.

A .38 round at close range makes a mess. McCall had never realised how much blood could come out of a body so quickly, but it was a headshot. The back of the woman's head had disappeared. Fragments of skull and brain matter were spread over a large area, but it wasn't until she had hit the floor that the red plasma began to pool.

The ringing phone McCall brought her back to reality. Brant looked over to his office phone as the noise of the electronic ring bellowed out of the open doorway. McCall's boss got up and walked to his desk. He didn't run. He figured that if it was important, they would wait, after all, they wanted him. After a moment of nodding and hand gestures, Brant came back to where McCall was sitting.

"That was Traffic. They said there was no footage of that alleyway. So, they are going to try and find the cab to find out where else it has been," Brant said, not feeling hopeful they could actually find that particular needle in such a big haystack. He looked around for a second, a confused look on his face.

"So, where's Steel?" Brant asked, suddenly noticing the British detective's absence.

"He said he had some stuff to take care of. Hopefully, he'll bring me back a coffee and a bear claw," McCall joked.

Brant smiled and nodded. "Well, keep me posted, Detective," Brant concluded, almost tempted to wait for the phone to ring again.

"Will do, sir. Will do," McCall answered as she watched the large bear of a man head back into his office. It was almost three p.m. according to the clock above the elevator doors.

Three o'clock and they had nothing. Forensics had a backlog, so the clothes that John Doe was wearing would have to wait their turn, according to their importance. *More time wasted*, she thought as she read the email from CSU.

She looked across at Tony's empty desk and wondered what he must be feeling. She had lost her dad when she was younger, but it would be nothing to compare to what he was likely to be going through.

For now, it was a waiting game to see what else might come up.

CHAPTER SIXTEEN

A SHORT MAN IN A BLACK SUIT AND DARK SUNGLASSES SAT on a bench in Washington Square Park. He was heavily built, as a result of spending too much time behind a desk and eating too many business dinners. Thinning black hair covered a large head, and a handmade suit from Chinatown covered his large frame. Even his shoes were a classy knock-off. But he didn't care. The fact they lasted longer than the original would have done, made them that much sweeter to wear.

The sun was high, and a slight breeze made the surrounding trees sway in unison as if they were dancing to the same tune. The large white marble arch was stained from years of weathering, which made it more magnificent. The park itself was a circular meeting place of grey concrete slabs that encircled a large fountain. Grass and wooded areas added to the pleasant setting around the two-hundred-year-old memorial.

Tourists walked around with their tablets and cell phones, taking shots to send to the web. The man shook his head as he bit into the sandwich, he had brought with him.

"Doesn't anyone own a camera anymore?" he asked himself. There was a squawk in his earpiece as someone gave a situation report, otherwise known as a 'sitrep'.

"We'll give him another five minutes. If he's a no-show we'll call it a day," he said, careful not to give away the presence of the microphone in his sleeve. He wiped his large brown head with a cotton handkerchief he had taken from his jacket pocket. He was nervous. Who wouldn't be?

The park was surrounded by three teams. They weren't here to arrest anyone. They were there for his protection.

The man looked at his watch. It was ten past three. "OK, people, he's a no-show. Shut it down." The disappointed man shook his head and gave the signal to collapse the operation.

He stood up and headed towards his car, which was parked on Thompson Street. The teams had broken off and disappeared into the mass of people. The man pushed through the crowds, his eyes scanning every face just in case. He was feeling the temperature, not from the sun, but from his own body heat, as his heart pumped the blood around his system like fuel for a rocket.

Then he saw the blacked-out GMC Yukon parked in a shady spot. The street was narrow, meaning there was not so much traffic. The man breathed a sigh of relief as he climbed into the back of the oversized SUV.

"OK, Tom, let's go," the man said, buckling up his seat belt and not really paying attention to the driver.

"Tom let's go!" he repeated, but the driver stayed still.

"What, you fell asleep on me again?" he said, tapping the driver on the shoulder. Tom's head fell to the side, with only the seat belt to stop it falling further. Suddenly the rear passenger door swung open, and Steel slid onto the seat next to the man. In one swift motion, Steel grabbed the gun from his holster and tossed it into the car's footwell. The bemused man was shocked by the speed of it all and sat with his back firmly against the car's door.

"Steel," he said in shock with his hand's half-raised.

"Hello there, Agent Hardy," Steel said with a broad smile on his face. "I've been waiting for you."

———

Agent Frank Hardy had finally calmed down after Steel's sudden and theatrical entrance. Hardy sat for a second whilst he gathered his breath. Steel handed him a bottle of water that was in the cup holder in the door. Frank Hardy snatched it from him and drank slowly. An angry look came over his face as he started to feel his heartbeat reach normality.

"We were supposed to meet outside, in public," Hardy growled.

Steel smiled and looked in the rear-view mirror. He found it amusing to watch the agents trying hard to blend into the crowd as they made their way back to their vehicles.

"Never been one for public appearances," John said, still holding on to the childish grin. Hardy reached into his inside pocket, pulled out a bottle of pills and flipped the lid off. He poured a tablet into his large hand and swallowed it down dry.

"Have you got an ulcer again?" Steel asked, sounding concerned.

Hardy shot him a look and smiled. "My ulcers have ulcers. All because of you." He laughed.

Steel nodded then shrugged. "What are friends for," Steel joked.

Hardy looked over at the unconscious body of Tom, the driver. "Did you have to slug him? I mean you could have made him go for a walk or something," Hardy grumbled, sounding worried about his driver. Steel knew enough to realise that all

Hardy was bothered about was how he was getting home without a driver. The chances were the man would wake up on a plane heading for Iceland or some outstation in the middle of Alaska.

"Are you pulling me back, Frank?" Steel asked. His smile had faded, meaning that he was no longer joking.

Hardy gave him a shocked look. "God, no. Since you left the others have found that they must do some work," the agent joked. "This case you're working on now. What have you got so far?"

The British detective sat back in his seat and looked at Hardy for a moment. He said nothing, just sat and stared.

"Oh, will you cut that bullshit out?" Hardy yelled, his face going red. "You probably had the whole thing worked out before you got in the car."

"Amber was one of yours, wasn't she?" Steel asked, just to confirm his suspicions.

"Yes. She was investigating some strange things we had discovered about the shipping company. We were seeing strange shipments being taken in and out of the country. Large amount of goods was being shipped out and distributed around the globe," Frank explained.

Steel just looked at him, puzzled for a second. "You think someone was smuggling something out in large quantities? What? Drugs? Guns? Cars?" John was hoping to get some clue as to what nefarious activities Amber was investigating.

"Honestly, we don't know. All I do know is that whoever is doing it is using the shipping firm. Who knows, maybe they are in on it, or the company is paying a hell of a lot for them to look the other way?" Hardy sounded angry. Not because the bad guys were getting away with it, but because Amber had died trying to take them down.

"She was a good kid, John," Agent Hardy continued. "She didn't deserve what they did to her."

John Steel nodded slowly as if to agree with Hardy's words. But something was bothering Steel about the killing.

"Uh oh, I know that look. What's up, John?" Hardy spoke carefully as if he was unwilling to break Steel's concentration.

"The murder of Amber made no sense," he simply said after a while.

Hardy now had a puzzled look across his sweaty, pale brow. "What do mean, made no sense? The bastards tortured her, didn't they? It was just a killing, Steel. Hell, you've seen enough in your time to know that." The agent took another sip from the water.

"Yes, I've seen torture before many times, by different cultures. But this was different. This was as though they wanted to erase her existence. Her face was cut up, teeth extracted and the skin from her fingers removed. This was a *deletion* not just a torture." Steel bared his teeth as he spoke. He could feel the hatred welling up inside him for those who had done this terrible thing.

"OK, let's say you're right. Why leave the body?" Frank asked, hoping not to hear what he thought Steel may come out with.

"Maybe it was meant to be a warning to those who knew what she was doing. You know—back off." Steel looked his watch. He had nearly overstayed his welcome.

Hardy saw a look on Steel's face that he had come to know quite well. "You have an idea who may have done this, don't you?" he asked calmly, sitting back in his seat. "I was almost waiting for that, 'and the murderer is' moment."

"I ... That is, *we*, think that Williams is back," Steel said, almost terrified to consider the prospect of that madman running around in the city.

"Williams?" Hardy thought for a moment. "Oh, yes, I remember. The psycho you were hunting before. He was the reason you joined the NYPD in the first place, wasn't he?" Hardy smiled at the irony of the situation.

"So, you think that the organisation is behind this?" Hardy asked.

Steel shrugged and shook his head. "In all honesty, I don't know. It could be SANTINI, but it seems too obvious to be him," Steel said, questioning his own instincts.

He wished it was the organisation, so he could take them down once and for all. Or at least hurt them badly enough to destroy them. But even that idea seemed wrong.

"So, what's your plan?" Hardy asked, hoping that his associate would suggest something simple.

"To carry on with the investigation. There's no point running blind. Just follow the evidence as we always do." Steel shrugged.

"OK, just keep me in the loop and by the way, Steel—be careful." Hardy smiled.

Steel gave a mocking look of surprise. "Why, Agent Hardy, are you concerned I may get killed or something?"

Hardy shook his head and grinned. "Chance would be a fine thing; you pain in the ass. No, I am just worried you're going to make a mess, the sort of mess insurance companies is afraid of."

Steel smiled and gave a quick joke-salute. As Steel went to get out the car the agent grabbed his arm.

"Remember, Major, you're *our guy*, not NYPD," Hardy said with a stern look on his face.

The other man just looked him until Hardy felt an uncomfortable feeling come over him. He quickly released Steel's arm without a word.

"That's funny, and I thought you had thrown me to the

LONE WOLF operation." Steel smiled and got out of the car, just as a large bald agent came around the corner. Steel moved casually towards the corner of West 3rd Street. Hardy turned to see the agent approach.

"Is everything OK, sir?" his colleague asked, not noticing the unconscious state of the driver. Hardy laughed at the whole situation. "Well, son, I guess you're driving me back, my driver seems to be otherwise, let's just say, *out of order*." Hardy laughed, looking back at the junction where Steel had disappeared.

"See you around, Major," the detective said, smiling to himself as they drove away back to headquarters.

CHAPTER SEVENTEEN

SUNRAYS POURED THROUGH THE LARGE WINDOWS OF THE suite of rooms that held John Doe. The luxury pad was high on the sixth floor. Steel had booked it, thinking it was safer than the usual kind of so-called 'safe house'. John Doe sat watching a rerun of an old movie on the large flat-screen television. He was sitting in luxury, but his mind was in hell. He had no idea who he was, what sort of life he had had before today. But the most disturbing thing of all was, he didn't know why he had been covered in blood, or even whose blood it had been.

So far, his only visitor had been Dr Davidson. He had been on a house call to check on John and to do some tests. The psychiatrist was still baffled by what had caused the amnesia. There was the head wound, certainly, but that didn't seem serious enough to have instigated such a harsh reaction.

Davidson had left at around three o'clock to get back to his practice. This left John Doe free to wander around like a caged animal. Sure, he was free to go, but to where, he wondered? He didn't know anyone.

The hapless man walked up to the window and looked out

across the city. There were people, cars, tourists. Life. He turned and walked to the telephone and picked up the receiver. Suddenly his thumb paused over the keypad. He smiled and looked up as if to ask God what he was doing. He shook his head then placed the receiver back down.

John remembered the doc saying his problem might have been caused by a massive traumatic event. But what could have happened? He was covered in blood, so if such an event had occurred, the likelihood was that this had something to do with it.

Davidson had told him that he was sure his memory would come back in time. But *in time* was not a real definitive answer. John Doe looked across at a pile of books Steel had brought for him, just in case, he got bored. There was a mixture of sci-fi, mystery and even some Shakespeare plays. John smiled at the irony of seeing the stack of mystery novels.

"I sure don't need any more mystery in my life," he thought out loud, reflecting on things. He sat back down and flicked through the TV channels until he saw the local news. Suddenly he stopped and stared. The news station was reporting on a local murder: the murder of a woman called Amber Taylor. His jaw dropped, but he pulled himself together quickly before changing the channel back to the movie he'd been watching, his face now impassive.

John stood up and stretched. He turned and tidied up the couch's cushions before disappearing into the bathroom.

In the room next door, three men sat at desks wearing headphones and checking the monitors in front of them. The six screens showed images of the various rooms in the suite, plus the stairwell and the elevator.

Steel had put John Doe under strict surveillance.

Because Steel didn't trust John Doe. There was something

about him that made the British detective nervous, and he didn't like things that made him nervous.

When he felt nervous, it normally meant trouble.

———

McCall walked out of the restroom. Too many coffees and hardly anything to eat had taken its toll on her. She returned to her desk and her computer, where she had been looking up anything she could find on Amber and Sharney Taylor. So far, there were only birth certificates, college information, and social security numbers that told McCall there were two of them. She turned in time to see Steel step off the elevator with a coffee and a bear claw. McCall suddenly had a strange look of mistrust as he handed her the coffee shop items.

"What?" he said abruptly, looking shocked at her lack of gratitude. "I thought you'd be hungry." He was looking hurt and somewhat confused.

"You're not bugging my desk, are you?" she asked, giving him a glare.

"Why would I do that?" He started to speak, but she just smiled and bit into the pastry.

Steel shook off her put-down and attributed her bad temper to her having low blood sugar. He looked at her monitor and saw the background check she was doing on Amber. He suddenly had that bad feeling of knowing something and not being sure whether he should share the information.

For he knew that Amber had been working undercover. But if he told anyone, that would lead to awkward questions. Questions he didn't want to answer, at least not right away.

The trouble was it was information that might help them to find her killer. If he was going to say anything, he was going to have to be discreet about it.

"So...have you had any luck in finding the sister?" Steel asked, waiting for a moment when McCall didn't have food in her mouth.

"Not yet. I don't think there was another sister. I think that Amber and Sharney are one and the same." She explained her theory with a sparkle in her eye.

Steel nodded as if he was going over her theory in his head. McCall scowled as she watched his bad acting skills.

"But then you've already thought of that, haven't you?" she growled.

It was true that he had—that was why he had met up with Hardy. He didn't want to give anything away to Hardy, not yet anyway. Steel had suspected that Amber had been with the agency. He also figured that she had taken both jobs at the hotel and the shipping company. What he didn't know was why work at the hotel? Sure, the shipping company was obviously a useful way to get information, but the hotel? There seemed no point.

Another question that bothered him was Tony's involvement, or indeed the lack of it. Was he just being used as a cover, a useful boyfriend to take her places, so she blended in with other people, or did she really care for him?

Steel watched McCall stretch off, her T-shirt clinging to her shapely form as she arched her back. He looked away, so as not to stare in admiration. McCall smiled at his almost-gallant display of restraint but knew he had seen enough before turning away. She smiled at the thought that she had put a sexy image into his head. It was almost a display of teasing on her part.

McCall knew that most men saw her as 'just a woman', so she had to work just as hard as her male colleagues to prove herself as good as they were. But she was smart and damned good at her job, and that's how she had got ahead. She had not used her looks or sexuality to get her shield, she had simply showed that she was just as good as any other cop out there, and Captain Brant had seen that.

She could have been anything in life, but she wanted to be a cop like her dad had been. Every male on her dad's side of the family had been a cop, but her mother had only produced two girls. McCall had been the tomboy of the family: as if she'd been chosen to hold up the tradition. In fact, it didn't matter to her grandfather that she happened to be a woman; what mattered to him was that the tradition of having cops in the family never died.

Steel looked up at the clock on the wall. "It's nearly five, are you going home for the weekend?" he asked McCall, sitting back in his chair. Sam McCall glanced up at the clock as if to confirm he was telling the truth.

"We've got so much to do here, and I shouldn't," she said, in an almost disappointed tone. Steel stood up and pulled the jacket from the back of her chair and held it up for her to put on.

"Don't worry. I'll cover the weekend. Besides I have a benefit, I must attend, so working here might give me an excuse not to go." He smiled.

McCall stood up and slipped her arms into the leather jacket. "Are you sure?" she said.

He scowled at her jokingly. "Go before I change my mind and I go in your place," he joked.

Sam didn't need to be told twice and bolted for the door. Brant walked out of his office and watched McCall almost skate across the floor to the waiting elevator.

"You said you'd cover for her, didn't you?" Brant said.

Steel nodded and leant back in the chair. "She needs some mother/daughter time. Time to clear her head." Steel was still watching as the door closed behind McCall.

Brant approved. "Yep, we all have to have some sort of outlet. So, tell me, Steel. What's your outlet?" Brant asked, not caring that he was invading the Englishman's privacy.

"Not this bloody engagement tonight, that's for sure." John Steel laughed to himself.

Brant placed a hand on his shoulder. "The Governor and the Mayor expect to see you there, Steel. You know? Shaking hands and smiling, taking one for the team and all that." Brant joined in with Steel's laughter.

"Yeah, well, I guess I will see you inside then, Captain," Steel said with a look of sudden distaste at the thought of all those false people he had to talk to.

"You're going to sneak in again, aren't you?" Brant asked, shaking his head. "I mean seriously, who sneaks into an event they have a ticket for?" Brant was confused.

"Simple," Steel told him. "Someone who sneaks in is the kind of person who doesn't want to world to know where he is."

Steel headed for the door.

———

The benefit event was a massive affair. Anyone who was anyone was there, as well as all the wannabes. Guests included actors, actresses and politicians. Of course, the District Attorney or the DA, and the Police Commissioner were hovering around, blending and rubbing shoulders with the great and the good. Outside the darkness was banished by the glare of outdoor lighting and camera flashes at the main entrance of the Waldorf Hotel. Park Avenue was full of limousines and state vehicles. News vans were parked down the street—out of view but close enough to transmit their signals. For the police it was a nightmare: security services were posted here and there, trying to blend into the crowds.

Steel stood across the street beside a prestigious looking bank and watched the chaos. He smiled to himself as he checked out the building. CCTV cameras hugged the walls, and there were tough-looking men in badly fitting tuxes at the entrances, checking purses and tickets. The main entrance was clear, but the other surrounding walls were under renovation. Scaffolding towered over everything, looking like a child's climbing frame.

To Steel, he regarded the practice of 'sneaking in', rather than entering in the usual manner, as good training as well as being a challenge. He had been trained to be a 'ghost', and lately, he hadn't had the opportunity to practise his skills. He wore an all-black tux and had rubber soles on his shoes: trying to sneak into a place while making a noise like horse's hooves didn't exactly work.

He headed for East 50th and the car parking structure. He noticed that one of the windows had been carelessly left open. He smiled as he brushed off the idea. *Too obvious. Besides you only leave the window open if you're in the room,* he thought to himself.

Outside, FedEx trucks were parked up, making deliveries for the party. Catering vans from various companies sat nose-to-nose on the side of the building, their logos bright and obvious.

Steel sneaked up to the furthest one, whilst blending in with a crowd of nosey tourists. He made his way to the truck and set off the alarm. Smiling, he blended back with the crowd then eased himself back to the parked trucks. Men with ill-fitting suits and earpieces rushed out to check out the commotion. Steel climbed up onto one of the trucks and hoped that the chaos had made the cameras zoom in on the guards' location.

On the third floor of the building, there was a flat roof.

Steel clambered the structure like a monkey up a tree and made for the shadows, which the two towering parts of the building provided. There were a group of people huddled around a bucket of champagne: obvious escapees from the function down below. Billows of cigarette smoke caught the breeze. Steel smiled as he saw their escape route: an open window that led into one of the hallways. He left the group, who were having more fun there than the other guest's downstairs.

As he stepped out onto the carpet, he brushed himself off and headed for the elevator. He was in. Not quite in the way, he had wanted to enter, but he'd managed it.

The lobby area was full of wives in new dresses that probably would never be worn again, husbands in rented tuxedoes and staff holding trays with flutes of champagne. Steel headed down to the ballroom, where the event was being held. It was a massive room with a stage at the far end and balcony seats going up two levels. Above them, was a huge chandelier that was around sixteen feet wide. Below, round tables stood lined up like soldiers on parade, each one able to seat five people. The seats had been arranged so that they all faced the stage.

Music played in the background, courtesy of a small string quartet on the stage. Steel passed a young waitress who smiled and offered him a glass of champagne. He returned her smile and took one of the flutes before entering the swarm of wealthy people. He sipped the golden liquid and scanned the room for any friendly faces.

He saw Governor Alan Childs talking to Mayor Tom Lawson. Each of them looked as bored as the other but cloaked their lack of enthusiasm behind fake smiles. Childs saw Steel and called him over, looking as if he had finally found someone of interest to speak to. Steel downed the champagne in one and placed it on a nearby waiter's tray, before picking up a fresh glass to dull the pain.

"John, my boy, glad you made it," said the heavily built governor. Childs was over six foot three with broad shoulders and an ever-increasing waistline. He was in his late fifties and had grey hair and a bleached smile. From what Steel knew of him, he was a good man, an honest man.

"Governor, Mr Mayor," Steel greeted them both.

Childs scowled at Steel.

"Now come on, John, we're behind closed doors now," Childs said, laughing.

Steel nodded a gracious defeat. "Sorry... Good evening, Alan and Tom," Steel said, raising his glass to them. "So, Tom, has he bored you with proposal plans yet?" he asked the Mayor, who was clinging to his scotch like it was his last.

Tom Lawson nodded and rolled his eyes jokingly. Alan laughed and slapped the poor man on the back. Lawson, who was around two feet shorter and thinner than the others, stumbled slightly at the impact.

Mayor Lawson was in his late forties and had inherited a family nest egg that could choke Godzilla. He, too, was one of the good guys. Lawson was ex-military, which had seen him through to the rank of colonel in the infantry. He was smart and intelligent. But most important of all, his face fitted.

Tom Lawson was six feet tall and had dark hair, chiselled good looks and an eye for the ladies. He was the full package. The ladies were queuing to be the next 'Mrs Mayor', but he was happy enjoying the movie star lifestyle as a bachelor. The three men spoke for a while about nothing. That was until something caught Tom's eye.

"Oh, sorry, gentlemen, it appears that Miss New York has become free," Tom said, raising his glass as a quick salute before gliding off in the brunette's direction.

"Think they'll be in page six tomorrow?" Alan asked, jokingly.

Steel smiled. "Page two at the most."

Alan laughed. Steel rubbed his right eye, finding that his contact lenses were itchy from lack of use.

"Didn't think you liked coming to these damned things," Alan remarked, looking around the room at people raising their glasses to him as if they were old school friends.

"I don't, but I have been told to keep up appearances. You know how it is." Steel suddenly caught a glimpse of a familiar face near a white-clothed table full of drinks.

"However, tonight could be interesting," Steel said as he gazed through the crowd at a tall woman in a red cocktail dress. Her fiery red hair hung down to her shoulders. He had not seen her face, but he was sure that it was Helen Adler, the woman he'd met at the shipping company.

Helen Adler stood at the bar waiting for her drink while a small blacked-haired man with a weaselly face hit on her.

"Excuse me, but is this man bothering you?" Steel asked in a sympathetic voice.

The man turned around to face the person behind him. His angry look faded as he stared directly into Steel's chest. Slowly he looked up as if he was counting each button on Steel's shirt. A look of fear appeared across Helen's admirer's face, as he gazed upon Steel's emotionless features. He stumbled backwards, almost crashing into Helen Adler. He stopped and turned to face her before turning tail and moving away quickly, afraid that John Steel might be her husband.

"Why, Mr Steel, you *are* a pleasant surprise," she said, provocatively biting an olive off a cocktail stick. Steel made a 'two' gesture as the waiter brought her drink: a large martini with a splash of vodka served in a bucket-sized glass.

"So, are you following me, Mr Steel?" Helen asked. Those

blue eyes moved slowly up and down his frame as if checking the cut of his tux. The waiter passed Steel his drink which he raised. "Cheers," he toasted. Helen raised her glass to return the gesture.

"I'm afraid not," he went on. "I am here on orders. They like someone from the precinct to come down and smile. It's good for PR apparently."

His words were a lie. But then, what could he tell her, a possible suspect? Could he really tell her that he was the poster boy because of his social status as Lord Steel? It was much simpler to leave her in the dark.

"Well here's to good PR," she said, raising her glass.

He gently clinked glasses with her, and their eyes locked on to one another. The music in the background was drowned out by the hum of conversation. Steel and Helen made their way to the far side of the room to a quieter spot, with her leading the way, deliberately, or so it seemed to him, but he wasn't about to argue. The dress fitted her as if it had been sprayed on. Steel had to admit that she really was a fantastic looking woman.

They sat at a table that probably belonged to someone else, but it was out of the way, conducive to quiet conversation.

"So, tell me, Detective," she began.

Steel shook his head. "Please, let's not be formal. Call me, John."

She smiled and nodded. "So, tell me, John, what other activities do you enjoy, to pass the time?"

He was about to answer when the lights began to dim, and a woman walked onto the stage. She was a tall blonde with a blue sequined dress. Her long blonde hair was arranged with fabulous twists and probably had been fixed with enough hair spray to be a fire hazard.

Showtime, Steel thought to himself. Everyone took to their seats, but Steel and Helen stayed put at the lonely table.

They talked for hours, finding time to dance whenever there was a break in the proceedings. Helen, like John Steel, was only there as a representative. For her boss at the shipping company, it was all about 'being seen' at the right places. It was a pity he didn't want to be seen himself, she thought.

However, on this occasion, she didn't mind. This time she was having fun. After one dance Helen led Steel out into the lobby. She turned and kissed him passionately. He kissed her back with equal enthusiasm. There was no room full of people, no music. Just them. They went up to her suite on the third floor.

"We're going to miss the dinner," Steel said as she pushed him through the door and into the room. He noticed a hunger in her, like that of an animal that has had its appetite suppressed for too long. She pulled off his tux jacket and let it fall. Her fingers passing over his shirt explored his body beneath.

"Why, Mr Steel, you do live up to your name, don't you?" she purred. Then she unbuttoned his shirt slowly as if she was unwrapping a special present, kissing every part of bare flesh as it was revealed. Steel pulled off his shirt and picked her up as if she was made of tissue paper. She gasped at the sudden use of his strength. They moved to the bed where he lay her down. Her eyes held that cat-like stare that she had noticed before. Steel moved on top of her, still half-dressed.

With a flip, she was now on top of Steel, and she could feel his hard body between her legs. Steel sat up, and they kissed again, their mouths and tongues exploring each other's. His fingers reached at the back for her zipper but found none. He pulled away from her with a confused look.

She smiled and stood up. "It's a side zipper, John," she purred seductively as she pulled the tag down and let the dress fall to reveal her stunning body. She stood there naked and gorgeous.

"I find underwear tends to get in the way," she explained.

Steel nodded, somewhat speechless, his mouth dry. Helen crept up the bed like a panther on the prowl and undid his trousers.

Their naked bodies were entwined in a passionate embrace, their hands holding onto one another as if never wanting to let go. Her face had a look of ecstasy as she felt all of him. His hard body brought her to the place that she longed to be, time and time again. Her painted nails clawed at his hard-muscular back as he slammed against her. Time meant nothing as their bodies became wet with perspiration and the heat of the moment. She grasped the bed covers as they lay on their sides, his body holding her close as he was lying behind her. She felt his powerful hands against her soft flesh. Just the feel of his tight body against hers was enough to bring her to a shuddering end. Her cries of passion were muffled as she bit into the pillow. They fell into each other's arms and laughed, gasping for air as though they had just run a marathon.

"I hope the diner's still on. I just worked up an appetite," Steel joked.

Helen slapped his bare chest and grinned pleasurably, like a cat that had gotten the cream.

Nearly two hours had passed before they returned and blended into the party, each going their separate ways. But they had not been missed. Steel headed straight for the bar. He was still sweating from their adventure's upstairs. A young waiter approached, and Steel ordered a large water with a double Johnny Walker Blue chaser.

"Thought you'd bailed out on us," said the familiar voice of the Governor. Steel turned after picking up the water and downing it almost in one. The Governor looked at him in surprise, saying, "You're drinking water?"

Then Steel picked up the double whisky.

"You had me worried for a minute, my boy," the Governor laughed. Steel raised the glass in a toast, and the two men drank.

"So, where have you been? You missed the dinner," the large man said, rubbing his belly. Steel's eyes scanned the room until he caught a glimpse of Helen standing with her boss and another white-haired man with a goatee. She looked around the room nervously until she caught Steel's gaze. Suddenly she looked back at her boss. Steel took out his cell phone and took a picture. As a precaution against losing his phone, he sent it to his desk as an email.

"Apparently, I was getting screwed over," Steel said. The Governor followed Steel's gaze then slapped him on the shoulder and laughed in a bellow.

"Well, my boy, it looks like you had a better meal than I did," Alan said, almost feeling jealous. As Steel watched, he noticed Helen's attitude towards her boss. It was not one of cooperation, and it was of antagonism and hatred. He could almost feel the loathing in her glare every time her boss wasn't looking.

At one in the morning, Steel decided to call it a night. The day before had been a long one. He was tired and just needed a shower and then bed. He had gotten a room for the night, so as not to waste time with taxis.

In the elevator, he noticed that his room number was just down the hall from Helen's. He held the brass tag tightly as if willing her not to be anywhere near. He felt used but didn't know why. Had she slept with him to achieve influence? He didn't know.

The doors slid open, and he found Helen sitting, crouched

upon the floor outside her room, crying, looking as if she was ill or in trouble. The key was in the door. For a second, he felt like rushing up to her instinctively and consoling her. But he stopped himself and deliberately strolled up to her casually, not turning or attempting to look at her. Sure, she was a beautiful woman. But one that he didn't trust. Was her breakdown an act? But if it was, then how could she have known when he was coming?

He turned the key to her room and then looked over to her. Her whimpering remained a shallow piteous sound. If this was an act, it was a very good one. Steel cursed himself and his gallantry and moved over to her. He stood next to her, bent down and helped her up.

She was drunk. So drunk that she didn't even know he had opened her door. Steel picked her up and carried her to the bed and lay her down. She stirred slightly and tried to kiss him. Steel smiled and helped her back to her pillow.

He smiled and picked up the phone and dialled for room service. He ordered Helen breakfast and a bloody Mary for the hangover. He watched her as she slept a restless sleep. As he looked across, he suddenly felt some other emotion towards her. He thought back to the look of hatred she had given her boss. And the emotion she displayed in the office whenever she was around him.

He suddenly felt something. He felt pity.

He felt that Helen was in trouble and that she needed help.

CHAPTER EIGHTEEN

A DEEP BURNT UMBER SKY COVERED THE CITY. THE morning began as any other. The garbage men had already been on their rounds early, leaving the streets clear for the usual mayhem to ensue.

Steel had stayed with Helen until the early hours before heading home. She had been in no fit state to be alone. He had been out of the door before the sun had broken over the horizon.

He entered his apartment and locked the door. The whole place was bathed in a blazing orange with the light of the morning sun. He hadn't really slept, but then he never did. Watching over Helen had been a welcome change to his usual round of nightmares. He stripped off his shirt and headed for the shower. The twelve o'clock shadow had grown darker on his chiselled jaw.

The British detective ran the shower until a cloud of vapour rose, almost filling the room. *First shave, then shower*, he thought to himself. In the kitchen, the sound of the coffee machine let him know it was time to get up. Steel wiped the mirror clean of its misty shroud.

"Here we go again," he laughed, and then lathered up his face.

Showered and shaved, he stepped out into the coolness of his open-plan sitting room and headed for the kitchen. He poured a coffee from the machine and got milk from the fridge. There was a note on it held on by a magnetic 'smiley' that wore a pair of sunglasses.

New toy for you. Don't lose this one. Steel smiled at the note and sipped the coffee. He ventured down the hall to the room with the coded door. He punched in the numbers then put his hand on the scanner before entering.

Moments later, he came out holding a cell phone. He searched through the new applications while he drank his coffee. There was a strange app icon with a first-aid sign. He smiled and tucked the phone away.

"They think of everything, apart from making calls better," Steel joked to himself as he pulled on a shirt, he found on a hanger on the coat rack. He pulled on the leather-and-wool jacket and headed out. He would grab breakfast on the way to the precinct.

Steel stepped off the elevator onto the hard laminate squares of the department's floor. Most of the desks were empty. Detectives were either out working a case or off for the weekend. Apart from the odd phone call, the morning was quiet, but Steel had found that most people tended to be inconsiderate and committed murders in the middle of the night.

He headed for McCall's desk to check on her messages. Her password was easy: the date of her father's shooting. As he scanned through the mass of garbage and laughable chatter between Sam and her friend Tina, the ME, all of it was dull.

The seven o'clock sky was already lighting up the Homicide department through the large windows, as he watched other detectives started to return, and the phone lines got busy. But he had other things on his mind. Things like: who was Helen's boss talking to at the party?

Steel sat in McCall's chair for a while, as he looked up at the murder board. They still had no idea where Tara had disappeared too. She could be miles away or injured or dead. Also, he thought about John Doe. Who the hell was he and why was he covered in blood? He wasn't in the system and CSU were backlogged, so the report on the blood wouldn't be due until at least Tuesday, so they had promised.

After his conversation with Agent Hardy, Steel had wondered what the real motive behind Amber's murder was. Deep down, he knew it made no sense. McCall was convinced it was Williams's work, but Steel was unsure of that. Yes, Williams was a complete psycho, but there was just something wrong with the way that Amber's body had been left. Williams liked to make a 'statement' with his bodies. Amber's corpse had just been abandoned in her apartment.

Steel looked up at the picture of Tara on the board. His mind began to speculate on what her involvement could have been. Had she seen everything or just found the body? He shook off the thought. Tony and Tooms were on her trail, and he already had enough to do.

He stood up, leaving the comfort of McCall's chair. His first plan was to go and check up on John Doe. Or rather not so much to check on him, but to evaluate the surveillance team who were watching him.

Suddenly McCall's desk phone began to ring. Steel hesitated before picking up the receiver, just in case this was news of another murder that had nothing to do with Amber's case. He gave in and answered. It was Dispatch, telling him that there had been another murder in the Village. First responders thought it may be linked. Steel wrote down the address and replaced the receiver.

John Doe would have to wait. Morbidly, Steel hoped that this new body was linked to their murder so that they could move forward. So far, they had nothing but questions and theories. Hopefully, this might answer a few of those questions.

———

The morning sun was bright, but a cool breeze kept the heat at bay for the time being. In front of the apartment building, members of the press and nosey onlookers gathered to try and get a glimpse of something. Steel smiled and shook his head. The press he could understand, for they had a job to do. But Joe Public wanting selfies with a corpse? Please.

Steel had no love for having his photograph taken. Normally he would just let McCall deal with the press, and he would just sneak in while they were busy with her. Hell, she had the looks and the body of a model, so she was already media-friendly. Plus, it was good for her career. But talking to the media was something he could do without. Especially in this situation.

John Steel sneaked around the back of the building and found another entrance via a fire escape which he was nimble enough to get into. Inside he found that the main activity was on the third floor. Uniforms were gathered there to prevent any unauthorised access.

At the entrance to the room, two large uniforms stood watch. A large bouquet of flowers lay on their side adjacent to the next room. Steel took note but didn't pursue it. It could have been nothing, but then it could be everything. First, he wanted to see inside before making that call.

He walked into the apartment and came out again and stared at the arranged flowers before turning to the uniformed officer closest to them.

"The flowers there, make sure nobody touches them, would you?" Steel asked the large officer. The man turned and looked at the innocent flowers and nodded with a shrug.

Inside, the small angry ME was crouched over the body of a white male, or at least what used to be a complete body. Doctor Eliot Bauer was on call when Tina Franks was otherwise engaged – in this case; she was busy back at the morgue with a boatload of new cases due to an accident. He was a slight man, medium height with a thin frame. The man was in his late thirties but looked older, possibly the lack of compassion for the living, or humour had something to do with it. His ravel coloured hair was styled merely by brushing, but his clothes were immaculate with pressed creases in his shirt and trousers.

"Morning, Doctor Bauer," Steel greeted the weasel-faced man, who just grunted back. Steel looked over towards a large black cop, who just shrugged. Steel smiled at the situation and crouched down.

"Not to ask the obvious, but what have we got?" Steel asked, looking at the blood-soaked corpse.

"White male in his late thirties. Several gunshots starting at the ankles and working up to the shoulders. The final shot was to the liver." The ME spoke, all the time having a strange, passionate look on his face, which Steel found disturbing.

"This was torture at a high scale. I figure the killer used a suppressor on the weapon because the neighbours didn't hear anything, also the lack of powered residue you would normally find. At a close range you would have powder burns, stippling of some kind, these are lacking here," Bauer said, pointing out the entry wounds with his pen.

Steel looked confused at the doctor's theory.

"They didn't hear screams?" Steel asked, also noting that there were no signs of the man having been tied up.

"He was drugged with the same stuff they used on your first corpse. Poor guy couldn't move but could feel everything. We still don't know what it is yet. But an impressive drug... don't you think?" The ME grinned.

Steel gave him a look of concern, then walked away towards the officer who had been first on the scene.

The cop was an average young-looking guy. His short black hair was cut with a military short, back and sides. Around him, CSU were dusting for prints and taking reels of film. Steel had noticed the place was untouched, meaning that there were no signs of struggle.

As Steel approached the young officer braced up, and this amused the detective. He remembered his days as a recruit in the army. Every sign of someone with command had made him flinch to attention. Several times he had incorrectly saluted sergeant majors thinking they were officers.

"Relax," Steel told the young man, smiling. The uniformed officer attempted to do so but waved his hands, not knowing what to do with them.

"If it makes you feel better, stick the tips of your fingers in your pockets." Steel smiled broadly, understanding the stress. The cop smiled too, nodded and slid them partially into his trouser pockets.

"So, tell me what you found," Steel asked the young cop. He closed his eyes so he could picture the scene as it was described.

"I got a call from Dispatch," the younger man explained. "The neighbours next door was fighting so I went to check it out. As I approached, I noticed blood on the door frame. I knocked on the door, but there was no answer. I got hold of the manager who let me in, and that's when I found—" The cop's face went white, and he held his mouth in a reflex action.

"Is this your first body?" Steel asked.

The cop nodded. Steel returned his nod and tapped a reassuring hand on the man's shoulder.

"You'll be fine. Now tell me what else did you see?" Steel asked as he turned away and looked around the room.

The officer looked puzzled as if Steel wasn't taking notice of him.

"Don't worry, I am still listening," Steel said, sensing the cop's puzzlement.

"I saw the body on the ground and so much—" Steel raised his hand.

"—Forget the body." Steel raised his hand. "What else did you see? Did anyone pass you in the corridor? Did any cars race off when you got here? Try to think of things that struck you in a split second when you first arrived," Steel explained.

The young cop thought for a moment, then shook his head. "No, sorry. Maybe I should have been more observant." The young cop was instantly feeling guilty.

"Trust me, that comes with practice," Steel reassured him. "Besides if there had been something wrong, you would have known it."

The cop nodded, and Steel walked away back towards the ME.

"Have you got a time of death, doctor?" Steel asked, hoping for a time frame that coincided with when most people were awake.

"I estimate between six and seven this morning. Oh, there is one more thing," the doctor said with a curious grin.

Steel noticed the two cups of coffee on the breakfast bar and the ladies' bag hanging on the high back tall stool.

"What's that?" Steel asked. "That he wasn't alone, and we

have a missing person? Or that this missing person was the killer?" Steel noticed the crushed look on the ME's face.

"Something like that—yes," he answered, before hurrying after the body.

Steel shook his head and smiled as he watched the man scamper away. Steel grabbed one of the CSUs and told him about the flowers. Steel's gut told him that the flowers had been a decoy: a way in. He had seen it in the movies, so many times he wondered if people still fell for it. But he had to be sure.

The bag was a brown leather Gucci. The long strap held it just below the seat. Steel picked it up in his gloved hands. The blue latex almost matched the black of his suit.

Inside the bag were the usual hairbrushes, car keys, a day planner and her purse. Steel checked the name on the driving licence and cursed his luck. The licence was in the name of Brooke Taylor. Steel sat down on the highchair and sorted through the rest of the purse. Cash and credit cards were all there. She had been taken, and Steel guessed that the blood on the wall outside belonged to her. He bagged the purse and walked towards the door. The handle had blood on it, and there was a fruit knife on the ground.

Steel figured that she had opened the door to someone carrying the bouquet. The guy probably said it was a delivery so as not to draw attention to himself. Steel saw the images in his mind as he set the scene like a small movie rerun.

How the door had opened, and the man pushed his way in. She would have struggled, maybe even got in a couple of hits before being overpowered. How the other agent had rushed forward and probably been hit with a Taser before he could get to his piece.

Steel frowned as the movie in his head revealed possible new evidence. There had been more than one of them. Two to three at the most.

Brooke had purposely cut her hand to leave a trail. She was a smart woman. Without the blood trail, no one would have even known about her dead partner.

The question now was, why did they take Brooke? And more importantly, did they know who she really was?

Steel thought back to the first crime scene. How Amber had been tortured.

Someone was looking for something.

What Steel could not figure out was why Amber's apartment had not been trashed. Normally the place would have been tossed, but it hadn't been. However, the furniture had been moved. They had moved the couch back to make more room; however, there were no marks on the carpet to suggest a secret place in the floor. Steel stopped for a second and cursed his stupidity. They had checked underneath the couch. Whoever had done, it had tipped up the couch and checked underneath.

But they had not found it, and they figured that Brooke had gone. This then led to even more questions.

The key ones being: who were they? And what was worth killing for?

CHAPTER NINETEEN

Brooke Taylor opened her eyes slowly. The last thing she remembered was the man at the door. A delivery mans. Brooke had been slicing an apple as she had answered it. There had been no time to react, and the door had been rammed open just as she turned the handle. She had taken the brunt of the full force and had been thrown against the wall from the impact. A metallic thumping sound had rung in her ears as she had lost consciousness.

Brooke had slipped away into darkness. Now she had woken up in darkness. She looked around, but there was no light to even make anything out. Her head throbbed from where the door had made contact. Brooke tried to raise a hand but found she was unable to move.

A sudden fear came over her. She was tied onto something. Her arms, legs and middle were bound by strapping. She struggled, but the pain in her head became intense. Brooke lay there for a moment. She felt like shouting out, but who would hear her? Her captors presumably.

The sudden tap of footsteps on a hard floor filled her ears.

Then she was suddenly bathed in light from a lamp above her. The illumination seemed intensely bright after so much time she'd spent in darkness. As her eyes adjusted to it, she looked around. An expression of terror crossed her face as she realised, she was on an operating table. The cold steel surface glistened, reflecting the light from above.

Then another sound filled her ears: the sound of music. Soft mechanical music from a music box or ... Brooke felt her soul freeze over. She had heard the tales about Mr Williams and how he loved to play his tunes for those who were about to meet him.

He drew near, and she struggled to break free of her bonds. He stood there partially in the darkness—only his lower half was visible. Brooke could feel her heart racing in her chest. All the stories she had heard about Williams never ended well.

She wanted the music to play on forever. They said that when the music stopped, his fun started. A tear rolled down her cheek towards her ear. She could feel herself growing faint again. The music stopped, but he stayed there. Motionless. Silent.

"What do you want from me?" She spoke almost softly. She wanted to shout, but she had no idea how he would react.

Williams disappeared into the shadows again. There was a click, and the table began to rise so that she was sitting in an upright position. The fear grew stronger, and her breathing became heavy

What the hell was he doing? she thought. The motion stopped, and Brooke stared forward as she heard his approach.

Suddenly there was a buzz from a cell phone. She saw the illumination from the device as he pulled it from a jacket pocket.

He sighed heavily. "I am sorry about this," he apologised to her. "You try and add a little drama to things, and this happens. Please do excuse me while I take this call, will you?"

So, saying, he turned his back to speak, almost as if he was trying to hide the conversation from her. He walked into the light, and she saw him completely for the first time. The thousand-dollar suit hugged his tall, thin frame. He had an elegant yet disturbing look about him.

"Hello ... Yes, I am with her now." He turned to face her and smiled and rolled his eyes as if he was bored with the caller. "No, I haven't asked her yet. Because I have only just walked in and—"

Brooke watched him as he talked. His body language was almost like that of a schoolboy who couldn't wait to go out and play.

"Yes ... Yes ... OK ... Right."

She watched as he answered but wasn't really listening. She watched as he made a 'yap, yap, yap' hand gesture.

"What was that? ... orry ... ery ... ad ... s-gle ... our ... aking up," He said, faking a bad line, then he rolled his eyes before crushing the cheap cell phone in his bony right hand – just in case, they tried again. Williams let the broken device fall to the ground, then brushed off his hands. As he walked up to her, Brooke noted his almost embarrassed smile. He raised a hand to gently brush away the lock of hair that covered a slight cut above her left eye.

"I must apologise for your treatment, Miss Taylor. My employees do not know the meaning of 'gentle and unharmed'," he said softly, then raised a straw that was resting in a crystal cut glass to her lips.

She stared at the clear water. Williams smiled and took a sip from the crystal glass.

"My dear, if I wanted you dead, you would not be here." He smiled and raised the straw to her lips. Brooke drank. The water was cold and refreshing. Williams looked up at the angry bruise, and his smile fell away. He turned and walked into the shadows. There was a slight buzzing sound, and then the whole room was illuminated.

Brooke's heart sank as she saw that she was in an operating theatre. The white-tiled walls and floor made for easy cleaning. A small table to the side of her was filled with many different devices for surgery.

Williams walked towards a door at the far end and spoke to a guard who stood on the other side of the entrance. They were too far away to be overheard. Brooke had a bad feeling. Why was she here, in this place? The door closed, and Williams slowly walked back. He was calculating something in his head, but his gestures gave away his thoughts.

Moments later, the door opened, and a large man dressed in black walked in and stopped at the entrance of the doorway. Williams smiled and turned to face the man.

"Are you the one who brought her in for me?" Williams asked excitedly.

The man nodded proudly whilst wearing a dumb smile.

"Well I must say, you did a great job," Williams said, ushering the man to come over. "Please join us."

The newcomer grinned broadly and strolled over, feeling like he was a king's champion.

"Yes, indeed, a fantastic job. Just one thing though—"

The man's smile faded as he saw Williams's agreeable expression turn into a scowl.

"Tell me. How did she get the cut on her head?" Williams asked as a mean grin crept over his face forcing his mouth to widen like that of a Cheshire cat.

"I ... I don't know, sir," the man stuttered in confusion. "It could have been when we kicked the door in—"

The man suddenly stopped talking, realising what he had

admitted. He stepped back slightly. He was at least a foot taller and much wider than Williams. But Williams had an air about him that could put the fear into anyone with just one glance.

"You see what I have to work with?" Williams said to Brooke, pointing to the man with a flat palm. "A simple task. Not much to ask of him, I thought. I told him to go and bring me the woman unharmed—that's what I said. Nothing too hard to do, or to understand, I would have thought," Williams said, his voice remaining calm.

"You do know what *unharmed* means, don't you?" Williams asked the large man.

"Uh, yes sir," the brute replied, almost puzzled by the question.

"Really? Are you sure?" he said, dragging the man towards the frightened young woman.

"*Unharmed!*" Williams said, pointing to the man. "Not *harmed!*" He pointed towards the cut on Brooke's head.

"Unharmed!" he said again, but this time pointing to himself. "Harmed." He laughed, pointing to the man. The man's face fell, and he suddenly realised where Williams was pointing. Williams laughed out loud as if he was joking, the big man laughed as well, mostly out of relief.

Brooke never saw Williams reach for the scalpel, but then neither did the man. Blood poured from the open wound at his throat. The big man grasped his neck in a futile attempt to stop the cascading red liquid. A gurgling sound came from the man as he dropped to his knees and then to the floor. Soon a lake of crimson had engulfed the man's corpse.

The terrified young woman remained still and quiet so as not to join the man on the floor. She had heard about Williams. Ever since he had made his first appearance on the triple murder case the year before she had heard his name mentioned. It was standard protocol to know about him. He wasn't governed by money or power. In fact, he had no real master. He enjoyed what he did, and that made him even more terrifying. Her body trembled with fear as he casually walked to the washbasin and began to scrub the man's blood from his hands. There was silence, but somehow the mood had lifted. He turned towards her, and he smiled as though nothing had happened. Williams moved up towards her and stared into her eyes. She saw a different man. His eyes were almost kind and surprisingly gentle. He stroked her hair and smiled. "Don't worry, my dear. No one will ever hurt you again."

————

Steel stepped off the elevator at the lower level of the coroner's office. He had decided before going to see how John Doe was doing, and he would see if Tina Franks had any new information. They had been waiting for the test results on John Doe's clothes. 'We've got a backlog', CSU had said. He was aware they had been swamped with work since a recent accident on the subway. Was it an accident or an act of terrorism? some had wondered, especially the press. A train had derailed and crashed into another one. There were hundreds of dead or injured. The papers were filling the public's minds with all sorts of tales of possibilities, most of which was heading down the terrorist route. The Feds weren't talking, and the police were under orders not to reveal anything either. The social media groups had spun their piece posing their opinion and asking for feedback. Some blamed the president for cutting costs, others the Mayor. It was a media circus. Unfortunately, it was one of those that would stay in people's minds for a blink of an eye until the next catastrophe happened. Steel thought it sad there could be a mass genocide in a faraway land, but nobody gave a shit, but if there was something at home...different story, the people wanted blood.

Steel stopped for a second and checked his cell phone for any messages. There was nothing, just junk emails. People selling things, service providers telling him of the latest deals. Steel put the phone away and looked over at a room full of sheet-covered bodies. He counted twenty at the most. He figured that these were only a few of the crash victims.

He shook his head and headed for the double doors of Tina's lab. An orderly came out of one of the other labs and passed Steel on the way to the changing room, his scrubs covered in blood. Steel turned and watched the man as he strolled away as if he was just strolling down the street without a care in the world.

This got Steel thinking. How was it that nobody had noticed John Doe walking around in a daze and covered in blood? But then some people don't want to get involved with strangers, just in case of any trouble—especially strangers who were covered in blood. He pushed through the double doors and walked into the lab. He found Tina standing over her latest 'guest'. It was the body of a young male with a GSW – gunshot wound – to the midsection.

Steel noted that the kid was in his late teens or early twenties. Anyway, he was way too young to be where he was.

"Hi, doctor, you're looking as radiant as ever," he said.

She looked up at him with one of those *really* looks. She was wearing a full-body suit and a full facial mask ready for the 'cutting' part of the autopsy. She already had streaks of fresh blood on her, and her gloved hands were covered with tissue from internal organs.

He smiled and leaned against the steel table that contained some sample dishes and scales for weighing body organs. He watched as she slipped her hand deep into the cadaver's open chest cavity.

"What can I do for you, Mr Steel?" she asked, but already knew what he was going to ask for. "If it's the test results, I am afraid you're gonna have to wait. They are backed up pretty bad up here," she said, pulling out the boy's kidneys, and putting them in a large stainless-steel bowl on top of some scales.

"Anything on the guy from the hotel?" Steel asked, almost hoping for some good news.

"Not much. I have got a date with him after this poor kid. What I can tell you is he wasn't shot. He was stabbed with something round," she said shrugging. "I will know more once I have cut him up." Steel nodded and headed for the door. "Thank you, doctor, a pleasure as always." He gave her a small bow and then headed out through the double doors. She stood there for a moment with the skull cutter clutched in both hands and a dreamy look in her eyes. She felt her knees tremble at the indecent thought she had just had. Tina smiled to herself and then proceeded to saw the top off the kid's head.

———

Tooms got off the elevator and headed for Tony, who was sitting at his computer. Tony had sent photographs of the missing woman – Tara Burke, to all the hospitals, train stations and airports. Tony looked up at his partner, who was biting into a chilli dog whilst holding another. Tony smiled and shook his head.

"Hungry?" he asked as Tooms finished the hotdog and sat down, readying himself for the other one.

"You know she will kill you," Tony advised him.

Tooms shrugged and smiled. "Only if she finds out," Tooms said, grinning.

Tony smiled broadly. "Shouldn't be hard. All she has to do is check your tie." Tooms looked down at his blue tie to see chilli sauce in the dead centre of it. "Oh, great! This was a present from her, as well," groaned Tooms, taking off the evidence and stashing it in a desk drawer.

"Anything back on Tara Burke?" Tooms asked.

Tony sat back in his chair and stretched off. "Nah, no priors, nothing on the system apart from her birth certificate. Her mom bailed out on her when she was eighteen. Real piece of work by all accounts. Used to beat the crap out of Tara starting from when she was little. Then she just up and left." Tony looked over at Tara's photograph on the board. She was a pretty little thing with a touch of hardness about her. Tony thought back over the recent past and realised that he had never met her. He knew most of Amber's friends but not her. But then again there weren't that many friends to know. He reached down to the picture on his desk of Amber. It had been taken on a summer's day. She was wearing a white blouse, blue shorts and a beaming smile. He mapped her face with an index finger.

"You OK, man?" Tooms asked softly.

Tony looked up at him and smiled. "Yeah, I am fine," Tony looked back at the picture. "It's just that I miss her, man, I really miss her."

Tooms nodded slowly. He had no idea how his partner felt, and in truth hoped that he never would. Tony looked up to see Steel walk out of the elevator. He didn't look happy. Tony nodded over to Tooms, just as Steel ushered them to follow him into his office. The two detectives stood up and followed Steel inside.

Steel held the door open and watched them sit in the

chesterfields opposite the large desk. Steel closed the door and headed for the desk and sat on its surface, facing them.

"I thought you were off to see Memory Boy?" Tooms asked, confused at Steel's manner.

"Doc Davidson is in with him doing some tests or something," John explained. "I stopped at the morgue instead, to see if they had anything. Looks like we will have to wait for the results a bit longer."

Tony nodded, but he was still curious. Steel was staring at him, and the British detective's face was like stone.

"What is it?" Tony asked, sensing bad news. Steel reached into his inside pocket and pulled out a small baggy with something like a piece of paper or a photograph inside it.

"Tony, I got some news today, but you aren't going to like it," Steel explained.

Tony sat back in his chair as if preparing himself for a punch.

"Amber wasn't who we thought she was," John elaborated. "Amber was an undercover agent. She worked for a government agency. Apparently, she was investigating something big." Steel watched Tony's reaction. He saw the look of searching, the familiar stare of trying to make sense of what had just been said.

"Did her sisters know?" Tony asked, then he took in the look on Steel's face. "Ah. I get it. There are no sisters? But wait, if that's the case, then who the hell is Brooke?" Tony asked suddenly.

"She was Amber's handler. But there's something else. She was abducted, and her colleague was killed. She was possibly the only one who knew what Amber was up to," Steel answered.

"So...someone found out what she was doing and killed

her?" Tooms asked, confused. "But if that's the case, why kidnap Brooke? Why not kill her?"

Tony was having the same thoughts.

"Amber was tortured," John went on, playing the probable scene through in his mind. "I think someone was looking for something, and I don't think they found it. That's why they took Brooke."

"So how does Tara Burke fit in?" Tooms asked.

Tony looked over towards his partner. "She must have seen something or walked in on them. She is probably hiding." Tony put forward his own theory.

Steel considered it carefully, then shook his head. "You know I think that we have been looking at it all wrong. I think Amber shouldn't have been there. Don't forget that she wasn't due to move in until the Monday. She probably walked in just as they were looking for whatever it was, they wanted. If anything, I think that Tara is more involved than we think." The more Steel thought about it, the more sense it made.

An angry look crossed Tony's face. He had just remembered what started the conversation: the news that everything had been a lie.

"So, what about the ex-boyfriend—me," Tony Marinelli growled. "Was everything a cover?"

Steel picked up the plastic evidence bag and looked at whatever was on the front of it. "You have to understand that working undercover takes a lot out of you. It makes you forget who you are sometimes. You need an anchor. Family, boyfriend, girlfriend. Something you can come back to. You need something *solid*. I think you were that for her." Steel passed over the bag to Tony. Inside it was a photograph of Tony and Amber together.

"CSU found it in her diary," Steel explained kindly. "If

nothing else, Tony, you have to remember that she cared for you."

Tony took the picture and held it for a moment. He looked up at Steel and nodded a 'thank you'.

"What now?" Tooms asked.

Steel's face became emotionless and cold. "Now, we find out why Amber had two jobs. And we find Tara Burke."

CHAPTER TWENTY

Brooke Taylor was blindfolded, then led away. She had been taken up some stairwells and down others, and along straight and winding corridors. It was an old trick. Use disorientation, so that the person has no idea how large the building is, or whether they are up fourteen storeys or deep underground. If she had escaped, she would have had no idea where to run, meanwhile giving ample time for her captors to find her.

Eventually, they stopped, and she heard a heavy metal door being opened. She was led in, and then the door slammed behind her.

Brooke ripped off the blindfold and stood ready.

She was alone.

The sudden brightness of the light stung her eyes. Brooke closed them quickly and let them adjust. Slowly opening them, she saw the room properly for the first time. It was a large space that had been created to be like the luxurious bedroom of a six-star hotel. A large four-poster bed was draped in a maroon silk covering with a matching throw.

The furnishings looked European and antique. There were no windows, but flat screens behind wooden frames gave the illusion of the outside world. Oddly enough, the landscape was of a sea view. Possibly seen from an Italian villa. She was in comfort. The ensuite bathroom had black marble flooring and brass fittings. The cast-iron tub sat in the middle of the room with a shower curtain surround. The drawers and cabinets were of dark mahogany.

She sat on the bed and just lay back. Lying on the bed was like relaxing on a cloud. She felt herself slip away into a state of complete serenity. At that moment, nothing mattered.

Brooke looked over to the far side of the room. She stood up and walked over to the heavy mahogany door. Her hand remained just a few centimetres away from the brass handle. She had no idea what was behind this. It wasn't the way out, for she knew that was behind her. It was probably another bathroom, and maybe even a room joined to that of another prisoner. She turned the handle and opened the door.

Her mouth fell open at the sight of the massive walk-in wardrobe. Then it suddenly struck her. This wasn't just a sudden snatch and grab. This had taken time. This had been planned over a very long period, or else she was the only one who had spent time there.

———

Tara Burke sat, staring at the television set. The news broadcast told of some story about the pension problem of some big firm. She had flicked through the channels a dozen times and found this one to be the most interesting. Besides, she hoped they would have more information on Amber's murder. She still couldn't believe that her friend was dead, murdered in their apartment. The press had shown her apartment building on the newsflash. But that seemed a lifetime ago. Now they were showing fluff pieces and sports.

She sat in a comfortable curled up position on the couch, her head resting on a stack of throw cushions. She looked over to a few clothes Kim had sorted out for her. Luckily the two women were around the same size. There was nothing much—just some T-shirts and jeans. But it was something new to wear. Tara found the gesture sweet but unnecessary, as she had her own clothes in the pink suitcase. Tara figured it was some kind of 'big sister act'. Kim had always tried to look after her since her mom had bailed out on her. Kim was the big sister she never had.

Tara picked up her cell phone from the coffee table and checked her messages. Still no word from him. She re-read the last message: *Where the hell are you, we must talk...* Tara looked at the desperate-looking words. Had he known something about what had happened to Amber?

She closed the cell and placed it back on the cold wooden table. The weather girl came on TV to tell everyone how great the day was going to be—she was a bubbly blonde with a tight dress that some guy must have picked out for the job. 'Clear with bright spells' was the prediction. But Tara didn't care. She wasn't going anywhere.

Kim had advised her to 'stay in and don't answer the door to anyone', something Tara intended to do anyway. Someone had gotten into her apartment and killed her friend and roommate. The news reporter put it down to a 'home invasion gone bad'. Tara was not convinced. Not after what she had found out.

The weather girl's report finished with a close and a smile. When the programme resumed, Tara saw the time in the top right-hand corner of the screen. It was nearly eleven in the morning. She was scared and bored—a bad combination. Tara stood up and headed for the refrigerator. She had slept through breakfast. *Wow,* she thought, *I slept through breakfast, never done that before.* She smiled at the thought. She was on holiday. Tara suddenly felt a bounce in her soul.

Now that she thought about it, she felt hungry. First, solve that problem, she reasoned, then she could tackle the boredom issue. She opened the fridge door and peered inside. The cold air felt good on her skin. So much so that she closed her eyes and just waited for a moment. Tara opened them and grabbed the milk container. Cereals were good. Chocolate cereal was better.

Tara sat back down on the couch. The spot was still warm from where she had lain all that time. She crossed her legs and began to spoon the chocolate squares into her mouth. Her eyes darted towards the TV screen as she saw the report of a murder. Her heart began to race. Some guy had been knifed in the Bronx. Her eyebrows raised in anticipation and she held the spoon full of coloured milk and cereal in mid-air, just in front of her gaping mouth.

The picture of the victim was that of some poor Hispanic kid with a rap sheet if a roll of toilet paper. She breathed easy and shovelled the spoon into her mouth.

Tara was worried about him. Had they found him? Had he given her up? She shook her head at the very thought of it. Besides even if he had, they had no idea where she was. She suddenly froze again. They might know where she worked. They might hurt Kim to get to her.

The worried woman cursed her situation.

It had been a good plan. A sound plans. But they had become greedy and careless. Now the people they stole from wanted their stuff back.

They wanted revenge.

———

It was around one in the afternoon when Steel had decided to go and see John Doe. The hours of searching for anything on Amber or Sharney Taylor were proving to be a nightmare. Tony had gotten an old address from the hotel where Sharney had worked – someplace on the Lenox Hill. The boys said they would check that out after they had gotten a warrant.

Steel walked out of the elevator onto the floor where they were keeping John Doe.

The silence suddenly hit him.

There was no sound of a blaring television, and where was the guard? A sudden rush of panic rushed over Steel as he ran for the guard's room. With one swift movement, he sped up then dove at the door with his shoulder. With a crash, the door swung open, and Steel rolled, pulling out his Barretta as he hit the floor. Steel rolled behind the nearest cover, which was the sofa. Steel brought up the weapon over the couch and aimed. Silence filled the air, nothing but his breathing and a muffled sound coming from the bedroom. Steel stood quickly and headed for the noise. There on the floor were the two policemen, and both had been stripped down to their underwear and bound.

The men had been duct-taped together back to back, and the silver tape pulled tight around their chest areas, as well as around their arms and hands. Steel cringed as he noticed the older cop appeared to be the hairiest man he had ever seen.

"Oh boy, that's going to hurt when it comes off," Steel said to himself. He smiled as he reached for his cell phone to take a picture. But his childish thoughts soon passed. Steel turned and ran for John Doe's suite of rooms. He called out for him, but no answer came back.

There were signs of a struggle. Small tables lay on their sides with shattered vases spread across the carpeted floor. A large bookshelf lay on its front, its contents fallen onto the floor before it. An armchair had been turned over, and the glass coffee table smashed. There had obviously been a fight. A struggle.

Steel examined the scene. It looked as if possibly two or more men had been sent to collect him. But the more Steel looked at the scene, and the more something nagged him about it. He looked over to the wall and realised something. He ran out and headed for the room with the surveillance crew. The door was closed but not locked. The three men lay on the ground or were slumped over their desks. They were out cold.

The detective then noticed the empty food containers from a Chinese restaurant that was located down the road from the hotel. He reached into his jacket pocket and pulled out a pair of surgical gloves. Suddenly one question hit him: *Why did they order out when they had a room service tab?* Steel turned and took out his cell phone. He needed paramedics and CSU. As he entered the room with the bound cops, he noticed the same Chinese food containers. He would have to wait until the men regained consciousness before they could answer any questions, but one thing was clear: if they hadn't ordered the food, then someone else had.

John Doe had suddenly jumped up some notches on the 'important person' scale. At first, he was a possible person of interest, and now he was a definite one. Not many people would go to such lengths to get to someone. They only reason they would do so was if they had done something bad to the wrong people.

Someone had laced the food and taken John Doe, but how did they know he was there? More importantly, who wanted him and why? Steel finished the call and looked the photograph of the cops tied up on the floor. But he didn't feel in a mood for laughing. These people were smart enough to knock out cops and get to their possible witness. More importantly, they were smart enough not to kill cops. Whoever it was, they were organised.

———

Tony and Tooms had gotten a warrant to search Sharney's – or rather Amber's apartment. It was a large place on East 60th Street: Lenox Hill. The location was perfect, as it was not far from the hotel where Amber had once worked. The two-bedroomed apartment seemed a bright and happy place.

The front door opened into a slim hallway. Just off to the side was a sitting room and the small kitchen sat opposite. The white walls of the hallway displayed paintings of flowers and landscapes. Several photographs of Amber with her family and friends hung in framed eight-by-tens. Further down were the two bedrooms and the bathroom was at the end. The wooden parquet flooring resembled oak, but Tooms had laid enough of the stuff to know it was a stained wood imitation.

All the doors had been left open, allowing the sunlight to illuminate the hallway. A fresh scent of lavender hung in the air from the automatic dispenser that was plugged into a nearby socket.

Tooms headed towards the sitting room, which was a few feet from the front door. A dark green three-seat couch was perched up against the left wall, and was opposite a large teak unit, on top of which stood a forty-two-inch flat-screen TV and a Blu-Ray player. Above the flat-screen, photographs had been arranged in an arch formation.

Several potted plants had self-watering systems attached to their decorative pots. It was obvious to Tooms that Amber wasn't planning on moving out. In fact, everything in the apartment said to him that she was going to return.

Tony opened the large refrigerator. The steel sides glinted as they caught the afternoon sun. Inside there were no perishables. In fact, there was nothing with a 'Best By' date on it. However, the cupboards told a different story. Most of the food was in cans or packages.

"Hey, Tooms, I think this was home," Tony said, walking out into the hallway. Tooms stepped out, holding a pink silk nightshirt up in front of himself as he studied it.

Tony raised his eyebrows. "Something you want to share, partner?" Tony said, trying to keep a straight face. He only wished he had a camera. That would have been worth at least two months' worth of bribery.

"Yeah, yeah, screw you," Tooms said. "Come take look at this." Tooms thought quickly change the subject. Tony smiled and followed his partner into Amber's bedroom. The room was large enough for the double bed and some other furniture. As he entered, he saw the window was straight in front of him, and the bed was against the right-hand wall. A pine dresser stood in the middle of the left-hand wall. A small stand mirror and several jewellery boxes cluttered its top. The fourth drawer of the six-drawer dresser was pulled out. This held various types of nightwear. Tony noticed Tooms had left a gap where he had parted the garments. "Ain't nothin' here," Tooms said, placing the shirt back in the gap, then quickly shut the drawer.

"Were you hoping to find something?" Tony asked, almost wondering what Tooms's reply would be, given the fact he had been caught looking in the underwear drawer.

"I don't know. Guess I was hoping for a gun, a badge maybe. Something to explain what's going on," Tooms said, sounding frustrated.

"And you thought it would be in her underwear drawer?" Tony pointed out, hiding the grin of satisfaction.

"Hey, I had been through all of the drawers, you just caught me at that one," Tooms said, hurrying out of the room.

Tony smiled. He was glad that Tooms was there, not just to help with the case, but for support. Just being in the apartment and seeing the pictures was killing Tony. But he knew he had to carry on. He had to find Amber's killer.

They had swept through the rest of the apartment and found nothing out of the ordinary. Tony reasoned that if she had been working for a government agency, had they already been through the place and cleared it of anything that could tie her to them?

As the two detectives made their way back to the sitting room, Tooms noticed the answering machine. The digital display showed that she had ten missed messages. Tooms looked over at Tony. Tony walked over to the machine and looked down at the red LED display.

"Are you sure you want to hear this?" Tooms asked his friend, a sympathetic smile on his large face. "It could be disturbing."

"Probably no more disturbing than watching you holding my dead girlfriend's nightclothes next to you as if you were trying them for size," Tony said, raising his eyebrows.

Tooms scowled. He knew Tony wouldn't let this one goes for a very long time. But it was a worth suffering the taunts to see him smile.

The black officer pressed the 'play' button on the machine, and they waited. The first two messages were telemarketers selling stuff. The next, however, was from Brooke. Her voice was trying to sound calm, but traces of anxiety broke through the façade.

"Hey there, sis," the recorded voice said. "Sorry we haven't spoken for a while; things have been a little crazy here. Look, call me when you can. OK?"

Tooms looked at his partner, who just stared at the machine in disappointment, almost as if he was hoping the machine would spurt out clue.

The next few messages were from some insurance companies who were hoping to catch a score. Tooms and Tony both scowled with disappointment. They had come up empty. They turned and headed for the door. They had wasted precious time following this lead, and now they had to backtrack and find something new. The machine announced the last message just as the two cops were about to leaving the apartment. Tooms had barely closed the door as the sound of Brooke's voice echoed through the rooms.

"Amber. It's me. Whatever you do, don't go to the other flat," they heard.

The door burst open again, and the two detectives rushed back inside. Tony began to speak, but Tooms raised a large hand to signal for him to be quiet.

"Do you hear me, Amber? Don't go to Tara's apartment. Go straight to Alpha location and wait for extraction." There was a background noise. It sounded like a car's tyres screeching.

The call went dead. Tooms grabbed the machine. He had a mixed look of anger and relief on his face. This was their first piece of data.

"What now?" Tony asked as he watched his friend wind the loose cables around the small device.

"Now we play this for Steel and see what he has to say. The

man must know something, or at least he'll have an idea," Tooms said with a hint of hope in his voice.

Tony nodded. "Let's see if we can trace the call as well. It may tell us where Brooke was, and who was driving the car that spooked her." He looked around the apartment for the last time. He frowned and then closed the door behind them.

CHAPTER TWENTY-ONE

STEEL STEPPED OUT INTO THE WARMTH OF THE afternoon sun. A cool breeze brushed his face as he stood for a moment as if he was basking in the bright sunlight. The roads were full of traffic, and the sidewalks crowded with passers-by.

Upstairs CSU and the paramedics were doing their thing now that Steel had left. There was nothing more for him to do, and if he'd stayed, he would only have got in the way. The CSU report would take a while, possibly a day or two, due to the backlog.

Steel pulled up the collar on his coat, so it wrapped itself around his neck. Autumn would soon be here; he could feel it in the breeze. The leaves on the trees had already started to turn brown. Steel thought back to his days back home on his English estate. He remembered looking up at the geese as they made their yearly pilgrimage to avoid the winter weather.

He looked at his watch. It was two in the afternoon. He knew he had to get back to the precinct and assign the various jobs pertaining to finding their John Doe. He had more than enough to do, and they were short on manpower due to one of their number having recently quit his job.

Steel walked to the kerb and raised his hand to hail a cab. Several drove past as though no one was there. He stepped back as a yellow cab stopped. Steel noticed the attractive redheaded woman in the back. He opened the door for her and assisted her out onto the sidewalk.

"Why thank you, kind sir," she said to him. She had a soft voice, and deep brown eyes you could get lost in. She wore a white skirted suit with a black silk blouse that was open enough to distract you. Steel climbed into the back of the cab and froze. Something had set him thinking: a scent of perfume. One he had smelt before. Twice before in fact.

But where?

"Where to, buddy?" asked the cab driver.

But Steel was a million miles away, searching his memories to try to remember where he had smelt that perfume before.

"Hey, buddy, if you're thinking about that chick, I am afraid that ship has sailed, my man." The black cabbie laughed. The man's slight muscular build showed under his open sleeveless denim jacket. The sun shone off his shaven head, showing the beads of sweat that had begun to gather there. Steel got out quickly and looked at the crowd of people. The woman had gone, but he remembered where he had remembered that perfume before. The first time he'd seen her was on a cruise ship, and the second time was in the Precinct, the female officer who had guarded the Chief of Police.

Just before she put a bullet through his skull.

'Missy Studebaker', or at least that's what she had called herself, he remembered. Steel got back in the cab. His mind began to work overtime. Why was she here? He remembered seeing her shopping bags: they were all from the same store.

"The woman you just dropped off. Can you take me to

where you picked her up?" Steel asked as he leant forward near the dividing window.

The cabbie smiled and winked. "Sure thing, boss," the man said as he wiped his brow with his sweatband that had the colours of Jamaica on it. Steel sat back and let the man drive quietly. He looked out of the window and took in the surroundings as they travelled to Brooklyn.

The half-hour trip was filled with odd burst of chatter from the cabbie. Steel didn't answer much, just sat and watched the world go by. He could have driven himself, but when you don't want to be followed, a car tends to make things difficult. With a cab, you can just jump out and walk or catch a subway train.

"This is where I picked her up," the driver said, nodding to a pet store. Steel pulled out his cell phone and typed in a search. He had noticed the name on the woman's bags as she left the cab. It was a boutique called *Le Bon Voyage*.

The search engine showed it was just around the corner from where the cab had stopped. Steel paid the cabbie and got out. The cabbie noted the generous tip and smiled, showing off a couple of golden teeth.

"You have a good day, boss, and I hope you find what you're lookin' for," he said. Steel waved him a quick salute and headed in the direction the map had sent him. The cabbie waited until Steel had turned the corner and then picked up his cell phone. He pressed the auto-dial and waited. After several rings, a man's voice answered in a dry tone.

"Yeah, it's Jamal," he said into the phone. "We have a problem. I just picked up a cop from the hotel. I think he recognised the asset." He sounded alarmed at the turn of events.

"Where is he now?" asked the voice on the line.

"He's headin' for the store. What do you want me to do?"

The cabbie was still watching the corner; just in case, Steel came back.

There was a brief silence from the other end.

"Nothing. We have this covered."

The phone went dead. The cabbie put his cell away and drove on. He wanted to be as far away as possible.

One of the shops Steel was near was a boutique. The store was an old building, built in the late '30s, he judged. The three-storey building had large windows and a fabric overhang. The store next to it was a mattress shop, and they were taking delivery of some double mattresses.

He stood for a moment. His eyes scanning the building and the surroundings, taking note of anything unusual or out of place. Steel waited as two bulky men carried in a mattress before heading for the store next door.

The inside of the boutique was a mix of clothing and strangely decorated furniture. Natural sunlight was aided by a few dimly-lit lamps. The ground floor was mostly filled with women's clothing and accessories. Old revamped furniture was strategically placed amongst the items for sale: old chairs covered with mixed gold and silver paint, and dressers with the same touch. Large and small picture frames hung on the walls.

Opposite the door was a long glass counter which displayed silver and gold antique necklaces, brooches and watches. Behind the display, cabinet stood a stunning Asian woman. She had a gothic look about her, with her long black hair and dramatic make-up. Her athletic form was clothed in a tight black leather corset and trousers. These were topped off by knee-high black leather boots and a long thin fabric trench coat.

She looked up at Steel as he entered and cracked a smile. He smiled back before starting his wander around, making out that he was a lost shopper.

"Men's stuff is upstairs," she told him, her tone soft but at the same time forceful. "But I doubt if it'll be to your taste." Her voice made the hairs stand up on the back of his neck.

"Oh, I have very adventurous taste in clothes," he said, smiling.

She raised an eyebrow and smiled subtly.

Steel looked up at the stairwell to the next floor, which was of large dark wood boards that had recently been varnished. "Thank you, I am just browsing," Steel replied.

Her eyes widened with interest. "An Englishman in New York. You're on holiday, I suspect?" she said, almost purring the words as she looked him up and down with approval.

"Something like that. I saw your shop and thought I would give it a look," Steel said, picking up a wooden jewellery box.

"Are you looking for a present for your wife or girlfriend?" she asked, walking past the counter and moving beside a woman with red hair and wearing almost the same outfit, who appeared to be trying to blend in with the surroundings.

"Neither, I am afraid. I am very single," Steel replied, using objects with shiny surfaces to spy around the room for other shoppers.

The sexy woman smiled broadly at the news of Steel's availability.

"Upstairs, you say?" Steel said, pointing towards the wide opening stairwell.

She nodded and crossed her arms as she watched Steel climb the stairs which fluted at the bottom and the top like a grand staircase. This gave character to the store, almost blended its combination of 'old' and 'new' decor.

As he made it to the top, Steel heard the door open and caught a glimpse of a woman dressed in dark blue, with hair to match. The first floor was not as spacious as the ground floor, and every available space was packed with items. Along the left-hand wall, clothes hung in sections separated by size. On the right were the small changing rooms, with only a simple curtain to hide the customers from view. In the centre of the room, statues and busts were mixed with strange furnishings. Directly in front of him, two large windows let in a stream of warming sunlight.

Steel stood at the top of the staircase and looked at the strange mixture of people. A large mixed-race man in his mid-twenties stood at the racks arranging some clothes. He turned to Steel and just simply stared for a moment before returning to his task.

"Charming service," he muttered under his breath, not surprised at the lack of customers. Steel looked around, checking price tags and sizes, trying hard to look like a customer and not a cop.

"You lookin' for anything particular or are you just – looking?" The man's voice was abrupt and unfriendly.

The detective smiled as he looked through some shirts.

"Oh, just browsing. I am sure I will find something interesting though," Steel said, still holding the smile.

There was a sudden yelling coming from downstairs. It was the woman who was at the till. She was asking the man to come down to her. Her tone was composed for show, but he knew that the man was going to be given a lesson in manners.

Steel looked around the room. Something was off. There was obviously another floor above, so where was the stairwell? He walked over to the changing rooms. He opened one of the curtains and found a chair and a long mirror that almost filled the wall. Steel checked the inside but found nothing.

Quickly he checked the next one but to no avail. He was beginning to think his theory was just a bad idea until he reached the fourth one. He walked inside the booth and looked around. There was nothing out of the ordinary. Steel leant against the mirror out of frustration. There was a click as he pressed against the mirror, and then it moved away like a door.

Steel smiled. He could hear the conversation between the man and woman grow louder. *Good,* Steel thought.

It was the perfect time to check the upstairs floor.

At the top of the dimly lit stairwell was another door, and there was a mechanical sound emanating from within. Slowly, he turned the handle, opened it slightly and peered through the gap. The area appeared to be empty, so he crept in and closed the door behind him.

It was a large room, with only supportive upright beams to break up the floor space. The surrounding walls were painted white, and the floor was of grey plastic tiles. The mechanical sound was being made by rows of large counting machines.

Steel walked over to one of them. There appeared to be around thirty machines and mechanical stackers beside each one. Each machine was churning out ten-dollar bills. One machine would bundle them into stacks of ten, and the other would bind them. Behind all that were large metal containers, which Steel figured held the cash. It was a fully automated system, a large operation with few employees to know about it.

The detective took out his cell phone and took photographs of the presses. He went to call Tooms and realised that doing so may not be the brightest move, not while he was still in the building. There were a handful of women downstairs and a man with an attitude. Possible civilian casualties if it went wrong.

This was a major operation, so there had to be back-up nearby just in case things went awry. Besides, this was more in the Civil Enforcement Unit's line than Homicide. Steel waited until he was outside to make the call to a detective he knew: the guy he had in mind was a heavy-handed son-of-a-bitch named Walter Cobb.

Steel made his way downstairs to the changing stall. He hoped they hadn't been looking for him, for that could complicate things. As he edged out from behind the mirror, he heard silence. This was a bad sign. He had taken several shirts and trousers into the booth with him as a bluff, just in case, he was seen coming out of it.

As he stepped out, Steel found himself alone: the large assistant had gone. Music played downstairs—some sort of classic and rock mix of Beethoven's Fifth with orchestra and guitars in a mix.

Steel walked towards the top of the stairs to find five women standing there looking up. Each of the women had almost the same style of clothing, but each had her own colour.

Even their hair was dyed in the same shade as their clothes. Steel noticed the Oriental woman standing at the centre, dressed all in black. The others were of brighter colours: red, violet, blue ombre, pink and white. As well as wearing the same style of attire they all had the same concentrated stare.

They seemed to be unarmed, but he knew better than to trust his judgement about that. If he was inclined to arrogance, he might have decided that they were only weak women and pile in. But from what he had seen drunken soldiers' wives do, he knew better than to underestimate their fighting skills. One thing that did worry him was the missing assistant.

Steel suddenly felt the vice-like grip around his middle, as the man grabbed Steel in a bear hug.

"Ah, there you are," Steel said with a slight loss of breath as the man squeezed, apparently to show off his strength. Steel looked down at the woman in black as she placed her right leg on the bottom step and leaned in slightly.

"Did you find anything interesting?" she asked. Her voice had a hard softness to it, and her eyes stared at his face as if she was looking for a lie.

"Well the shirts were quite nice, but the other things were really an eye-opener," Steel said with a smile. The man squeezed again in defiance of Steel's mockery. But the man thought he was stronger than he was.

"Who are you...a cop?" his attacker yelled to show off his authority, of which he had none. The woman stared into Steel's face, but this time the look was different. This time she was sizing him up.

Steel suddenly got bored with the cuddling and scraped the inside of his boot down the man's shinbone. The hugger screamed and released his grip slightly. Steel leant forward and brought his head back. There was a scream of pain, and a loud cracking sound as Steel's head crunched against the man's nose. He released Steel and stumbled backwards before falling to the ground, blood pouring from the wound on his face.

Before Steel could react the woman in blue was already on him. She landed a roundhouse that he barely moved for, causing him to spin. She made several more kicks, which he was able to block. As she made another kick, Steel managed to grab her leg. A look of surprise crossed her face, and he just gave a quick grin before tossing her into the changing rooms.

As she flew from his grip, he received a sidekick to the back from the woman in red and then a sweeping kick from the woman in white. Steel hit the ground hard, making a dull thump. He looked up and rolled just in time before Red's heel came down where his crotch would have been.

Steel got up into a crouched 'ready' stance. This wasn't just five against one. This was five *highly trained ass-kickers* against one. The woman in red made a spin kick to either knock him off balance or distract him from seeing the woman in pink rush up behind him. Neither worked. He waited until the last moment and then dived out of the way. The woman in pink took most of the kick to the side of the head and was thrown to the side. The red woman roared in anger. Steel simply smiled and shrugged. This made Red enraged, and she lost her head. She charged, despite the woman in black's command to stop.

She made several impressive attacks with both feet and hand punches. But Steel blocked them all until he found the right moment, and then grabbed her leg and sent her flying into the booths along with her colleague.

Steel let out a muffled grunt as Blue let loose a hard kick to his midsection. He stumbled backwards slightly from the impressive power shot. Blue spun to make another hit, but Steel dropped to the ground in a press-up position, just as her leg passed over him. He spun around on the ground and swept Blue's legs from under her. Blue let out a brief cry of pain as her head met with the flooring.

Steel stood up, almost ready for the next shot. White and Pink didn't disappoint. The two women took turns in hammering at Steel with kicks and punches. The woman in black stood at the top of the stairs and watched as she realised something. This man was only blocking their attacks. He was doing everything he could so as not to hit her girls.

However, the detective knew he couldn't keep up his lack of aggressive tactics, and that had to do something. He had worked out that each of the girls appeared to wait for each other, and that they wouldn't both kick at the same time. He waited for Pink to kick, and then he suddenly backflipped out of the way and landed badly on his front.

Pink's kick landed full into White's stomach, sending her halfway across the room. Steel stood up but managed to drop backwards, just as the large mixed-race guy swung a mannequin's leg at Steel's head. This missed Steel but landed full onto the back of White's head. Steel watched angrily as the woman fell. Steel slid and managed to land under her to break her fall.

"Silly bitch got in the way, her own damn fault." Those were the man's last words. He grabbed at his throat, which had suddenly been pierced by a strange-looking throwing knife.

The much-battered detective stood up. Blood flowed from a couple of scratches on his face. The woman in black walked forward, and he moved back towards the window. The sun felt warm on his back. The sunlight poured in, turning the blood pools into white coloured liquid.

Steel and the woman in black started to circle one another, each ready for the other's move.

"So, you never answered the question," she asked him. "Are you a cop? A Fed even?" Her voice had something about it that made the hairs stand up on the back of Steel's neck. There was something about her that Steel found arousing. Maybe it was the look, the voice or perhaps just the fact that she was dangerous.

"I guess telling you that I was just a guy out shopping wouldn't wash?" Steel said with a smile.

The woman in black smiled back and shook her head. "Sorry, but you can drop the accent now," she said, impressed with what she thought was a fake accent.

Steel kept smiling, even as the two gunmen walked into the store and opened on Steel and the woman in black. She stood defiantly as the shots rang out, but Steel grabbed her and pulled her through the window.

As they crashed onto a pile of old mattresses from the store next door, they heard the gunfire and saw the wood and brickwork splinter away above them.

"How did you know there were mattresses here?" she asked with a surprised look on her face.

"Truthfully —" Steel said with an innocent look on his face.

Her expression changed to one of shock. "You mean you didn't know?" she screamed, as Steel dragged her off the mattresses just in time. A hail of 5.56mm rounds ripped the mattresses apart. Then there was silence, and two bodies fell to the concrete in front of them, each of them with a knife in their backs. The woman in black looked down at the men who had fallen from the window and spat on their corpses. She looked up to see the other girls standing in the window. She nodded at them; they returned the gesture and left.

"So, Mr Shopper, who are you?" the woman in black said, turning to face him, only to find an empty space. She looked around in shock. He had gone, and there was no way out of the courtyard but up or through the back entrances of the stores. She smiled to herself, looking forward to a better encounter in future with her mystery man.

CHAPTER TWENTY-TWO

A BLACKED-OUT BENTLEY 'FLYING SPUR' LIMOUSINE cruised down the gravel driveway which seemed to be a mile long. Tall ferns lined the way, ending in two sandstone lions on tall mounts which faced the oncoming traveller. The car pulled up to a two-hundred-year-old mansion. A relic from after the civil war, whose sandstone walls were tarnished with age, but held its magnificent appearance. Surrounding the structure was green lawns which were cut off by tall bushes and stone wall archways. Rose bushes sprung from ornate arched frames while smaller ferns sat in Grecian style plant holders.

The huge vehicle pulled onto the gravel driveway which encircled a fountain and a small grassed area surrounding it. The car stopped outside the front entrance, and the occupants waited for a moment before the doors opened. The driver got out and opened the passenger door on his side. Williams got out of the town car along with three of his large henchmen. The former straightened out his grey pinstriped suit as he looked up at the huge mansion.

The sun beamed down onto the grounds, giving the estate a

friendly feel. But this was not a friendly place. Williams started for the steps, but his guard dogs waited outside. Company rules decreed that no weapons or 'gorillas' were allowed. He entered the main lobby and smiled at the splendour of the antique carvings in the woodwork, admiring the paintings and tapestries. The outside of the mansion had been altered a bit over the years, but its interior was maintained in its period splendour.

Williams could spend hours just walking around the old place, but duty called. He took off his black trench coat and handed it to the butler, or maybe it was just some guy dressed in tails who was collecting coats. Williams thanked the man and headed inside.

The left-hand corridor led down a long stretch. But he didn't mind, and it gave him time to study the art on the walls. Behind him, on the other side of the lobby, was the ballroom which was fitted out as the 'relaxation room': a place he loathed to go. It was tradition for all members to go there after business and just talk casually amongst themselves. The trouble was Williams disliked all the people he encountered there. He found them to be lacking in any sense of honour or actual purpose. In his opinion, they were all conmen, killers, thieves, spies and terrorists. An organisation who sought to gain power, control and money. They weren't after world domination, for that sort of aspiration gets you noticed. It makes you a target for the security agencies. This group preferred anonymity to hide in the shadows.

Williams appreciated the finer things in life, whereas these people just wanted the best for its own sake. He had worked for these people for many years. Back in the old days, the founder had given the organisation a purpose, had set rules that were never to be broken—a code, even. But the newcomers had come in and made it their own. Perverted what it meant to be

SANTINI. Williams often smiled at the brilliance of the name. It did not spell anything, nor did it for that matter represent anything. The name was more of a distraction than anything. It was a deliberate ruse because it made the worldwide agencies think that they were looking for a person or a family, not something less trackable.

He walked down the long corridor and headed for two men. These big-framed guys were standing on either side of two large wooden doors. As he approached, they opened the doors to allow him entry. The huge room was long, with oak-panelled walls, and the floor was carpeted with a blood-red carpet with a thick pile.

Williams stood for a moment and took in the beauty of the room, admiring the white high ceiling and the works of art that adorned the walls, and the crystal chandeliers whose lights were reflected in the long oak dining table. The table's top was polished, so it glistened as if a layer of glass had been placed upon it. Twelve red velvet-backed dining chairs surrounded the table, six per side. At the far end, at the head of the table, was a sixty-inch monitor.

The psychopathic expert torturer looked around the room at his colleagues and gave a false grin. There was none of them worthy of his time or conversation, apart from one. Williams's eyes lit up at the sight of a new person at the table. It was a beautiful looking woman, who must have stood at six foot eight and who had the build of a Russian shot putter, or maybe one of the WWF fighters. She had long black hair and hands bigger than those of most men. Her black skirted suit covered a white blouse and an ample bosom.

Williams saw there was a free space next to her and hurried towards it before anyone else could, nudging others out of the way as he went. They all stood behind their chairs, waiting for the signal to sit. Various shapes and an almost gyroscopic view appeared on the screen, while lines of contrasting colours spiralled and danced across the black background.

"Good afternoon, everyone, please be seated," said a voice emanating from the many speakers around the room. Everyone sat and waited for the voice to speak again. Williams thought the whole thing was very theatrical, but it preserved the leader's identity, and, in some ways, it was kind of fun.

"Mr Forbes. Your report please," the voice went on in a British accent: an accent Williams considered to be fake—another 'hiding place' for the head of operations.

A tall thin man with blond hair and an expensive grey suit stood up. "Our operations in Africa have been a success," Forbes began. "Also, the crashing of the four aircraft over the past week have seen shares fall worldwide, and so we have made a nice profit from that." He waited for a moment for some sort of pat on the back. Then he looked around and sat down, confused at the silence.

However, Williams took no notice of him or anyone else, as he was leaning against the arm of his chair and staring deeply at the woman next to him.

"Mr Charles. Your report please." The voice was speaking more slowly this time, and his tone was filled with disappointment.

A short, stocky man with black hair and a blue suit rose from his seat. He took a sip from the water and wiped the sweat from his brow. His face was red with embarrassment. Or it could have been fear.

Charles swallowed hard before starting his speech. "Well ... Uhm," he began. His gaze landed on Williams, who was oblivious, as he was too busy staring at the huge woman next to him, the adoration in his eyes like that of a smitten schoolboy.

"Well...uhm, what, Mr Charles?" demanded the voice. "Did you lose the package?"

As the words came from the speakers, the lines and shapes on the screen danced in tune with the tone.

Mr Charles began to panic. He knew he had to say something. In desperation, Charles pointed towards Williams, who was still lost in his lascivious thoughts about his Amazonian neighbour.

"No, sir," Charles floundered on. "Mr Williams lost the package, and he has failed to recover it." He was almost proud of his lie.

"Is this true, Mr Williams?" asked the voice.

At first, Williams did not react. Not until he had that burning feeling that everyone was watching him. He sat up and wiped the drool from his mouth.

"I am sorry. What was the question?" he said, confused. But his confusion cleared when his gaze fell on to Mr Charles's smug face. He knew at that moment that he had been set up.

"Is it true you have lost the package and have not recovered it yet, as Mr Charles has explained to us?" the voice said, in a tone that was strangely calm.

Williams also picked up on this apparent calmness, and he wondered why it was. After all, they all knew that failure was not an option.

He smiled and stood up quickly, almost forcing his chair backwards. He bowed his head to the large monitor, banking on the instinct that a sign of courtesy and a lack of fear would work in his favour.

"As our good friend Mr Charles has explained, the item in question was stolen, not lost," Williams explained succinctly. "However, steps have been taken to track down and recover it." He looked across at Charles, and his smile turned into an evil glare, his mouth opens wide, showing his teeth with every word.

"However," Williams went on smoothly, "I would like to

point out the loss of the item was down to *someone else's* lack of judgement." Suddenly his arms flew about, and his voice was raised, as though he was delivering a sermon. "But I do not blame anyone, and I blame circumstances. I blame—" Williams glared at Charles for a moment before continuing, "—I blame sheer bad luck. And I also blame the person whose idea it was to put everything on a flash drive that was in the shape of a dog. That said, I expect to have the package back soon. Before next Friday at least." Williams looked around the room, then down at the neighbouring woman as she stared up at him. He smiled at her, which made her look away in disgust.

Feeling he had finished his statement, he bowed low to the monitor, like a conductor who had given the performance of his life. His bow was not given because of any great respect he felt for their leader, but as a ploy so that he could get a better look at the woman next to him. This act only resulted in the woman landing a giant paw across his face, causing Williams to disappear onto the carpeted floor below.

The meeting continued for another hour. A long hour, in which Williams just wanted to leave. He knew that afterwards, they would all have to go into the large 'relaxation room' and pretend to get along.

But tonight would be different. Tonight, he would have the large woman to use his charms on.

The meeting closed, and everyone bowed to the monitor. Williams didn't want to do so, because he felt it was quite a stupid thing to do. But then he remembered what happened to the last person who had neglected to show respect. How could he forget? He still had the video on his cell phone. The guy was run through with a sword and then left to bleed to death. The thing about polished tables is that the blood seems to flow faster. Williams smiled to himself as he remembered everyone backing away at the sight of the oncoming red tide.

The two heavy doors opened, and the assembly began to retire to the relaxation room. Williams waited until the woman next to him turned to leave, and he followed, next to her. His charming conversation was one-sided. She had given her report earlier, and that's when he found out that she was German. Her accent had made him tingle. But now, standing beside him, she said nothing.

He liked the challenge. He knew that she was simply toying with him, or at least that was what he was telling himself. As they entered the lobby, a man with a silver salver stopped Williams.

"A message for you, sir. Most urgent," the tall thin man said. Williams watched in torment as his prize glided off to the room full of men and their hungry obsessions. Williams took the envelope and stared at the wax seal covering the fold. He thanked the man and opened it slowly. He knew these messages did not come very often. In fact, according to his reckoning, it had been at least ten years since the last.

He broke the seal and pulled out a folded piece of paper. The six-by-four sheet had a spider-headed emblem embossed into the paper. Williams began to smile wickedly as he read. His gaze moved across to where Mr Charles was standing. He was talking to another smaller man whom Williams did not recognise. Williams refolded the paper and placed it back into the envelope. Slowly he slid it into his jacket pocket and walked into the room as though he was floating on air.

Williams spied the woman sitting next to the bar, and she was very alone. To her amazement, he simply walked up to her and kissed her on the lips. Everyone looked at them for a moment and then carried on with their conversations.

She was about to slap him but stopped herself. She saw the menacing grin he wore, and she backed off slightly. She was afraid. There was a glint in his eye that she feared.

"My apartment, twenty minutes," she said. "You bring the champagne." She turned and marched out of the mansion. Williams danced towards the door, singing and kicking his heels as he went.

This will be a night to remember, he thought.

———

Steel walked into his apartment. His bloodstained hands left trails on the door as he moved inside. The bright light of the afternoon sun illuminated the area. He moved to the bathroom slowly, his body hurting all over from the beating and the fall.

He was glad that the mattresses had been there. In fact, it was probable cause to buy a lottery ticket after an experience like that. Steel walked into the bathroom, causing the automatic lights to come on. He looked in the mirror at his scratched face and shredded clothing.

Feeling every muscle in his body scream in pain, he removed his jacket and shirt. Blood flowed from a couple of wounds on his arms and chest. Opening one of the bathroom cupboards, he took out some tweezers and iodine. He dug the tweezers into his flesh and pulled out the mini shards of glass that were keeping the wounds open. He turned around and was amazed to see in the mirror that his back had not sustained any cuts.

Taking the bottle of iodine, he poured some onto a cloth and dabbed his wounds. He winced at the biting pain of the sterilising fluid. Steel reached inside the cupboard once more and pulled out a 'skin stapler'. Carefully pulling the skin together with the tweezers, he began to use the dissolvable stitches on the worst of the wounds.

He stood and looked at himself in the mirror. His body was full of taut muscle, and there were plenty of scars, six of which would never heal, either emotionally or physically. Steel turned on the shower and let it run for a moment to allow the hot water to flow. He stripped the rest of his shredded clothing from his muscular form and stepped inside the shower cabin.

The warm water cascaded over his body. He felt the strain in his muscles start to slip away. Even though he was fully trained in combat, the mileage always took its toll. He put his hands on the wall and leant forward, completely immersing himself under the hammering water.

Steel had sent Cobb a text and the incriminating pictures of the money-counting operation before he had left for home. By now the place would be swarming with cops in tactical gear and others on standby. But Steel was sure there would be no sign of the women. They were smart enough to be 'in the wind' by now. The money, however, was another story. There were thousands of banknotes there. Too much to move unless they had a truck hidden somewhere.

In a way, he was glad that the Oriental woman had gotten away. Sure, she was on the wrong side of the law, but she just had something about her that intrigued him.

The cab carrying Steel stopped outside the precinct. Steel paid the driver and got out. The warmth had been replaced by a crisp wind. Steel walked calmly inside and headed for the elevator.

He stepped out onto the dull floor of the Homicide department to see Tooms and Tony jokingly checking their watches. Steel adjusted the bridge of his sunglasses with his middle finger and smiled.

"Where you been, man? You've been gone most of the day!" Tooms barked. Steel checked his watch. It was nearly four o'clock.

"Sorry. I had to go home and change clothes after a spot of

'store assistant' trouble. They were looking to make a quick killing," Steel said the words with a straight face.

Tooms shot him a look. The sort of look that said, *should I be looking for bodies?* Tooms knew Steel had a way of attracting trouble, or else he just was good at finding it. He had a good track record for being in the wrong place at the wrong time, though the people whose lives he saved would probably disagree.

"But those are the clothes you went out in," Tooms remarked, looking at Steel's black attire. Steel looked down at his black suit and shook his head.

"Never mind, I don't want to know," Tooms said, giving up before something weird started.

Steel noticed the strange expression that Tony was giving him. It was almost a 'begging' expression.

"OK, what do you want? It's not the Ferrari, is it?" Steel asked curiously. The American detectives looked at one another with child-like expressions.

"You have a Ferrari?" Tony asked quickly, almost forgetting what he wanted to ask Steel.

The British man smiled and shook his head. "No, but it was interesting to see how quickly you would lose your attention span." Steel grinned as he quickly bent down and grabbed the answering machine.

"Don't tell me, the answer to everything is on this, and you want me to decipher it because you think no one but me can do it?" Steel said, waving the machine about.

Tooms and Tony looked at Steel with gaping mouths.

Steel's grin faded. "Really ... Look, I was just joking, guys. I thought it was just an answering machine from your home or something." Steel said, looking at the machine in his grasp. "So...you think there is something important on this?"

The two detectives stood up and gave Steel a serious look.

Steel nodded and headed for his office. "I'm the only one who can find out, I guess," Steel said. Tooms and Tony raced for Steel's office and the comfort of his chesterfield armchairs. Once at his desk, Steel placed the machine on top and plugged it into a nearby socket. The leather of his 'ship captain's' chair creaked as he rested his still-aching body onto it. He looked at the two detectives sitting opposite him.

After he had listened to the tape, Steel sat back in his chair and tapped his fingertips together in a thoughtful gesture. His face held a concerned look.

"Who else has heard this?" Steel asked. Tooms and Tony looked at each other and shrugged.

"Nobody. Why?" Tony asked. Now he felt an uneasy feeling creeping up his spine.

"Keep it that way. In fact, if I were you, I would burn it and never speak of it again." Steel's face was like stone.

Tooms could tell that something was very wrong.

Tony started: "But—"

"—There is no 'but', Detective," Steel growled softly, interrupting him. "This tape never existed."

Tooms looked at the door behind him and then back to Steel. "Why, what does it mean?" Tooms asked in an almost whisper. Steel leaned forward over his desk, the others following his every move.

"You don't want to know what the truth about this, Tooms. It is something ... Well, something terrible." There was fear in Steel's voice.

"You don't have a friggin' idea, do you, Steel?" Tooms asked, keeping the tone of fear in his words. Steel looked Tooms in the eye and shook his head.

"Haven't got a bloody clue."

Tooms sat back, catching his breath. "You're a real asshole, you know that, don't you? You nearly gave me a friggin' heart attack!" Tooms boomed.

Steel smiled and sat back, smugly.

"Hey, what can I say? It's been a bad day, I needed cheering up," Steel watched the two men scowl at him. The smile faded as he looked over at the large electronic murder board. He looked at Amber's photograph. She had been a looker: young and very good looking, which made Steel think.

Why was she in the agency? And how did all this mystery fit together? He turned towards the two detectives, who were still scowling at him.

"So, we know that Amber was working for the government, we also know that Brooke was her handler," Steel said, standing up and heading for his drink's cabinet. He grabbed three bottles of water from the small fridge and tossed two of them to his colleagues.

"How did you know she was an agent?" Tony asked, cracking the seal on the bottle.

Steel shook his head as he sat down. "The last call on this machine were instructions, not a warning as such. Plus, most 'spooks', as you like to call them, have someone watching their back. Getting intel, doing background checks, and so on, while the asset plays the part." Steel looked over at the picture of Brooke. He saw something in her eyes. She looked like a woman who had a lot of experience.

"We need to find out who took her and hope she's still alive," Steel said, looking at the hands-on his smartwatch. It was nearly four o'clock. He reached into one of the drawers of his desk and pulled out a yellow legal pad. Taking a pen from his pocket, he started to make a list:

Amber, John Doe, Brooke, Tara. Steel tapped his pen on the pad in frustration. Something connected them all. There was no way the murders and abductions had happened coincidentally. Steel lifted his arm and dramatically slammed the pen into the thick pad.

Tooms and Tony jumped out of their seats and reached for their weapons.

"What the...? Have you gone crazy, man?" Tooms yelled, still holding his hand over the pistol grip of his Glock. Tony had drawn his and was looking at Steel, waiting for more sudden movements.

"None of it makes sense," Steel growled as he stood up, his chair giving out a creak of protest.

"It's like a puzzle with most of the pieces missing and no picture to follow," Steel said, but his tone had calmed slightly.

Tony re-holstered his weapon with shaky hands.

"We have a missing John Doe."

"What...John Doe is gone, what the fuck, did he walk out or summit?" Tooms said in surprise.

"Sorry..." Steel started; his trail of thought broken by Tooms's outburst. "– no, he was kidnapped, someone drugged the guards and took off with him," Steel's words were casual as if it was a daily occurrence. Tooms and Tony just sat opened mouthed, wondering how he could be so calm. "OK, John Doe...we don't know who he is, or where he had been to get blood on him. We don't know whose blood it is because CSU is backlogged." Steel looked up at the murder board with his hands behind his back. The way he stood made Tooms think of his old platoon sergeant major.

"We have a missing woman, who was maybe a witness to something, and a government agent who is also missing," Steel said, almost chewing on the words as they came out. He was mad. Not that he was showing it.

"You asked me why I was late? The answer is, shall we say, painful," Steel said, rubbing his right shoulder. "Today, I was outside the hotel, where John Doe was taken. There I met a woman." Steel watched as Tooms and Tony leaned forward for some juicy details. He smiled and shook his head.

"I thought I recognised her. I didn't know where from at first. I got the cab driver who had brought her there, to take me to where he'd picked her up. It was a boutique in the Bronx. I did some snooping around and found the top floor full of counting machines." Steel turned to face the two men, who were taking in every word.

"Don't tell me you blew it up?" Tooms said, causing Tony to smile. The British detective tapped his pocket to check that his cell phone was still there.

"No, I called a friend in Task Force. They are probably in by now. Not that they will find much." Steel shrugged. Tony shot Steel a curious look.

"Let's just say, the people involved are ready for anything." Steel looked back to the board with a faraway look.

"So, where did you know the woman from?" Tony asked. "Was she an old girlfriend or something?"

Steel turned to them and shook his head, his face stern. "What if I told you she was the cop who was guarding the chief when she called herself 'Missy Studebaker' on that cruise ship last year?" Steel watched as his colleagues' jaws dropped.

"Now, you see why I followed her." Steel watched the two detectives nod, whilst wearing blank expressions.

"Don't worry," he reassured them. "We won't be chasing her. We have enough to do. Besides, she is probably long gone by now." He knew that 'Missy Studebaker' was just a part of their mystery and finding her would waste valuable manpower and time: time that Tara and Brooke didn't have.

Steel wondered what her connection was with the store. He knew she wasn't working for SANTINI: that had been proven when she'd murdered the Chief of Police. However, there was another organisation that was working against

SANTINI. One that was more power-driven—and more sinister for that matter. Steel tapped an icon next to Amber's picture, which was in the shape of a file. It opened and showed the crime scene.

Tony just stared before looking away. Tooms's eyes glared at Steel for his lack of compassion.

"Hey, man, you could have warned Tony before Poppin' that open," Tooms growled.

Steel turned slowly to face him, his face as impenetrable as stone. A shiver ran down Tooms's back.

"I am sorry. But I understood that we were here to catch her killer," Steel said calmly, but his tone had a hard edge to it.

"I'm looking at the pictures because there is something in them that is bothering me. What it is, I do not know." Steel said as he turned back to the board. He looked at Tara's furnishings in her living room. At first look, it appeared to be a normal single woman's apartment. Ordinary.

"How are we going trying to find Tara Burke?" Steel asked without breaking his gaze from the board.

"All patrols have a copy, so do people in public transport. It's a long shot, but someone might have seen her leave," Tony said, taking a mouthful of water.

Steel shook his head. "She isn't leaving. I have a feeling there is more to Miss Burke than meets the eye." A disquieting feeling tore at his gut as he stared at the photographs.

"She is in hiding. We've just got to find out where." Steel touched the photograph of Tara on the monitor, causing it to enlarge.

Tooms shot Steel an 'unconvinced' look. "What makes you say that?" he asked.

"Simple. We haven't found a body." Steel turned to look at them.

The two detectives knew he was right.

Steel checked his watch: half-past four. "OK, you guys, you can take off. It's been a long day. We hit it again tomorrow. With fresh eyes." He returned to his chair.

Tooms and Tony raised their bottles as if to wish him a 'goodnight' and headed for the door.

Steel watched them as they left the room and then waited for a moment. He took another hit from his own bottle and leant back in the chair. His gaze fell onto the enlarged picture of Tara. He looked at her eyes. They had a sadness to them. No, not sadness.

Pain.

Given her past, it was understandable. Her father had split when she was little, and her mother beat the crap out of her until she was old enough to take herself off. By all accounts, she was a good kid. Worked hard, paid her taxes. No criminal record whatsoever.

But still, something struck him that didn't fit right. In addition to the unexplained abduction of Brooke. Why take her? Steel took another sip from the bottle. The cold liquid felt good as it flowed down his throat. Steel tapped the bottle as if he were playing an instrument. A thousand thoughts cascaded through his brain.

Steel reached into his pocket and pulled out his cell phone. Finding a number in the contacts list, he pressed the autodial and waited.

"Yes, it's me. We need to talk," he said, sitting back and crossing his legs, feet on the desktop. He waited for a moment and then took a mental note of the address.

"Roger that. See you then." Steel closed the phone and sat finishing the rest of his drink. His eyes were fixed on Tara's image.

"What really happened that night?" he said to the picture, almost hoping she would speak.

CHAPTER TWENTY-THREE

THE NEXT DAY BROUGHT A BRILLIANT BURNT UMBER-coloured sunrise. A fresh breeze carried gently on a westerly wind. Joggers and dog walkers had filled the park early to beat the masses that would soon congregate. It was seven o'clock on a Sunday morning. The sound of birds in full song blended with the background noise of early-morning traffic.

A young female jogger made her way around the lake. She had to beat the time it normally took her to get to the boathouse. Her effort wasn't being made for any other reason than a personal goal. Her grey-and-pink cotton shirt and shorts fitted well enough to show some form without being restrictive. Her long brown hair was held high at the back in a ponytail. The sound of her music from her cell phone blared in her ears via the wireless earplugs. Her feet hammered the concrete as she went.

She preferred this time of day to any other. It was cool, and most people were still in bed. Her view was locked forward, like a racehorse with an eye on its goal. Sweat began to collect and pour from her forehead. Her breathing was steady: in through the nose and out through the mouth. She had the boathouse insight. *Not far now, just a little more,* she thought. Her arms were pounding the air as she pumped out the strokes, matching her footwork. She ignored the pain in her thighs as she headed for the finish.

Finally, she ground to a sudden stop and put her head back and laid her hands on her slender hips. Sucking in the cool air, she walked around, shaking off her aching legs. The cool breeze tickled her bare flesh as it swept across the water. Pulling up her wrist, she checked her time. It was a good one: at least two seconds faster. As she looked down the path, a handsome man dressed in a blue T-shirt and shorts jogged past. He looked back with a smile as he continued. The woman's smile was lost to the back of him as he disappeared across the path and past some rocks and bushes. She scowled at the lost opportunity and jogged slowly on.

Taking a path from the boathouse, she headed for Azalea Pond, then reached a group of bushes, stopped and backed off. The mass of green was shaking as though someone was moving through it.

"Who's there?" she cried out, wishing she had her can of mace.

The bush continued to shake. At first, she thought it was the man she'd seen before. Something seemed very wrong. The bushes were in a small area under a tree. It was a good place to make out with a partner without being seen.

"Hello, who is there?" she said, creeping forward slowly, curiosity pulling her on. Her hands parted the bushes that were like a curtain of foliage. Her breath became shallow, and she could hear her heart pounding.

The branches parted and she was suddenly knocked back by what seemed to be a large black mass of sharp beaks and feathers. She screamed and fell to the ground as the huge flock of crows swarmed past her like a black cloud. She stood up and brushed herself off.

"Stupid birds," she said to herself. As she turned to leave, something in her head stopped her. That curious feeling had returned. Slowly she made her way back to the place and parted the foliage curtains once more.

Her scream was loud and piercing. People across the park heard it and came running. Her screams continued. She couldn't stop her screams any more than she could stop staring at what she had found. Her eyes were wide and fixated, unable to break free from the sight before her.

———

Steel had risen early. He had already been on his eight-mile run and was now in his building's gym. It wasn't quite Gold's Gym, but it held enough equipment for what he needed. Besides, membership was included in the residency package.

The gymnasium room was long with white walls and a wooden floor for easy cleaning and to create a good visual effect. The right-hand wall was virtually all mirrors, in front of which were some of the machines. To the left were twelve bike machines and five units for 'rowing'. At the far end was a stand with the free weights and loose weights for the bars. In the centre, a couple of benches sat ready for use.

The well-muscled detective sat on the bench and finished the last of his reps with the free weights. He had done around two hours in there to stretch out the discomfort in his muscles caused by the beating. He let the dumbbells drop from his fingers and onto the padded mat. As he dabbed the sweat from his brow with his towel, two young women came in and debated which piece of equipment to start using, oblivious to anyone else in the room. One of the women had short brown hair. She saw Steel in the mirror and tapped her friend on the shoulder. They watched as Steel started his second set of exercises with the fifty-kilogram weights.

The second woman brushed her long black hair with her fingers as she watched him in the mirror.

Steel paid them no mind. His thoughts were a million miles away, and the pain from the workout was aiding his concentration.

He finished his final rep and stood up. His T-shirt was soddening from the sweat that clung to him, showing off his muscular form underneath. As he put the equipment back, he turned and saw the drooling women, who were still standing at the machines. He walked past and bowed slightly.

"Good morning, ladies, wonderful day isn't it?" he said. He caught their reflection in a mirror. They just stood nodding as their eyes followed him. He smiled to himself as he waited for the elevator. All the while, he could feel the women's stares upon him. It felt good.

The doors opened, and he stepped inside. The only thing on his mind was a cool shower and a good cup of coffee. The doors closed, and with a small shudder, he started to ascend.

Steel caught his reflection in the elevator's mirror. He turned and looked at himself. He was almost unable to understand the attraction he seemed to have for women.

As far as he could judge, he was an average looking man who had turned into a freak. Steel looked deep into his own eyes. The blue contacts covered his cold, lifeless emerald-green eyes: eyes that most men could not bear to investigate. He also noted the wounds on his body from where he had been shot all those years ago—six holes in a strange 'V' pattern.

'The mark of the phoenix', his old mentor had called it. 'The mark of a dead man walking' was what Steel called it. Six 'through and throughs', each of them narrowly missing a major artery or organ. Either the shooter had been a bad shot, or the lack of a lethal shot had been done purposely. Steel reckoned that the shooter had just wanted him to die slowly.

No one had known that the gardener had been nearby to save him.

He looked at himself and remembered what it had been like to be normal. To have a family life. Things like that had been taken away from him. His master told him that everything happens for a reason. That everything has a purpose. Steel couldn't understand that. He refused to believe it.

The elevator came to a stop, and he ventured out into the hallway and headed for his apartment. One day he would understand everything, but for now, he had work to do.

Steel had showered and changed into a black suit but didn't wear a tie. He pulled on the quarter-length suit jacket and headed for the kitchen. The coffee machine had stopped making the unhealthy 'choking' noise, meaning that his brew was ready. On the refrigerator was a post-it notes. He smiled as he read the message: *New suit is ready. Look after it. G.*

Steel made his way to the room at the end and punched in the code and entered. Moments later, Steel came outstretching his arms and shoulders, as though he had tight-fitting underwear. He wore a big smile and new glasses.

There was a buzz, and his cell phone danced across the kitchen's breakfast bar as it vibrated. He picked it up and answered it.

"Steel... how fast you can get to the boathouse in Central Park?" the voice in his ear said. It was Captain Brant, and he didn't sound happy. Steel looked at his fresh cup of coffee and then at the wall clock.

"Twenty minutes, I guess, why?" Steel asked, hoping there'd been a break in the case.

"We got a fresh one for you," said Brant. "It may be connected."

Brant hung up, and Steel cut the connection and finished his coffee. He was almost afraid to find out what this new development might be.

It took him around fifteen minutes to get there, and he used the time to think, to review the case so far. He figured that the 'fresh one' that Brant had referred to was likely to be the body was one of the missing people and was assuming that was why he'd been summoned.

The ME's truck confirmed his suspicions that it was indeed a new body that had been found. The question now was, whose body was it? As he approached the yellow tape, he saw Tooms making notes in his notebook. Tony was talking to a pretty woman dressed in grey-and-pink jogging gear.

A uniformed officer lifted the tape as Steel approached. Steel nodded a thank-you as he pulled on a pair of black surgical gloves.

"What have we got?" Steel asked as he met with Tooms. Tooms nodded towards the bushes.

"A female jogger thought she was scaring off a peeper or creep. Hope you haven't had breakfast yet," Tooms said, leading Steel to a break in the foliage. As they pushed through the natural veil, Steel saw the ME and some of the CSU team. Tina Franks was kneeling in front of something he couldn't quite make out. But then his view was mostly engaged on the two CSU people who had their backs to him as they were trying to gather air. Tooms stayed at the entrance to the gap they had just come through.

Steel felt the hairs on the back of his neck begin to tingle something was badly wrong. As he approached, he saw something that used to be a person. The sex of the corpse was impossible to determine, as it had been badly burnt. Steel knelt next to Tina, who said nothing at first. He certainly wasn't going to push her either.

He took out his small camera and took some shots. *Always take a camera with you,* was one of McCall's unwritten rules, and Steel had always found it to be good advice, as it meant there was no delay whilst waiting for the lab to send up the photos. He could feel the emotion coming from Tina. Sure, she had obviously seen a lot of dead bodies. But none before quite like this one.

Apart from being burnt, it looked as if the body had had its skull smashed in to prevent any reconstruction. The teeth and the flesh on the hands had been removed. Even for the battle-hardened Steel, this was a bad one.

"Are you OK?" Steel asked, placing a reassuring hand on Tina's shoulder. She turned, smiled and nodded. He stood up and offered his hand to help her up.

"Sorry, Steel," she told him. "I can't give a TOD as the liver has been removed. DNA may be a problem because of the burning of the body." She shrugged and shook her head. "Someone went to a lot of trouble to hide this person's identity. The ribs have been smashed, and so has the pelvis." She pointed out the broken chest cavity and pelvic area.

"They didn't want us to know if this is a male or a female," Steel said, shocked at the depths of depravity the killers had sunk to. He turned to Tina with a hopeful look.

"But you can, can't you?" he asked, looking into her deep dark eyes. "You can find out who this was."

She smiled. "I will see what I can do but no promises." Her voice rang with uncertainty. It would take a miracle, or there was always the slim chance that the killers hadn't been as thorough in covering their tracks as it appeared.

The orderlies carefully bagged the remains and took the

body away, leaving CSU to sketch, photograph and measure everything, while Tooms took the jogger's statement.

Steel stood for a moment and took more photographs of the small area. There were no scorch marks on the ground. No blood or signs of a struggle. Everything was undisturbed, apart from the immediate area where the body had been found. The British detective shook his head.

Something was wrong, very wrong.

Why go to the trouble of making ID impossible, but leave the body where it was sure to be found? It didn't make sense, just like everything in the Amber case. Steel was certain that this fresh body had something to do with the Amber case. He also had a suspicion of who it was. He didn't need tests to prove that it was most likely to be their John Doe, the amnesiac man who they'd done their utmost to protect.

They were being played with. Someone was purposely making them chase their tails.

And he was going to find them.

———

Back at the precinct, Steel sat at McCall's desk and sorted through the statement of the girl jogger and those of the officers who had been overpowered and drugged whilst supposedly babysitting John Doe.

There wasn't much information to be found. The jogger girl had not seen anyone, and they were still waiting for any footage from security cameras nearby. The cops had all said the same thing about the food delivery to John Doe's apartment, and that the delivery guy had told them that the precinct had sent the food. The delivery guy had disappeared, but according to his boss he often disappeared on his days off, probably blowing his earnings at a local strip joint.

220

If the body was that of their John Doe, why did they want him, and why did they try to conceal his identity? Steel looked over at Tony, who was calling Traffic to try and get the footage from outside the hotel. Tooms was yelling down the phone at some guy from the parks and recreation department for the CCTV footage, if any, of the whole area.

Steel could feel his head spin every time he thought about this case. It made no sense. None of it. A dead undercover agent who had two lives, and who got killed in an apartment of a now-missing waitress. Meanwhile, her handler goes missing, and a man who was walking around covered in blood may have been partially skinned and barbequed to conceal his identity.

The agency had no idea what their operatives had been working on – or at least that's what they had told Steel anyway. But one thing was for sure: the Trent Shipping Company was at the heart of it.

Steel stood up quickly, forcing McCall's chair to slide across to the next desk. Tony and Tooms looked up at him. Steel seemed calm, but they knew something was eating at him.

"Where are you going?" Tony asked, covering the mouthpiece of his phone.

"Off to clear my head," Steel said, rushing down the stairs.

Tooms and Tony looked at one another and swallowed hard.

Steel stood outside the precinct building and took in the warmth of the morning sun. The wind had died down to a pleasant breeze. The volume of foot traffic had increased. Tourists and families spending quality time hurried past. He stood and watched, hoping for an epiphany to strike. He smiled to himself, wondering what McCall was doing at that moment. Having brunch with the family, no doubt.

He recollected the painful memories of his own past summer holidays—or 'leave' as they called it in the service.

Brunch on the patio whilst watching his little brother and sister play. Staring into those beautiful eyes of his darling Helen, whilst his father talked about work.

His thoughts were a million miles away. He was so distracted that he did not hear Doctor Davidson yell a greeting.

"Mr Steel...are you alright?" Davidson asked, staring at Steel, almost wishing he knew what the detective was thinking about.

Steel shook his head as if to bring himself back to reality. "What?" he asked. "Sorry, doctor, I was miles away. Good morning." He smiled. "What brings you to this neck of the woods?" He thought he already knew the possible answer.

"I heard about what happened at the hotel. Is everyone OK?" Davidson's tone was one of genuine concern. But Steel detected something else in his face. A tiny flash of fear was visible in his eyes.

"Have you found John Doe yet? Or do you know who took him?" Davidson continued.

Steel just stood there for a moment, quiet and motionless. Then he shook his head, with a grim look on his face.

"No, we don't know right now. However, we did find a body in the park," Steel explained.

Davidson's eyes widened. "Is it him?"

Steel wasn't sure if Davidson's question was one of concern for John Doe's safety or whether he was worried about how easy identifying the corpse was going to be.

The detective shrugged. "The body was ... unrecognisable. We are waiting for the ME to do her magic." Steel looked down at the doctor. "If it is John Doe, it only means that he was involved in this case, as we suspected he was."

Davidson nodded as if to concur with the theory.

"Did he tell you anything?" Steel asked, hoping for any snippet of information the doctor could give him.

The psychiatrist investigated space, trying to compute the situation.

"Doc, did he tell you anything at the hotel?" Steel repeated.

Davidson shook his head. Then he shot Steel a look of horror. "I never met him at the hotel. I was ... Oh, God. He's back, isn't he?" Davidson cried out, nearly collapsing to the ground. Steel managed to catch him before he hit the hard concrete.

"It would appear that he is back, yes," Steel replied calmly. "But why he's back I have no idea. Doctor Davidson, you might like to consider taking a short vacation far away from here. I hear there's a package deal to Mars." Steel smiled as he spoke.

"I may just do that, Detective." Davidson appreciated the humour and the advice, fussily straightening out his clothes after his near fall. "There happens to be a conference in Paris, and I was looking for a good reason to go." He smiled.

Steel nodded and looked across the sea of people. "To me, that sounds like a good enough reason to go. You might like to consider staying on for another week afterwards."

Steel's words were more than just a friendly suggestion, they were a warning, and Davidson knew it. The two men shook hands, and then Steel watched the strange doctor turn and hail a cab.

The detective knew that Davidson would be safe while he was out of the country. But better still, with Davidson out of the way, Williams would be unable to do his 'doppelganger' double act. Steel still couldn't believe that Williams and Davidson were twin brothers. But their futures had been sealed when their mother had sent Davidson away. Davidson had gone on to become a good man, a respectable doctor. His brother had become something else—something evil. On Steel's first case with the NYPD, he had seen first-hand what Williams could do, how he could pretend to be Davidson in order to gather information. Williams was cunning and a perfectionist. He also had an ego as big as a planet.

A yellow cab stopped, and Davidson got into the back seat without looking back. Steel smiled as he watched him, nodding to himself. He saw the cab take off and disappear into the mass of traffic. Then he turned and ventured back inside the station house.

CHAPTER TWENTY-FOUR

Tara sat in Kim's apartment, flicking through the channels on the television. She had vacuumed and dusted just out of boredom. She knew making the noise was a risk, but she had done it the same time the neighbours above had done theirs.

It was the longest she had been still that she could remember. Normally she was on her feet for twelve hours a day. But now she had time on her hands, and it was starting to get to her. Tara knew she couldn't stay there forever. At some point, she would have to make a break for it. Trouble was, where could she go, Canada maybe, Mexico? But then there was the question of how would she get there and what she would do for funds?

She picked up her cell phone and checked for any new messages. There was nothing, only the ones she had seen a thousand times before. He hadn't sent anything for days now, and she was worried. Worried they had found him, and he had ended up like Amber. Worried, he had given up on her.

The worried woman grabbed the cushion from behind her

and hugged it tightly. She felt alone and scared. He had left her with the problem, and she would have to decide: to go to the cops or to go ahead as planned. Tara looked up at the front door as she heard a sound coming from the hallway. *Only the neighbours*, she told herself. Her eyes were glued to the door handle, waiting for it to turn.

The news came on TV with a top story: *Body found in Central Park* was the headline. Her eyes widened as she switched her gaze. The female reporter stood with the park behind her. Yellow police tape showed the area along with a dozen uniformed officers making sure nobody tried to get a closer look at the crime scene.

A sudden bad feeling flowed through her veins like lead. The reporter had said an 'Unknown person'. Why person? Not male or female but ... *person*. Her imagination took hold, and she felt sick. What state had the body been in for its sex to be difficult to determine? Tara got up and went to the kitchen for a glass of water. Her nerves were shot.

She downed two glasses then leant against the aluminium sink, her head bowed.

If the body was his, what had they done? Was she going to be next? She looked back to the television set and watched the rest of the newsflash. As the reporter spoke, Tara could tell that the police hadn't divulged many details to the media and that the information she was giving was largely just speculation. The police had obviously blanked her efforts to find out more.

Tara sighed as her clear head was trying to make sense of it. Fear had begun to affect her thoughts. One thing was certain for sure: she had to get out. She had stayed here too long.

———

Steel stepped out of the elevator. He had just gotten off the phone with Alan Cobb. The police team had found cash, the machines and a dead black guy in the boutique premises that they had stormed, thanks to his tip-off. But the women were gone. Cobb told him that he reckoned there was at least around three to four million dollars on the premises. Steel had smiled when his friend had asked what had happened before they'd arrived. A room torn apart by gunfire often leaves a shocking impression. Steel had said nothing, just let his friend's imagination run riot.

The loss would hurt someone. Probably not for long but enough to pinch. Steel hoped it was SANTINI, the organisation that had murdered his family. The people who had hunted him for so long. The ones he was now determined to see burn in hell.

But something nagged at him. It was 'Missy Studebaker', or whatever her real name was. She was with the other organisation, so was the boutique theirs? Regardless, the money was off the streets, and someone had a bloody nose. If they were in the middle of an organisation 'turf war' the Feds knew about it. That part was obvious, and it would explain why Amber was working two cases. But why did Brooke have reservations about telling the company what was going on? Did she suspect someone in-house to be a mole?

He couldn't know the answers to any more questions without Brooke. If she was alive, there had to be a reason for her survival, since they had killed Amber.

Steel had put his phone away with mixed feelings. Sure, it was a good bust, but the perpetrators had gotten away. Whoever they were.

The detective looked across the field of empty desks. It was Sunday, and most of the team were at home or out on a case.

He walked over to Tooms and Tony and sat on the edge of Tony's desk.

"Feel better now?" Tooms asked.

Steel nodded as he looked over at the murder board. It still made no sense. He shook off the negative feelings that were clouding his thoughts.

"OK, guys, go home. There is nothing more you can do today," Steel said, watching their mouths fall open.

Tony suddenly felt a strange, happy feeling. Had the great detective John Steel given up on the case? Tony smiled to himself, just waiting for him to admit it. This great man with the strange theories and the even stranger methods, who was now evidently stumped.

"So, are you just giving up?" Tony asked, trying to force Steel to admit it.

Steel stood up and shook his head. "No. I said there is nothing that you guys can do. It's Sunday. I am sure Tooms wants some family time," he said.

The Tooms didn't need to be told twice. Before Steel could say another word, he was halfway to the elevator. Steel smiled and shook his head as he watched Tooms disappear into the elevator before the doors closed.

Tony felt bad. Part of him hoped that Steel had given up. This great sleuth, the man with all the great ideas, was finally admitting defeat. But he hadn't done so, and that tore a little in Tony. Sure, he liked Steel but felt that there was something surreal about him. He was more like a comic-strip hero than an actual cop. What Tony really didn't like was that Steel had *everything*: money, the title 'Lord Steel', pertaining to some family seat in England, and great looks that made women fall at his feet. Whereas all Tony had was a lousy pension plan and a dead girlfriend.

Steel turned towards Tony. He could see something in his eyes. A sadness of sorts.

"You don't have to stay, you know," Steel pointed out, heading for the break room.

"I am not leaving until we have Amber's killer," Tony growled.

Steel cracked a smile from the corner of his mouth and nodded. "You and me both, Tony. Come on, I'll make you a coffee." Steel raised his cup and turned as he headed for the smell of freshly brewed beans.

Tony took a seat and watched as Steel poured the steaming liquid into two mugs.

"I heard that the Task Force made a big bust this morning. A boutique full of cash and counting machines," Tony began, smiling suspiciously as Steel passed him his coffee. "It wouldn't be the same place that you were talkin' about, would it?" Tony quizzed him.

The other man just smiled and blew on his hot coffee. Steel sat down on the chair opposite Tony. His head was full of possible situations, but without solid data, they were all only theories.

"We need to find Tara. She is the centre of all this, I can feel it," Steel said before taking a sip.

Tony nodded. He had the same feeling.

"If you're right and she is here, she's gonna make it difficult for anyone to find her," Tony noted.

Steel knew he was right, and he just hoped since they couldn't find her, maybe nobody else could either.

CHAPTER TWENTY-FIVE

Mr Charles lay on his back. He was enjoying the quiet of the pool as he lay on the inflatable, which looked more like a floating chaise longue. He smiled with his eyes closed, thinking about the meeting and the look on Williams's face.

He had stolen from his organisation and had gotten away with it: whilst they were chasing their tails busying themselves over the lost data stick, they had missed the money transfer from the people in Berlin. They would find out about it sooner or later, but he wasn't worried. Once Williams's credibility had been crushed, he could blame Williams for almost anything now. He could even blame Williams with aiding the man who had taken the stick. How else would the man have known how to get into the safe?

The pool was inside a large glass conservatory which was attached to his seven-bedroom mansion. He loved money but loved demonstrating his wealth to others even more. His garage was more like a parking lot for classic cars. Charles was unmarried. He loved wealth too much to share it with someone who might try to take it away.

He could feel the warmth of the sun as it glared through the glass ceiling. The cool water lapped at his fingertips as it splashed onto the buoyant chair. All was good, and the eight security guards would make sure that he was safe.

Mr Charles hadn't stayed long at the meeting. Listening to all the pointless pleasantries and watching Williams drool over the huge German woman had made him feel nauseous. Besides, he had other matters to see too. Much more important matters, such as tying up loose ends.

There was a sudden noise from the sitting room, which joined onto the pool room via a sliding door. Charles looked up and over to where the sound had originated from. It had been a slight metallic clatter as if someone had dropped a key or some other small object onto the wooden flooring.

Charles shook it off, reasoning that his ears were playing tricks on him. He closed his eyes and went back to his daydream.

He looked up quickly.

It was the noise again, but this time it was closer. Very close, in fact. His eyes became wide, and he scanned the room, searching. There was someone there. It could be one of the security guards, but generally, they stayed outside.

Charles's brown eyes found nothing to tell him that anyone else was in the room. Gently, he used his hands as a paddle and started to turn himself around in the water. Charles half expected to see a masked man with a weapon standing ready. However, he was alone. He breathed a sigh of relief and paddled over to the metal stepladder. Charles reached for the polished steel railings and froze. Paranoia crept into his mind. The sudden thought of Williams seeking revenge filled his thoughts. In his smugness, he had forgotten what sort of man Williams was.

That had been a mistake.

He stared at the shine on the polished metal: what if Williams had wired the bars? *Water and electricity don't play well together,* he thought to himself.

Charles snapped his hands back and jumped into the water, opting to climb out using the side. Unfortunately, lack of exercise and an overindulgent lifestyle made the climb more of a sight of amusement than an elegant escape.

The flabby man stood up and hurried over to his bathrobe, which lay on a sun lounger. The fluffy white cotton clung to his skin as he pulled it on. Charles looked through the open doorway into the sitting area. It was large and modern. The whole mansion was early 1900s, but he had modernised the interior.

The antique wood panelling and staircases had been replaced with bright white walls and gaudy furnishings. Expensive art hung on the walls, its sole function being to advertise his wealth rather than demonstrate his artistic preferences. The house was an extension of his own personality: large and empty.

Charles moved slowly into the house. His bare feet left wet impressions on the wooden floor as he crept forward. The place was quiet, too quiet. He wanted to shout out but held himself back. Doing so would only alert the intruder to his presence. That was, of course, if there was an intruder, which he doubted.

The unnerved executive could feel his carotid artery pulsate with every heartbeat. His hands trembled with fear. He didn't know why. He looked out through the sitting room window and saw his guards, who seemed calm and undisturbed. Nothing seemed to be untoward. Nevertheless, he had a gut feeling that something was wrong.

Charles moved quickly through the sitting room and into the hallway. He cursed the slapping noise his bare wet feet were making on the polished wooden floor. He stopped for a moment and took off his bathrobe and tossed it to the floor and stood on it. Charles rubbed his feet on the soft cotton then headed off towards his study, leaving the trampled robe on the floor.

He needed to get to his desk, where he kept his gun. Pool water splashed off his body as he moved, leaving droplets on the floor and nearby wall. He felt a surge of relief as he entered the room. Rushing over to his desk, he pulled out a nickel-plated Kimber Carry .45. Now that he felt the weapon gripped tightly in his hand, he felt safe, confident.

A large bang from the floor above made him look up in terror. Charles gripped the weapon, and his strength returned. The sound had come from one of the bedrooms upstairs. More precisely, his bedroom. Carefully he made his way out of the study and headed for the brass bannister rail of the marble staircase. His movements were slow. Each step was taken as if he had a lead weight attached to his ankles.

Beads of sweat began to form and mix with the pool water. Charles wiped his eyes as a few drops of the mix trickled into his eyes and began to burn like acid.

Charles stopped at the top of the winding staircase and looked towards his door. There was an eerie silence, which was only broken by the sound of his erratic breathing. He crept forward towards his door. He could feel the gun in his hand begin to shake the closer he got. He stopped suddenly.

Soft music was coming from within.

At first, he couldn't make out the tune because of its low volume. But it was definitely music. Slowly he turned the handle and opened the door. The curtains had been drawn, and the only light was from a few candles that had been arranged around the large bedroom.

He walked in, feeling slightly confused. What the hell was

233

going on, he wondered to himself? In the darkness, he suddenly caught sight of a pair of long legs in black stockings. Red high-heeled shoes and a black-and-red Basque completed the picture. However, the woman's face and shoulders were bathed in shadow.

"Oh, I do hope you're Mr Charles," came a sultry female voice.

Charles couldn't stop himself nodding enthusiastically, almost as if he was making a special point of his identity. His eyes fixed on this vision of beauty in front of him.

"Who are you?" he asked, but he wasn't really interested in the answer. His jaw was slack, and his grip was slacker. The gun fell from his hand as his arms came to rest by his side.

"Me?" she replied. "I am just a present from the management for all your hard work." Her voice was like a siren's song, drawing him closer. He stumbled forward as though under a hypnotic spell. Charles watched as she moved onto the bed, her perfect form suddenly held in a dim light. He moved steadily forward, the drool starting to form in the corners of his mouth.

"Come on, Charles, I don't bite...well, maybe a little." Her voice and laugh were intoxicating.

"P-please call me Charlie," he said, fumbling his words and his steps. She patted the bed next to her, and he obeyed by climbing up like a small puppy. She opened her legs slowly and pressed the chest piece of the Basque together.

"Come to me, Charlie, show me what you have got!" Her words tingled down his spine.

He climbed between her legs and moved forward, a huge grin across his face. This was the stuff of dreams or those sexy 'fake' letters to men's magazines. Her body was gorgeous, and he wondered what her face was like. Why did she keep it hidden, he wondered?

But it didn't matter. He looked over at the hand, restraints on the bed's headboard. Devices he had used before on many a young woman! Indeed, he had a perverse taste in sex. He was a little man that liked to hurt women because it made him feel good. A man who liked to watch others 'feel the pinch'. He couldn't wait to see how this one would fare.

"Let me see your face, my dear, let me see where I will end this night," he growled with a sudden burst of authority.

Suddenly her powerful legs shot up and locked around his neck. He struggled, but she was far too powerful for him. He started to lose consciousness.

"What are you doing you bi—"

She applied more pressure, cutting off his words.

"A certain someone sends his regards." She laughed as she heard something crack in his body.

"Whatever he is paying you I will double it," Charles begged, hoping it would be enough for her to let him go.

"I doubt it. His fee was very high." Again, she laughed as she squeezed a little more.

Charles could feel the air leaving his body.

"I will give you anything!" he gasped with the minimal breath he had left. "What did he offer you?"

"He said I could take you down and kick your ass as a punishment for all the women you ever hurt your sick bastard." As she spoke, she squeezed his neck, ever more powerfully.

He tried to claw at her, but her legs were long. As he slipped into darkness, he heard something else: Music. But not from the stereo. It was from a pocket watch.

As the darkness took him, he prayed that this would be how he died.

———

Mr Charles awoke to blackness. Blackness and the silence of the grave. There was a chill in the air. At first, he thought he was outside. Then he felt the cold of the metal on his back, the restraints on his arms, legs and chest. Before he had been groggy from his ordeal, but now he was very much awake.

He struggled to break his bonds but to no avail. Charles stopped and listened. There was a slight tapping noise. He froze, his heart began to pound against his chest. And then it came the music. The distant sound of the musical pocket watch.

Charles knew what the music meant: it was the signature of a madman. The last sound a person would hear before he started his devilish work. Charles looked as small pools of light appeared as the madman approached. Finally, a large lamp came on over Charles's head, and he could see himself and his perilous situation in detail. He was bound to a special table with his arms and legs spread out. Tubes of medical chemicals had been inserted into his neck and just above his collarbone.

"You can't do this to me, you psycho!" screamed out Charles in a futile attempt to scare Williams. The latter said nothing, just looked down at the bound man and stroked his hair, as if to comfort him.

"The council will find out what you have done, and you know the rules," Charles yelled desperately. "No one member may hurt any of the others." The desperately scared man hoped that his show of authority would sway his torturer from doing something terrible.

Williams looked at Charles and gently smiled. "I guess you're right. There would be questions, certainly. But then I could always say you ran off to South America or something. Oh, I know how about Australia?" Williams said with a sudden excited look as if something else had popped into his head.

"You know I have always wanted to go to Australia," the

crazy doctor continued in a conversational, friendly tone. "Kangaroos, the wide-open spaces."

Charles looked up at his tormentor with a confused look. "What?" he asked.

Williams looked down at Charles in some excitement and slapped himself on the forehead. "Sorry, I do apologise, I was away somewhere else for the moment. Silly me. Now, where was I?" Williams said, looking puzzled. Then that callous grin of cruelty came over his long pale face.

"Oh, yes, I remember now. I could lie to the council, but that's not my style. That's more ... yours," Williams went on, his face only inches away from the other man's. Suddenly he shot upwards and walked backwards. As he did so, the circle of light grew bigger, and five women dressed in scrubs entered the circle. Each of the women had different coloured hair.

Two of them walked towards Williams, holding out a surgeon's gown, which he stepped into, and another tied it up at the back. Two others held out a pair of surgical gloves and pulled them over his long bony fingers. Charles realised with horror this was not a scare tactic: they were getting him ready for surgery.

"Williams, you maniac, when the council find out about this you are a dead man!" Charles spat his words. His misplaced overconfidence in his dire situation showed on his smug, fat face.

His enemy froze for a moment and looked as if Charles had struck on a valid point.

"You know, Mr Charles, you are absolutely right, they would find out. That leaves me no alternative, I guess," Williams said disappointedly, turning and walking away.

Charles grinned. He had beaten the executioner. The great Mr Williams had been denied his pleasure.

Suddenly Williams stopped and turned with a smile. "Of

course, if I showed them what I had done, I guess that would be different. Don't you think?"

With that, all the lights came on, and Charles saw for the first time the dreaded 'operating theatre' that he had heard so much about. Above him was the viewing gallery, inside which all the members of the council were standing, watching the proceedings.

Two of the women pulled out a large table from the wall, on which was a large monitor. As Charles watched, he realised with horror that Williams had been given permission to do his terrible business.

They all watched as the strange dance of multi-coloured lines twisted and swayed with every pitch of tone.

"Mr Charles," came the words from the loudspeaker that accompanied the picture on the screen. "You know the penalty for stealing from us. Not only did you steal from the organisation, but you also tried to incriminate one of your own colleagues. You know the punishment for this. I found it only fitting that you should face the man you accused." The lines onscreen were hard and jagged to match the words.

"Let this be a warning to you all," the voice said in roar of displeasure. "Mr Williams, you may proceed."

The star of the show gave a low theatrical bow and then turned to the gallery.

"Ladies and gentlemen, there are refreshments at the back, and for those who are squeamish...and the bathrooms are down the hall," he said with a smile. Williams then walked back to the wriggling Mr Charles. Williams pushed the remaining air from his gloves and smoothed them out over his fingers.

"Don't worry. I am not going to hurt you. I give you my word," Williams said once again, stroking Charles's hair.

The tied-up prisoner looked up; half confused. "Then why am I—"

Williams placed his index finger onto Charles's lips to silence him and slowly shook his head.

"Do you remember those young girls you raped and brutalised?" the psychopath went on. "Some of them took their own lives, and some ended up in a clinic. And some, well, let's just say... I got to them just in time." Williams stood back and revealed the line-up of the five women who had been assisting him.

A look of utter terror-filled Charles's face. Each woman held a bone saw. Each of them also had a look of utter contempt on their faces.

Williams walked around to the other side of the table, his hands behind his back. Charles was too transfixed on the women.

"I would like to say this was not personal, but I would be lying," Williams said with a kind of pleasure, as each of the women took her place standing beside a limb.

The tall, black-haired woman stood between his legs and held what appeared to be a rusty kitchen knife with a serrated blade. She winked at Charles and smiled. "Oh, lucky me. I won the toss," she said, and as she spoke, the other women moved in.

Revenge burned in their eyes. There were a piercing scream, and all the people in the gallery looked away. All apart from the large German woman, who was now staring into Williams's eyes with a lustful hunger. He stared back with equal pleasure. He smiled wickedly and headed for the door.

CHAPTER TWENTY-SIX

Steel and Tony arrived at the apartment where Amber was found. Steel took the keys from his pocket and headed for the lock. The guard was gone, but the police tape remained. He looked over at Tony, who had a wary look on his face as if he really didn't want to go in.

"If you can't do it, I will understand," Steel said in a soft, reassuring tone. Tony felt almost insulted at the accusation. But the more he thought about it, the more he realised he was angry with himself, for if he couldn't bear to go into his dead girlfriend's apartment, he was letting her down. Tony gave Steel a shallow nod. Steel cracked a smile from the corner of his mouth and nodded back. He slipped the brass Yale key into the lock and turned it until they heard the click of the bolt release.

"You think we missed something?" Tony asked as they entered.

Steel said nothing at first, he simply headed for Amber's room. As Tony entered, he saw the huge stain where the blood had soaked into the floor. He stopped and stared for a moment.

Flashback images of Amber's mutilated body lying on that spot returned. Steel stopped and looked over at Tony. He knew what he was going through.

"Tony," Steel gently called over. He knew that the more Tony relived that moment, the less likely he would be able to stick around. Not that he should have been there in the first place.

"Hey, Tony," Steel yelled loudly: since the soft approach didn't work, he'd decided to play it rough.

Tony looked up at Steel with an almost dazed look.

"Listen, Tony. This time you're here for Tara. If we find her, it may lead us to Amber's killer. You take Tara's room I will check Amber's," Steel explained.

Tony shot him a puzzled look. "I thought you just said we were here for Tara. So why would we look in Amber's room? We never found anything last time," Tony said, missing the point.

"No," John went on patiently. "I said YOU'RE here for Tara. You said there was nothing at her other apartment, so the chances are there may be something here we have overlooked."

Tony nodded and walked over to Tara's room, opened the door and walked in. He didn't know why they were there. He had already checked the room days ago to try and find out who the roommate was. He pulled on a pair of latex gloves and started to search for anything he could find. There'd been no visible signs of her having a computer, so he hoped for at least a diary.

Steel entered what had been Amber's room. Most of her stuff was still in boxes that took up that main part of the sitting room. The room was decorated in a ghastly pink colour, and there was not much in the way of furniture. A double bed rested against the left-hand wall facing the window. The wardrobes were built into the walls to save on what little space there was.

There was a black canvas holdall and one of those armoured suitcases. Steel noticed that there was fingerprint powder residue on the lock. He smiled at the CSU's thoroughness. He looked around the room. Apart from the stacked boxes, it was tidy. Steel walked out and headed for Tara's room, where he found Tony with a handful of Tara's panties.

Steel coughed and raised an eyebrow. Tony turned quickly and looked at Steel, then realised what he had in his grasp.

"Not very appropriate, but needs must I suppose." Steel smiled.

Tony just stood there, his mouth opening and shutting like a carp out of water. He turned red then shoved the underwear back in the drawer.

"I didn't find anything, how about you?" Tony said quickly, hoping to deflect Steel's crude humour away from himself. Steel looked back at the sitting room then returned his gaze to Tony.

"The place has been searched, so if there was something here, it has gone."

Tony looked blankly at Steel, reflecting that his claim that the apartment had been tossed didn't fit. "How do you work that out?" Tony asked. "The place isn't trashed. It looks normal." He looked around the room for signs of tampering. Steel walked over to a small dresser and picked up a tiny music box with a figure of a ballerina on its lid. He turned the key and let the tune play.

"And that, Tony, my friend, is what worries me. There are two possibilities. One they searched the place while nobody was here. Or two, they did it after Amber had come in. They managed to leave everything where it was, and doing that after you've killed someone ... Well, that's takes nerve." Steel put down the music box.

"You see, whoever did it was careful enough not to draw attention to the fact," Steel noted as he walked back into the sitting room. His gaze fell onto the blood pool, and his own personal memories came flooding back. He closed his eyes as if to hold onto the image of his wife's smiling face. Steel was glad of his sunglasses to hide his pain.

Unlike Tony, Steel had not revisited the scene where his loved ones had died, which was the attic in his father's mansion in England, where he had lost his mother and wife. Sure, he had been home, mainly to uphold the formalities of the estate he had inherited. But he had never once ventured up those cold-looking stairs. He had ordered that during the renovation the attic was to be left as it was. It was more of a shrine now than a storage space.

"Are you OK?" Tony asked on seeing Steel standing there motionless as if he was in a trance. Steel turned slowly and nodded. Tony noted something different about him. Something dark, as if a haunting cloud had passed over him.

"I am fine," Steel reassured his friend. "I was just remembering something from a long time ago. It doesn't matter." He smiled and headed for the boxes that were stacked near the kitchen. Tony shook his head and went back to searching the bedroom.

Steel had looked through most of the boxes and found nothing but everyday items. Each box was labelled for convenience. But he could not find anything worth dying for in any of them. He had hoped for secret compartments and hidden data sticks but came up empty. All she had were pots and pans and a load of clothes. Even the suitcase was just a suitcase: no false bottoms.

The British detective leaned against the door frame of

Tara's bedroom and watched Tony rip the room apart. He had searched through books and jars of creams. Neither of them knew what they were looking for, but Steel figured it wasn't anything big. Only information or data was likely to attract the unwanted attention of scary people.

The chances were if the other organisation was behind it all, the mystery involved something worth a lot of money or that could be used as 'leverage'. Tony slammed the last drawer shut and looked over at Steel with an angry glare.

"There is nothing here, Steel," Tony growled. "We just wasted half a day lookin' for nothin'!" He wished that McCall was there: she was someone whom he felt something for.

"We have learnt nothing, Steel, so are you friggin' happy?" Tony barked.

The other man rocked his head from side to side. "Actually, yes. I am feeling quite good. However, I sense you are not." Steel moved away from the door's wooden frame.

Tony's mouth fell open with surprise. "How the hell can you feel good about this?" He walked around, trying to stop himself leaping over and strangling the smug Englishman.

"For one thing we know whatever it was they were looking for, they never found it," Steel explained, talking softly. "Secondly, I'd say that unfortunately your girlfriend was killed by accident."

Tony's tearful wild-eyed stare shot over towards Steel. A look of bewilderment was carved into that stout Irish/Italian face.

"How can you be sure they didn't find it?" Tony's voice was close to breaking. "Maybe they found it on her and killed her."

"No. If they had it, why take Brooke? And why is Tara missing? I think we have been looking at it all wrong. I think that Tara has what they are looking for, and Amber walked in at the wrong time. Remember someone telling us that Amber wasn't due to move in until Monday? I think they mistook Amber for Tara. I think Tara walked in after they had gone and now, she is running scared."

Tony investigated nothingness and weighed up what Steel had just said. It made sense, but it didn't change the fact that Amber was dead. In fact, if her death had been an accident, it made things worse.

———

Steel had told Tony to go home. It was Sunday and would be limited to witnesses he could talk to due to the weekend closures. Besides Tony was still shaken up after having been in the apartment. Steel had planned to go back to the precinct and wait for the ME's report on the body from the park.

The British detective stood outside in the warm sunlight and watched Tony's police-issue Dodge Challenger disappear into the mass of traffic at the crossroads of Ninth Avenue. He stood for a moment and looked up and down the street as he pulled on a pair of leather-and-neoprene gloves.

Tomorrow everyone would be back at work. There was a lot of investigating to do, and the body in the park meant even more activity. Neither was it helpful that the accident earlier in the week was tying up the labs with urgent tests. He started to head towards Eighth Avenue.

From the corner of his eye, Steel saw a yellow cab pull up. Curious, he stopped and turned just in time to see a fabulous brunette get out and start struggling with her shopping bags. Steel smiled and shook his head at the damsel in distress. As he approached, Steel took note of the driver: a large black guy with dreadlocks and a strange knitted hat.

"May I be of assistance?" Steel asked politely.

The woman giggled and nodded. Steel noticed that she kept her face away from him or else blocked it from view whenever possible.

"Oh, thank you so much," the woman said in a southern accent as Steel placed the bags on the ground.

All the while, his alarm bells were ringing.

"Hey, do you need a taxi, man?" asked the driver in a joyful tone.

Steel stepped backwards to give the woman space to sort her bags out, but all the time, he took care to never look at her directly.

"No, thank you," Steel said to the cab driver. "I don't have far to go." He had not noticing the air-powered dart gun that the cabbie had just aimed out of the window. There was a dull thud of gas being released as the weapon was discharged. Steel grabbed his neck and pulled out a small dart.

"Oh, bugger," Steel said, looking at the small projectile. Immediately he started to feel the effects of the drug, but he grabbed for the cabbie, nonetheless. Steel still had some fight left in him, and he intended to use it on the driver. The cabbie yelped as Steel approached and wound the window up. Groggily Steel made it to the cab's door and raised a white-knuckled first. The safety glass of the driver's window exploded into small fragments and Steel began to drag the screaming cabbie out before the woman hit him three more times with the dart gun. Steel lay on the ground, with the bleeding cabbie pulled halfway out of the window.

"We stickin' this crazy motha in the trunk, man," yelped the driver as he fell out of the broken window. "I ain't riskin' him wakin' up and killin' me!"

The woman smiled and took off her wig: it was the black-haired woman Steel had encountered at the boutique. She knelt close to the unconscious man at her feet. She smiled and kissed two fingers and then placed them onto Steel's ruby lips.

"Sweet dreams, my white knight. Dream well," she crooned to him.

CHAPTER TWENTY-SEVEN

STEEL AWOKE SLOWLY. HE FELT COLDNESS ON HIS SKIN. That was when he realised; he was naked. He was bound to something cold ... Something metal. He didn't try to struggle; he could feel it would be pointless. He was bound with his arms and legs out to the sides. Everything was black, and there was a clinical smell in the room.

Above him, a bright light came on, followed by the tap, tap, tap of expensive shoes. The single light on above him revealed he was bound to a strange metallic construction, shaped into the letter 'X'. He was upright and exposed, in more than one way. The tapping came closer until the walker stopped and he heard a whispered discussion. Suddenly all the lights came on, and there stood Williams and the black-haired woman from the boutique.

Williams took one look at Steel and turned to the woman. She just shrugged and smiled broadly.

"Keres, my dear, I asked for him to be unharmed... not undressed, but I see now why the ladies think so much of him," Williams said, laughing and raising an eyebrow.

"Why of course, sir," Keres said, fumbling over her words as she grinned. "After all, there is so much of him ... I mean, he is very muscular, sir."

"I also had to make sure he wasn't armed," she said almost innocently.

Williams rolled his eyes and walked up to Steel with an embarrassed look. "I must apologise, John, it would appear, my assistant, Keres, has taken a shine to you. Once you've gotten dressed, please do join me upstairs." His voice was apologetic and sincere. This was not the man Steel was used to: the madman – the killer, no, this was a civilised man, the complete opposite from the man Steel had first encountered a year ago . Williams smiled and walked back towards the doorway.

"Keres, please ensure that our guest is well taken care of, and bring him to the study, will you?" Williams saw a glint in her eye as he spoke. Her gaze locked onto Steel's impressive physique.

"Oh, don't worry, Mr W, it will be my pleasure," she said and waited until she heard the door close behind her. As she approached, her metal high heels gave a loud tap as they impacted on the tiled floor. She moved slowly as if to enjoy the view for a moment.

Keres looked up at Steel. There was a purposeful glint in her eye. She moved close to him, almost nose to nose. Steel wondered what she had interpreted Williams's commands to mean. He felt something cold against his stomach but was unable to look down to see what it was. The brunette's hand moved across his muscular chest, her fingertips paying special attention to the scars from the bullets' exit wounds. She had a sad look as she touched them, almost as if she could feel the pain, they were a reminder of. Her other hand was held firmly behind her.

John Steel had found himself in many tight spots before,

but none like this. By this stage, after his capture, he had usually devised a way out of the situation and was already making plans to carry out an escape.

But this time it was different. There was something sinister and oddly surreal about all this, and it was all her doing.

"I think your boss wants me alive," Steel said, confused about the whole situation.

"He also said that I have to take very good care of you," she purred. There was a clicking sound, and then Steel felt the X-shaped contraption he was attached to begin to move down to a horizontal position.

"And, my white knight, I intend to take vvveeery good care of you indeed." Her words were followed by the sound of a zip being pulled down, followed by the soft flapping of clothes hitting the floor.

———

Williams sat in one of the red leather chesterfields that faced a large marble fireplace. He took out his pocket watch and checked the time. They had been gone for over an hour – almost two. Normally he would be worried, knowing what he did about Steel and what he was capable of. However, Williams also knew that Steel was curious, and Williams had sparked Steel's curiosity by bringing him there.

He was about to get up and find out what was keeping them when the two oak double doors opened and in walked Steel and Keres. Williams noticed Keres wore a particularly wide smile and walked with a swagger.

"I hope Keres didn't give you a difficult time, Mr Steel?" Williams said, walking over to a large drinks cabinet that was housed behind a wall panel. The mirrored back glistened as it reflected the small lights above.

"Oh, there were a couple of hard moments, but I'll live." Steel smiled and Keres bit the nail on her right index finger. Williams looked at them both in the mirrored back of the wall panel and shook his head with a smile. Picking up two large-bowled brandy glasses, Williams turned and walked towards Steel.

"You may leave us now, Keres, thank you." Williams's words were soft and gentle. Keres nodded and swaggered out of the room, closing the double doors on her way out.

"Please, sit down," Williams said, handing Steel a glass. Steel took it, and both men sat before the roaring fire.

"We're drinking Domaine des Forges, bottled over three hundred years ago. Preserved since the eighteen hundred. The cost, astronomical," Williams said, before putting the glass under his nose and inhaling the aroma. His eyes closed as he savoured the strong hard smell.

"Such a thing should be savoured and enjoyed." Williams looked over at Steel, who was admiring the golden colour in the firelight. Williams smiled comfortably, reassured in his estimation of Steel's character. He knew from their first meeting that John Steel was much like himself – a different side of the same coin.

"This is all very nice, Mr Williams, but can we get to the point? I don't think you brought me here because you wanted to catch up on old times." Steel lifted the glass to his lips and sipped the ageing cognac. He had noticed a woman's handbag on Williams's desk, meaning that Steel's arrival had interrupted something.

Williams smiled and raised his glass. "Quite so. To the point then," he said, crossing his legs underneath him and sitting like a child. As he did so, Steel noticed that Williams was wearing odd socks. One was black and red stripes, and the other was yellow and blue.

"John, you're investigating the death of Amber Taylor... yes?" Williams asked, wriggling around on the chair, trying to find a comfortable position.

"I can't really say. Why, what's your interest?" Steel asked, suddenly getting a bad feeling.

"Well, if any of your colleagues are investigating the case, tell them to be careful. It isn't at all what it seems," Williams explained, leaning forward.

Steel sat back in his chair and looked suspiciously at Williams. This wasn't what he had been expecting from Williams. He had been anticipating a very different sort of warning.

"Why the concern? Surely having us killed would be a very good thing from your point of view, wouldn't it?"

Williams looked mortified. "John! How can you say that after all, we've been through together?" Williams raised his bottom lip over his upper one and gave Steel a sad look, like a disappointed puppy.

Steel laughed and took another sip of brandy.

The psychopath's face became serious, and he uncrossed his legs and leant forward. "Let me explain. The other 'organisation' you are following in this regard, the ones I told you about before, well, they are dangerous and out of control. You know our methods, but them ... Let's just say they have no rules, only objectives and no one ever gets in their way. They need to be stopped. And unfortunately, fate has chosen you to stop them." Williams appeared to be talking matter-of-factly as if he was describing the finer points of an ordinary business. His usual maddening tone had gone.

Of course, Steel had seen first-hand precisely what the 'organisation' could do, and he could see that Williams was nervous.

"So, what do you want us to do, stop investigating this murder?" Steel asked, smiling and shaking his head.

Williams's face, however, was like stone. The orange glow of the fire reflected in his corneas, giving them a demonic look.

"No, Lord Steel. I want you to watch your back and prepare for war."

Steel woke up with a strange taste in his mouth and feeling slightly disorientated. He blinked several times as his vision started to return. He found himself lying on his side, looking at what appeared to be a television screen. The smell of fake leather and the sensation of movement beneath him told him he was in the back of a car.

He sat up and immediately felt as if he had been out all-night drinking bad cocktails. He touched his brow: it felt cold and clammy. His vision came and went, almost as if his eyes could not focus. He knew something was wrong. Steel had already figured that they would knock him out for travel purposes, but this was something else.

It appeared to be almost dawn. As he looked out of the window, he saw everything had that blue tint of pre-dawn light. As they travelled through the nearly empty streets, Steel noticed small orange shards of light breaking through between the buildings.

"What time is it? And where have I been all this time?" Steel demanded. The driver in front of him said nothing. He just shot a smile at the rear-view mirror and cupped his ear, as if to signal that he had not heard what Steel had said.

The detective felt something roll against his thigh. Looking down, he could make out it was a bottle; however, the label was a blur. He picked it up for a closer look.

He could feel the refreshingly cold moisture on the clear plastic. Cracking the lid, he carefully put the neck to his lips. The liquid was cold and still, and he hoped it was water.

Steel went on inhaling the liquid until the plastic screwed together under the vacuum, as he sucked out every drop of the contents.

"Where are you taking me?" Steel yelled, angry at himself for letting his abduction occur.

"I was told to take care of you. Don't worry, I have the address," the driver said.

Now wider awake, Steel realised that he was in the back of a yellow cab. As Steel listened to the cabbie's voice, he thought he recognised him, but couldn't place where from.

"Who put me in here?" Steel asked. He didn't really want to know. He just wanted to hear the man's voice again.

"Some pretty lady. She gave a good tip as well."

Steel smiled as he worked out it was the same cab driver who he'd met before, but why was he been so secretive? Surely, he would realise that Steel would recognise him. Unless of course, he had something to do with his present condition.

Without the cabby noticing, Steel took off his watch and pressed a button on its side. The hour marks started to glow green and Steel stuffed the watch down the back of the seat. Slowly, everything began to spin. He knew he was in trouble. Reaching for his phone, Steel pressed the 'medical app'. From its base, a small pin shot out. Quickly, Steel stabbed himself in the chest with it. His breathing became laboured, and his chest began to burn.

"Let me out," Steel growled. He still had strength but very little. The cabbie looked in his rear-view mirror and saw Steel pull out his Berratta Storm Bulldog. The cabbie's eyes widened as Steel aimed it at him.

"Let me out now, or you won't be around to spend the tip," Steel growled.

The taxi screeched to a halt and Steel opened the door and fell out. Steel could hear the scream of brakes from the other surrounding cars and could feel the wind from the river. He realised that he was on the Brooklyn Bridge.

Slowly he stumbled towards the metal railing. As he reached the edge, he stuck his fingers down his throat and then vomited hard onto the concrete walkway. As he held the rail, he felt a bit of metal bright against his skin. Quickly, he used the sharpness of it to cut his hand and then clenched his fist so that the blood would ooze from the wound. A cascade of fresh blood flooded over the railings.

Steel knew he didn't have much time. There was a peeping sound from his cell phone. He smiled, climbed up over the rail and let himself drop. People rushed over, and women screamed.

But all any of them saw was a man in black disappearing into the murky depths of the East River.

CHAPTER TWENTY-EIGHT

DETECTIVE LEWIS COREMAN WAS NEW TO HOMICIDE; IN fact, he was a new detective altogether. The last detective in his job had quit because of personal reasons. Coreman was ambitious and full of himself, and for some reason, the brass saw fit to promote him to detective.

Some said he was promoted on posting: a cunning ploy by his D.C. captain to get him away from the other cops. But he didn't care; he had gotten it.

He was of medium build and medium height. He wore styled brown hair and a grey Armani suit. He dabbled in stocks, but his main money came from Daddy. He was a rich kid whose encounter with a judge, made sure he was given a choice: go into the military or the police. The army had rejected him, but luckily his father had pulled some strings and got him into the police academy. His only saving grace was that he was a computer whiz, and he liked everyone to know it.

Coreman checked his reflection in the monitor. He smiled and nodded, admiring his own idea of good looks. His clean-shaven round face was proportionate to his stocky bulk. The floor was clear because most of his colleagues had not come in yet. He had been there since five a.m., and most of the night shift had already headed home or were out on cases.

He sat back and stroked his desk as though it was made from gold. He smiled and looked around, but there was no one to brag to. Suddenly one of the night shift detectives walked up to him and handed him an address.

"You're up for this, newbie," the tall, thin, ageing detective said as he slung his jacket on.

"Where we are going?" Coreman said excitedly.

The ageing Tooms laughed. "Well, I am going home to my wife, and you are going to check that out. It's a possible suicide. There are lots of witnesses, so I would hurry your ass up before they all go home," laughed the veteran.

Coreman sat open-mouthed for a moment before looking down at the address. *One times white male, possible suicide. Brooklyn Bridge.* Coreman stood up. If he waited around, witnesses and evidence would be lost. He smiled nervously and headed out. This was his first case, and he sure didn't want it to be his last.

———

Coreman had taken a cab to the scene—it was quicker than filling out the paperwork to take a vehicle, he could do that later. What's more, driving there would have been his first time driving in New York—after all, he had been a cop D.C. The three lanes of the bridge had been put down to two so that the forensic teams could do their work in safety. He got the cabby to pull up close to the scene. He sat for a moment to gather his thoughts. Coreman looked at the chaos of the situation: uniformed cops trying to wave on curious onlookers in their cars.

There wasn't much press, just a couple of freelancers trying to get something to sell. It was an old story, so why should there be? It was just some guy who woke up hating himself and took a dive. It would have been hot news if he had gone on the rampage with a weapon. Coreman spotted the ME's wagon and the CSU's vehicles. There was a huge blacked out SUV parked up next to the railings for easy access to their equipment.

Beads of sweat started to collect around his collar. He was in charge. The thought had just sunk in. This was his mess to sort out. His eyes were fixed on the situation. His hands gripped his A4 organiser until his knuckles became white.

Suddenly there was a loud knock on his window, causing him to jump. He looked over to find a veteran uniformed cop staring in. The cabbie wound down his window and faced the officer.

"Good morning, sir, I am afraid you're going to have to move along, this is a crime scene," the cop told him. He was polite, but his tone rang with authority.

"Don't blame me, officer, I am just droppin' this dude off," said the ageing black cabbie.

"I am Detective Coreman," said Coreman, showing his shield. His voice was stern and almost arrogant. He got out of the cab and passed the cabbie a twenty-dollar bill. The driver took off quickly, assuming he'd been given a big tip. Coreman scowled at the misunderstanding, but he had other things to worry about.

Coreman walked briskly, heading for the ME and the CSU, who were camped out together, with people busy taking samples.

"I'm Detective Coreman, so what have we got?" he asked, hoping for a quick end to his first case.

"I'm Tina Franks, the ME," replied the busy medical

professional. "As for what has happened, well, Detective, that's your job. All I know is we have blood and a missing body. A man was seen jumping into the East River early this morning." Tina gave him a look that said, 'your turn'.

Except he didn't have one, he was clueless. He cursed the other detective for landing this one in his lap. He looked around for a moment, gathering his thoughts. *Eyewitnesses*, he thought, after all, someone had phoned the cops. He thanked Tina and hurried off to the uniformed officer near their squad car.

"Who called it in?" Coreman asked the veteran cop. The cop smiled and took out his notebook. Coreman felt the man toying with him as he slowly flicked through his notes.

"We were just finishing our patrol early this morning around six when we got flagged down by a couple in a car," the officer readout. "They had just come off the bridge. They said that there was some guy getting ready to jump off the bridge after getting out of a yellow cab. There are some more eyewitnesses over there, next to the other squad car."

Coreman looked over to another squad car at the other end of the cordon. Beside it, there was two officers and two couples, each officer interviewing one of the couples, keeping away from each other as to get individual accounts. Coreman looked around to see if there were any close circuit cameras, and he spotted at least two. He made a note in his book: *Contact Traffic for any footage they may have.* There had been plenty of cell phones with footage which the CSU teams had taken in. Tina Franks was all done picking up her samples of vomit and blood, which she needed due to fact that the witness had said the man had thrown up before jumping. Coreman put it down to a drunken jilted lover who couldn't let go. When he had spoken to the first responding officer, it turned out that he hadn't seen much, but had just responded to someone flagging him down.

Unfortunately, by the time they had gotten through the traffic, the man had gone.

The keen new detective smiled to himself: his first case alone, and he was breezing through it. This was one way of getting the captain's attention. He walked back to Tina Franks like a man who had already cracked the case.

"Well, Dr Franks, you and CSU have taken samples. Seems to me to be an open and shut case. A man gets drunk after been dumped by his girlfriend; he can't take the disappointment, so he jumps," Coreman said confidently.

Tina just looked at him and said nothing. She looked around the scene. To her mind, something was wrong. The vomit and the blood. Sure, she could understand the throwing up if it was the result of a drunken last moment. But the blood? Her gaze halted on one spot at the railings. She found the place where whoever it was had apparently slashed themselves and took another sample. It was a small piece of metal that was sticking up out of the rail. It was only a tiny thing but was enough to cause a nasty scratch.

The ME looked at it for a moment, realising that their 'jumper' must have slashed themselves on purpose because of the whereabouts of the piece of metal. She said nothing at first. As usual, she would test things first then inform those in authority of her findings later.

———

Coreman had made it back to the precinct and was going through some of the footage from the cell phones. By the time Tony and Tooms had arrived, he had watched around twenty images.

Tooms and Tony walked over and introduced themselves. Coreman greeted them politely and told them of the suicide case he'd attended. The three detectives gathered around Coreman's computer as he began to watch the next footage. This was the best one yet. It was clear and close. Close enough for Tony and Tooms to recognise the jumper as Steel.

"I mean seriously what sort of moron decides to jump off a bridge?" Coreman laughed. "I mean really, what a loser!"

Tooms ripped the man out of his chair and pinned him against the back wall. "That 'loser' happens to be one of the best detectives that we have," said Captain Brant as he walked up to the group. He had just seen the same footage on the news. Tooms let the man drop to the floor, and he backed away before he did something, he would later regret.

"Son, you have a lot to learn," Brant said softly. "Right now, lesson one is don't be here when McCall gets here. Because if she finds out what you just said, she will shoot you." Brant held his hands tightly together so that he couldn't shoot him himself.

Coreman nodded and ran for the elevator. Tony looked over at Brant. "I want this one boss."

Brant said nothing at first, he just stared at the frozen image of Steel on Coreman's computer.

"I got a better job for you, Marinelli," Brant said with a lump in his throat. "Figure out how to tell Sam that Steel is dead."

———

For McCall, Monday morning brought a grey skyline and a cold biting wind. She had left her mother's house in Boston early, in order to beat the traffic. Plus, she wanted to get an early start on the case. Some German pianist called Richter was blaring from her stereo. Steel had lent her the CD a week ago, but she kept forgetting to give it back for some reason.

She pulled into her usual parking lot and eased the

Mustang into her parking spot. She had been such a good customer the owners gave her a nameplate. It was a simple thing. A licence plate with *SAM McCALL* stamped on it.

McCall turned off the engine and just sat for a moment. The weekend had been great, fantastic even. However, now it was time to go back to work. McCall stared into her own eyes in the rear-view mirror. She had to get back into the mind step. Time to be a cop again.

McCall closed her eyes and took a deep breath. As she exhaled, her eyes shot open. She was back, and she was ready. She locked up her car and clicked the remote again for the alarm. The lights flashed twice to indicate the activation.

As she headed towards the precinct, she couldn't help but wonder how far the boys had progressed with the case during the weekend. McCall was hoping she hadn't missed anything important. She smiled at the thought of Steel having already wrapped up the whole case and the dirtbag being in a cell. McCall laughed and shook her head at the stupidity of the idea. Nothing could have happened, because he hadn't blown anything up, as he had a habit of doing.

As she walked into the precinct, she picked up on the mood. It was like she had walked into a wake. Every cop either looked angry or lost. McCall waved at the desk sergeant and smiled as she always did. But he just stared at her and shook his head.

Something turned in her gut. Something bad had happened, and she should have been there. McCall didn't bother waiting for the elevator; she rushed the stairs. As she reached the top, she saw Tony and Tooms talking with Captain Brant. She froze for a moment. She was confused. Everyone was there, so what was the problem?

Everyone was there except for Steel.

As she walked towards the three men, she felt her legs grow

heavy. Tony looked up and caught sight of McCall. His eyes said it all. She went to sit at her desk but missed the chair completely. The men rushed over and found her just sitting on the floor, her eyes moving from side to side as if searching for something. Tony and Tooms grabbed an arm each and helped her into her chair. She looked over at Steel's office door, expecting him to walk out with a smile and a coffee mug. Except he didn't. She looked up at Brant with watery eyes. She wanted to do something: scream, yell, smash something. But all she could do was sit and look at Brant.

Outside the clouds were getting greyer, and the wind was picking up. There was a storm coming. McCall had gone from the emotion of shock to anger. She was now pacing up and down the floor of the large briefing room. Brant, Tooms and Tony were sitting at the long desk waiting for Tina to arrive back from the morgue. Detective Coreman hung around by his desk, almost afraid to say something, in fear of the wrath of McCall.

"So, what happened?" McCall asked.

Tooms looked over at her as she paced up and down with a face like thunder.

Joshua Tooms leant forward, using his elbows as support, saying, "From what Detective Coreman explained—"

"—Who the hell is Coreman?" McCall interrupted.

All three men turned and looked at the stocky detective who was cowering at his desk. Coreman felt himself being watched and looked over with a slightly panicked look. Brant waved him over.

"Detective Coreman is Jenny Thompson's replacement, the 'apparent suicide' was his case," Brant explained as Coreman walked in sheepishly. All of them stared at him with an almost hateful gaze.

"Tell them what you found, Coreman," Brant said in a soft

calming voice. Brant knew what the kid was going through; they all did. But at that moment all their memories of his first day had been clouded by hate. Not for him personally, but that wasn't to say that if he now said the wrong thing, his life would become unbearable.

"Well, early this morning, I was given the address of a possible suicide. On arrival, I saw that the first responding officer had—" Coreman stopped talking, finding that everyone was staring at him with menacing eyes.

"Oh ... Right." Coreman gulped. "Well at around six this morning, a yellow cab was seen to make an emergency stop on the bridge, and the passenger got out. Eyewitnesses and several cell phone videos have film of the passenger throwing up, and then he purposely seems to cut his hand. After which he jumps from the bridge." Coreman's eyes darted around from person to person, hoping for a response.

"I looked at the best footage, and it was Steel," Brant said sorrowfully. He looked into McCall's eyes as they turned red but refused to tear up.

"The ME found traces of blood and vomit at the scene," Coreman continued, aware that all eyes were upon him. "She suspects that whoever the jumper was, purposely threw up and the cut was a result of the climb over the railings." Beads of sweat started to collect on the back of his neck. McCall's glare was the worst; her eyes searing like laser beams. He chose not to identify the jumper as Steel. It was Brant's idea not to say his name, and now he knew why.

"Traffic is sending over any footage to and from the bridge for around that time, also any footage around the area. Harbour patrol are sweeping the area, but due to the current this morning they are not feeling hopeful." Coreman looked at his notes. He couldn't bear to look up at them with their scowls of judgement.

Coreman had thought being the newbie would come with some sort of unpleasantness—having to get the coffee, being the guy who bought the takeout food, doing that sort of menial job to earn their respect. But he never imagined that his first case would be the death of one of their own, and it sucked.

"Did we find the cab, the driver? Have we found...?" McCall started to say but quickly stopped as Brant gave her the famous 'be quiet' stare that most parents must use.

"In spite of this, we still have cases to finish," Brant went on grimly. "Now I know it's a blow and it is a lot to take in. However, we've got to carry on." He looked around the room at the pained expressions. He was feeling the pain as well but couldn't show it. He had to be strong, to set an example.

"Coreman, you will remain on this case," Brant said calmly. He could feel McCall's disappointed look but ignored it. "Tony, you stay on looking for our runaway witness."

Tony nodded and got up to leave, but Brant raised a large index finger and made a downwards motion. Tony smiled and immediately sat back down.

"McCall, you and Tooms have the Amber case and the body in the morgue. Find out if Steel is ... was ... right, and whether the body is indeed our John Doe." Brant looked around at the gathering of detectives. He wore a doleful expression instead of his usual angry one. Sometimes, McCall thought, to be captain, you had to have a good 'angry' face. *No one fears a happy captain*, she thought.

McCall stood up slowly. She looked over at Coreman, who was trying to stand up to look tall. She moved towards him and extended a hand. As he took it, her hand closed around his in a vice-like grip. She looked into his eyes.

"Welcome aboard, Detective Coreman," she told him. "However, if you mess this up, I will make sure you spend the rest of the year in vice, undercover." McCall released her grip and walked away without turning around. Tooms smiled and put a massive arm around the young detective's shoulder.

"Welcome to the team, man," he simply said then went to work.

Coreman just stood there and felt his stomach turn.

This sure is a bad first day, he thought.

CHAPTER TWENTY-NINE

TARA PACED UP AND DOWN THE APARTMENT. SHE HAD been there for days with no contact with the outside world apart from Kim, and she had to honest – as much as she loved Kim as a friend, it was beginning to wear thin. It had been far too long since his last message, far too long without a word. On several occasions, she had almost sent him her address but had deleted the message every time. She kept remembering the newsflash about the body at the park. She knew it was him. She didn't want to believe it, but it had to be. Why else wouldn't he have called? Yesterday Tara had taken the battery out of her phone after watching some cop show: in the drama, the bad guys had caught up with the witness using the phone's GPS.

She was street smart; she had to be. She grew up alone in a bad neighbourhood with only a few friends. Tara knew she would have to leave soon. She thought the best time was when Kim was at work. She couldn't risk any questions.

"Where will you go, what will you do?" Tara could hear Kim's voice now asking the sort of questions that would get her into trouble. She would leave a note, that was the simplest way. The less Kim knew, the better.

Tara went to the kitchen and looked for some paper and pen. It took at least fifteen minutes before she found something, an A4 pad and pen in an old sideboard, which had probably a result of Curb mining – the art of finding furniture on the street that you need. She closed the drawer to the sideboard in the sitting room and carried the A4 pad and pencil over to the couch. The note was simple: *Thanks Kim for everything, I will be fine just need to get away for a while. T.*

The worried young woman folded the paper in half and wrote Kim's name on the front to make it stand out and left it on the coffee table. Tara got up and headed for her bag, which lay in a corner next to the television set. Washed clothes lay folded next to the pink case. Tara looked down at the case and thought for a moment. No one knew where she was. She was safe. Then she looked up at the flat-screen TV as the news came on. It was a recap of the 'body in the park' story.

She bent down and set to packing up her stuff. It was nine in the morning, so she had plenty of time. Luckily Kim wouldn't be back until late.

It took only minutes to find and pack her stuff away. Her clothes had been washed and freshly ironed. Given the amount of time she'd had to kill, she could have redecorated Kim's apartment. Tara took one last look around the room, almost as if she was saying goodbye to her family home. Suddenly she caught her reflection in the glass of a photograph that hung on the wall.

Tara raised her left hand and touched her beautiful red hair. A tear rolled down her right cheek and hung onto her chin for a moment before falling onto her black T-shirt. She headed for the bathroom and searched the lower cupboards. Finding what she was looking for, Tara Stood up straight, she investigated the mirror and then at the package of hair dye.

She smiled for a brief second before thinking: *well, they say blondes have all the fun.*

———

Early that morning, nobody had seen the small black hovercraft speed towards the bridge. Its matt black shell and blacked-out windows, along with its sleek space-age look went unnoticed.

Nor did anyone see it slowly and silently pull up and snatch Steel's limp remains from the black depths of the murky waters. Even though people were looking down at the blackness, they never saw anything. Not even the ripples in the water.

The craft slipped away down past the Governors Island and then past Gravesend Bay. Once it had hit open water, the beast opened and headed north towards Southampton and Mecox Bay. The trip took an hour. By the time the hovercraft had reached the bay, the sun was just rising over the horizon. The vessel turned towards Mecox Bay and headed towards the beach and onto the strait. The craft sped across the sand without leaving a trace of its actions.

As the sun broke free from the horizon, the craft was on Hayground Cove and moving fast. As it reached the large boathouse, it slipped inside, and the automatic doors slid down.

An old Oriental man in a white suit watched silently for a short time while another man approached.

"We have him, sir. Where do you want the—" The man stopped talking suddenly, and the Oriental character shot him a stare. The man swallowed hard and stepped back.

"Take him to my office, I will take care of things there." The Oriental guy was in his late fifties and had an air of fear about him. The man bowed slightly and walked away with some urgency.

Well, Johnny, what have you gotten into this time? the man thought to himself, smiled and shook his head before heading towards a large mansion in the distance.

Tara walked out of the bathroom, drying off her new styled hair. It wasn't the best job in the world, but then it wasn't green either. She had cut it shorter just to add to the disguise. She looked in the mirror to check the result. She smiled. Somehow, she preferred the new look to the old.

Out of the corner of her eye, she caught another newsflash on the TV. The report was that of someone jumping from the Brooklyn Bridge earlier that morning. Tara turned to watch. The grainy footage appeared to be from a cell phone. It showed a man falling from the bridge into the river. The reporter said it was thought to be a detective who was working on the Amber Taylor case. Tara froze. She felt faint and nauseous. She sat for a moment and just watched as they played more footage. The female reporter's tone was full of played emotion – possibly to enhance the report, people loved emotional stories. Tara stood up suddenly. She knew she had to go, but first, she had to get back to her apartment. She needed the money she had saved and her passport. Tara picked up her suitcase and headed for the door. *Time to go,* she thought to herself. Tara knew she had to leave for Kim's sake. If they could kill a cop, what would a waitress's life matter? She placed her hand into her jacket pocket and pulled out some crumpled bills. She didn't have much money, only a few dollars. Tara looked over to the small kitchen and the china cat cookie jar that sat happily on a shelf next to a basilikum plant. She knew Kim kept some money aside for that rainy day. Tara took down the large white cat and stuck her hand inside. There was around six hundred in various bills. Tara took a hundred and slipped an IOU into the jar before placing it back. She had enough for a cab to take her to the nearest subway. Tara knew she couldn't afford to be seen on the street, so a taxi made sense. She was alone, and she was scared. However, she had to be strong to see it through. She still had a chance to make it out alive.

The scared young woman walked out into the sunlight and slipped on the sunglasses. She pulled her jacket's hood up over her hair and headed off. Next stop, back home.

———

Williams sat in a small, darkened room. There was only the light from the twelve flat-screen televisions to illuminate the space. It was a ten-by-ten area with nothing but an old cloth chesterfield armchair, a small side table and the twelve different-sized television sets which had been arranged to make huge screen. Mr Williams watched as the news reporter told of a detective who had jumped to his death earlier that morning. He watched the footage that had been shot on a dashcam. Williams watched as a yellow cab screeched to a halt, and a man dressed in black got out. The man stumbled, then made himself throw up before jumping over the rails into the water.

Williams's eyes squinted in displeasure. The remote in his right hand made a loud cracking sound as he squeezed the life out of it. He sat for a moment and tossed the crumpled plastic remains into a shadowy corner, with the others that had suffered the same fate.

"I really must stop watching television," Williams grumbled as he reached over to the small side table to where an intercom unit sat beside a crystal glass decanter set.

"Crystal," he said into the intercom, his gaze still on the arranged televisions. No answer came.

"Oh, Crystal," he said again, as he sung the words in a mocking tone. Still, there was silence. Williams rolled his eyes, stood up and headed out of the room.

Williams opened the heavy wooden door and walked out into Crystal's large secretarial office. The whole place was redolent of a 1960s British government office, with wooden wall panelling and red leather on the doors. Various potted plants sat on top of grey metal filing cabinets. She had chosen the style of furnishings herself when she first started. A stack of books by authors such as Le Carré, Ian Fleming and Graham Greene lay lined up on wall shelves above a deep burgundy leather couch.

Crystal's employer stood in the doorway for a moment, unnoticed by the pretty blonde secretary or her tall visitor, who at that moment was sitting on the antique oak desk whispering in her ear and grinning. Williams watched and gave a little smile at the delightful display. *Ah, young love,* he thought to himself. Then his face became serious and had a touch of displeasure.

"Obviously you are working for free or have very little to do," Williams's tone was full of wrath, but the volume didn't break above his normal speaking pitch. The man shot up onto his feet and stood rigid, as though a pike had been inserted through his body – Vlad the Impaler style.

Williams walked around the scared man, looking up at him as he did so. The man stared forward, his line of sight above Williams's head. He had heard things about Williams and didn't want to end up like Mr Charles.

"Do you have something to do, Donald?" Williams asked. His tone had become softer but still rang with disapproval.

"Uhm, well, sir—" the man started, his mouth opening and

shutting in a panic, almost as if his brain was censoring any stupid words that were about to come out.

"Well here's some good news, Donald, I have a job for you. Find the cab that took Mr Steel to the bridge and bring the driver to me. How's that?" Williams smiled.

The man smiled awkwardly and set off for the door. "Uhm ... Just one thing, sir," he stuttered, "my name's not—" The man's sentence was cut short, for he realised that Williams didn't care. If he told him that his name was Donald, his name was Donald.

"What cabbie and who is Mr Steel?" 'Donald' dared to ask. But then he saw a look in Williams's eyes, then noticed the watch had been drawn from Williams's pocket. He decided there should be no more questions. "OK, no problem, boss, I am all over it." And with that, he was gone.

Williams opened the watch and checked the time. He wore a large grin as he sat on the corner of Crystal's desk.

"I do like him. Nice catch for you, my dear." He grinned at her and planted a small kiss on her left cheek, then he stood and headed for his office. On the way out, he raised a hand as if he was going to speak.

"—No problem," Crystal spoke first. "We have a batch of spare remotes heading in tomorrow. In the meantime, you have a spare next to your coffee, Mr W, sir." She grinned smugly.

Williams said nothing. He didn't need to. It was as if she knew already. He returned to his office and sat in his leather-bound chair, and it creaked with age. As he looked over at the two chairs facing the fireplace, his smile faded.

Even though Steel was an adversary, a thorn in his side, he was ultimately the only person he could call a friend. The only one who would not lie.

Williams thought back to their conversation that had lasted most of the night. They had talked about everything apart from work. That night they had been just two men enjoying a quiet drink by a blazing fire and sharing confidences.

The distracted man unknowingly picked up the remote and snapped it into two. Suddenly the door opened, and Crystal stood in the doorway, an angry glare on her face. Williams looked down at the carnage at his fingertips.

"Oops," he said shamefully.

Crystal walked over, carrying a strange-looking doll and placed it onto the desk. Williams looked at the ugly looking thing, then at Crystal.

"What the hell is this, my dear?" he asked with a panicked look, almost afraid to touch it.

Crystal picked it up and pulled the head off it. "It's called a stress doll. It's cheaper than a remote, and you can put a face on it." She pointed to the small plastic window where the face should be. Williams picked it up and pulled off its arms and then smiled.

"My dear, what would I do without you?" he said with a childish grin. Crystal left him alone with his new device and sat her desk. She smiled at a naughty thought that had just entered her head and then got back to work.

———

McCall and Tooms were heading for Bob's Diner. Something Steel had said had stuck with McCall. Perhaps they were looking in the wrong place. Maybe Amber simply had been in the wrong place at the wrong time.

The sun was high and blazed through the windshield, making driving difficult in some areas, because all she could see was the bright light and nothing else. She turned onto the FDR to avoid the brunt of the sunlight which was now behind them, but despite this, as they passed the mass of glass-fronted buildings, the sun reflected into the collage of windows causing a blinding a strobe effect, making McCall to close one eye. Traffic was its usual nose-to-tail gridlock, and Sam was sure that she had hit every traffic light they had come across. Steel's death had pissed her off, and the traffic wasn't helping settle her temper. Tooms had offered to drive, but the knifepoint stare she gave made him back off.

Steel had always maintained that the waitress was the key, and maybe he was right. They had been blindsided by Amber's agency job. It made everything make sense: *undercover agent killed on duty*. However, she knew things were never that simple – that neat.

Amber had been ripped apart to get answers from her. The problem was, maybe she didn't know what those answers were.

"Do we know who Tara Burke's previous roommate was?" McCall asked, breaking the silence. Tooms looked over at McCall with a blank expression which suddenly changed as he caught on to her trail of thought.

"The people who broke in were looking for someone – or something," Tooms said, pulling out his cell phone.

"What if they just got the wrong one? What if they didn't know the old roommate left?" McCall completed Tooms's thoughts. Tooms pressed the speed dial for Tony. After a short wait, Tony picked up.

"Tony, can you find out who the previous roommate of Tara's was?" he asked his friend. "Thanks, man, later." Tooms put the cell away and made himself comfortable in the Mustang's leather seat.

"He should have an answer in a couple of hours."

McCall nodded a response. Her concentration was locked onto the old lady in the Hummer SUV in front of them.

"Seriously, couldn't she have found anything bigger?"

McCall said, shaking her head as all they could see through the rear window was a pair of arms and the bob of her hair.

Tooms finally let out a laugh, which made McCall take her eyes from the road for a second.

"What?" she asked, trying to get rid of the urge to stick the siren on. Tooms just shook his head and smiled at the situation.

"You're not gonna put your lights on, because that old gal will panic, and we'll have a whole lot of shit to explain." His humorous reaction wasn't so much because he knew what she was thinking; it was the fact that he had had the same idea.

Eventually, the old woman pulled onto a side street and disappeared into the traffic. McCall cracked a smile: she had to admit that the image was quite amusing. She looked over at the Sat Nav on the display screen of the all-in-one media centre. The diner wasn't far, only around fifteen minutes away.

McCall parked on the other side of Adam Clayton Powell Jr. Boulevard, next to some electrical supermarket. The crossing led straight to the diner's front entrance. *Great access*, McCall thought. They got out of the car and headed over. Tooms's belly let out a growl, almost as if it knew they were close to food. McCall gave Tooms a surprised look, to which he just shrugged and smiled.

"Didn't you have breakfast?" McCall asked, then stopped and looked at her watch. It was quarter to twelve. She smiled and shook her head.

Inside the diner, it was starting to get busy. Three waitresses were running about taking orders, while a new chef tossed the burgers in the back. Kim was at the till making up some old guy's check. Her smile was broad and accentuated by the ruby red lipstick. McCall had to compliment her on her tactics: *big smile, big tip.*

The diner looked fuller and cleaner than the last time she was there. The staff even had new uniforms. McCall headed over to Kim, who was busy shoving a five-dollar bill into a glass jar that had a slit in the lid and had a handwritten sign held on with tape. *Tips are always welcome* was written in thick black ink and fancy lettering.

"Miss Washington, the place looks great, where did the money come from?" McCall asked suspiciously. Kim smiled as the two detectives approached.

"Detective McCall, are you guys stoppin' by for a free lunch? It's the least we can do after you got rid of that nasty son of a bitch." Kim said, passing some menus over. McCall could see Tooms eyeing up the three huge burgers that one of the waitresses was taking to a city worker and his crew. Tooms held his stomach as it rumbled into life. Kim smiled, and McCall gave him a swift elbow to the side.

"Well, our dirtbag boss made the mistake of putting everything he had stolen off of us, and his suppliers in a kitty," Kim explained. "Unfortunately, he named it 'Diner petty cash'." Kim shrugged and raised her hands.

McCall gave her a confused look. "So, how did you get hold of it?" McCall watched her closely as she prepared another check, this time for a couple sitting at the back. The detective was impressed that Kim knew they were ready to pay without them even telling her.

"As smart as he thought he was, he wasn't." Kim had a skip in her voice. "The restaurant is actually in my name. If something happens, I take the fall. Nice of him, don't you think?"

"I didn't find out until he got locked up," the waitress continued. "That's when a guy from the bank came around here. It appears that our boss had wanted to put this place up for his bail, but he couldn't because he had forgotten about what he had done. The bank guy explained the situation. Later, I found the checking account details and checked it out. Even that was in my name. I mean, what an idiot." Kim laughed, passing over the check to a brunette waitress.

"I paid off all the restaurant's debts and got new help. Now we are rakin' its in." Kim smiled broadly as a middle-aged priest came in and sat in one of the stalls. He waved and smiled back.

McCall's smile faded, and she pulled out her notebook. "Kim, have you seen or spoken to Tara since the last time she was on shift?" McCall spoke softly but with a serious tone.

Kim shook her head. She didn't pause to think about it. "No. Sorry, but the last time I saw her was on that horrible day. I take it you have no leads on her roommate's killer?" She suddenly scowled at McCall. "You're not thinkin' she did it, are you?" Kim looked angry.

"No," Sam reassured her. "But we think she may be in a lot of trouble, and we would like her to come in for her own safety." McCall's tone and facial expression was full of concern.

However, Kim shook her head. "Look, I am sorry, Detective, but I have no idea where she is. I would love to say she has family someplace, but she ain't." Kim's face lit up as she had an idea. "Did you try her old roommate?"

"No, not yet, do you have a name? Maybe an address?" McCall said calmly, not wanting to give away the secret calculations she was making in her head.

"Sorry, Detective McCall, I don't have an address, but his name is Jake ... Jake Harding," Kim told her, smiling again.

"I don't suppose you could give us a description of this Jake Harding?" Tooms asked, his eyes darting back and forth to the kitchen.

Kim thought for a moment and disappeared to a noticeboard that hung on a back wall. It was full of photographs of the staff with tourists, and a couple of famous people who

278

had dared to eat there. She returned, holding a photograph to her chest.

"Here, this was taken last Christmas," Kim said, smiling as she looked at the photograph briefly and handed it over to McCall, who took it and smiled graciously.

However, Sam's smile faded as she recognised the man from the photograph.

"And this is Jake Harding, her former roommate?" McCall asked. She passed the photo to Tooms.

"Yes, why?" Kim shot Sam McCall a confused look, suddenly feeling her legs begin to shake. "What's happened?"

The look on McCall's face turn to one of those you see just before giving bad news. Kim thought she was going to puke.

"The man in the photo was found wandering the streets. He had lost his memory." As McCall spoke, Kim's eyes lit up.

"Unfortunately, he was covered in blood and had no memory of whose blood it was," Sam continued. "He wasn't far from where Amber was murdered." McCall watched as Kim's legs became unstable. It struck Tooms that for some reason, she was overly concerned. Was its fear for Tara or fear for their John Doe?

"He was taken from a safe house and possibly killed, most likely by those who had killed Amber," Tooms said, hoping for a reaction, and he got one.

Kim threw up before she fainted. All the patrons looked over suddenly, more concerned about getting their food, than Kim having received bad news.

"It's OK, folks, she got some bad news, that's all," Tooms explained to the worried-looking customers. They all grumbled at the lack of excitement, and those who had stood up to look retook their seats. Two of the waitresses came to her aid, one holding a glass of water while the other helped her to a seat. McCall took the glass and smiled at the small Hispanic girl.

"Here, drink this," McCall said, holding the glass to Kim's mouth. She was still shaken up and slightly dazed from the shock. Kim took a couple of sips before pushing McCall's hand away.

"Are you sure it's him?" Kim asked, her voice full of emotion. Tooms looked down at McCall, interested in what she would say.

"We don't know yet. We are still waiting for Forensics to make an ID. But at least now we have a name, so thank you." McCall's smile was gentle and warm.

The unhappy waitress stared into McCall's large gentle eyes and felt almost at ease.

"And what about Tara. Could she be—?" Kim looked away. She didn't want to say those words, the words nobody ever wants to hear. McCall held Kim by the shoulders and squeezed slightly, a comforting trick her father had done so many times.

"We don't know, but I have the feeling that she is somewhere safe. She seems to be a smart woman. So no, I don't think she is dead."

Kim looked up at McCall and smiled as she wiped away a small tear from her left cheek.

McCall stood up and looked down on Kim. "Please, if she contacts you, get her to call me. We can keep her safe." McCall turned just in time to see Tooms pick up a wrapped burger. She scowled at him as they made their way out.

"When the hell did you order that?" she asked him, confused. Tooms just smiled and opened the door for her.

"Hands quicker than the eye, McCall, hands quicker than the eye!"

CHAPTER THIRTY

A COOL WESTERLY BREEZE SKIPPED ACROSS THE LAKE. There was a calm silence in the air. High above, wandering seagulls hovered in the warm sunshine, scouring the land for their next meal. Anglers sat on the riverbank; carbon-fibre rods held on stands as their masters sat idly. In the distance, cars hurtled past on the freeway that led back to the city. Southampton was green and open. As part of the Hamptons, it smelt of money as much as it did of fresh air. There were large estates with long drives—some were so long they almost seemed like freeways.

Some people had moorings on the lake: long wooden piers that held expensive weekend playthings. Long-nosed powerboats, with shiny white hulls and padded seating. One large estate had a helicopter pad; its dull, grey concrete was adorned with a large yellow circle and a large painted H in the centre denoting the helipad. A black Dauphin helicopter sat proud on its grey concrete. The shine of the gloss frame made it glow as brightly as the midday sun. A man on a sit-on lawnmower powered past, paying the world around him no mind. He seemed content on his red machine.

A pair of blue dungarees covered his red-and-blue chequered shirt. A blue Yankees baseball cap hid most of his features. A black beard with streaks of grey made him look older, probably older than he really was. He drove on, lending his gaze to the TV show on his tablet that sat on a handlebar mount. The sound of the blades trimming above the acres of grass was the only noise for miles. The house itself was late 1900s: a large sandstone building, with tall windows and a grey tiled roof. A gravel turning circle for the drivers encircled a statue of Eros. Rose bushes and small hedgerows broke the lines between gravel and grass.

The inside of the house had been kept to its original design. The walls were half white plaster above, with the lower part covered with dark wooden panels. Sometimes there was just the panelling. Polished brass fittings and works of art were scattered throughout the place. Thick, heavy maroon carpeting stretched across the public room areas and winding staircase to the upper floors. The hallways and corridors remained bare wood, with only a thin layer of wax as cover.

It had more of a 'stately home' feel to it than that of a private dwelling. Above the main entrance, a stone coat of arms sat proudly: a shield with a chevron centre. To the left was a crown, to the right a gryphon. Below was a strange-looking eagle. Some may even have called it a fiery bird of prey. The same crest was etched into the wood of the thick bannister rails. But there the words stood out. Written in a deep engraved scrolling script were the words: *In Causa, Invenire Vires,* meaning *In Cause, we find strength.*

The house was seemingly quiet. Staff moved about following their daily routines. The sound of a radio from the kitchen was only a murmur. A man in a black suit exited the kitchen, stopping halfway to converse with the two women chefs inside.

"You know I only have eyes for you, ladies," he said.

They laughed, and he went on his way, leaving the door to close slowly on its hinge. The middle-aged man was of average build and height. His expensive suit fitted well, and his stay-bright shoes glistened as they caught the light from the windows. He carried a large tray that held a coffee pot, milk and sugar in silver set. A large domed food cover sparkled, polished to perfection. He headed down a corridor that seemed to have a hundred windows. He felt the warmth of the sunlight, and it felt good. To his front was a doorway to the dining room. To his right, there was another door that resembled one of the panels. The man pushed the door open with his foot and took the stone staircase down to the old cellar.

The cellar was strangely warm. Not a humid, stifling warm, but a comfortable warmth. Its thick heavy walls were straight with six rooms on either side. The doorways were arched with heavyset wooden doors. Several of them housed wine in environmentally controlled conditions: one room was for red wines and another for whites and champagnes.

He headed casually for the last door on the right. He stopped in front of a heavy steel door. This had a keypad entry, which was embedded in the wall next to the door. The man balanced the tray while he typed in the numbers. He should have put the tray down and stood ready for any eventuality. He should have remembered who was inside.

Everything happened lightning fast. The man looked up in surprise as the door was ripped open. The tray was thrust upwards into his face. He yelled as the hot coffee covered his left side, the scalding pain making him cringe. Then the heavy tray came back at him, this time under control. Its impact sent him hurtling against the opposite door. He was dazed and confused. Two powerful hands grabbed his jacket and threw him into the cell. The door slammed shut with a metallic thud that echoed around the cellar.

The newly imprisoned character in the black suit sat on the floor against a small bed. He tried to stand but found his legs could barely hold him. A shaky hand checked his forehead for damage, and he sighed with relief at the absence of blood. He took a moment to get his head straight, then sucked in a lungful of air, kept it for a moment then released it slowly. Carefully, he stood up, using the wall as support. He smiled as he stood confidently. The smile faded as he noticed the control panel at his side had been destroyed. Quickly he checked his pockets: his wallet, sidearm and car keys were missing. The man sat down heavily on the bed. He had no contact with upstairs, and his guest had just broken out. Looking at the tuna sandwich on the floor, he just shrugged. Knowing he would be there a while, he decided to tuck in.

Almost an hour had passed until someone came down. It was a waiter who had sounded the alarm. He had noticed the signs of struggle as he went to get the wine for the evening meal. The tray that was leaning up against the wall had a strange imprint on the metal. The coffee set was strewn across the concrete floor, shattered. They found the man on the bed, with his arm folded underneath his head. His face was swollen, and the signs of scalding on his skin told them the story of what had happened.

Later, an old Oriental man sat in a high-backed chair. It was almost a throne, made of gold-coloured wood, with red velvet cushioning. He was in his mid-sixties, possibly older, as his healthy complexion hid his years. His office was huge, a twenty-by-twenty space with dark wood bookshelves covering the walls. To the left, a large blue marble fireplace with a brass guard broke up the dark wood and the blood-red carpet. His desk was made of ebony and had Oriental carvings. The telephone was made of brass and green marble, and the desk lamp was designed as an ebony dragon curling around a woman, whose outstretched arms held the silk shade. A strong smell of incense hung in the air, plus there was the scent of flowers and some sort of wood aroma. The old man sat with his eyes shut. His index fingers were pressed together and held against his lips, almost as if he was meditating, or contemplating.

The door to this office opened, and an injured man stepped in, limping, a cold, damp cloth held close to his face. The Oriental man said nothing. He just sat there with his eyes still closed.

"Uhm sorry, sir," the unfortunate guard fumbled with his words. "Lord Steel ... Lord Steel, he—" He was nervous at having to deliver his news.

The old man opened his eyes and smiled. "It's not your fault," he told his servant. "We underestimated his will. Something is driving our boy. At least we know he has all his instincts back. He knows friend from foe." The old Oriental man stood up and walked over to the injured guard and rested a small hand on the man's shoulder.

"How do we know that, sir?" the man asked his employer.

The old man smiled again. "Because, if he didn't, you'd be dead."

The guard swallowed hard.

———

Tony had waited in line for a hotdog for what seemed like forever. Even though the sun was giving off a pleasant warmth, standing around almost motionless made him aware of the slight crisp wind. Five people stood in line, and he was number four. Impatiently, the crowd looked over at the woman who getting served. Tony looked over at the cart and noted the way her food was being stacked up. She was a short, thin lady, somewhere in her late eighties Tony estimated. Her long fake leopard-skin coat was old and had seen better days. She paid and left with her arms full of food. Tony turned and watched her as she headed towards a group of other pensioners, who were sitting across the road in a large eight-seater cab.

He smiled and shook his head as he heard the suddenly raised voices about who got what. The next woman was quick: 'a dog with onions' was all she wanted—a small, but simple request, that took less than a minute. Tony smiled as he neared the stall. He didn't need to order, for the tall man behind the counter smiled and pulled up one large dog with 'the works.' Tony paid as well as sticking a five-dollar note in the tips jar before saying his farewells. He stopped before entering the precinct and looked around at the busy life before him. People and traffic were moving at different paces, but all had the same sort of purpose. As he watched, he saw someone in the distance. The figure looked like – Steel. It was just a shape of a person because it was far away, but it looked like the detective. As the figure grew closer, Tony grew excited as he saw the figure walk past on the other side of the street. Tony went to call out but stopped himself as he realised his mistake, remembering his friend's demise. Tony remembered the footage he had seen from the cameras. There was no doubt it had been Steel that had plunged from the bridge. Despite this, the hooded figure had Steel's build, even the way he carried himself had something familiar about it. Tony remembered that Steel liked to disguise himself, but this wasn't him, not this time, he was gone. There had been witnesses who had seen him jump – or fall!

The stranger was just a tall guy dressed all in black with a long black coat with a hood. The hooded figure was scruffy, his clothes worn and dirty. Tony shook his head to clear his thoughts. Why was he seeing the ghost of Steel and not that of Amber? Why was he missing John Steel more than his deceased girlfriend? Tony shrugged and stepped inside the large old building of the 11th Precinct. The hooded figure stopped and looked across at the precinct, almost as if the man was deciding. The cowl of the hood placed the man's face into shadow, and the long cut of the coat covered all but the military-style boots. The figure just stared for a moment. Passers-by just seemed to move through him as though he wasn't there. A tour bus hurtled past, and he was gone.

Inside the building, Tony sat at his desk just as there was an electronic *ping* from his computer. He placed the hotdog down on a clear space of his desk and searched for the email he had just gotten. He smiled as he saw that it was a message from Traffic, with five attachments: it was the CCTV footage from the bridge—five views from different cameras. Three were street views, and the others were from the bridge. Coreman was at the ME's trying to get anything from CSU on any of the cases. Tony had sent him because he was a new face, a face that hadn't pissed them off – yet.

He played the footage in turn. The street views seemed uneventful: just lots of early-morning traffic. Then he opened the next attachment and sat back to watch. Grabbing his meal, he settled down for another hour of nothing. Tony went to bite into the bread and sausage when he stopped. His mouth was still open as he saw the yellow cab stop suddenly and a darkened figure got out.

Tony leant forward and placed the hotdog back down as he watched. He saw the figure bend forward and throw up, and then climb up onto the ledge. Tony stopped breathing. His eyes were wide as he was watched the final moments of Steel's life.

He moved closer to the monitor, still holding the same breath as if he was afraid to exhale. His unblinking eyes focused on the darkened figure until it vanished from view.

Detective Tone Marinelli sat back in his chair, feeling as though he himself had felt the impact of Steel's body hitting the water. He looked around, almost panicked at what he had seen. He wiped the moisture from his eyes: tears that had formed from staring for too long. Finally, he released that stale breath that he had been holding onto.

His eyes went back to the screen. Now the taxi had gone, and people had started to gather. Tony couldn't do anything but watch. His instincts told him to stop watching and find that cab. But he was frozen. He had just watched his friend jump to his death, and he was lost as to what he should do.

Tony's desk phone began to ring. The sudden alarm made him jump, bringing him back to reality. It was Tooms. Just a quick call to say they were going to Kim Washington's apartment. It was a friendly check-in, but Tony knew that Tooms had other motives for calling. Tooms was worried about him. Ever since they had found Amber, he knew he had been different, unfocused. By rights, he shouldn't have been on the case, but everyone had managed to convince the captain that his relationship to the victim wasn't a problem—everyone, including Steel.

The phone conversation was short. Tooms had asked if he had anything new. Tony had lied and said, "No." Not so much a lie, as a holding back of information for the right reasons. He couldn't risk them being unfocused if there was a situation. He could see McCall had taken Steel's death badly, even though she tried to hide it. He would wait until his two colleagues were back.

Tony looked back at the monitor. His head had lost its

muzziness. He was thinking clearly again. He picked up the mug and drained the last dregs of the hour cold coffee.

"OK, Mr Cab Driver, where are you, and who are you?" Tony muttered, going back to look over the footage again. This time his focus was on the cab. The driver had been the last person to see Steel alive. The cabby knew where he'd picked up Steel from, and thus where he had been. If they could find the driver, maybe they could find the killer.

The process was long. He had to send the footage to the Tech department so that they could look for anything they might have on the cab. On his monitor, all the images were too small to see things properly, and he didn't have the software to enhance the views. A young guy in a grey suit and yellow T-shirt and white deck shoes had worked on his computer. In the half-hour Tony had waited he had looked hard at the street cams, trying to detect the direction from which the cab had come from.

Tony looked up to see the tech guy approach with a brown folder in his hand. Tony almost forgot about the pencil that he held in his mouth, making him look like a dog with a bone. As he began to talk, the yellow HB fell to his desk with a small clatter. He ignored it and stood up.

"Did you get anything?" Tony asked, almost excitedly.

The man smiled and handed over the file. Tony opened the flap and flicked through the pictures.

"Thanks, they'll be a great help," Tony said, looking up at the man and smiling broadly.

Tony retook his seat and began to search through the blown-up stills. The smile faded as he saw that it was Steel getting out of the cab. Then he froze at one of the stills. He could see what appeared to be Steel forcing himself to be sick, by sticking his fingers down his throat. Had he known something?

Tony shook off the thought and concentrated on the cab. There in one still was a shot of the cab's rear. He had the licence plate and the medallion number from where it was sprayed on the trunk. Tony put the pencil back in his mouth and ran the medallion number through his system. It didn't take long before it spat out a name and DMV photograph.

"OK, Mr David Kidd, let's see where you're at." Tony's voice was muffled by the stick of wood and graphite. The cab belonged to a company on the West Side. Tony grabbed his gun and his badge. Taking his jacket from the back of his chair, he swung it on and headed for the elevator. Tony took his cell phone from his pocket and pressed the fresh number on the speed dial.

"Coreman? It's Tony. Meet me at this address."

CHAPTER THIRTY-ONE

THE AFTERNOON SUN BEGAN TO COOL, AND THE TRAFFIC IN Harlem began to build up. For most, it was time to head home, and for others, it was nearly time to start the late shift. New York – like so many other cities, was always on the move: alive and active. Shift work and tourists kept the city in momentum. But for a few of them, it was never-ending, such as double shifters, or those with too many jobs and not enough time to do them. The economy was in a bad place, not enough cash for people to live but the government asking for more. Cuts to police, the military and small business had left its mark.

The sea of yellow metal washed down the busy streets as taxis carried their fares. The sidewalks were awash with people walking hurriedly for *that* station, to catch *that* train. A movement of people oblivious to others, who were busy in their own little worlds. What better place to hide?

The hooded figure moved amongst them almost as if he wasn't there at all. He moved with ease through the crowds of people, moving no quicker than a normal stroll. His body would twist and turn gracefully to avoid those awkward shoulder impacts.

This lone character made his way to a darkened alley. Clouds of white steam rose up from the subway vents, successfully concealing his entrance into the passageway. The passage he walked down was long, the breadth of the two adjoining buildings, which also gave him plenty of shadows to disappear into.

Eventually the alley it led to took him to a group of old warehouse buildings, one of which had three roller doors. It was an old building, built in the late '40s. The doors were new, but it seemed as if the green of the paint was faded and weathered camouflage for the untrained eye. The figure hurried up to the building and climbed the fire escape to the roof, before disappearing. The red brick construction stood four storeys tall and was untouched by graffiti. The street itself had an unloved feel about it. Bits of paper and a couple of paper cups danced across the concrete, carried by the wind like an invisible child was kicking them around. The breeze was a slight and from the west. The apparent normality of the place was broken by one of the roller doors screeching open. As it reached a good height, a blacked-out Aston Martin Lagonda SUV nosed out as the door began to come down again. The car's heavy, snub-nosed front made it look angry and foreboding. Its thin, almost *peering* headlamps added something animalistic to the vehicle. The paint finish was a strange matt black. There were no chrome or bare metal parts. This vehicle had been built for stealth and power. It took off into the distance with a throaty roar of its V12 engine and a scream of tyres.

The street was silent once more. The breeze picked up again, chasing more garbage down the street.

———

McCall had forced her car through the maddening traffic. She had parked the Mustang at the nearest available spot, which was halfway down the street. The street itself was calm compared with the main highways. But the volume of parked— or in some cases abandoned—cars discouraged people from staying long. McCall pulled her coat tightly around herself as the westerly breeze picked up. Even though the buildings acted as a windbreak, the cold air always found a way.

McCall was hoping for some good news from Tony after the phone call. He had said something about a breakthrough on the cab, but she had learned not to get her hopes up. She had found out far too often that life often has a wicked sense of humour.

She rechecked her notebook for the address of Kim's apartment. The red-brick building looked like all the rest, apart from the fact that the fire escapes were painted dark green.

The detectives made their way up the small steps and towards a wood-and-glass door. The door was also green but not wide. Tooms held the door open for a young blonde-haired woman who was struggling with her luggage. As she finally managed to pull her pink suitcase out from the doorway, she nodded at them. Tooms smiled back and entered the hallway while McCall stepped to the side to let the woman drag her case down. The woman smiled at McCall. She wore overly large sunglasses that covered her eyes and part of her face. McCall returned a sympathetic smile, feeling almost jealous of the woman, who was obviously going away on a trip.

As McCall entered the small lobby, she stopped dead. She turned slightly, almost as if a voice in her head had just called to her. McCall ran out, just in time to see the woman get into a yellow cab. Everything seemed to slow down, almost as if she were watching a movie. The woman turned slightly before getting in, and her face had turned pale with the fear of being caught.

McCall had reached the bottom of the steps, just as the cab's door closed. That's when she saw the driver, who was smiling at her. She felt a chill as she realised this was a victorious smirk and not an expression of friendship. His dark skin seemed to shine as the sunlight reflected off it. His long dreadlocks were falling over his shoulders, the multi-coloured beads matching his woollen cap. The driver stepped on the gas just as McCall's hand was near to the door handle. She began to run after the cab but lost it as the driver turned onto the main street. McCall went to reach for her gun but stopped herself in time. She could see the headlines now: *Cop shoots cabbie.* The press would have a field day. She just stood and watched the exhaust fumes until they faded into nothing.

Tooms came running out. He wore a confused look as he followed her gaze down the street.

"What's up?" he asked, looking around to see what the problem was.

"I think that was our girl. She's dyed her hair, but I know it was her." McCall cursed herself. She looked up at Tooms with a frown. He knew that expression meant that things had just gotten worse.

"What...what is it?" he asked, almost afraid to know.

"I think we just found the cab that dropped Steel at the bridge. The problem is, she's in it," McCall said, turning back to the main street. Their only hope now was that Tony did indeed have something. If not, then they might be looking for another body sometime soon: the body of Tara Burke. McCall felt her jacket pocket vibrate and pulled out her cell phone. It was a text message from Tina Franks at the ME's office.

"Tina's got something for us," McCall said, showing the

phone's display to Tooms. He nodded, and they both headed back to her car. There was no point trying to chase the cab. It and the girl were long gone. Tony said he had something on the driver. McCall felt a ray of hope. Even though things seemed bleak, they were starting to look up. Now they had leads to follow.

———

Tara rearranged her seating position and put on her safety belt. She didn't look back. She didn't want the cabbie to think there was anything wrong. Tara looked out of the window. Watched the world go by.

"So, where'd you wanna go, miss?" the man shouted back through the intercom system in the dividing safety glass, his gaze directed firmly on the traffic ahead. Tara noticed the man was completely secure. She figured he had been held up too many times. Tara had heard about cabbies getting rolled over by bogus fares, some of the many stories she had heard at the diner.

"Grand Central, please," she replied, leaning forward to make herself heard. The driver nodded, and she saw him smile in the rear-view mirror.

"Good time for a holiday. Going somewhere special? Jamaica or Hawaii, perhaps?" He laughed, a tone of jealousy in his voice.

She smiled broadly and shook her head. "No, just visiting family upstate," she lied, but she concealed the truth well. Almost as if she believed there really was someone out there for her.

"Family is very important. I myself have a wife and three beautiful daughters," he said proudly, pointing to a photograph that was taped on the dashboard. It was of a pretty woman with three young girls. The eldest must have been around fifteen and the youngest five. Tara smiled at the photograph. She had dreamed of having a family with the right man someday. A home with a white picket fence and lots of kids playing in the yard.

Her smile faded, and she stared out of the window. From then onwards, the only conversation was from the cabbie. She couldn't believe a man could talk so much. She just stared, but not out of the window, but into her dreams. She saw only those white picket fences.

The vehicle hit a small pothole which crashed Tara back to reality. She pulled out her phone and checked for any new messages. The inbox only held the last message, one she had received days ago. She closed the phone down and looked up at the driver, who was checking something on his phone. Curiosity got the better of her. Tara leant forward as if to check something in her case. That's when she saw the display on his phone. Luckily the thing was massive, and the words were clear: *Package on route.*

Tara sat back in a panic. Something was badly wrong. She reached for the door handle, but the deadbolts were on. She tugged frantically at the opening handle, but nothing happened.

She was trapped. They had found her.

Tara looked over at the driver, who was smiling proudly. His head was rocking side to side as if he were singing to himself.

Tara took off her seat belt and leant back to kick out the windows. This made the man laugh even harder. Her shoes struck the glass, but the window just rocked with the impact. Now she was sweating with fear. Beads of fresh perspiration poured out of her with every effort. She started to feel faint.

The world began to spin. All the while, the cab driver's voice boomed through the intercom.

"Don't worry, miss. You give them what they want, and I am sure everything will be fine." His voice had a skip to it—as though he was getting off on her dilemma.

"Who are you? Who are they?" Her words began to slur, and she slipped into her dreams.

All she could see were those kids and the picket fence.

———

A throaty wail filled the corridors as the sound of James Brown's music blared from one of the rooms at the city morgue. McCall and Tooms stepped out of the elevator and was greeted by a chorus of "You gotta, gotta, give me some..." as they walked briskly towards Tina's door. Tooms looked down at McCall, who was grinning and shaking her head in disbelief.

"I guess she's done with her backlog," McCall announced, recognising the tune as a victory announcement. As they entered the room, they found Tina pouring a coffee from her small machine that was on a long table next to her desk. She hadn't noticed the two detectives standing in her office's doorway, watching as she shook her shapely rear in time with the music.

"I thought it would have been champagne you were drinking," McCall shouted over the din. Tina turned and smiled happily before turning off the stereo. Tina looked fresh, but there was a sadness in her eyes that didn't match the smile. The smile faded.

"Backlog done, CSU and this office have done the impossible again." Tina's words sounded victorious. However, there was something in her body language that didn't match her apparent joy.

"OK," she began. "First we got the blood work from the shirt. It's a match to Amber." Tina passed a brown file to McCall, who opened it up and held it so Tooms could read it as well.

"So, he killed her?" Tooms said, almost disappointed and confused.

"No. It just shows he came into contact with her, but he was there." Tina picked up another file. "This is the report on Amber. She was drugged. She had high doses of some weird cocktail. A mix that renders the patient conscious but unable to move. She was completely awake while they butchered her." Tina was almost in tears as she explained the way she figured they had done it. "They had started at the feet and worked upwards. Taking their time so that she didn't pass out."

Then she picked up another file. Her hands were trembling as she handed it to McCall. As McCall took it, she felt Tina's grip on the thin brown card, almost as if she didn't want to show her. McCall looked into Tina's glassy eyes.

"I am sorry," Tina spoke with a soft broken voice. McCall opened the file and just stared at the figures and long words.

"We checked the vomit and blood found at the scene on the bridge. I think he did it on purpose so that we would have something to work on. He knew he was going in the river and knew the chances of us getting anything if his body was found," Tina tried to explain without hurting McCall's feelings. She could see McCall was rocking on her feet before Tooms pulled round a chair for her to sit on.

"From our analysis, we found that Steel had snake venom in his system. I can't say how he got it, but there was traces of bottled water in the vomit. My guess is he drank a laced glass of water. The dose was high, so without treatment, he would have been dead in minutes, maybe an hour." Tina sat on the stainless-steel operating table. She could see the pain in McCall's eyes.

All the time, McCall had found comfort in the fact that Steel's body had not been found. She had almost been expecting him to turn up in some damned disguise like he had done on their first case together. McCall shook her head as if denying it would make it untrue.

"I am sorry, Sam. He's gone, and he's not coming back." Tina fought away the lump in her throat.

McCall nodded and shot her a quick sympathetic smile. Apart from her red eyes, she was solid. Her mind was on the job and if that meant grieving later then so be it. Tina walked over to a table on which lay the body of the agent from the hotel.

"This guy, however, is a different story. Gunshots starting at the feet. We thought this was a slow and methodical job." Tina voice sounded as if there were more questions than answers. "The gunshot to the head was first," she said, pointing to the medium size bullet hole in the man's skull.

McCall shot her a puzzled look. "If he was already dead, then why do this?" McCall asked, suddenly wishing she hadn't come here. She looked over at the peaceful-looking corpse. Even after so much suffering, he still looked at ease. McCall closed her eyes for a moment, trying to take everything in. Sorting it all out like a murder board in her head. Suddenly her eyes opened. There was a shocked look on her face.

"We ran his prints, he worked for the Feds, but nobody's saying who else he was working for." Tina's words rang with a hard tone. She was sick of the body count on this case.

"This was a cover-up," McCall said, thinking as she talked. "They wanted Brooke, but they wanted someone else to think they had interrogated the agent as well. Someone grabbed Brooke while she was in a safe house. They thought she knew something because she was Amber's handler." McCall paced about like a tiger in a cage, her mind computing all the new data. Then she looked up—the scared look was back.

"The question is...who's got her?" her words trembled as one name sprung to mind, and she just hoped to God she was wrong.

Mr Williams.

CHAPTER THIRTY-TWO

Tony pulled up outside the taxi company's premises. The once pale blue sky was becoming a darker, with streaks of purple gathering on the horizon. Cloud formations had begun to taint the once clear heavens. The evening would be a cold one, but the night had been promised to be dry. The front passenger door opened, and Coreman got in. Tony said nothing at first. In fact, he didn't even look around to acknowledge the new detective, for his gaze was on the cab company's garages, and he was watching the vehicles coming and going.

They were looking for a Checker Sedan: a big old car used back in the '50s through to the '80s. The sort of car you expect to see in an old movie or cruising around Cuba or some other place south of the border. Tony didn't need a picture. He had one firmly in his mind, but he needed something to show around.

Tony took out a picture of their suspect and passed it to Coreman to look at. Coreman took the piece of paper and looked at the DMV photograph. He had to admit that the man did look serious, but then, with the restrictions made on what identification photographs should look like, everyone looks like a criminal. No smiling, no glasses, you just must glare at the camera. The older of the two detectives had spoken with Tooms earlier after he had found the right taxi firm. Tooms had told him to stay put until he and McCall got there. Smiling to himself, Tony had remembered the three-way conversation. Tooms had been the relay for McCall, passing messages back and forth. He had reckoned McCall had been driving at the time.

Tony leant forward, his fingers gripping the leather of the Dodge's steering wheel impatiently. They had sat still for a long time and had seen vehicles come and go. Some of them three or four times. But there had been no Checker insight.

"Come on," Tony said, getting out of the car. Coreman looked at him strangely, almost speechless at Tony's action.

"Sorry, but Tooms told us to wait," Coreman said nervously. Tony looked at Coreman who was still sitting in the car.

"I'm just going in to get a look, maybe get an idea where this asshole might be," Tony growled. He was regretting having Coreman there. The man was green, but that was only the 'first-month blues. That awful first month when you don't know how to act, or what to say. The first month of getting coffee for everyone and being looked at with suspicious eyes. *Will he make it? Will he be able to handle himself?* or more importantly, *has he got my back?* Tony's regret was more a question of *has he got my back?* the other questions were, at that point irrelevant.

The two detectives crossed the busy road and headed towards the cab office. Tony resisted getting his shield out: the last thing he needed to do was to spook anyone. Looking around, he guessed that most of the drivers were there illegally, without the correct permits, but that was someone else's problem. Tony put a strut into his walk and hoped the new guy wouldn't fuck things up.

The cab company's garage was large, with enough room for around twenty-five vehicles. There was a small office in the corner with two large windows and a blue wooden door between them. The whole place reeked of exhaust fumes and fuel. A couple of drivers were heading for another room next to the office. Tony figured that was a restroom or locker room.

Tony could see inside the brightly lit office. A woman with sky-blue hair and a love for doughnuts sat at a control desk. There were two phones, a stick microphone and a computer with three monitors on a long pale wooden desk. Behind her sat a smaller man at another desk. This also had a phone and a monitor. He was in his late fifties, wearing a bad Hawaiian green shirt and an even worse comb-over. The little guy appeared to be the boss. He wasn't the owner, merely the ringmaster.

The senior detective had around fourteen steps to walk in which he had to come up with a good cover story. He knew it was a risk not waiting for McCall and Tooms, but he knew he had to do something, and sitting in the car wasn't getting things done. As they got to five feet away, Tony was happy, for he had a plan. However, time would tell if it was a good one.

Tony knocked on the door and waited for permission to enter.

"Come in!" yelled a surprisingly deep voice—presumably it was the only man they'd seen in the office, or so Tony hoped. He opened the door, and the two men entered, both smiling broadly.

"Yeah, what do you want?" the small fiftyish man in the Hawaiian shirt said, shoving half a Cuban cigar into his mouth. He had a Rolex and enough gold on his fingers to open his own pawn shop.

"Sorry to trouble you, but we are looking for one of your drivers, we need to talk to him," Tony began cheerfully.

The man gave the two detectives a suspicious glance. His eyes were large, and so was his dome-like head, from which miserable black strands of hair hung down.

"Sorry, don't know him," the man growled, leaning back in his chair.

Tony shot the man a confused look.

"But we—"

"—We were hoping he would be here," interrupted Coreman quickly. "We have the badge number for him, you see. We had just come back from our honeymoon and left something in the cab. We have looked all over, and yours is the last one to check. Please!"

Tony shot Coreman a shocked look, then smiled and put his arm around the new guy in a loving gesture. The small guy shook his head in disgust and waved them forward.

"So, tell me, what you two lovebirds got?" the man asked. The woman smiled at the two men affectionately. Coreman passed over a scrap of paper that had the cab's medallion number on it. The man took the paper and typed the number into his computer.

"8Z56, yeah, that's old David Kidd's rig." The man looked up at the clock, noting that it was nearly five. "He should be back any minute now." He chewed on the hand-rolled tobacco.

Tony smiled and thanked him before leaving the office. Coreman gave a quick, friendly wave and followed.

"Nice job in there, newbie," Tony said, heading for the way out. Coreman just smiled and nodded. He was almost afraid to speak in case he ruined the moment.

They waited for another fifteen minutes. Both men leant against the wall like schoolkids waiting to see the headmaster. The crisp wind forced both men to pull their jackets tightly around them, but all the while, they didn't falter from their observation of the street. Tony looked over to see a yellow cab approaching. He looked at the licence plate and the illuminated sign on the roof. 8Z56 stood out on the freshly washed vehicle. Tony looked at the car for a second, puzzled. Behind him, on the street, McCall had parked. Both she and Tooms were heading his way fast.

"What we got?" McCall asked as she ducked in with the rest of them.

"We got eyes on the taxi, were just waiting for the coast to clear," Coreman said proudly.

"Have we got a name for our guy?" she asked. Her voice was hard, with a hint of blood lust.

"David Kidd," Tony answered, his gaze fixed on the group. McCall looked over at a group of cars and their drivers, who were laughing and joking at shift change, sharing stories of their busy day. McCall walked in. The others followed close behind.

"I am Detective McCall; we're looking for David Kidd." She spoke firmly, with not a hint of emotion. If she hadn't bottled everything up, the next move could be her last as a cop. McCall looked at all the men who were just standing there. Their expressions had faded into stone.

"I am David Kidd, what's the problem, Detective?" one of the men said to her. McCall shot a look at Tony, then back to the man who called himself Kidd.

"Sorry, is your cab number 8Z56?" she asked, confused. Kidd looked at her, puzzled.

"Yes, that's my number, and my cab is over there." He pointed to a yellow Ford Crown Victoria.

"Thank you, sir, sorry for the inconvenience," McCall said, before turning and heading off. Tony looked at the drivers and then at McCall, a look of complete confusion on his face.

"Hey, McCall, what's going on? We got the guy!" Tony

yelled as he chased after her. McCall stopped and looked round to face Tony.

"Tony, we saw the guy today on film. He was driving a yellow Checker Sedan, and this guy has a Ford Crown Victoria. Also, I know it's not our guy because the person we saw was a black guy with dreadlocks, while your guy is a three-hundred-pound Hawaiian," she growled before heading back to her car.

———

Tara Burke began to stir. Her eyes felt heavy, and her vision was blurred. She could feel the movement of the car as it thumped along the busy streets. If anyone was to look inside, they would think she was drunk or tired. The world around her seemed to move slowly, the sounds muffled as if she was listening to them from underwater. Her eyes felt heavy, and all she wanted to do was sleep. Slowly her eyes closed, and she was under.

The vehicle hit a large pothole, causing Tara to stir. She had no idea how long she had been under or where she was. She felt the cramp in her extremities and the muscle tension in her fingers and toes. She needed to move them, or she would scream out in pain. Careful not to make any sudden movements that would alert the driver, she tried to move her fingers first. One by one, she made slow movements that were luckily unnoticed. She felt a slight relief as she felt as if the blood began to flow once again.

Her body felt heavy, as though her clothes were made from lead. Whatever he had given her had played havoc with her muscular system. Maybe that was the idea so that if she did wake up, she couldn't do anything because her muscles wouldn't work. But somehow, she could move. It was painful, but she could do it, and what's more, her vision was improving. Unfortunately, all she could see was the rear seat of the car. Either he had moved her, or this was how she had fallen. She smiled to herself. She remembered those cop programmes, where the guy had got to the trunk by burrowing through the back seat. She thought about getting inside the trunk and then popping it open.

Tara stuck her hand between the backrest and the seat. Then felt a surge of disappointment as she hit a hard metal surface. Moving her hands slowly, she felt something else: something cold and round. Slowly she pulled it out. It was a Military style smartwatch. It was mostly made of carbon fibre, including the face. However, what stuck out most was the fact that the hour numbers were glowing themselves instead of being constantly illuminated.

Suddenly the sounds from outside the car had changed and so had the lighting. The whole car grew dark as if they were in an alleyway or inside a building. Quickly she tucked the watch into her pocket. The car began to slow down.

Her hastily conceived plan was simple. When he opened the door, she would roll onto her back and bend her knees. As he leant in to grab her, she would kick him as hard as she could and escape. Tara knew that she would have only one shot at this, so it would have to count. She got herself ready. Her breathing started to become erratic, and her pulse began to race. Tara didn't know if it was because of the drugs in her system, or if she was just plain terrified.

Tara felt the weight shift as the driver got out. She closed her eyes and took a deep breath. She heard the slam of his door and the crunch of his footsteps as he approached. She swung herself around and got herself into position. The movement of him leaving the car and walking to her door only took seconds, but for her, it seemed like hours.

She heard the click of the door handle. Quickly, she opened her eyes and mustered all her strength to go into her legs. If she was going to die, she would die fighting. Her eyes fixed on the door, waiting for the man's face to come into view. Suddenly she thanked all those hours on her feet at the diner, it had given her strong thighs, and she was going to use every inch of power she had on that face. She saw it in her imagination, the door opening, the cry of pain as her small heels encountered his nose and mouth, Tara envisaged the man falling back grasping his bloody wounds, possibly spitting teeth. She was psyched up, her body tensed like a coiled spring. She was ready for him. Tara gasped in horror as the door behind her opened. He had come in from the other side. She looked up at his grinning face. She wanted to scream, but she knew it would do no good. If anything, it would only make him feel more powerful.

"We have some talking to do... Questions and answers," he told her, laughing as he bent down to talk to her.

"I agree," said another voice.

She saw the sudden panic on the man's face as he looked around. She watched the driver stand up from his crouched position. As he did, so there was a scream, and the man were ripped from the ground and disappeared.

Tara lay there for a moment, wondering if the beast was coming back for her. Her breathing became more erratic. She closed her eyes and calmed herself slowly. Something she had taught herself to do as a child: a method of calming the fear of when her mother came home drunk. She slipped into happy thoughts. Her imagination led her away, on a beach somewhere. Probably somewhere she had seen photographs of once. She was listening to the sounds of the water on the sand, and the seagull's overhead. Tara's opened one eye. A look of confusion crossed her face, for the cries from the birds was strange... Almost like sirens.

Her eyes snapped open. Painfully she sat up and saw the approach of two black-and-whites. Flashes of red and blue filling the alleyway.

She smiled softly. She was safe.

For now.

The alleyway was becoming dark with the setting of the sun. Shadows that had once kept to the edges were now growing. Draping everything like a grey cloak.

———

McCall pulled the Mustang up to the garage where she usually parked when they got the call. Uniform had picked up a young woman in an alleyway. The cops had checked the plate number, and it had flagged up as McCall's suspect vehicle. It had taken her twenty minutes to get to the scene, hoping the driver was with them. She had left Tooms at the precinct. He said he had stuff to do, but she figured he just wanted to check on Tony. She didn't object to going by herself. It gave her time to think.

McCall had parked the black GT 500 near the mouth of the alley. People had begun to gather. They reminded her of hyenas near a kill. Most had cell phones on long poles, normally used for those ever-popular 'selfies. She pushed her way through the crowd, her jacket pulled tight around her, holding off the sudden chill of the evening. A female uniformed officer lifted the yellow crime scene tape and nodded a respectful greeting. McCall returned the nod and headed for the alley.

The dark of the passage was disturbed by the headlamps of the black-and-whites and flashes from the roof-mounted lightbars. This had no real purpose, apart from the fact that it made it difficult for the public to take photographs. McCall smiled at the officers' ingenuity.

McCall found the four first responders. Two of them were at the other end of the alleyway holding off those members of the public who had nothing else to do but make their lives difficult. McCall thought back to when she was a uniform. People didn't have smartphones with photographic options back then; all they had was cameras.

She always figured that if people would just do as they were told and move off, police wouldn't need to guard crime scenes so heavily. For her, the worst type of 'rubberneckers' were the souvenir takers: the morbid ones, who collected items from scenes of murder and carnage. For them, getting some souvenir from a scene was like having an autograph from a famous star, and for the cops, it was a nightmare. Most of the time, what they took was something insignificant—for instance, a bottle or a magazine. However, sometimes it might be a key piece of evidence, and that was the problem.

She thought back to the case of a serial killer who was almost not convicted because some interfering idiot had taken vital evidence from the scene. The killer found out about this and baited the man. In fact, the souvenir hunter, Henry Corp, nearly went down for the murders himself because he was in possession of the incriminating items. Unfortunately for the real killer, he had been so keen to set up Henry that he had left his fingerprints behind, assuming Henry would also be careless enough to leave his own. But Henry had been careful and worn gloves. So, the killer got the lethal injection, and Henry got a suspended sentence for hindering a police investigation.

McCall headed for two uniforms who were standing beside their black-and-white. The male officer was tall and medium built with short black hair. The woman cop was just a couple of inches shorter, with red hair and a slim build. They were both in their late twenties but had lost that 'rookie cop' that some young officers just couldn't get rid of.

"Detective McCall," the officers greeted her with a fond welcome.

"Hi, Wellman, Osborne," McCall greeted them back. Detective McCall had worked with them before and knew that they were good cops, with bright futures. She had hoped that Karol Osborne might have made it upstairs to their department as a detective, but they got Coreman instead. Wellman was one step away from SWAT. McCall had no idea why he wanted to join that crack division, but then it was his personal goal.

"What have we got?" McCall's gaze shot around the scene. There was a taxicab, its doors wide open. CSU were all over it, taking fingerprints and photographs.

"We received an anonymous tip that someone was about to get murdered in a taxicab," Officer Wellman explained. "They gave a location and a plate number. After what had happened with Detective Steel, we thought it may be connected. When we got here, we found a woman on the back seat, but no cab driver."

"We figured he took off when he heard the sirens," Osborne added, but McCall saw some doubt in her eyes.

"But?" McCall pressed.

Osborne looked around and then over towards the cab.

"The woman said he was..." She paused as if she was searching for the correct words to use without sounding crazy. "...That he was *taken away* by something."

"Taken away?" McCall asked. "What? You're saying that some guys tackled him or what? What do you mean taken away? How exactly?"

She looked at the two officers who both had the same expression. It was one of those looks that said, 'I knew you wouldn't believe me'. Then almost together, the two detectives looked up, up to the rooftop. McCall followed their gaze, and then her mouth fell open. Quickly she slammed her mouth shut and shook her head.

"Where's the witness now?" McCall asked, pulling on a pair of latex gloves.

Osborne pointed to an ambulance that had been reversed in, that was almost acting as a second barricade to stop onlookers getting too close. McCall nodded and headed for the taxi. At first, she didn't know what to think. Was the driver just a serial killer and had nothing to do with their case? If so, it meant the worst scenario imaginable: two cases running parallel—the odds of which were more than Mr Spock could predict.

As she came closer, she saw the taxi's medallion number on the trunk: 8Z56.

McCall's heart skipped a beat.

It was the taxi she'd seen taking Tara away earlier that day. She looked over into the back of the ambulance. There sat a woman with short blonde hair.

There sat Tara Burke.

CHAPTER THIRTY-THREE

The taxi driver woke up with a start. There was a searing pain in his feet. Below him was a bright light. So bright, in fact, that he couldn't see anything else. His head throbbed as if he'd woke from a massive hangover. He didn't remember much. Just the sensation of been ripped from the ground. After that, there was nothing.

The driver tried to move but found that he couldn't. He was bound tightly. Then, with horror, as his head began to clear, he realised he was upside down. He was strung up like meat heading for the slaughter.

He looked forward and saw blackness. The only light was that of the single bulb socket above his feet. The blackened-out lampshade was made to channel the light downwards in a column of light. His arms were stretched downwards, held tight by a chain that bound his hands together, and was secured to the floor via a heavyweight.

Sweat poured out of his body, mostly caused by fear. The room was silent apart from the driver's frantic breathing. His body was shaking from all the adrenaline that was being pumped through his veins. He tried to look around, but there was only blackness beyond the pillar of light that surrounded him.

"Who's there?" he yelled out. "I know someone is there... Come out!" He was trying hard not to show his terror. The silence continued until it became unbearable. The driver thought he would start bleeding from his ears as he strained hard to pick out a sound.

"What did you want with the girl?" asked a deep gravelly voice. The driver spun his head around as far as he could, hoping to get a glimpse of whoever was talking. But there was only darkness.

"Sorry, man, she was just a fare. I picked her up, and I drove her to her destination." The man's lies were almost convincing...almost.

"What did you want from the girl?" the male voice asked again with a hint of anger.

"Look, man, I don't know what you mean! The chick asked for a cab, told me to drive to some alleyway. I thought she had something goin' on," the driver cried out as sweat poured into his eyes, the salt causing them to sting.

"The girl. Tell me the truth please," growled the voice. "And I won't ask again."

The cabbie started to panic. His courageous attitude had washed away with the oceans of perspiration.

"I don't know, man, I am just the driver, that's all! I get a call, and someone picks them up or drops them off," he yelled, foamy spit spluttering from his desperate mouth.

"What do you mean, them?" asked the voice from the shadows.

The cabbie then realised that he had just crossed that line you should never cross. The line between ignorance and just plain 'covering your ass'. He swallowed hard.

"I get a call. They tell me to pick someone up, and that's what I do. They normally give me an envelope with cash and a picture of the person and instructions. That's all I know, man, honest!" He was almost in tears.

"The cop. Why did you kill the cop?" asked the voice. This time the words seemed to be delivered more calmly.

"You mean the guy on the bridge? No...no, that wasn't me, man. I just picked up the dude and drove him to his hotel. The man started raving and waving a damn gun. I stopped and let that crazy motha go, man." He shook his head as if to convince the stranger of his story.

"Who do you work for?" asked the deep, hard voice.

The cabbie said nothing.

"Who do you work for?" the voice asked again.

A thousand things went through the cabbie's mind. Most of his thoughts were about his death. Once his employer found out about this, he was as good as dead.

"Who are you?" the cabbie yelled out of frustration.

Was it the cops? The Feds? The local nuns' choir.

"I am Batman," said the voice. The cabbie investigated the blackness with a confused expression.

"What...Really?" he asked, then kicked himself for falling into the trap to make him look stupid.

"No, you idiot. I am something much worse," came the voice.

And then from the shadows walked a man in an ankle-length trench coat. The figure pulled back a cowl to reveal a stony face and a pair of sunglasses. Fear gripped the driver as he stared at Steel. He wanted to scream. To yell out for help. But his mouth quivered and flapped and gave no sound.

"Now, tell me about the girl and why you tried to kill me," Steel told him, his voice growling with satisfaction.

The cabbie looked over at the menacing form of Steel. He

felt the warmth of his own urine flow down over his naked body. The driver spat and gagged as it passed over his face and into his mouth and nostrils.

Steel just stood there, his long black coat almost reaching the ground. The light from the lamp was reflecting in those damned sunglasses.

———

McCall drove Tara back to the precinct. She had decided that the thought of nearly a thousand cops in the building might make her feel safe. McCall could see that Tara was well shaken up, but she guessed it was because of something other than her recent abduction.

Detective McCall sat in the chair next to Tara's in one of the briefing rooms. Tara sat nursing a fresh cup of black coffee that McCall had just brought in. McCall let her just sit for a while in silence. There was no point getting straight to it. Firing questions at her at this stage would just make her distrust McCall and clam up. This was another reason why they weren't in one of the interrogation rooms.

The colour had returned to Tara's once-pale cheeks. Her eyes were less bloodshot, and she had that 'human' look about her once more. Tara was scared. Her edgy movements as someone walked past the windows spoke volumes. What she wasn't saying, was why she was scared. Of course, her fear could easily be attributed to being abducted by a madman. But McCall thought differently. Tara was troubled by more than the abduction, something even more terrifying than the death of Amber.

"How you doin'?" McCall finally asked. Tara looked up at her with innocent, frightened eyes.

"I'm a little shook up, but I am fine thanking you," she

responded before taking a sip from the hot coffee. McCall gave her a reassuring smile and placed a comforting hand on hers.

"Are you ready to tell me what happened back there?"

Tara thought for a moment at the question. Then nodded slowly.

"Well, you saw me get into the cab," she began. "The driver asked me where I was going. I thought he was just a regular cab driver; had no idea he was some psycho killer. As we were travelling, he must have drugged me or something because I passed out..."

McCall nodded as she listened to Tara's account of events.

"...When I came to, I felt as if I couldn't move, there must have been something in the drug. I don't know. He parked up and got out. I planned to kick him when the door opened, but I wasn't figuring on him coming from the other side. I can still see his sickening smile as he looked down on me. Then suddenly someone said something to him."

McCall shot her a puzzled look.

"Someone else was there?" the detective asked. "Did you see them?"

Tara shook her head. "No, I couldn't see anyone. But I don't think it was *someone*. Sounds crazy I know, but it was more like a *something*." Tara spoke, looking slightly bashful.

McCall sat back in her chair and gave Tara a disappointed look. "More like a *something*? So, tell me, Tara, what did this *thing* look like?" McCall was disappointed, half expecting a monster story from this woman, who she realised had to be deranged.

Tara shrugged and shook her head. "I don't know. All I know is that whatever it was, it took him away." Tara felt stupid admitting she'd something so patently impossible. She knew that any second McCall would be standing up and walking out, and Tara wouldn't blame her if she did.

"So, someone drags away your attacker, but you don't see anything. Really. How's that possible? How could you *not see* the man being dragged away?" McCall said, her tolerance wearing thin. "OK. So which way did they go?" She leaned forward, resting her arms on the desk.

Tara simply looked up and pointed. "He went ... Up." Tara held her upwards gaze. She gave a little smile as she recalled the man's screams as he disappeared.

"What are you thinking about?" McCall asked curiously, thinking that Tara's reaction was somewhat suspicious, to say the least.

"The man. As he was being carried up, he screamed like a girl," Tara said, her gaze falling back on McCall.

McCall said nothing at first, just sat back in her chair, her thoughts racing to one conclusion. She decided: *if you're going to hit her with it, do it now.*

"Tell me about that night with Amber," McCall dived straight in.

Tara didn't know why she suddenly felt herself looking shocked. After all, she had been waiting for the question ever since they had sat down.

"I had just finished a double and was heading home. It may sound strange, but I was looking forward to one last night alone," Tara started to tell her.

McCall leant forward, a confused look on her face. "So, you didn't know she would be there?" McCall quickly made a notation in her notebook.

Tara shook her head and took another sip from the coffee. "I wasn't expecting her until Monday. She said she had stuff to sort out before she could move in," Tara explained.

Sam made some more notes before laying the pen next to the notebook. "Sorry, you were saying you'd just finished work?"

"That's right. I got my usual train. It was around ten when I got to my final stop. I remember getting a text from my boyfriend. He was asking where I was. I figured he had tried the house phone and had gotten worried when nobody had answered."

McCall made a quick note of the times Tara had just given. She sat back in her chair, taking the pad with her. She crossed her right leg over her left, using her knee as a support for her yellow legal pad.

"When I got to the building, everything seemed normal," the witness continued. "Well, until I got inside the apartment anyway." Tara looked down at the steaming dark of the coffee, but all she could see was her own reflection.

"Is that when you saw Amber's body?" McCall asked gently.

Tara looked up at McCall and shook her head. "No, the lights didn't work. I thought there had been a short or something. The great thing about living alone is you know where everything is. We get a lot of blackouts in my building. Normally because of the gamer freak upstairs who sucks so much juice. I know where every table, chair, even lump in the floor is because the floors are coming apart. I headed for the side dresser for a flashlight. When I tripped over something, I knew there was trouble." Tara stared back at her coffee.

McCall could see how painful it was for her to remember that night.

"The floor was wet. At first, I thought the guy upstairs had left his bath running again." She looked back at McCall with a smile. "He gets so involved in his damn games he forgets stuff. Do you believe the landlord has put twelve fire alarms in the guy's apartment?

McCall returned the smile, reminded of her own occasional difficulties with neighbours.

"I ... I remember the front door opening and my boyfriend coming in. As he opened the door—" Tara closed her eyes tightly, as if she was trying to delete the memory.

"That's when you saw the body?" McCall finished; almost sensing Tara would be unable to say it.

Tara nodded. The tears began to stream down her cheeks. "He pulled me up and held me tight. It wasn't until later that we realised we were covered in blood. My boyfriend—"

"—Jake Harding?" McCall said as if to confirm the name Kim had given to them.

Tara nodded, looking somewhat confused that she knew his name.

"Well, Jake told me to get changed and to pack a case. He also told me to lay low. He thought you guys may think I was guilty and burn me for the murder. So, I packed a bag and disappeared." Tara took another sip from the coffee. She watched McCall as she scribbled down some notes.

"And what about Jake, what happened to him?" McCall asked, knowing full well that he was at the morgue.

"I don't know. That was the last I heard from him. I thought it had all been too much for him and he had bolted." Tara shrugged and then for the first time set down the coffee mug. She frowned and shook her head.

"You know it's funny when I heard there was a body found in the park. I hoped it was him." Tara looked over towards McCall, who just sat there with an expressionless face.

"You were hoping for closure. If he was dead, you knew he hadn't left you alone with this."

McCall's words caused Tara to nod as she wiped away another flood of fresh tears.

"Tara, do you know why anyone would want to kill Amber?"

McCall had successfully managed to place Tara in that

comfortable spot. She had persuaded her to talk about that night. Tara felt at ease, unpressured. If she was ever going to get answers from Tara, now was the time.

Tara shook her head. "She worked for a big shipping firm, overseas stuff. It was a shipping company, not the CIA." Her voice trembled. It could have been because of tiredness, stress or emotion. Or more likely avoidance.

"OK," Sam went on gently. "So, Amber had no enemies that you knew of. How about you?"

McCall had been saving this question. Tara pushed her hands underneath the table out of sight. The unsure shrug and the biting of the bottom lip spoke volumes. Tara said nothing more. She just stared into that coffee cup and dreamt of that beach house. Just her and her man alone together.

McCall stood up and walked out of the room, leaving Tara to her thoughts. Captain Brant was waiting outside near her desk.

"You get anything?" he asked, popping some gum into his mouth.

McCall stopped and looked back at Tara, who hadn't moved. "Well, I think I know why our John Doe—or should I say Jake Harding—was covered in blood. They were a couple."

Brant raised an eyebrow at the revelation.

"She says he came for her at the apartment. The lights were off, and she must have fallen into the blood. When he picked Tara up off the floor that's when the blood was transferred," McCall explained.

Brant nodded. It was a good theory and would explain why he had blood on him. What it didn't explain was were had he been from ten that night until McCall had found him the next day.

"Well, she's a witness, where you gonna put her?" Brant asked.

Sam McCall shrugged and shook her head. She was out of ideas, or more precisely, she was busy trying to figure out what Tara was into.

"Use the safe house that Steel set up, it's already paid for. But don't tell her about her boyfriend having been there. If she knows something, she will spill it eventually. When she feels safe enough." Brant spoke with the benefit of years of experience, making McCall wonder how many times he had used the same tactics.

Brant and McCall looked over towards Tooms, who was approaching fast. He wore a childish smirk, looking like a child with a secret.

"Guess where our John Doe used to work?" he asked, his glances bouncing from McCall to Tara.

"I don't know where?" McCall asked impatiently. Tooms nodded towards where Tara was sitting.

"He worked at the diner?" Brant asked.

Tooms smiled and shook his head. "No, better than that. He worked at the same shipping firm as Amber did. In a different department but for the same company."

McCall looked over at Tara, who was still staring into her coffee. "Funny she left out that part of the story," she growled.

———

As the hour hand of her watch moved towards the five, McCall stared at her murder board.

The information was getting better. Thanks to Tina's time of death—more usually referred to as TOD—she was able to make a good timeline. Photographs of the scene were accompanied by lines and scribbles of information. Jake Harding was still a suspect. Sure, he was dead, but that didn't make it any less likely that he could be their killer. It just meant someone was 'cleaning the house'.

Tooms walked up behind her. She could smell the mixed aroma of the hotdog and the fresh coffee. She turned as he handed her a freshly filled cup.

"Where's Tara?" Tooms asked, afraid of losing anyone else connected to the case.

"Tony has taken her to the hotel." She saw his sudden look of concern and smiled.

"Don't worry. There will be two female officers inside with her all the time. Plus, four men outside in the hallway. Also, no take-outs allowed!" Her words were confident. But after all, last time they had been taken by surprise, they weren't expecting anything to happen. He was only a John Doe at the time, and they weren't aware of his importance. Tara, on the other hand, was different. They knew there was a real threat to her life, and they would be ready for it.

But something was bothering McCall. Tara had said there was no power to her apartment. McCall picked up the desk phone and called CSU. She spoke to some young guy. She requested someone to go to Tara's apartment and dust the fuse box for prints. It was a longshot, but sometimes longshots paid off.

"Anything on our flying taxi driver?" McCall asked with a smile.

Tooms shook his head. "Not for the moment, but I got the uniforms to look. Who knows, maybe the Batman left something behind?" Tooms smiled. He, like McCall, thought Tara's account of the cab driver's disappearance had to be a tall tale. She had probably seen the driver run off when the cops arrived but was too scared to say so. McCall looked over at the clock. It was late, and they were both tired.

"OK, that's enough for today. We'll pick it up tomorrow," McCall said, pouring the coffee into her thermos mug.

Tooms headed for his desk. Home time always sounded good.

"See you tomorrow, Sammy," Tooms said, pulling on his jacket.

"See you tomorrow, big guy," McCall answered as she watched him head for the elevator. She looked at the empty chair next to her desk.

"Good night, Mr Steel," she whispered, almost hoping he could hear her.

CHAPTER THIRTY-FOUR

Steel walked out into the darkness. He had left the cab driver dangling like a piñata. He hadn't learnt much from the man apart from the discovery that he had terrible bladder control and he was indeed just a driver, not otherwise part of the organisation.

It was a simple set up. He gets told by cell phone who or what to collect and he does so. He then knocks his passenger out with some drug, then leaves them in the alley where Steel had caught him. The cabbie didn't even know who he was working for; he just got paid a lot of cash to drive and not ask questions. Looking at the man, it was no wonder that they never told him anything. If he'd added just a touch more pressure, he would have sung for longer than Mick Jagger in a live performance.

The enigmatic British detective had made an anonymous 911 call to the police and ambulance services, telling them the driver's whereabouts. The cops could have him now. McCall would certainly love to talk to the guy.

Steel made his way through the darkened streets of the city.

He couldn't risk being seen. In a way, the killers had done him a favour, for they had made him invisible. There is a certain freedom in being dead. Nobody is looking for you or expecting you for that matter.

Of course, he couldn't return to his apartment or go back to the station. He was now officially a ghost. He was back to doing what he was good at being a shadow.

Steel headed for his other safe house. It was an old abandoned power plant in Glenwood. A place he had seen about a year ago while working on another case. The machinery had been stripped away, leaving the rusted metal skeleton and the graffiti-covered red brick walls. This massive structure had been left abandoned. Now, he had a use for it. It was in a convenient position, close to the Hudson River. Everything of any value had already been ripped out and sold for scrap. New windows had been fitted on the inside; the old ones left on the outside. This gave the place the appearance of being abandoned. New, heavier doors had been fitted but made to look like the old ones.

Inside it was a different story. On one of the split levels, he had three computers and five large monitors. One room had been made into an armoury, another a bedroom of sorts. There was a shower room and a wardrobe. This was a safe house wearing the disguise of a ruin. The Aston Martin SUV was parked in one of the special bays next to several other vehicles, including a motorcycle. The power was from several generators that were stored in a larger room that once held the building's own generators. This electricity was completely off the grid.

When he first came over to the States, John Steel had acquired several places that no one else was interested in. Of course, his name wasn't connected to them, just in case, he needed a bolthole. They were places he thought would come in handy. Places that the agency didn't know about.

It had taken nearly a year to renovate this one. All that time plus a lot of money to turn the power plant into a base of operations: his own personal 'bat cave'.

Steel headed for the split-level section. This large area was set out as a war room. As well as the five computers and large monitors, there was a long metal table with a coffee machine and a couple of mugs, next to which was a grey fronted refrigerator, mainly used for milk and bottled water. Opposite a large flat-screen television was an old brown leather couch.

He took off his long trench coat and hung it on an old wood-and-brass coat stand that stood next to the metal staircase. Steel prepped the coffee machine then switched it on. There was a bubbling noise and then the whirring of motors, as the water was being passed over the ground coffee. He filled one of the cups with coffee, milk and sugar, then headed for the couch. As he fell onto the leather, it squeaked under the sudden pressure. He stretched out, using the armrest as a cushion. Closing his eyes for a moment, he inhaled the fresh smell of caffeine.

He let himself reach that comfortable place, that moment before slipping into a deep sleep: something he often didn't have time to do. He opened his eyes again and sat up. Taking a well-deserved sip of coffee, he stood and headed for one of the computers. He downloaded the picture of the cabbie who'd abducted Tara from his phone to the computer and started a search. The facial recognition software kicked in and started running, using all the standard databases. Steel took another sip before stripping down to the waist.

Steel stepped into a long room which had once been one of the main halls. To the side, there were walkways on many different levels. But now it held a strange assault course: eighty feet of multi-levels which came back on itself so that the start point was eventually the finish. There were long thin walkways, ropes, large jumps and long drops. It was a combination of an urban cross training track and a military assault course. Some of the latter, he had taken from the British Parachute Regiment's 'piece of terror'. This training area was punishing, but good for keeping you agile.

Steel strapped on a sports watch and started the timer. He bolted off to a ramp that went up around twelve feet at a ridiculous angle. He attacked each jump and apparatus with ease. His movements looked fluid, as though he was making no effort at all. His tight muscular body felt alive again, he felt the blood flow to his taut frame, and it felt good.

Finally, he dropped around eight feet and grabbed a horizontal bar. As he did so, he swung off and landed with a roll. As he came up, he threw two throwing knives at two targets, each one on either side of him. Steel stood up and stopped the watch. The whole thing had taken him five minutes. *Not bad for a dead guy*, he laughed to himself. But it was not his personal best. The knives had struck home. One was in the guy's head, and the other target had got it in the throat. He smiled, crunched his neck from side to side, rolled his shoulders and headed for the shower.

The water from the shower felt like tiny bullets hitting his skin. The mix of the hammering water and the steam from the heat was almost therapeutic. He turned the water from hot to cold: skin shock treatment.

He dried himself off and then changed into another set of clothing that was hung up ready. Black BDU trousers, a black long-sleeved top and military-style boots. They fitted well and were comfortable as well as practical. Steel made his way back to the couch and the coffee he had left. It had cooled to the right temperature. Steel headed over to another computer which was piggybacking from his own at the precinct. This held all the footage that the precinct had collected from that morning at the bridge.

He knew he had been poisoned; the question was when? Williams hadn't done it; he had made it clear he needed Steel alive. It wasn't the taxi driver, for he didn't have the stones for it. Then he remembered the driver saying that he 'just picks the people up'. They wouldn't trust him enough for him to pick Steel up at the house, for then he would have to know their location. It must have been at the drop-off point. Steel took a sip from his coffee as he moved over to the murder board he had recreated on a large smartboard.

Steel had to go back to the start, to Amber's murder. Everything that had happened was as a result of that. Abductions, bodies in the park, even the attempt on his own life. *Find out the why and you will find out the who*, he thought to himself. As Steel took another sip from the coffee, one thing dawned on him. The driver wasn't working for Williams, but what if he worked for the other organisation? It would make sense. If this was the case, where was Steel dropped off for the cabbie to get to him?

His head began to hurt with all the questions, or it could have just been the anti-venom and other medications rushing through his system. He sat down hard on the couch and stretched out once more. He needed rest, if only for a little while. He had to let his body recover. As he slipped into a deep and troubled sleep, one thought came to the forefront of his mind. Who was the girl in the cab?

And what did they want with her?

———

The next morning brought an early shower. Dark clouds hung in a blackened sky. McCall had got up early to take a run. A three-miler, just enough to blow away the cobwebs and give her brain a kick-start. The rain was light, not even heavy enough to get the store windows wet. But it was cool to the skin, which helped her to pound out the miles. Her plan was to do a quick run and then a workout at the station gym.

Despite everything, she felt good. They had Tara, and she hoped that would be the start of the good things to come. They had an ID on their John Doe and a location of where he worked. Tony was checking out the man's apartment that morning to see if there was anything relevant to the case, but even with all the progress, it still felt hollow.

It was nearly five by the time McCall reached the precinct's gym. Today was 'bag work' to relieve some tension. She felt that kicking the shit out of a four-foot bag was therapeutic. If she didn't hit the bag, then some other poor bastard was going to get it.

Sweat ran down her back, halted by the skin-tight Lycra bodysuit. Her hair was bunched up in a ponytail, giving her the look of a warrior. As well as relieving stress, the exercise helped her to think. One person that kept coming to her mind was Tara Burke and her statement. She was either lying about something or just holding back. McCall knew she would have to speak with her again, but she needed something that would tip the scales.

Tara was a smart woman. That had already been proved. She had been smart enough to hide out, and she had been smart enough to know it was time to run again.

Unfortunately, the bad guys were smarter.

McCall landed one final upper kick to the bag and grabbed her water from her own equipment satchel. The water was still cold. She smiled as she peeled away the sides of the sock which encased the bottle: a trick that Steel had taught her. Put a cold bottle in a sock, and it acts as a thermos. She had scoffed at the idea at first. In fact, she had no idea why she had done it now.

She took a mouthful of the liquid and swallowed hard. The cold fluid left an almost burning sensation, but it was simultaneously refreshing.

The glamorous woman detective showered and changed at the precinct—there was no time to travel back home. She sat at her desk and put her favourite coffee mug down on her coaster. The white china mug had an 11th Precinct logo on one side and on the other was her name printed out using a print label maker. The two-inch strip simply read: *McCall's Mug. Hands off.*

She opened her emails. There was still no word from CSU about whether there were any prints on the fuse box at Tara's place. Tooms was waiting to hear back from the uniforms, after their house-to-house questioning of the people in the apartments near the rooftops close to where the taxi driver had disappeared. McCall was still having a hard time with the whole 'flew away' business—Tara telling them that the cabbie had been spirited into the sky—but then she supposed that anything was possible given the right equipment. Tony had just walked in and was heading for the break room. He looked angry, but she knew it was a thing him and Tooms had going last one in gets the coffees.

She waited until Tony had sat down and checked his email before approaching him. It was pointless asking the guy what he had before he had checked. McCall closed her messages. The long list of mind-numbing trivial items could wait—she had more important things to look out for. McCall rose from her chair and wandered over to them, coffee cup in hand.

"So, what have we got?" she asked, sitting in the chair next to Tooms's desk.

"CSU are working on the taxi, no hope of any pictures, all

the surveillance cameras in that area had been vandalised ages ago," Tony told her, rocking in his chair as he spoke. "The lab did come back to us. The blood on Jake Harding's clothes was Amber's. Which confirms the story Tara told you?"

"Let's look at that alley again, anything you can pull up," McCall had a lively bounce in her voice as if she thought things were looking up. "He must have taken her there for a reason. My guess is he has used that location before." She felt as if they were on a roll, and she hoped it was just the beginning of the breakthroughs.

"Tooms, you look more closely at Trent Shipping. It appears that our Mr Harding also worked there."

Tooms raised his eyebrows at McCall's revelation.

"Funny, they never mentioned that they had an employee missing when Steel and I spoke to them," she commented, smiling deviously. The people at the shipping company were all a little too smug for her liking.

"Pleasure to rip 'em a new one for you, McCall." Tooms smiled before taking a bite from the bear claw; he had brought in. Loose almonds fell onto his desk as he tucked in.

McCall smiled. It was like watching her nephew eat, and he was eight years old.

She looked across to her murder board, concentrating mainly on the picture of Tara. Tony noticed the long stare.

"I am heading off to Harding's apartment later," Tony told her. "The manager said it wouldn't be a problem; actually, he was asking how long before he could re-rent the place." Tony shrugged miserably. "All heart, eh?"

McCall smiled and shook her head. "I'll be with Tara this morning. She's got some blanks that need filling." McCall's voice had a stiff tone to it. Tooms knew that tone all too well. His wife had it whenever the kids weren't telling the truth about something.

McCall stood up and stretched off. Her body ached from the workout. *No pain, no gain,* she thought. She'd have preferred the gain without the pain, but hey.

She headed for her desk and pulled her gun from the top drawer, then relocked it, then pulled on her jacket and left.

"Call me if something comes up," McCall shouted as she headed for the elevator. Tooms just gave a quick salute, knowing she wouldn't be listening for an answer anyway. She bypassed the elevator and took the stairs. *Today will be a good day, but not for someone,* she thought and smiled as she headed for her car.

Central Park was full of life. Joggers, strollers, people taking that scenic route from one side to the other. The sun hung high in a picturesque blue sky. The only evidence of the early morning shower was a light film of water on the parked cars. The air smelled fresh, and the grass appeared greener than usual. The park was full of motion, of people hurrying around. All except one. It was a man in a hooded long leather-and-wool coat, who strolled along a path next to a lake apparently without purpose. To his left was a row of green benches, which curved round, following the contours of the path and grass verge. Steel stopped at the last one of a row which was next to an old-style streetlamp. Using a gloved hand, he wiped away the dampness from the bench, then sat and looked out over the lake.

The morning light made the blue still waters glisten. A family of ducks swam past in single file and dragonflies skated low, close to the water. Behind him was a mass of bushes and then a tree line. To his left was Bow Bridge, with its white arched cast-iron walls and six flowerpots. Each urn held an explosion of colours. He had a straight line of sight of the path to his right and the bridge. The running path that branched behind him, near the bridge, was no concern. If his view was blocked, so was theirs. But nobody was looking for him, and it was just his own paranoia that made him pick the spot: a very public place with good fields of vision.

Sure, he was dead, no one was looking for him. However, he was looking for someone. Steel pulled out a paper bag from his pocket and picked at the loaf of bread inside. He tossed the pieces towards some hungry birds. The pigeons happily pecked away at the free meal.

"I prefer ducks myself," said a low husky voice. It was the sort of voice that came as a result of using whisky as mouthwash and having alcohol breath as a result.

"Really? I am a swan person myself," Steel replied.

He wasn't moving, apart from the slow tossing of the bread. "They're majestic birds. Calming to watch."

The homeless guy sat next to Steel and offered a bottle in a brown paper bag. Steel didn't react, just carried on tossing the bread.

"There's a warehouse you might be interested in. Someone is providing weapons to small-time street gangs. Selling them cheap to flood the system. Someone wants to cause some trouble, methinks," Crazy Gus said, handing over a small piece of paper discreetly.

Gus looked to be in his seventies. But he probably just looked old because of his filthy appearance and the chemicals he poured into his body. He wore an old US army M65 combat jacket. The 'Screaming Eagles' insignia was dirty but intact. But the name shield had been removed, almost as if he wanted to forget who he used to be.

"Any ideas who this *someone* might be?" Steel asked, almost for confirmation of his theory.

Gus just looked at Steel and laughed, knowing full well that Steel had the answer. Steel smiled and nodded slowly, feeling almost foolish at having tried to trick the old-timer.

"Is there any word on the street about why someone wants a woman called Tara Burke so bad?" Steel asked softly, tossing another piece of bread at a fresh batch of birds.

Gus looked up for a second, almost as if he was asking permission from God to answer the question. "No, but I can ask around. Maybe there's some chatter on the East Side." Gus took a swig from the bottle. Steel had no idea what his friend was drinking, but the smell made him wince.

"Gus, I am surprised you remember anything at all after pouring that stuff down your neck," Steel joked.

Gus just laughed and went back to his drinking. Steel tucked the piece of paper away into a pocket and pulled out a folded hundred-dollar bill.

"You look after yourself, Gus," Steel said, shaking the man's hand and passing the bill in the palm. Steel stood up and straightened the long coat.

The old man watched as Steel walked away, making sure he was near crowds of people, trying to mask his escape. He smiled and tucked the note away without looking.

———

The warehouse was tucked away in Gowanus, Brooklyn. The red-brick monster was once a powerhouse, and now it was a disused shelter for the homeless and junkies. It overlooked a canal and the 3rd Street Bridge.

Inside the building were fifteen men who were all dressed in black three-quarter-length leather coats, jeans and black T-shirts, standing around impatiently. Mr James was the leader of the merry band. He was a large man, with a military-style haircut and a bulge in his jacket from the twin .45. It was a strange weapon, comprised of two 1911s put together, creating one beast of a gun.

He looked at his watch as he chewed on a toothpick. They were late. The deal was meant to have happened twenty minutes ago. His men were scattered around in tactical positions, armed with Heckler and Koch 416 assault rifles and SFP9 pistols. James touched the earbud in his right ear. It was the 'overwatch' on the roof sending a report.

"Roger that," he spoke into his sleeve, then looked over to the two men at the main doors. "Open her up, our guests are finally here."

There was a scrape of metal on metal as the massive doors were opened. Then a roar of engines which echoed throughout the structure, as two blacked-out GMC Yukon SUVs tore inside. With them was a box-body truck designed for house removals. It was a rented vehicle that they had no intention of returning.

The vehicles stopped, and fifteen black guys got out. They were an up-and-coming street gang, hoping to make a name for themselves. To do that, they needed what the big man had. The gang leader stood around six foot one, and he had broad shoulders. He wore a pinstriped suit and white Nike trainers. A blue baseball cap covered his shaven head, and round sunglasses hid his eyes. With him, as he approached were two massive hulks of men, each one standing at around six foot four and with the massive build of giants.

James said nothing at first. He just stood and sized up the men. He smiled to himself. The muscle that the man had with him was more useful for scare tactics than action. Their frames were too large, which made them slow moving. Sure, if they got hold of you, they could do some damage, but he knew he could have those men on the ground and screaming in no time at all.

"You're late, Mr DX," James said, spitting out the toothpick. "We have a schedule to keep, and you are messing with that."

"Relax, man, we got de money, yam got de goods, so everyone is happy." Mr DX spoke with a slow Jamaican accent. He smiled and waved at the driver. The man got out of the SUV and walked over with two aluminium briefcases and laid them flat on the bonnet of the SUV. DX clicked open the catches and opened each of them up, revealing three million dollars in cash.

"So, you got sometin' for me?" DX's smile was smug.

James waved behind him, and two men moved to the truck and opened it up. The vehicle contained large military cargo crates. There were enough automatic weapons, grenade launchers, grenades and ammo to start a small war.

DX smiled broadly and nodded. "Very nice, man, very nice."

The black guy's smug grin bothered James. His instincts told him it was a set-up. The voice inside his head told him to put a bullet into every one of the assholes. But that was not the plan, and those were not his orders.

"So, man, what if I told you I am walkin' out with me money and de guns. I know you can't stop me. I know dat yam boss has told ya to just deliver de stuff." DX held a Desert Eagle semi-automatic handgun up towards James's head, and his men had already pulled out their own automatic weapons. But James just stood there, saying nothing. Just staring at DX and his smug grin.

"You could kill us all and take everything," James told him calmly. "You could just leave us alive and take everything. But I also know that you're a smart guy and the last thing you want to do is to upset my boss and his organisation. Because you know that if you become a problem, he won't kill you and make you disappear. He will make your death public and very messy." James put another toothpick into his mouth.

DX's smile changed slightly. "Hey, man, you know I was just messin' with ya, man! We're cool, man, we're cool!" DX tried to hide the slight wobble in his voice. He stood tall and opened his arms, as though everything was on the level. His men put their guns away and went to load up the weapons. James tossed the keys of the truck over to one of DX's men.

"Let's just call it a gift," James said, chewing on the new stick of wood. He knew cross loading the merchandise would take time and the sooner he was away from the vermin, the better.

DX smiled again, and his driver handed over the case.

James watched as DX and his men drove out of the building. He hoped he would see DX again, just before he put a bullet into his brain. DX and his men sped along the road, along 3rd Avenue, and back to their own little hideout. The sun was cool, and a fresh breeze made what little vegetation there was sway.

They had their prize and, unknown to them, they also had a stowaway. A figure blended in with the darkened underside of the truck. For the gang, it was a good day that was going to turn bad.

CHAPTER THIRTY-FIVE

DX AND HIS CREW PULLED INTO AN OLD ABANDONED warehouse in Brooklyn that served as a distribution centre. The multi-level complex had offices on two levels, and the centre was open spaced with a clear view all around. The place was barren, apart from some office furniture and the odd leftover crate. Scratches of paint hung onto rusted metal, and glassless frames were caked in dust. Power was stolen from a nearby transformer, giving light via the only working lamps. Above, a glass skylight held off the elements. The one reason DX had scouted the place, was that it had a working roof and it was miles away from prying eyes.

As the vehicles rolled in, there was a cheer as if it was from a pack of animals. Armed men covered most of the levels, while the rest of them stood on the main floor. DX's SUV pulled up near a staging area. He got out and raised his hands to quieten everyone down.

"Today we have the power to take this town, tomorrow we take the city," he yelled out. As he raised his hands, the two mountains of men opened the back-shutter door to the boxcar to reveal the weapons. The mob howled again, the sound echoing all around. Then the music started to play from a huge stereo in a corner. There were speakers positioned all around, the sound system creating a massive din.

This noise was a distraction that Steel welcomed. High above on the roof, the resourceful ex-soldier had wondered how he was going to open one of the movable skylight panels so that he could get in. The squeak of rusted metal would certainly have got the attention of the guards below.

Carefully, he opened the skylight. He winced at the first metallic screech. He stopped for a moment, looking down at the guard who seemed to hear it. Slowly he moved the skylight a little more, chancing to go a little further. There was another screech followed by powdered rust falling onto the guard. Steel looked down, his heart racing, expecting the guard to look up and see him at any minute. But the man stayed firm, and his gaze fell to the party below. Steel opened the skylight enough to get through, and then clambered down, using the building's metal frame for hand and footholds. Now he had a clear view he could make out where everyone was.

There was a guard at every corner of the top floor, just as there was on the second. The first floor would be easy to break into. Using the offices as cover, he could take out the guards. However, the second floor was more open, and there was much more danger of being seen. Luckily all the lighting was from the skylight, and this created shadows and dark corners, which were good enough to disappear into. Good enough to allow him to wait patiently for that right moment.

The guards were lackeys, totally untrained. Just thugs with guns told to stand and cover them from above. Sure, if most men came in and found so many guards in position, they would think twice. However, Steel wasn't most men.

———

The guard called Laurence stood, rocking on his heels, listening to the party that was in full swing below. He didn't even have his gun in his hand. He had just slung it from its strap across his back. He felt the cold metal of the MP5 machine pistol against his back through his thin shirt. He leant on the railings and looked down. There were several women who had been dragged in with promises of cash, but most of them were here for the drugs. Each one would be given a free sample, after which they would be easy pickings. Laurence pushed himself off the rusty metal and paced about for a while. He was dying for some action, ready for something to happen. He walked over to the dark corner and stopped. His overexcited imagination stopped him from going closer. The movie he had watched the night before had given him a sudden fear of the dark. It had been some weird zombie flick about the last man on earth or something. He smiled at his foolishness and turned around to walk back to the railing.

He didn't have time to scream. Something grabbed him from behind. Something strange and leathery covered his mouth to prevent him from screaming, just before he was dragged into the shadows.

———

The second guard – a man called Jamal, stood at his post, this was to the right of where Laurence had once been guarding. He leant on the railings and looked down at the party, as did the other guards. They had nothing to fear: any attack would come from the main door. So before reaching them, they would have to get past the two heavies guarding the main entrance.

Jamal never noticed Laurence disappear. Nor did he see his

two other colleagues fall to the same fate: something darting out of the shadows and ripping them into it. He smiled as one of the men below started dancing with one of the drugged women. She hung in his powerful arms like a ragdoll.

"Man, I am missin' the friggin' party while I am stuck up here," he complained to himself, sucking his teeth in annoyance. He wasn't a big man – eighty pounds at the most. He wore a pair of army cargo trousers, a white vest and some over-sized sport shoes. A red-and-blue bandana covered his head as if he was some guerrilla fighter of the '70s.

"Well, we can't have that, can we?" came a voice from behind him.

Suddenly he was being pushed over the side. The rushing wind caused by his fall pulled at his cheeks. His eyes widened, as all he could see was the dusty concrete rushing up towards him. At the last moment, he closed his eyes, as if not seeing it would make it hurt less. His screams made everyone clear a space. Then he felt the tug on his leg. He had stopped moving. There was no pain, just a swinging sensation. Carefully, he opened his eyes. The ground was close enough for him to clear the dust with his breath. He felt dizzy, nauseous. He vomited before he passed out.

Everyone stopped and just stared at Jamal as he swung like a broken builder's plumb line, his face covered in puke. Steel used the distraction to get to the first level. He was hoping most would venture upwards to the second floor, to find out who had done this.

As he tucked himself into one of the offices, Steel watched a stream of armed men rush upwards. He noticed some familiar-looking crates that had been piled up. Ammunition, 5.56, 9mm Lugar and 7.62. There were pine crates stacked up separately. One had black stencilling on it that said: *S4GIA Handle with care.* These were military pineapple hand grenades. The other had *M18, smoke grenades* stencilled on them. Steel smiled cunningly as he hatched a plan.

There was only one way up. The other staircase had fallen down years ago and was lying on its side on the ground floor. This left a large hole and a long drop. The floor above was a grated metal walkway that served no actual purpose apart from providing access to the crane that once straddled the walkways.

Steel had found a powerline that had once given life to the crane. Now it was held above the metal flooring at the other end of the walkway. A thin wire held it firm. A wire that was also threaded around the railing and attached to the wall. All it needed was a foot to kick it.

The armed gunmen ran about checking the upper floor, making their way down towards the other side. Steel looked at his watch. The second-hand quickly approached the twelve. He smiled wickedly.

The men on the level stopped and looked towards a sudden noise—a strange singing coming from the far corner. Three of the men ran towards the sound, their guns at the ready.

There was a flash of blue and sparks sprayed down from the upper levels. Light bulbs exploded from the power surge. Steel watched the chaos from the safety of the concrete office. Women screamed in panic, and the rest of the men yelled orders from the floor below. Gunfire rang out as the electrocuted men involuntarily squeezed the triggers on their guns as their muscles tightened. The others dived for cover, some of them too late as they caught the stray rounds. One man caught two in his body armour, hurling him through a window and into an office. There was a burst of light as he fired back out of anger, but all he managed to hit was an old fire extinguisher on the wall. There was an explosion of a white cloud and the sound of coughing. Steel smiled at the pandemonium he'd orchestrated and moved in towards the downed man, giving him a swift punch to render him unconscious.

DX was angry, confused and frightened. He thought at first that the attack had come from the mercenaries, who were coming back for their weapons. The women that was able to ran out of the main door, causing the guards to run in. There was a clatter of metal as if tin cans were hitting the concrete. Seconds later there was a hissing noise like air escaping, followed by thick smoke rapidly filling the room from the smoke grenades Steel had thrown. DX let out a spray of automatic fire onto the first floor. Sparks flew as 9mm bullets impacted with hard concrete and steel supports.

The eight men below were now enveloped in the thick white smoke. The air was too thick to breathe, causing them to cough and splutter. Steel knew he only had a small window of opportunity to do what he had to do. He adjusted his sunglasses and jumped into the fray.

He moved quickly. The noise of the shouting and jostling men gave him cover, so there was no need for him to sneak about. Each one of them was expertly taken out, knocked unconscious by using the quickest method: either a neck holds or a punch.

That only left DX.

The smoke had stopped pouring from the now-empty grenades. The thick clouds were starting to thin. To disperse enough for DX to see a figure approaching him, but not giving him enough time to do anything about it. It only took one punch, square in the face. He was unconscious before he hit the floor.

———

The police had received an anonymous call, that there was reports of gunfire in an old warehouse. It didn't take long for SRU to get there. Uniformed patrol units in the area had also been tasked with securing the area. The orders 'hold but do not enter' were very specific. Police helicopters were there in minutes, circling above, ready to give orders if need be. Thermal scanners were hot and ready. Tactical ground teams headed for the entrances while the second team prepared to abseil down through the roof.

The plan was to get inside the place quickly and easily. The anonymous tip had told them about the weapons, and the SRU teams were ready. 'Flashbangs' were fired into the building. After the first set of explosions, the teams moved in single file, one man on the other, like some Roman legion battle stance. The glass above shattered as the aerial teams swooped in.

The cries of 'CLEAR' soon died down, and the teams looked down at the men lying on the ground. All were zip-tied and had duct tape fastened over their mouths. Everyone looked down, astounded to see what had been done, all of them intrigued.

"What the...?" one of the men in the unit said, looking upwards. The others were just as shocked and amazed. There were twenty-eight men all lying down in a row, all except one of them. DX was hanging upside down from the ceiling. A rope had been tossed over a high beam, and he had been pulled up and fastened to the rear of the truck. The teams searched the area. It was a massive haul that would soon make the evening news. It was a good bust. One that the police commissioner would be getting his best suit pressed for. The only information that would be missing would be that the violent gang of hoodlums had been found neatly gift-wrapped.

From a distance, Steel observed the bust. He watched as

the gang members were led into secure vehicles, ready for transport. Ambulances were also present to take care of the women.

Steel smiled. It was a fantastic sight. He had shaken the tree.

Now all he had to do was wait to see what would fall.

———

Tooms and Tony went back to the alley. The place where they'd found Tara and the cabbie had been spirited away. This time they took to the rooftops. They wanted a bird's-eye view of the situation. High above, they could get an idea of entrances and exits. The place they were above was a fast-food joint, which suited Tooms just fine. The stench of burnt oil and fats made Tony want to throw up and caused Joshua Tooms to drool. Tony had wondered how his partner wasn't suffering with a weight problem but remembered that Tooms hit the gym as much as he could, so none of the food turned into flab.

Being at roof level brought with it a biting wind, but the overview was perfect. It was a straight line past the main street to the next row of buildings. There was no way the cabbie could have been taken either way by road without being seen. Tooms and Tony stood at the edge and looked down. They were directly above where the taxi had been, and ultimately where the cabbie had vanished.

"Any ideas?" Tooms asked, leaning over the drop just that little bit further before pulling himself back.

"I may have one," Tony replied, crouching down and inspecting a spot where the concrete had been scraped by something.

Tooms looked down to look at his partner. "What you got there?"

"Not sure." Tony looked towards where Tooms stood. "Check over there, see if there are any more scuff marks, would you?"

Tooms looked around and immediately found the same sort of marks near where he was standing. "What the hell are they?"

Tony shook his head – he had no idea. He pulled out his phone and called CSU. Hopefully, they would come up with something.

"Let's get CSU to rip this place apart. Hopefully, they'll be able to find something. But I bet my badge this has something to do with the driver's flying act." Tony waited for someone to answer his call. Tooms smiled and headed downstairs to get something to eat before the CSU arrived. Tony shook his head as his partner disappeared down the stairwell.

When he got through to the CSU call desk, Tony spoke to some young woman with a bubbly voice. He told her the address and the exact location they were at. He could hear music in the background, possibly from a MP3 player or phone's headset. The conversation was short but to the point. Moving back to the scrape marks, he decided to take some photos of his own. If he had to leave before the crime lab got there, he would have a record of what he saw. Just in case.

The sun was high, but there was a haze which blocked out most of the heat. It was still the morning. He knew that by one o'clock it would start to get warmer.

Tony pulled out his cell phone again and sent a quick text to McCall with an update. As a small gust of air swept past him, he closed his eyes briefly. A sudden memory of a day in Memorial Park filled his mind: a Sunday morning with Amber. They had just been on the ferry to Liberty Island. He smiled as he saw her face. Saw her fantastic smile and those ruby lips. A sudden buzz from the cell phone in his hand woke him from his daydream. It was McCall. CSU weren't coming.

A patrol unit had found the cab driver.

The cabbie's body had been dumped in the river, and a river patrol had found him. McCall stood behind Tina as she examined the body. Uniforms were taking statements, and Coreman was with the patrol unit. McCall just stood there, looking down on the corpse. The man's eyes were open and held a look of fear. McCall took secret pleasure to think that he had suffered before he'd died.

She was ashamed of feeling that way. Almost. She had seen that look in people's eyes before. A long time ago, on another case. There was only one man who could scare anyone that much – Mr Williams. This turned out to be a double revelation. Firstly, it confirmed her fear that Williams was back. And secondly, this body told her something else: that the cab driver wasn't working for him. McCall noted the wounds on the man's body. He'd had information ripped out of him. If Williams was his employer, why would he do that? He would already know the man's secrets.

"So, what's this guy telling you?" McCall asked, kneeling next to her friend, Dr Tina Franks.

"Well, someone went to work on him that's for sure," the ME told her. "I will know more when I get him back to the shop. I would say he's been dead less than twenty-four hours. As for the cause of death. Um..." Tina looked closely at the body, which was covered in cuts. She shrugged. "Sorry, Sam, that I will have to get back to you on. Whoever did this know what they were doing." Tina Franks's voice held a terrified wobble. McCall knew then that her friend had come to the same conclusion: that this had been the work of Mr Williams.

Tina's assistant helped bag the body and carted it off to the

ME's wagon using the gurney. McCall stood and watched her friend climb into the black van and drive away. She said nothing at first, just took time to take in the scene. A sudden cold breeze brushed past, carrying her hair upwards. With a gloved hand, she brushed her hair from her eyes. The choppy water looked cold and unforgiving.

She found it curious that the body hadn't been weighed down, merely tossed into the water like the piece of trash that he was. It was almost as if it was a message for someone.

The midday weather had changed. The wind had brought dark, unwanted clouds. The breeze had become stronger and constant. There was a storm coming.

Steel sat in his lair, working busily on the computer. He was pulling up what he could on recent gang incidents, especially those involving weapons. At the power station, he had enjoyed a nice talk with DX. He was surprisingly chatty, but then Steel had learnt that most people would rat on their grandmothers if they were under the right powers of persuasion to talk. Someone was supplying gangs with weapons. Steel didn't know why, and DX wasn't much help, even though he had told him when the next shipment was meant to be.

The computer gave some reports on gang activity: a couple of robberies and shootings, all of them involving handguns. Steel was looking for something else. The weapons that DX had bought were military grade. If the gangs were using these sophisticated weapons, they might aim to attack banks or money transports.

Steel sat back in his chair and took a sip from his mug of Yorkshire tea. His cold emerald green unshielded eyes scanned the pages, only to find nothing useful. Steel pulled DX's phone from his pocket and plugged it into the computer. The plan was to copy the phone's memory and leave it somewhere for McCall to find. He smiled at the thought of his colleagues' reactions. They had been through a lot together recently. He only regretted his decision to remain dead to the world for their sakes, and he would have let his friends know he was alive, but the risk of his cover being blown was too great. It was a choice he had made with regret but also a sense of ease. He knew the pretence wouldn't have to be for long – just long enough for whoever was responsible for all these things to make a mistake.

He looked over at the screen, to see the message: *Transfer complete.* He unplugged and re-pocketed the phone. The data would have to wait. He had people to see. Standing up, John Steel took his long coat from the coat stand and pulled it on. Given its bulk and size, it was surprisingly light. He took the sunglasses from the wireless charging station and slid them on as he headed for the door. He needed to find out if DX had been lying about the other drop with another gang. If it was indeed going ahead, he had to shut it down.

———

David Adams sat behind his desk. He was busy writing an email to a client. He stopped, picked up his whisky glass and downed a mouthful of Jack Daniels as he read it through. His eyes suddenly darted over to the heavy wooden door of his office, as it burst open, and a small thin man walked in with two larger men. Adams's secretary ran in after them.

"Sorry, Mr Adams," she apologised, "I tried to stop them—"

Adams just raised a gentle hand and nodded with a smile. Reluctantly, she left the room and closed the doors behind her. Adams sat back in his chair, and the leather squeaked under the shift of his weight.

"What do you want?" Adams growled as he looked the man up and down.

The short man was in his mid-fifties. His blond brushed-back hair was hidden by a grey fedora, round-rimmed glasses matched his oval face, and a grey handmade double-breasted suit emphasised his slimness. His two henchmen looked like a couple of bouncers from a bikers' bar, with their shaven heads and short beards. Leather gloves hid whatever tattoos they may have had on their hands.

"Our employer is not happy with you, Mr Adams, not happy at all," said the man, who was known as Mr Kidd. He poured himself a drink from Adams's private bar. Mr Kidd chose the Napoleon brandy, filling the small bowl glass up to halfway.

"Why?" Adams asked. "The shipment went out today as ordered. Those kids should be getting ready, if they haven't shot each other, that is."

"Yes, I know it went out today. But it was also found by the police. The men and the weapons are in custody now. This is only one of several mistakes you've made." The sinister Mr Kidd spoke softly, but there was something about him that terrified Adams.

"You're talking about the disk, right?" Adams blustered. "Well we know who's got it and we're tracking her down right now." Adams's voice was filled with a mixture of confidence and fear. Kidd shot Adams a look that made him sit back in his chair, almost as if he had been punched.

"The woman you are referring to is also in the hands of the police. Oh yes, and while we are on the subject, who ordered the death of the cop?" Mr Kidd asked with a sneering tone. The door opened, and Mr James from the warehouse exchange walked in. There was an expression of confusion on his face as he expected Adams to be alone. Adams scowled at Mr James, almost as if his Number Two had been keeping secrets from him.

"Do you know anything about a hit on a cop?" Adams yelled at Mr James.

Mr James smiled smugly. "Oh, yes, sir. He was the boyfriend of that Amber woman. I figured she may have said something to him about the disk."

Kidd nodded and smiled. The man's smug grin broadened as he felt he had got one over on his employer.

"Interesting idea," Kidd told him. "But wrong."

Mr James suddenly looked shocked at Kidd's revelation.

"You see, firstly, that was the wrong cop," Kidd explained patiently. "And secondly, Miss Taylor had nothing to do with the disk. You, my dear boy, have made a grave error. One that could cost us dearly."

Before he realised what was happening, Mr James was suddenly picked up by the two men and thrown out of the second-storey window. His body hit the ground just in front of an eighteen-wheeler that was coming around the corner. His screams lasted a second or so, quickly terminated when there was a screech of brakes.

"Sort out your mess, Mr Adams. Get the woman, get the disk and get rid of the *correct* cop." Kidd tossed a piece of paper onto the desk. Adams picked up the small scrap. Written on it was an address of a bar.

"How do you know he'll be there?" Adams asked, confused.

Kidd said nothing, just headed for the door with his men behind him. Adams blew out a lungful of air and sat back in his chair as if a great weight had been removed from his chest. He thought for a moment, then picked up his cell phone. He searched the contacts on the display and pressed the autodial and waited.

"It's me," he said when he got through. "We've got trouble.

Get your ass back here. We have to talk." Adams threw down the phone and rocked in his chair while he combed his hair with his fingers out of sheer frustration.

High on a rooftop of one of the warehouses, Steel knelt in cover. Massive billboards that advertised the company covered the flat roof. It was the perfect nest for him to set up. There was a foot-wide gap between the roof ledge and the bottom of the billboard, where Steel had secured a folding parabolic microphone. 8k digital cameras were also located on the roof, capturing images from the office and the surrounding areas. A small laptop with an external hard drive had recorded everything: including the criminals' plans to get Tony.

Steel waited. The bottom of his long coat spread around him and covered the ground below him; his cowl pulled tight over his head. He was invisible, just the way he liked it.

Twenty minutes later, a car pulled up into the parking lot. Steel looked over at the car, but only made out the nose of the Camaro. Steel looked over at Adams's office through a pair of special binoculars which were also connected to the laptop. Everything he saw was being recorded. Suddenly the door swung open, and Adams stood up, blocking his view of the visitor.

"This cop will be at this address tonight. Make sure it looks like an accident," Adams told the man.

"Well, bars can be rough places, especially if you've had too much to drink," replied the visitor.

Both men laughed.

"Just get it done." Adams's tone turned serious. He knew this job couldn't be messed up, for if it was, he would be joining his bag man under a truck.

"Don't worry. He's as good as gone."

The sound of the door closing signalled the man's retreat. It also told Steel that he had to find Tony immediately and shadow him all night. He could have warned McCall, but if his plan was going to work, he needed to stay dead, just a little while longer.

The resourceful detective plugged in the cell phone to the laptop and closed its weatherproof case. Now he could watch the feed from his lair. It had already been risky, just getting down there once. Coming and going would only tip someone off.

Besides, he had eyes and ears on the compound.

Now, he was one step ahead.

CHAPTER THIRTY-SIX

McCALL SAT AT HER DESK AND RE-READ THE CASE FILE. To most, it would seem like a Lee Child or Micheal Connelly novel. Undercover agents, assassin taxi drivers. But it wasn't, and it was reality. A harsh reality. It was also one of the hardest cases they'd had. Not because of the complexity of it but because of what they had lost.

McCall thumbed her notes on the yellow legal pad. For every opening, they found they also encountered a brick wall. Their John Doe had wound up crispy in Central Park, Brooke Taylor was missing, and the taxi driver had ended up as fish food. Their only lead was Tara, and McCall wasn't taking any chances there.

She took out a copy of Amber's reference from her previous employer: top of her class at NYU and a master's in business administration. The write-up was everything an employer could want, which of course screamed a cover story to McCall. For her, there was a bit too much icing on the cake. Most of Amber's life was a fabrication, not so much a lie as a deception.

But McCall had to wonder, how did Tony fit into that aspect of her life? Was their relationship also a fabrication?

She looked over at the empty desks where Tony and Tooms normally sat. They were still out trying to locate any eyewitness of the body dump. She knew it would be pointless, for the people were pros. They would have got rid of the body late at night in a darkened spot. CSU were doing their thing with current shifts and so on. This might give them a location of the dumpsite, but then it might just be another diversion to head them off down another road.

Sam lifted her cup to her lips and took a sip. The aroma of freshly brewed coffee carried into her nostrils. It was strong and pure. No milk and no sugar. After a while, she tossed the paperwork back on to her desk, then stretched off her annoyance. McCall looked up at the wall clock above the captain's office door. She had worked through lunch, and now her blood sugar was punishing her for it. She stood up and headed downstairs to the street.

The sun was bright, and the buildings blocked most of the breeze. She pulled her jacket on and headed for a hotdog vendor. She had never seen him before, but she was glad he was there. She stood in the queue of four people. A young couple were at the front. McCall noted their body language and figured it was their first date. Next was a short woman with a Chihuahua dog sticking out of a large handbag. Its large eyes glared up at McCall with cruel intent.

The next few people didn't take long as the dogs were already practically ready. The maintenance worker directly in front of her ordered a dog with all the trimmings. The smell of the food made her stomach growl with impatience.

"Just a dog with onions please," she ordered as she reached the front of the queue that had built up behind her. The vendor smiled and nodded.

"Coming right up," the man told her cheerfully. He was in his late fifties, with a large, stocky build. His black hair was neatly cut, and underneath his apron, he wore blue jeans and a chequered shirt. The front of the cart was colourful, and *Vince's Hotdogs* was written in gold lettering on a red background. Small US flags on wooden poles blew in the breeze on top of the food stall.

"There you go, Detective, it's on the house."

McCall smiled and headed for the precinct. Suddenly she stopped and turned back. How did the man know she was a detective? Her shield was in her pocket, and she doubted he had seen her come out of the building. Even so, that didn't mean anything. McCall looked over at the stall. The older man was gone, and a man in his mid-twenties was now serving.

She scanned the area, hoping for a glimpse of him, but he was gone. She looked down at the food in her hand. A sudden look of suspicion crossed her face. Who was he and why the act? McCall decided to toss away the hotdog in case it had been laced with something. As she headed for the wastebasket, she noticed one of the napkins had writing on it. She removed the napkin and noted a message that had been written in ballpoint pen: *We need to talk. Come to the zoo at 18.00, come alone.* Alarm bells sounded in her head. This could be – and most probably was – a trap. On the other hand, who wanted to talk to her? And about what?

The alarm bells remained, but her intrigue was greater. The best possibility was that he was a witness; the worst scenario was that he was the killer. Either way, she needed to know, but she wasn't going alone—she was curious but not stupid.

She shrugged and ate the hotdog before heading inside the precinct. She figured there was nothing wrong with the food. What would be the point of send a message in a hotdog if you're going to poison it? As she bit into the dog, she rolled her eyes with pleasure. There was nothing wrong with the hotdog; in fact, it was perfect.

McCall returned to her desk, feeling her light-headedness subside. The food had filled a small gap, but she still felt unhappy about something. She looked at the murder board with its lines and photographs, but one thing stuck out to her: Trent Shipping. There was something about that place that didn't sit right with her. Everything seemed to revolve around that place. If it had been a thriller on TV, the set-up would scream that its connection was too obvious. But this wasn't a television show, and so what if it seemed too obvious a link? It was a start.

She grabbed her badge and gun from the top drawer and threw on her jacket. It was around three o'clock. She had time. After leaving Tooms a quick note on his desk, asking him and Tony to meet her at the statue in front of Central Park at five, she headed for the elevator and moved out into the busy streets.

———

Becca sat at Amber's old computer, arranging the files for the meeting that was due to take place later that day. She felt uncomfortable with the task, as it was normally Amber who did it. But Amber was gone. All the information she required had been put into specific folders on the desktop, making her life a lot easier. Amber had been a thorough person, someone who liked to ensure that everything was user-friendly and easy to find. Just in case she wasn't there for some reason.

Becca printed off page after page. Graphs and charts, world plans with route markers and locations. Becca arranged the folders she was creating for the meeting so it would follow the protocol for a PowerPoint presentation. She opened file after file. Becca was amazed what Amber had set up. Everything the company shipped abroad through their office was catalogued, and charts had been made ready for just an event. As she searched, she came across a strange-looking file. Curiously she opened the file that had no name, only a question mark. At first, she thought it was a miscellaneous folder. A place Amber may have junked the unknown, or just the unimportant files.

The young woman's mouth fell open. The files were of imports to Eastern countries that had trade embargos or that were involved in civil wars. The logs said it was mostly machine parts and farming equipment involved, but her gut told her otherwise. The more she read, the more she was convinced that Amber had been using the company to smuggle weapons. Her heart sank at the thought. Her best friend and mentor was an arms dealer, and she had had no idea. A sudden thought made her feel ill. She had unknowingly become part of it, whatever 'it' was.

Becca made a copy of the file because she knew she had to show this to Adams. Had she just discovered the reason why Amber had been killed? She looked at the telephone on the desk. Her thoughts were all over the place. She needed to talk to someone, she needed to share this horrible secret, but she didn't know who she could trust.

She caught sight of a small business card next to the phone under a piece of clear plastic sheeting. Even though it was with many others, this one stood out because of the police badge. She remembered the handsome cop who had given her the card. She took the card from under the sheet and picked up the handset and dialled the number. The sound of ringing seemed to go on forever until it went to voice mail.

"Hi, Detective," she dictated to the answering machine. "This is Becca from the Trent Shipping Company. Look I've found something disturbing, could you please come down here or we could meet somewhere? I think I may have found out why Amber was killed."

She held onto the receiver for a moment, her eyes still glued to the computer screen. She felt alone. The meeting would be on in thirty minutes, and she had to get the room ready. Becca put down the receiver and stood up, grabbing the files and heading for the door.

As she left the room, the door swung shut on its automatic closer. The computer screen still showed the open file. Suddenly the taskbar came on and showed the files that were being downloaded. The screen flashed and then showed the message: *Files deleted.*

Becca headed for the second floor. The conference room was down a long corridor on the left with a fantastic view of the car park. As she approached, she saw Adams enter with someone she couldn't make out. She took a deep breath and headed for the entrance with a sense of purpose. Becca stood in front of the door and raised a clenched fist, ready to knock. Her hand froze just inches from the timber as she heard Adams's raised voice.

"I told you to clean this mess up!" he ranted at somebody. "Find that disk and take care of the woman!"

Becca's heart stopped. Had she been so wrong about everything? She felt as if she was frozen to the spot, her legs grounded and unable to function. A tear of terror rolled down her cheek as she saw the doorknob begin to turn. Adams would see her there. He would know she had heard everything. She looked down at the stack of files, on top of which was the report she had found. If she was discovered with that, she was as good as dead.

The latch clicked, and the door began to open. She began to shake as the adrenaline began to surge through her veins. The last breath she took, she was holding onto, almost afraid to let it go in case he heard her. Her top half was as good as down the corridor and already in the car park, but her legs held fast onto the same spot. Sweat from her brow was cascading down her forehead. Her eyes stared at the door with utter fear.

Suddenly from within the room, a desk phone rang. The door closed, and the next sound was that of Adams asking: "What?"

Becca almost stumbled as she was released from her anchor. She had control over her legs once more, and she used them. As fast as she could, she hurried to the lobby and the car park. She needed to distance herself from this place and from him. She needed the cop; the handsome one they had called Steel.

The terrified woman stared at the sea of vehicles, but only saw hers: a small red Datsun that was parked next to one of the several large lamps designed to help drivers find their cars in winter months. She strode along at a fast walking pace, the paperwork clutched to her chest. She was running on autopilot, not hearing or seeing anything but her car.

When she reached her vehicle and tried the door handle, she remembered that the car was locked, and the keys were in her handbag, which was upstairs in her office. Becca fell to her knees and screamed to herself, shocked she had made it this far, only to fail now. Then she heard a voice calling her. It was Brad, the security officer, a stocky man with a doughnut belly and beady eyes behind round glasses. He was in his late fifties with more hair on his body than on his head. He was Adams's 'suck up', guy.

"Becca," he told her, "Mr Adams is looking for you. He wants to see you right away."

Becca stared up at the man who just stood there with his hands on his hips, trying to look important. It was as if he didn't care why she was on the ground: his lack of interest in others was a trait he was renowned for.

She stood up and wiped her eyes. She knew she was done for. The way back would seem long, but it would also be the last journey, she knew that.

"Do you know what he wants?" she asked, almost as if her breakdown had never happened.

He just shrugged and pointed towards the main entrance. He was a man of few words and a lack of personal hygiene. As they neared the building, there was a roar of a Ford Mustang and a screech of tyres as McCall brought her car to a quick stop. Becca turned quickly and recognised Detective McCall. Suddenly Becca ran for the Mustang's passenger side door, to the guard's amazement. Brad rushed around to Becca as fast as his legs would take him.

"Drive, Detective! Please, just drive!" the scarred woman yelled.

In a flash, McCall picked up on the mixture of fear and relief in Becca's eyes as the guard tried to open the passenger door that Becca had just slammed shut in his face.

The Mustang's engine roared again, the tyres spitting gravel as they zoomed out of the car park.

Brad looked up at the second-floor window to see Adams looking down at him. The guard swallowed hard and looked away as he re-entered the building.

———

McCall had put Becca into the safe house suite. She could see that the Trent Shipping employee was terrified about something, and the way she was grasping the documents, meant that they were part of her problem.

Detective McCall took Becca to the empty bedroom in the

suite, where she curled up and fell asleep. The confrontation with her employers had been too much for her system and had worn her out. McCall would leave it for now. Tomorrow she would press Becca for the answers. Tomorrow, she would find out what was so damned important about the paperwork she had fallen asleep holding. But right now, she had a meeting to get to.

———

The sky had turned a deep purple as the sun began to creep into the horizon. The traffic was heavy as people travelled home after a hard day. The zoo had been closed since half-past four, but the park itself would be open until one in the morning. Sam McCall stood at the large, bronze statue of General William Tecumseh Sherman. She looked up at the glinting metal representation of the Civil War hero and smiled. It was more than a statue that she loved: it was a reminder of courage in the face of adversity.

Tooms and Tony had already signalled that they were set up and out of sight. They never made contact directly just in case they could be seen and communicated with her via quick text messages. The entrance to the park was full of people, and the traffic on Fifth Avenue was stacking up, almost to a standstill. The whole place was a tactical nightmare. If someone wanted to take her out, this would be the time. Car horns blared wildly, and engines revved impatiently. McCall headed down the path towards the zoo, passing several nannies pushing expensive prams, as well as people who were out for an evening stroll.

The entrance was in sight. Green gates barred the way, and billboards in wooden frames showed timings and prices. Many people were passing, but no one was loitering. A tall black guy

STUART FIELD

with a string shirt and baggy jeans was trying to sell off his music CDs—ten dollars was the asking price. A professional-looking cover was on the insert, but that didn't make his music worth it, that's if there was anything on it in the first place. He approached McCall with a smile. A smile that faded as she moved her jacket to show the shield on her belt. He raised his hands in a comical surrender and backed off.

She didn't have time to harass him, not that she would have done anyway—after all, the guy was trying to make a living. McCall stood by the entrance and looked around. There was nothing that looked off. Mainly joggers and dog walkers. She looked at her watch. It was now ten past the hour.

"I would say he's a no-show," McCall said quietly into the hidden microphone.

"Oh, I wouldn't say that," said a voice behind her. She spun around quickly, one hand on the pistol grip of her custom Glock. Her eyes widened, and her mouth fell open.

"You!" she yelled.

"McCall, who is it?" screamed Tooms from his hidden position. "McCall! McCall." He moved quickly the moment after he had lost sight of her. Tooms and Tony came running, only to find a blank space where she had been standing, talking to the black guy who was selling CDs.

"Are you the cops?" asked the CD seller. Tooms scowled at him and showed his shield.

The man held his hand out. On his open palm, he held McCall's microphone and earbud.

"The guy said he wanted to chat to her alone," the black man said, shrugging. Tooms grabbed the gear and pulled the man in close, practically dragging him off his feet.

"What guy?"

364

Williams wore a black pinstriped suit with stay bright shoes, and a blue tie with tiny pocket watches embroidered into it. In his leather-gloved right hand, he held a silver-tipped cane, for no other reason than he could. McCall walked alongside him, still unnerved by his presence. She could have brought him in, but he knew she wouldn't do so. She was curious as what he wanted from her. McCall wanted answers, and confinement in a six-by-four would have made him as mute as a monk.

"My dear Samantha, you are looking positively radiant. Have you done something with your hair?" Williams had a skip in his voice and a grin on his face.

"What do you want?" McCall said, cutting to the chase.

Williams's grin broadened. "Ah, always straight to the point, no foreplay. Very well. I want you to catch whoever killed Miss Amber and our Mr Steel." McCall was slightly taken aback by his interest in the deaths of both Amber and Steel.

"Frankly, I thought you were the killer," McCall admitted. "If so, it would have made things easier, but then things are never that easy are they?"

Williams shook his head. The smile had gone. "No, I am afraid that was someone else's doing. Steel was a great adversary to the point of him being a friend. Amber was ... let's just say she was an old acquaintance. Someone whose company I will miss and whom I wish I had known sooner."

McCall shot him a curious look. Had Williams had a crush on Amber, she wondered? Already the conversation was beginning to make her head hurt.

"It's funny," the psychopath went on, "the night Steel met his fate we had a chat. I had warned him to take care. And I'm giving you and your team the same warning. You see, there is an organisation who would like nothing better than to see the world burn. It is them I ask you to be wary of."

Williams stopped talking for a moment and looked across the green of the park's open space. An ocean of grass with large oaks was spread out, bordering the concrete pathways. The fingers of his left hand fondled something in his waistcoat. She knew it was his pocket watch. Something she had longed to forget.

"Detective, you need to watch yourself on this one," he continued. "Miss Taylor was an undercover agent at the shipping company, that I know you are aware of. We—or rather I—believe she found something out, and for that, they killed her. The organisation wants nothing more than to keep their plans secret. Something is about to happen and what she found out confirmed this." Williams pulled his fingers from his pocket and smiled at McCall.

"I know this is a strange situation, Detective, and I know you don't trust me," Williams told her. "And I know you want nothing more than to arrest me or shoot me. But I also know that your instinct is telling you that I am right."

McCall scowled at him. He was right on all accounts, most of all the 'wanting to shoot him' part. However, everything he had said made sense. She looked into his eyes and saw a kind of almost sadness. Somehow Steel's death had affected him as well. If that were true, she pitied the person who had killed him.

"After Mr Steel left the other night, he found himself in a cab," Williams revealed as they set off walking again. "I found this curious, as a limo had been arranged to bring him home."

"Yes, we found the cab driver. Someone had taken him for a swim."

"So, I heard. I also heard that you found a woman." Williams's tone growled at the mention of her.

McCall suddenly became uneasy. "It was just someone of

interest in Amber's murder, a witness," she said as if to dismiss her importance.

Williams stopped abruptly and grasped both McCall's arms in a vice-like grip at the wrists. His eyes were burning with redness. "Detective, that woman has something I want. If I have it, I can end this business before it starts."

McCall stared into those menacing blue eyes and froze. In her mind, she was back to that terrifying day, the first day they had met.

Williams released her and stepped back, his arms out to his sides, and his head bowed in an almost regretful gesture. "Forgive me, Samantha, I am sorry for the outburst." His voice was calm and apologetic. "There is a war coming, and your city is caught in the middle of it. You need to choose aside. Is it not better to do battle with one enemy and ally with the other? Is the enemy of my enemy, my friend – or my enemy?"

She thought for a moment. What he was proposing was unthinkable, but also frighteningly logical. If there was a war, the police couldn't possibly fight both organisations. For a start, they didn't even know who both were. Suddenly from behind her, she heard Tooms yell out her name. She turned and yelled back: "Over here!"

When she turned to face Williams, she found he had gone. She looked around at the expanse of the park and couldn't see him anywhere. Tooms and Tony caught up with her and looked around, confused and wondering what she was searching for.

"Where the hell did, he go?" McCall asked.

"Where the hell did *who* go?" Tooms replied, confused.

"Williams," she told him, leaving the two men with blank expressions.

CHAPTER THIRTY-SEVEN

THE NIGHT SKY WAS MADE DARKER BY THE BLANKET OF cloud cover. The chill breeze had turned into a biting wind. Tony had been in the Irish bar on East 4th Street since nine o'clock. He had been in there every night since Amber's death. He had gotten a favourite spot – a quiet table in a corner where he could sit, virtually undisturbed.

It was an old place with bare brick walls, oak fittings and fixtures, as well as dim lights and the smell of Guinness and stale beer. The tavern had been around since the late '90s and Tony had spent most of his youth in there. It was his second favourite place in the world, of which he'd seen plenty since he'd been in the army – the first being his childhood home, which his parents still owned. By half-past ten the tavern's capacity had swelled, and this for him was a cue to leave. Sure, he wanted to drown his sorrows, but then again, he didn't want to risk losing his badge. It was all he had. The fresh air was sobering as the wind hit his bare skin like a thousand needles.

He headed towards Lafayette Street and past the strange multi-storey car park. It was a towering structure that placed vehicles into mechanical booths that held each one and stacked them upon one another securely. A man sat in a pay booth, which was a grey metal box at the entrance to the small lot. The attendant was a young guy who was busy watching a film on his laptop while he waited for someone to pick up or drop off. The lot itself was dimly lit, but the illumination was enough for the man to see the vehicles.

Tony pulled his coat tightly around him as he turned the corner. He headed towards the parking lot. The alcohol had thinned his blood and made him feel woozy. Probably too woozy. As he walked, he found himself beginning to sway, and his vision became blurred. He didn't remember having anything more than his usual three double shots and a coffee. As he neared the lot, he looked at the reflection of a passing car.

The four men behind him had been standing at the bar near the door. Now they were behind him. It could have been a coincidence, but he didn't believe in those. He began to open his pace. The footsteps behind him hammered on the concrete, meaning they were matching his sudden burst of speed. In a sudden quick movement, he headed into the lot, hoping the man in the booth would see him, but he was engrossed in a film on his laptop.

Tony stood his ground but was unaware of the two men who had come up behind him. It was now six against one, and the one was in no condition to punch a feather, let alone six men. Suddenly the lights of the lot flickered. The six men looked around to see what the problem was but detected nothing but shadows. The man in the booth looked up from his laptop in time to see a darkened figure move from man to man, knocking each of them down and then disappearing into the blackness. The men screamed as they were being dragged into the dark. In the end, only one man stood alone – Tony Marinelli – that was until he fainted.

369

The lights went out for a few seconds. As they came back on, the drunken man was gone, and six bound men remained. The attendant looked back at the superhero movie he'd been watching to see the same type of scene in the film. His eyes rolled, and he fainted in his chair.

———

The next morning Tony woke up with a massive headache as if hammers were banging at his brain. It took a moment until he realised that the banging was coming from his front door. He got up slowly and headed there as quickly as his body would allow. His mouth was as dry as a dessert, but his eyesight had improved. He opened the door, and Tooms stamped into the hallway wearing an angry look.

"Tony! Man, you look like shit!" he told him.

"And good morning to you too, Joshua," Tony said, turning and heading for the kitchen.

"Is this a problem I should know about?" Tooms asked, picking up Tony's newspaper from the mat in the hallway.

"I didn't get drunk if that's what you mean."

"Really? So, you had a bad pizza then?" Tooms said, taking a seat at the breakfast bar.

"I think I was drugged last night."

"Drugged? What the hell for?" Tooms asked, looking suspiciously towards Tony's ass.

"No, I wasn't raped, asshole. But six guys tried to take me out last night."

Tooms raised an eyebrow at Tony's revelation. "Did it happen in a parking lot on Lafayette by any chance?" Now it was Tony's turn to raise an eyebrow, before downing a bottle of water.

"Come on, Rambo, we got a crime scene to check out,"

Tooms said, standing up. Tony looked closely at his watch and groaned.

"Tooms, it's five in the morning!" Tooms just shrugged and smiled.

"Yup. It's breakfast time. You can buy me a coffee on the way."

Tony wore his sunglasses on the way to the crime scene, even though the weather was overcast, and it looked like rain. For him, everything was as bright as a summer's day. He was on his second cup of coffee and his second bottle of water. Tooms was on his third bear claw. Tony's apartment was on Broadway, so he had to take Spring Street and go up on Lafayette. The traffic was already getting heavy, despite the early hour. They found an open spot to park and decided to walk to the parking lot. Tooms thought the cold air would mask Tony's already pale complexion. Yellow crime scene tape and plastic barriers held the public back. Tooms shook his head at the thirty or so people who had congregated around with cell phones held high, taking photographs. One of the uniforms recognised Tooms and Tony and let them through. The lot was almost empty apart from the CSU techs, the ME and a couple of detectives. The parking lot attendant was busy giving his statement and didn't notice Tony's approach. The lead detective was a man called Sam Cryer, a good detective from the 8th Precinct. He was a huge man in his mid-fifties with broad shoulders, a huge barrel chest, grey quiffed hair and a moustache to be proud of. The man looked like one of those small-town sheriff types, from somewhere in Texas in the 1900s. Tooms went up to the man, and they embraced like the old friends that they were.

"Tony, I'd like you to meet my old training officer, Sam Cryer. Sam, this is my partner, Tony Marinelli." Tooms spoke proudly. The two detectives shook hands. Tony had trouble keeping hold of Sam's giant hand in a grip, so he just let the other man do all the work.

"What brings you down here, boot?" Sam said, laughing. "Are things so slow uptown you gotta come down here?" Tony looked over at the ME, who was kneeling beside six covered bodies. Lakes of deep red covered the concrete but were largely restricted to around the upper part of the covered bodies. Tony had figured that they had all taken shots to the head.

"So, what you got, Sam?" Tooms asked, trying not to reveal all his cards just yet.

"Someone decided to tie these guys up and then give 'em an extra eye socket," Sam said, pointing to his own forehead. "Bit of an odd place to do it, but I guess someone was trying to make a point." Tooms looked over to the attendant, who was sitting sideways on to them. The man looked shaken and drained from the night's activities. He was wrapped in an emergency blanket and nursing a cup of something that Tooms could only presume was coffee. A female uniformed cop was taking his statement. She was a cute black woman with high cheekbones and large glistening eyes. Short compared to Tony, minute compared to Tooms. She had two bars on her sleeves – obviously a veteran to the streets.

"Did he see much?" Tooms asked, fishing for information. Sam smiled at his old rookie's attempt to get information.

"Yeah, a ghost. Could have been a big bat, might possibly even have been Dracula."

"What?" Tooms asked in an insulted tone. Sam nodded towards the attendant.

"The guy was watching some superhero flick when some drunk guy walks in, followed by six other guys. The lights flicker, and before he knows it, the guys are gettin dragged away into the night. Of course, he faints and wakes up early this morning to find six fresh ones in his lot." Sam made circles with his index finger at the side of his head.

"If you ask me, he saw the whole thing, and he doesn't want to join them," Sam added, chewing on his cigar.

"Well you may have another witness," Tony said, his gaze not leaving the covered bodies. Sam stepped back slightly, surprised at the news. He looked around, briefly hoping to see someone lurking, waiting to make an appearance.

"OK, where are they? In your car?" Sam asked, looking towards their vehicle. Tony shook his head and opened his mouth to speak. He had no idea how to even start with an opening. Not only was he a witness, but he was also going to be a suspect.

"That's the guy!" the attendant yelled suddenly, pointing at Tony. "That's the drunk from last night!"

Sam stood open-mouthed at the news. "So, do you want to explain what the hell you were doing last night?" he asked suspiciously.

"Don't worry, Sam, he couldn't have done this," Tooms said confidently. Sam scowled at his old partner.

"Whoever did this was highly trained and nimble," Joshua Tooms added.

"Yeah, so? Isn't he highly trained and nimble?" Sam growled out his words. Tooms shook his head.

"Trained yes, but nimble? No. He said he was drugged last night, probably to make him an easier target. Besides, I've seen him fight, and I tell you a handcuffed guy of ninety could take him out."

Sam laughed, partly at Tooms's theory, but more so about Tony's inability to fight. Sam looked Tony up and down and nodded.

"Yep, guess you're right, but we're still gonna need a statement," Sam said before spitting the loose bits of cigar that had collected in his mouth. Tony nodded, struggling to remember as much as he could.

"Well, there's not much to tell. I had a couple of drinks at the Irish bar around the corner until it started to get full, then I left. As I got outside, I started to feel off, like I'd had too much. That's when I realised something was wrong. As I headed home, I noticed the four guys who were standing at the bar, but who were now on my tail."

Tony watched as Sam made some notes in his brown-backed notebook.

"So why come here?" Sam asked curiously.

"I knew there was a watchman at night. I figured he would help or call the cops. Boy, was I wrong?" Tony nodded towards the shivering kid who was beside the medics.

"So, you took them down yourself instead?" Sam asked, almost hoping to trick Tony into a confession.

"In truth, I only saw the four guys, and I never saw the two behind me. I stood my ground, hoping to intimidate them."

"I guess that didn't work out for you either?" Sam joked. Tony didn't smile. His gaze fell back to the six men who were now being placed into the coroner's body bags.

"The last thing I remember is the lights going out," Tony admitted.

"That's when you fainted, you mean?" Sam nodded and made a notation.

"No. That's when the lights went out. They flickered and then went out. I'll never forget the screams those men made as they were being dragged off." Tony spoke with venom in his voice. He could tell this friend of Tooms's had already made his mind up about what had happened, and it didn't involve some ghostly phantom.

"I woke up this morning at my apartment," the unfortunate detective went on. "I have no idea how I got there or what happened to the men. For all, I know the attendant could have done it." They all looked at the cowering man and, almost as one, shook their heads and said, "Nah!"

Sam thanked them and gave Tony his card, just in case something came back to him. Tony and Tooms took off back to the precinct. They had a case of their own to solve, and this one was all down to the 8th and Sam Cryer to sort out. Tony didn't doubt that they would be stopping for coffee. Tooms's stomach had already growled twice, so it had to be close to breakfast time. Tony took one more look at the lot's entrance, hoping for some inspiration. But he could remember nothing more. Only those screams of the men as they were dragged away.

"What are you thinking about, partner?" Tooms asked, popping a stick of chewing gum into his mouth.

"I'm thinking we need to see that roof. I think that our taxi-driver-grabber is back."

———

Steel sat at his computer with a large glass of something green. It was blended vegetables and fruit with three raw eggs added for good measure. He was checking out the feed from the monitoring devices pointing at the shipping company's main building. All the phones had been tapped, and Adams's computer hacked and cloned. If Adams got an email, so too would Steel. The whole of Steel's lair had been rigged for security just in case of unwelcome guests. Outside cameras had been set up with motion sensors and lasers. Williams had warned him to watch his back, and he had been right to do so. The other organisation – SANTINI's rival, had tried to get rid of him. Tried and failed, but so far, they didn't know that. Steel still wondered why Williams was helping him. He reasoned that maybe the psychopath thought it was a good way of getting rid of the competition without being involved. If it all went wrong, Williams's organisation would be blameless. But there was something else. The way Williams had spoken to him was almost full of admiration, no, he had talked to him as if Steel was a friend. Steel couldn't rule this out; after all, they had many encounters together. Maybe a strange relationship was forming. A kind of Holmes and Moriarty complex.

John Steel turned in his chair and faced another screen. It was a computer monitor, on which was Amber's records. He was unable to ask for them officially, so he had hacked the system instead. She was born in Virginia in 1982. An only child who had never known her father, raised by her mother until 1998, when her mother had died of cancer.

Tara Burke's life was not much different, apart from the abuse. Tara's mother was an alcoholic with a hatred for the world – and Tara. According to her file, Tara was 'accident-prone'. Back then, child abuse within the family had been a taboo subject, something to ignored rather than dealt with as it is today. Tara had slipped through the cracks in the system. However, Tara was a survivor. Now, she had her place and a job, which made her a winner. More than her mother ever had. Steel noticed that McCall had put her in John Doe's old room. It made sense; the place was paid for, so why not? Steel took a mouthful of the putrid looking cocktail as he opened a file on Trent Shipping. It had photographs from newspapers as well as copies of personnel files. One photograph was of a fundraiser for a children's home. Six men stood together, proud smiles on their faces, while in the background were several of the staff who had helped to make it possible, including Amber. Steel had seen several of the people when he had set up the surveillance gear, but two he had not. All of them were business types with nothing on their minds but money. Nothing in the files told him anything much, but he was hoping the file he had taken from Becca's computer would do so. He had deleted it for her safety. If Adams found out she had it, or indeed had even seen it, she was as good as dead.

Steel started to close the picture when something in Tara's open file caught his eye: a photograph of a Christmas at the diner. Quickly he picked up the ten-by-eight and held it next to the monitor. He leaned in closer to make sure, and his mouth fell open.

"Well, I didn't see that coming," Steel gasped, then gave a smile.

CHAPTER THIRTY-EIGHT

McCALL GOT OFF THE ELEVATOR ON THE FLOOR THAT HAD been specially secured. Two cops stood at the elevator and another two near the suite's door. Captain Brant had boosted the security due to what had happened to the second witness. The sound of McCall's footsteps echoed down the hallway due to the ferocity of her pace. She was mad, and it was written all over her face. So much so that the plainclothes cops never stopped her. She held her shield up for all to see, and her eyes fixed on that door to the suite. The door swung open just as Tara was coming from the shower with nothing but a towel around her middle and another round her head. There was a large selection of breakfast dishes laid out on a glass dining table.

"You could knock?" Tara said sharply, shocked at Sam's sudden entrance.

"I could also throw your ass in jail and let some tattooed thing make you her bitch," McCall snarled as she slammed the door behind her. "So, save it."

The angry detective walked over to the breakfast table and

lifted the silver domed lid on one of the plates: eggs Benedict sat there, steaming with freshness. The other plate contained a 'full English' breakfast.

"Glad you're enjoying your stay," Sam McCall told her sarcastically.

"Is something wrong, Detective? Maybe you could use some breakfast? After all, the department is picking up the tab." Tara smiled smugly.

McCall rushed across and grabbed her by the arm and thrust her into a nearby chair. "The tab for this was paid for by a cop who died trying to find you, so think about that while you're ordering your next meal!"

Tara sat back into the chair as if she was trying to hide within its cushioned back.

"Sorry ... I ... I didn't know." Tara was trying to sound sincere but failing. McCall had the urge to toss her and the breakfast out of the window, but she wouldn't feel any better for doing it—after all, it would have been a waste of good food. Besides, McCall believed that Tara had no feelings because she'd always been hard. Her mother probably taught her that feelings get in the way.

"So, are you going to tell me what is really going on?" McCall said, her tone had calmed as she moved the plate with the bacon towards her.

"I told you everything, I swear," Tara said.

"Why don't I believe you? Why is it I'm getting the feeling that you're missing something out?"

Tara shrugged and shook her head, a look of confusion and innocence on her face, but McCall knew she had practised that one, possibly since birth. McCall reached into her jacket pocket and pulled out her cell phone. She checked the display and then her messages.

"I've got to go, but we'll continue this discussion later."

McCall had a worried expression on her face as she slid the phone back into her jacket pocket. She turned and headed for the door. McCall didn't turn back as she left; she just let the door click shut behind her. Tara moved quickly to the dining table and picked up her cell phone. After looking around, she typed a text message, then hurried into her bedroom.

Meanwhile, McCall entered the room next door where the surveillance team were sitting. The large monitors showed the suite, each of the rooms, the hallway, stairwells, and elevator. McCall stood behind the two operators and leant forward.

"So, what was it, a call or a text?" She smiled wickedly.

"A text, then she went to her room," said one of the men.

"How long before we get the text?" McCall asked, feeling smug.

"A long time. We don't have it cloned. It's not her phone," the technical man answered.

McCall stood up and gave the man a puzzled look. "So, who the hell's phone is it? And how did we miss it?" McCall growled, looking back at the monitors. Then she saw Becca lying peacefully as she slept. "Tell me you cloned Becca's phone when she arrived?"

The two men looked at each other and simultaneously shook their heads.

———

Across the street, the hooded figure of John Steel crouched on a rooftop like some strange gargoyle. The leather arms of his long trench coat glistened in the morning sun. The lower half was splayed out, almost blending into the treated roofing. His rangefinder binoculars peered through the un-curtained windows, taking in the view of Tara. A beeping sound from his cell phone made him look down at the screen.

Suddenly a message came up, saying: *I have what you want. Fifty Million. Shipping yard, one hour.* Steel nodded to himself, filling in the blanks. The number she had sent the message to, it had belonged to the Trent Shipping Company. He knew something had bothered him about Tara. It still did, but he didn't know what it was. Something he had found on the computer didn't help his gut feeling. Slowly he sneaked off down from the rooftop and slipped away to the street. He couldn't risk telling McCall anything, not yet. This one was going to be messy, so much so he wanted his colleagues far away from the whole business until the end. He wanted to get more intel before calling in the cavalry. McCall had good instincts, but this was bigger than she could possibly have realised.

The same thing applied to Tara. The young woman thought she held all the cards because she had something they wanted. What she didn't realise was that she was up against an entire organisation, not just one person.

She wasn't in control; they were.

And there was no way that they were going to pay.

———

McCall made it back to the precinct. The techs said they would get back to her as soon as they had anything on the text message. She found Tony and Tooms in the break room making coffee. Tooms was finishing off a hotdog. He screwed up the wrapper and just missed her with his long shot. The ball of paper went into the waste bin effortlessly, to his delight. Tony raised a cup at McCall, and she nodded. She still wore the pissed-off look she had brought back from the safe house.

"So, how's our runaway doing?" Tooms asked. Her look said it all, but she answered anyway.

"She's living it up at someone else's expense. She sent a text to someone, and the techs are trying to track it down. The clever bitch used Becca's phone." She took the cup from Tony and sat at the table. "She knows more than she is saying, that's for sure." Tooms nodded in agreement. He had had a bad feeling about her since the first time he had seen her. "Tara is up to something. I can feel it." Tony passed Tooms his coffee and then joined them at the small table.

"How's Becca coping?" Tony asked as he dropped two lumps of sugar into his coffee.

"She was sleeping," Sam replied. "I didn't have the heart to wake her, not yet anyway."

Tony kept looking over towards Brant's office. He was waiting to brief him on the things that had happened last night and this morning before One Police Plaza could. Tony had already spoken with Brant briefly, so he had a heads up. But Brant didn't have the full facts because Tony himself didn't have them either. McCall could sense that Tony was uneasy but didn't push him for details on the incident, though she planned to do so later.

McCall got up and moved back to her desk. Her thoughts were of Becca and the way she had run away, terrified and jumped into McCall's car. Becca hadn't said anything, just looked petrified all the way to the hotel. She was still clutching the bunch of company documents when she fell onto the bed in her new room.

Sam decided to wait until the surveillance team told her that Becca was up and awake before talking to her. In the meantime, she had other work to do. Coreman was busy downtown. They were out of Steel's special coffee, so he was given the task of getting some more. She thought it was a bit much to make him run errands like that, but then he was a rookie detective after all, hell, when she got her shield she had to put up with all sorts of crap.

McCall had hoped to ask Adams some questions, but Becca had ruined that plan. If she went back to the shipping company now, she'd be questioned herself for abducting one of his employees, and she had no time for that. As far as she could tell all roads led to that shipping company. Either they were very bad at covering their tracks, or someone wanted the police to look at them closely.

Samantha McCall looked up from her desk as she watched Brant head to his office. Tooms and Tony were waiting outside, like school kids waiting for the principal. She leant back in her chair and watched with strange curiosity as they went in and partially opened the door. Through the window, she saw the two detectives waving their arms around in explanation. Brant seemed calm. He merely sat in his chair and listened, but McCall knew him to be the man who often listened quietly first to what you had to say, and *then* tore your head off.

Brant picked up the receiver of his desk phone and dialled a number, while the two detectives took a seat on the couch in his office. Brant put down the receiver and waved them out. His face was full of anger, but Sam knew that their boss wasn't mad at the two detectives.

"What's up, guys?" she asked as the door opened fully and they came out. "You didn't crash the car again – did you?"

"Nothin' much," Tooms told her. "Tony just had some trouble last night ... Wait... What do you mean, crash the car again?" McCall smiled at Tooms's shocked expression.

"Trouble," she asked them. "What trouble?"

"Some guys tried to jump me last night that's all," Tony said, trying to make out it was nothing.

"Two on one, not very sporting. I hoped you kicked their

asses," she said proudly. Tony just shot her an awkward look and walked towards his desk.

"Don't worry about it, and he just gets easily embarrassed," Tooms joked and followed his partner. Tooms felt bad about not saying anything to McCall in explanation, but Tony had asked him not to. At least, not yet.

McCall looked back at the notes on her desk. She was still waiting for Tina's report on all the bodies. The crash had caused a massive backlog, which had put everything on hold. They had even got extra help from the FBI labs to try and sort through the evidence for the hundreds of cases that were still waiting.

Sam looked at the empty chair next to her desk and suddenly felt utterly alone. She missed Steel sitting there and rattling off his strange theories. Smiling, she looked back at her notes. After the meeting with Williams, things were starting to seem more complicated than she had at first thought. This wasn't a random killing of an undercover agent. This was something much more.

She checked her messages on her phone. Tina had left a text, saying: *I need you here ASAP.* McCall stood up quickly and slipped her jacket on. Tony and Tooms looked up at her as she headed out.

"Tina has got something, I'll be at the morgue," she yelled back without turning around. She had a bounce in her step. She figured that Tina might have found something that could break the case. She might even have found something that could lead to Steel's killer as well.

———

Steel walked through the streets as though nothing was amiss. His long black coat was carried by the wind, causing it to flap like a ship's colours. Even though the hood of his coat was covering most of his face, he blended in with the crowd, almost as if he wasn't even there. Tara's text bothered him. Even he knew it would take longer than an hour to get that much money together. That was unless she knew that Adams had that sort of cash available. A meeting at the company was the worst idea in the world: one woman alone on their home turf. He knew they would have her in seconds. Snatched and never heard of again.

He knew the place, but he didn't know all the players, including the organisation's hitman, the man who had killed so many people to cover their tracks. Whatever information it was that she had, it was big. Fifty million was a big chunk of change. Steel was heading back to his lair. He had blueprints to look at. If he was going in, he had to have a plan. There was too much cover, too many places to put snipers. With a compound that size, they didn't even have to be good shots to kill efficiently.

All he had to do was identify the right spots and take out the men before the confrontation even started. These were amateurs, merely workers with guns. However, he couldn't afford to take any chances. Even the worst shot in the world just needed that one lucky hit. He had to be ready.

Steel threw off his coat to the side. It landed onto the office chair, causing it to turn slightly. He touched the huge touch screen monitor, which came to life in the blink of an eye. He touched an icon that had *Plans* written underneath it. The screen changed into a blueprint-type sketch of the compound. Around the side were several areal photos. Each photograph was alined with specific areas on the blueprint.

In the centre was the main building with the parking lot to the front. To the left and right a row of five large warehouses, each standing lengthways. To the back were the heavy cranes and the loading area. Huge metal ISO containers stood ready for packing or unpacking, behind this was a rail track next to a loading station. Steel took note of several buildings that would be handy for getting bird's-eye views. The main building itself looked as if it could be a fortress. Once lockdown was initiated, not much would be able to get through. He would have to move quickly, which meant travelling light.

Anyone could go there with guns strapped to every part of their body, but that meant carrying a lot of weight and webbing gear makes a lot of noise. A simple two-weapon choice with plenty of ammo was always a good plan. Steel looked over the plan again. He would need 'eyes on' first. The thermal vision would be good to pick out the hidden few. Steel walked over to a gun rack and picked up a custom-built Desert Tactical Arms SRS sniper rifle. The .338 Lapua Magnum's magazine was a rear fit, which meant there was a place for a swivel foregrip. The barrel was just one long silencer. The Bullpup weapon was compact and easy to move with. It was also an upgrade from the original version which was bolt action; this new type was semi-automatic with a ten-round magazine. Steel smiled and tucked it into a kitbag, along with a silenced Heckler and Koch VP9 pistol and several magazines for each weapon.

He was hoping his surveillance gear would go unnoticed on the roof of the opposite building. The build boards next to the nest hadn't changed in years, so the chance of that happening now were slim. However, it was a good vantage point for a rifleman. Steel had camouflaged the equipment well just on the off chance, but he had to assume the equipment could be compromised at any time. "Always have a plan B, sometimes a plan Z could be an option," Steel's old Army instructor used to say. "Never assume, always secure." Words to live by, and Steel had. As well as the nest by the build boards, Steel had set up a secondary nest with equipment. Plan Z.

Since McCall had picked up Becca, Steel had to imagine Adams was desperate and would cover all his bases. Steel walked over to a rack of clothing equipment and picked out some more appropriate clothing to wear. Something more tactical and bulletproof. He picked out a tight-fitting bodysuit that had magazine pouches enlaced into the thigh parts of the legs and a belt unit that looked like a bat belt because of the pouches. Steel grabbed a small rucksack – ammo bag for the .338. He had to be ready for anything.

He just hoped that they weren't.

CHAPTER THIRTY-NINE

Tara paced up and down in her room, unaware of the surveillance team who were watching her. She had to think of a way to get out. She looked at her watch. Twelve minutes had gone since her call. She picked up her rucksack and grabbed a chair. Standing on the chair, she pulled out a small disposable lighter and held it under the fire alarm. She winced in pain as the thing began to get almost too hot to hold. There was the loud shriek of a fire alarm. She smiled and tossed the red-hot lighter onto the floor, just as the door suddenly burst open.

The security detail gathered the two women and hurried them out towards the back stairs, knowing full well that the elevators would be shut off automatically. As they hit the lobby, there was a mass of hysterical people pushing and shoving to get out. Rational people suddenly turned to self-preserving animals rushing to leave the building. Security staff were standing at the door working hard to calm and marshalled the people out in a single file, through the entrances.

Tara saw her chance to escape as a large surge of women

collided with the detail. As the detail made it outside to safety, the men looked around hurriedly.

Tara was gone.

Upstairs in the surveillance room, one of the men made a call to McCall.

"Detective?" he told her. "Yes, you were right. She's made a break for it."

———

Williams stood outside Brooke's room. He knocked and waited for an answer. Even though she was officially a prisoner, he somehow made her feel like she was a guest.

She answered with a, "Come in", and waited to see who would enter. Brooke smiled as he entered and gave a small bow with his head.

"I hope you'll forgive this intrusion," he said softly. He stepped aside to allow two women to enter. One carried a dress of red lace and silk, with high-heeled shoes to match. The other had a make-up bag and hair styling equipment.

"I believe you like opera?" His words had a mix of pleasure and anticipation of the answer.

"Yes...yes, I do." Brooke looked around at the women as they made themselves busy arranging the equipment, ready to get to work.

"I have a small engagement, after which I am hoping you will join me at the National Opera House," Williams told her. Brooke was taken aback by the gesture. Confused, but flattered.

"Aren't you afraid I will try to escape?" she asked with a childish grin. Mr Williams just smiled and shrugged.

"I think I would be disappointed if you didn't at least try," he spoke softly. She thought for a moment, before giving a large grin and nodding.

"Then thank you. I would love to go."

"Good, it's settled then. I will leave you ladies in peace." Williams bowed again and left, locking the door behind him. Brooke smiled, calculating that it might be a way to break out. The National was a great place to draw attention. But she knew that he would find some way of keeping her quiet. Perhaps he'd use the threat of snipers, or the murder of her family. She knew he was anything but stupid, which made her wonder why he was doing all this. Was she a prisoner? Or just a heavily guarded guest?

Williams headed down the long corridor slowly, his hands tucked behind his back. He was strangely quiet, almost as if he had received grave news. Halfway down the long corridor, beside a photograph of a woman and a baby, he stopped and pulled out his cell phone and pressed the speed dial. His eyes locked onto the picture on the wall. It was at least twenty years old, if not more; the texture was old and grainy, no high-end high definition camera was used. The ten-by-eight lay in an ornate gold frame. It was next to several other pictures, these being of the same baby as a child and then as a young woman at school.

"It's arranged," he muttered into the phone. "Now it's time for your part."

Slowly, he tucked away his cell phone and carried on back down the unlit corridor, whose only illumination was the stream of light that flooded through the French windows. Williams went along like a man in his nineties, his movements weak and feeble as if he had to drag himself across the wooden flooring.

Soon he reached his office. He poured a large brandy then sat down hard in his office chair. Williams's eye transfixed into space, as though something had appeared in the empty corner of the room. His gaze went far beyond the confines of the room.

There was a knock on the door. Williams's silence caused the caller to knock again. Williams said and did nothing, merely stared into the golden liquid in the glass. The young friend of his secretary walked in with trepidation, the look of fear for entering without being summoned evident on his face.

"Did you find the taxi driver?" Williams asked, his gaze still fixed on the aged liquor.

"Uhm... yes sir," the nervous young man replied. "Unfortunately, it was while the police were pulling him out of the Hudson."

"I see. So that's a no then really... isn't it? You found a corpse that used to be him but was not really... him."

The man squirmed where he stood, almost terrified at giving the only answer he could.

Slowly, Williams turned to look over at the pale, shivering man. Williams's eyes held a callous, unnatural look. Angry, but at the same time touched with playful excitement, almost like a cat who was having a psychotic moment.

"I gave you a simple task. Not much to ask, I would have thought. I asked you to bring the taxi driver to me." Williams sighed, the brandy swirling in the glasses as he rotated the crystal with his hand as he sat back into his chair. He looked over to the roaring blaze in the fireplace. The flames leapt up from the crackling, over-seasoned wood.

"Find me the waitress, alive and unharmed. Can you do that?" Williams asked.

"Yes ... Yes, sir, no problem." Instantly, the man cursed himself, as the promise slipped from his lips, realising that what he had just said had sealed his fate.

Williams peered around the side of the tall back of the chair, a broad grin on his face.

"Oh, I do hope so," Williams's voice tore through the man's soul, almost causing the man to piss himself where he stood.

Mr Williams sat back into his chair, the sound of his cackling laughter continuing even after the door had been closed. The man was sweating buckets as he left. He knew if he messed this one up there wouldn't be enough left of him to be found in the Hudson. The sound of his running filled the corridors as he sprinted.

He had to find that waitress.

———

Tara needed to get up to town and had less than an hour to do it. The Metro was the best way, but not the safest. Muggers were the least of her problems. Not that they had ever been a problem in the past. The people who had killed Amber were after her and most probably knew where she was. If she took the train, she would have to ride it until the end, allowing plenty of time for someone to do something. She would have to keep an eye on all the passengers, see who stayed and rode the train. See who was looking suspicious and who just stuck out as different from the norm.

The worried young woman hurried down to the subway station. She soon blended with a crowd that had gathered at the turnstiles. It was a large group of fifteen people, probably students at NYU mixed in with people trying to be on their way. She waited her turn as the tickets slid into the slots of the waist-high turnstiles. Green arrows on the top of the scanner flashed as each ticket was approved. Tara looked at her watch: she had a good forty minutes to get to the compound.

A disapproving beep signalled that the man in front's card was either damaged or had just run out of credit. His friends laughed at him and waved mockingly. Tara rolled her eyes. She couldn't afford to make a scene or be identified, just in case the cops had put out an alert for her.

Then a nearby Metro cop took the man's ticket and checked it. Slowly he entered the piece of card into the slot. The light showed green, and he thanked the cop with an embarrassed grin. As the man's friends heckled him, Tara moved through the stall. She knew her card was new and hoped for no dramas. Tara faced away from the cops as she tried her travel card. The light turned red and spat the card out. Calmly, she repeated the process only to have the same response. She grabbed the card and rubbed it between her hands as if she was trying to warm up the barcode. For a third time, the scanner beeped angrily and returned her card. Tara felt the cop approaching behind her.

"Trouble, miss?" asked the same cop. Tara turned slowly and handed the card over, all the time trying to keep her head down so he wouldn't recognise her later. He took the card and checked the date. He slid the card in slowly and smiled at her as it showed green. She thanked him and scurried off towards the green line. Immediately, the cop lost his smile and pulled the radio mike on his shoulder towards his mouth.

"Control, this is Two-Zero Charley. We have a positive ID on the woman. She's heading uptown on the green line."

"Copy that, Two-Zero Charley," a woman's voice responded. The cop went back to his post, his eyes turning to the next horde of people.

Tara moved quickly onto the platform and looked around for a place to blend in with the crowd. She knew that if she just stood around, she would be picked out instantly. Her best bet was to join a group. She smiled as she spotted the group of students that had gone through before her. Carefully, she nuzzled next to them enough to appear to an outsider as if she was one of them. The group was so large that even they never noticed the extra member amongst them. Hiding in plain sight was always the best camouflage.

There was a rush of air and the sound of metal wheels clattering on iron rails. The train was on approach, and soon she would be rich. She smiled to herself as the train screeched to a halt and the doors slid open. A crowd of people pushed past, their eyes mostly fixed forward, looking at nothing but the stairs, down, and avoiding all eye contact whatsoever.

Tara had often wondered why everyone on the Metro avoided looking at one another. It was almost as if giving someone the wrong stare would get you into trouble. It was the same with elevators. Whenever she had gone into one of those mysterious boxes, she found everyone suddenly backed onto the walls, almost as if the sides had been magnetised.

The ride was a long one. Every time the train stopped and exchanged passengers, Tara would make a mental note of who was new and who had stayed put. From what she could see, everyone was getting off, all except two men. One was a young guy in his twenties, medium build with red dreadlocked hair and a goatee. The other was in his forties, tall with black styled hair, and wearing a blue pinstriped business suit. Neither of the pair paid her any notice. The suit was busy reading the *Financial Times* and the other guy was playing some game on his cell phone.

Tara looked out of the window. Flashes of electricity lit up the darkened tunnel. She rested her head against the cool glass and stared into the nothingness of her mind. Her memory slipped back to that fateful night when this whole thing had started. That cold, wet night when she had found her friend dead on the sitting-room floor.

There was a screech of metal on metal as the train began to slow. The walls began to get brighter from the lights of the approaching station. Tara's weary gaze rested on the glass and the reflections of the people gathering to get off. Tara's eyes wandered from person to person. She was spying on them as the shuffled about, eager to find a spot. Suddenly, Tara felt her heart almost stop; she had caught a glimpse of what she thought was her boyfriend's face. An image that lasted but a second, caught in the reflection of the glass. She turned quickly, only to see a woman with a child in her arms. Tara's gaze shot back to the window and hurriedly, scanned the crowd for any sign of him, hoping that using the reflective surface wouldn't draw attention to her.

Tara's heart began to pound in her chest with excitement. A sudden feeling of hope rushed over her as her eyes checked out every person who had gotten off. The feeling slowly faded as the train pulled away. He was gone – dead, the police had said so. Her imagination had given her false hope, or indeed may be false hope had tricked her imagination.

She looked up at the map on the arched information boards on the upper walls. There were another five stops to go. She sighed and looked back out of the window. She was tired of running. She was tired of being scared. All she wanted now was to disappear and have a good life.

The journey took another fifteen minutes. Each time the train came to a station, Tara checked the people's faces. The suit and the red-haired guy had gone two stops ago. Now only a fresh batch of faces kept her company. Finally, the train came to her station. She rose from her seat as the train came to a grinding halt. As the doors slid open, she was carried by a wave of people to the bustle of the platform. The smell of diesel and warm metal filled her nostrils. The overpowering smell of too much perfume emanated from a large older woman in front of her. Tara pushed her way forward, wading through a sea of men and women who were all desperate for the freshness of the outside air.

The bright light of the morning sun was welcoming. A breeze carried the smell of the city with it: a mixture of the traffic and food stalls. Tara checked the time. It was a quarter-too, and she still had a way to go. She had no money for a cab and hitching wasn't going to happen.

Her plan had been too hasty, and Tara wished at that moment that she'd thought it through properly. Tara knew that she should have called while she was getting closer. However, it was too late now. She had to see it through. She let out a determined grunt and pressed on. Tara reckoned that she had at least a forty-minute walk. *Too late now*, she thought to herself.

A large black SUV pulled up beside her; the window was down. She stopped for a second and looked over. At first, she thought it was some rich tourist looking for a monument or a hotel. She leant in and spoke with the driver and then got in. She smiled to herself at her good luck. The driver was going her way. Now, at last, things were turning around.

CHAPTER FORTY

McCALL WAS PISSED. THE LAST REPORT SHE HAD GOTTEN was at the subway where Tara had got off the train at East 143rd Street. The techs had come through and traced the text. The message was obvious, but even before that, McCall had a gut feeling about the woman. The 'tail' had lost Tara at the top of the stairs, and now it was up to Traffic to find where she may have gone.

The cynical detective knew that Tara was travelling light on cash, so that removed the possibility of her taking a cab. Unfortunately, the techs could only find the text. The number she sent it too was taking time to find. McCall paced up and down, growling under her breath at another stroke of bad luck.

She stopped and looked at the murder board. There were too many bodies on there for her liking and not enough suspects. The few there were, all had alibis. She looked at each picture once more, hoping something would leap out her, something she had missed before. They were all linked somehow. Her eyes moved over towards the photograph of Adams. He looked smug and arrogant even in his six-by-four photograph. McCall turned and headed for her desk. Her coffee had gone cold by now, but that didn't bother her. Coffee was coffee.

McCall stood in front of her desk and flicked through her notes while drinking her hour cold coffee. Just as she lifted the cup to her lips, the desk phone gave off a dull electronic ring. She picked up the receiver and waited for the next big bit of bad news.

"McCall... Homicide," she said, then listened as one of the security guys for the witnesses explained about the documents Becca had brought with her.

McCall had thought they were just every day meeting presentations for the board. She sat down hard as the other cop explained what the documents meant.

"Are you sure about this?" she asked. "Why didn't she... Never mind. We need those documents sent to Financials ASAP," McCall said. She listened to the person on the other say their " will do's" McCall sighed before speaking again. "Don't let her out of your sight. Great, thanks." McCall shot up out of her seat and pulled her gun and shield from the top drawer of her desk. She clipped on the gun holster and shield onto her belt and arranged them, so they sat correctly. Tooms and Tony looked up in surprise at her sudden movement.

"What's up?" Tooms asked, getting up and hurrying over to her, his jacket already in his hand.

"Get your stuff together. We're going to pay Mr Adams a visit." She looked over towards Tony, who was getting out of his chair.

"Tony, see if you can get a warrant to search the Trent Shipping Company."

Tony gave a quick salute to the order and started filling out the request form on his computer.

"What's it for?" Tony asked as he opened the form.

"For all the records and data in Amber's office. Computers, hard copies, you name it. I want it. Also, get SRU to meet us there."

Tooms noticed her eyes sparkling with joy.

"I think we've found a motive," she told them, "and I think I know where Tara is heading." She said nothing else, just headed for the elevator. As Tooms caught up with her, he could see her satisfied grin.

"So, what's the plan?" Tooms asked. "Bust in with loads of cops and scare the hell out of him?"

"Sounds like a plan. Get some uniforms to come with us just in case the bastard causes any problems." Tony could see in her eyes that she hoped that Adams *would* be a problem. She was blaming him for Steel and Amber's murders. A guy with that much money wouldn't do time; he'd probably get off with a fine and community service.

As the elevator doors opened, they saw Brant looking his usual gloomy self. He saw the excited looks on their faces and chose to ride down with them. McCall and Tooms stepped inside the elevator and stood either side of their huge captain.

"I take it you have something?" Brant asked while facing forward, his body rigid.

"Becca, the woman who worked with Amber, she had some documents that implicate the Trent Shipping Company in smuggling," Sam McCall explained.

"Smuggling what?" Brant asked her.

"By the look of things, just about anything, to anyone. Mostly containers to Africa or Middle Eastern countries. Usually places with trade embargoes. Could be guns, drugs, even people. He doesn't care. If it makes a profit, he's into it."

Brant nodded but kept his statue-like stance, almost as if they weren't having the conversation. "So, you think Amber stumbled onto this?"

McCall shook her head. "No, sir, I think it was her job to find it. We know she was working undercover. She must have found something when she was working at the hotel, and that's why she changed jobs."

"So how does Tara Burke fit into all this?" Brant asked as he watched the numbers on the panel illuminate, showing the floors they were passing.

McCall shook her head and shrugged. "In truth, sir, I have no idea. Maybe they were friends. Remind me to ask her when we find her again," she said awkwardly.

Brant shot McCall a look that made her step back slightly. "What do you mean, find her... How the hell did you lose her?"

"They lost her at the Metro," McCall told him. "We're checking traffic cams now, just in case she got picked up." Brant gave a usual scowl and nodded.

"What's your plan for Adams?"

"We're gonna sit on the place until the warrant comes through. Make sure he doesn't disappear anywhere." McCall's voice almost purred at the thought of taking Adams down. Williams had warned her of the potential danger, that's why she was taking back-up. Tony was also on the phone with SRU. If it was as bad as Williams had explained they needed plenty of firepower.

"Watch your back you two, and make sure you get that son of a bitch," the captain told them. The doors slid open, and the two detectives strolled out. They never looked back as Brant watched them walk away. As the door slid shut, he suddenly had a bad feeling that one of them wasn't coming back from this one.

———

The SUV dropped Tara off on the corner near the entrance to the compound. The driver hadn't said much. Normally she wouldn't take rides from strangers, but there was just something about this driver that felt right, safe. He had worn a black suit that must have cost more than she made in two years, and the SUV must have cost a bundle as well. And since he didn't have 'axe murderer' written all over him, she took a chance.

But she did wonder why he had stopped to pick her up and why he just happened to be going that way. Those questions had only just come to her, questions she should have asked before getting into the car. However, she was there, and she was safe.

The wind had begun to pick up, blowing loose dust into the air and creating a funnel. From where Tara stood, the yard looked empty. Everything was still, no movement of any kind. No people were wandering about, no trucks moving – nothing. In fact, the only movement was that of the large cargo train that had just pulled in at the back of the compound. Tara shuddered as she had the feeling someone had just crossed her shadow.

Her eyes took in the surroundings, scanning the buildings for any signs of life, but she found nothing. Slowly, she moved forward, the wind pressing against her, almost as if it was trying to push her back. Even though she managed to walk casually towards the large main building, she was terrified inside, wondering if she had thought this through properly.

Tara moved past the security gate. Peering inside she saw the small one-person box was empty. The wind howled as she moved across the large empty parking lot. She looked around, constantly turning as she went, hoping to see someone – anyone. Tara began to get a bad feeling in her stomach, but there was no going back – not now.

She arrived at the entrance of the main building. Its towering walls cast a huge shadow which covered most of the buildings behind it. She tried the main doors, but they rattled in her hands. Both doors were locked. Her feeling of uneasy was now screaming for her to run – and keep running. Tara looked at her watch. It was now noon. She tried the doors once more, before cupping her hands to block out the daylight as she peered through the glass doors, but all she saw nothing but emptiness.

She was about to head back to the parking lot when she heard a noise: the sound of metal banging against metal. Slowly, she edged around the main building and headed for the warehouses. Tara felt alone, and her body trembled with emotion. As she neared the corner of the building, she saw the rows of warehouses, in front of which stood columns of ICO containers, stacked up ready to be shipped. They were laid in three rows, each was three high, with each row was seven containers long. She looked down one of the lanes to see the door of one of the warehouses swinging freely with the breeze.

It was like a bad horror movie. Tara knew she shouldn't go there, but she felt drawn somehow. Slowly, she headed for the door; her back held firmly against the cold metal of the containers as she steadily made her way.

High above her, on the roof of the main building, a sniper had her in his sights. The bolt-action hunting rifle was made more for hunting game, but the .303 full metal jacket bullet would do the job regardless. His fingertip paused on the trigger as he waited for the signal. His target was a good two hundred metres away. At that range, he couldn't miss. He held his breath and waited.

He smiled at the thought of taking her head off. The crosshairs of his rifle were following her figure, resting on different parts of her body. He could go for a kidney shot, or maybe just take her apart piece by piece. However, he had his orders: shoot to kill but only on the signal. He was already loaded and ready to go. He smiled again, disturbing thoughts rushing through his mind.

The sniper never heard Steel come up behind him. Steel's gripped the shooter's chin and the back of his head. It was a swift motion. A quick lift and twist-action followed by a sudden crack as the head separated from the Atlas bone in the neck. Tendons broke and ripped. There had been no sound; it had been a quick and silent death.

Steel swung the sniper rifle off the dead man's shoulder and lay down next to the fresh corpse. Using a pair of laser rangefinder binoculars, he scanned the area, searching specifically the places he had noted on the plans.

The two snipers on the far warehouse roofs each took a headshot: a simple kill at four hundred metres. The next two were on the roofs of the containers. Each one of them was lying down flat until the signal was given. A quick shot to the base of each of the heads made sure that they stayed down. The SRS sniper rifle made little noise, a meer sound of the metal on metal as the action worked and a gentle sound like gas escaping from the suppressor. No sound, no mussel flash.

With the snipers gone, Steel knew he was going to have to move. The containers would provide cover and plenty of shadows. The top cover had been taken care of, so now it was a matter of minimising the numbers. Steel slung his rifle and took the sniper's 9mm Glock 17 and a couple of spare magazines he had found in the man's jacket pocket. Steel slid out the magazine from the pistol grip, pushed down on the top bullet with his thumb. It was stiff with little give, a good spring, little chance of feed jams. The clear magazine showed the clip had the full fifteen shots. Steel replaced the clip then slid back the top slide on the pistol enough to see the glint of the top round in the chamber — fifteen in the mag – one in the pipe.

Steel made his way down using the outcrops of the building, such as window ledges or anything that gave enough grip to hold onto. He didn't have time for staircases.

As he touched down onto the hard concrete, he rushed over to where Tara was going. The warehouses were large and multi-levelled: good for a killing ground. Steel made it to the middle one and clambered up the side. He had to get high, and he knew the best vantage point was the roof. When he made it to the sheet roofing, Steel moved quickly and silently. His goal was the open window near the centre. It was a maintenance hatch as well as part of the skylight. He looked around at the other warehouses. They all lined up, with enough room between them all for the large forklifts to go about freely. At the far end, the train that had pulled in stood motionless as the crew waited for it to be unloaded. It was a long snaking thing with a mix of boxcars, containers and fuel pods.

Steel neared the small window hatch and looked inside. One guard was right below him – a small, stocky man, who was probably one of the workers and not a gun for hire. His long black hair and beard fell onto his red-and-blue chequered shirt. His arms, covered with tattoos. He was a rough-looking guy who looked more at home with a knife rather than a gun.

The black-clad intruder slowly opened the hatch, holding his breath as though it would help. A sudden squeak of metal made Steel freeze the motion, but luckily the man below didn't flinch. Slowly, Steel carried on until the hatch was fully open. He couldn't understand how the man had not heard the noise, for it had been loud enough. That's when he saw the earbuds. The guy was probably listening to the ball game. Steel smiled at his good fortune and eased himself down behind the guard. Steel could tell that the man wasn't interested in being there, he'd probably been told he'd get a bonus in his wages if he just stood there with a gun.

Steel threw aside palm at the man's neck. He watched as the man's knees buckled and then caught him before he slammed onto the metal flooring. Steel stayed in a crouched position; his long coat splayed out over the grated metal. He looked around for more gunmen. There were two more, and they looked as uninterested in their jobs as the first. The man at his feet carried an MP5K—the short 9mm weapon had a double magazine and a red dot sight. It was a fine weapon for close quarters but wasted if you didn't know what you were doing with it.

John Steel took off one side of the shoulder strap and pulled it from the prone man's body. Picking up the machine pistol, he reattached the strap and slung the weapon. If he were correct, the men would do one thing if challenged: run. He looked down to see Tara heading across the floor towards the exit. The men on the other side of the building just looked down at her and did nothing. Steel had begun to wonder if Adams had any real fighters with him. If he did, they were probably as close to him as possible, and he was as near to a getaway plan as he could be. Adams was in it for the money, nothing else. If there were any wet work, he would get someone else to do it. He watched as Tara exited the building. Quickly he headed across the walkway to a pile of crates. These were only stacked, thus forming a perfect step way.

As he hit the cold concrete, he looked up at the men who just stared down on him as though nothing was amiss. These men were bait: a reason to make someone to open fire and alert the others. But he wasn't going to give them that chance. He wanted to catch them unawares.

Slowly, he edged out of the building and ran across the open ground towards the next warehouse. This time a perfectly parked truck gave Steel the boost he needed to climb to the roof. Carefully making his way to the apex, Steel noted the buildings around him. There was nobody, the place was quiet and still. This worried him because it meant that if there were men out there, they were taking cover. As Steel reached the apex, he suddenly hit the deck as a large blade came flying overhead. He rolled as the blade came crashing down, creating sparks as metal hit metal. Steel looked over to see a huge thin man wielded the huge machete.

The man was around six-foot-five, large hands with long fingers gripped the massive blade. The man was slightly bent at the shoulders, giving him a ghoulish appearance. His face was long with a pointed nose; his eyes were sunken and dark, and rat-like teeth protruded passed thin pinkish lips. His naked upper half was covered with scars and tattoos on pale, leathery skin.

He smiled at Steel, who just shot him a surprised look back. The blade came down again and again. Each time, Steel rolled, and the sparks flew. The blade smashed down, and Steel rolled back onto the blade, locking it into position before landing a double-footed kick onto the man's chest. The man flew back but landed on his feet. A menacing grin crossed the man's face as he pulled out another blade from the sheath on his leg. Its blade was long and brutal. The eighteen-inch length glistened as the sunlight caught its polished sides. Blood grooves in the shape of a dragon were cut into the solid frame. The jagged teeth of the top serrations looked animalistic.

Steel could have shot him, but the noise would carry and alert them to the invasion if they didn't already know about it. Steel picked up the dropped machete, and the two men circled each other. The larger man lunged forward, and with a rear spinning motion, brought the blade around. Steel rolled and gave an upwards kick, catching the brute under the chin. The man didn't even flinch, instead carried on the movement, spinning like a tornado. Each time Steel did the same but targeting different parts of his opponent, trying to find his weak spot.

As Steel kicked up once more, but the man grabbed Steel by the leg and swung him like a ragdoll. Steel skidded across the roof, sliding towards the edge. Panicked, Steel drove the blade into the metal to try and stop his descent. There was a loud squeal of metal on metal. As Steel got to the edge, he brought the blade down again, and he felt it plunge deep into a weak spot.

The man looked down at Steel angrily, disappointed at his opponent's luck. Slowly he strode over to Steel, who was half hanging over the edge, fighting to clamber up. The man reached down and picked Steel up by the knife arm. He held Steel high and smiled. Grabbing Steel's other arm, he began to pull. Steel felt his arms being pulled out of their sockets and let out a cry of pain. This made the man grin even more. Steel pulled all his strength together and brought his arms inwards. A shocked look covered the brute's face, stunned as he was at Steel's power. That second of amazement and lack of concentration cost the man dearly.

Steel pulled his knees up and hooked his feet on the man's belt. Leaning back, Steel broke free from his grip and at the same time delivered a double chin-kick. The knifeman stumbled backwards, disorientated. Steel quickly jumped up and gave him a double flat kick to the chest. The brute stumbled and hit a weak spot in the roof. There was a loud scraping noise as the section of roofing gave in, and the man fell, screaming. Large, heavy sheets of metal followed, crashing down on the man, burying him under the debris.

The detective didn't stop to find out if his attacker was alive or not. Tara was walking into a trap, and she didn't know it. He knew the tell-tale signs. The way everything was laid out, the lack of innocent people, in fact, the lack of anybody apart from the odd few.

He raced to the roof's edge just in time to see Tara approach a covered walkway that was surrounded on either side by stacked wooden crates, ICO containers and large cargo containers. Steel guessed that this was the load-on and load-off point for the trains. Two large cranes loomed overhead; their thin-looking frames silhouetted by the afternoon sun.

Tara moved slowly towards the strange walkway. The wooden construction would have looked more at home on the side of a lake, rather than in a haulage company's backyard. She stopped around twenty feet shy of the entrance. Her stomach was telling her to run right now and get the hell out of there. But she had business to attend to. Down the centre of the eight-foot-wide path, wooden crates no more than four feet square had been stacked up to form an L shape. These zigzagged all the way down, forming a chicane. The lack of wind or even a slight breeze gave her an uneasy feeling. It was almost as if the world was holding its breath in anticipation.

Everything that had happened had led Tara up to this point. Her choices were clear: stay or leave – it was simple. But each choice had consequences. Either she could leave and run for the rest of her life, always looking over her shoulder, or she could move on down the path, and it ends. One way or the other, it ends today.

She felt alone and tired. The strength she had displayed over the phone at the hotel was almost gone. The emptiness of the compound was designed to do one thing: to smash her confidence, instil fear into her heart, and most of all, make her feel utterly alone.

Then she saw something. Someone was moving forward. The person was cloaked in so much shadow that delineating its gender was impossible. There was just the hint of movement heading her way.

Tara stood frozen to the spot. Her body pushed her to start running, but her legs were as firm as the Statue of Liberty.

Suddenly the stranger stepped out of the shadows but remained on the wooden decking of the walkway.

Tara's eyes widened, and her mouth fell open.

"You!" she yelled out. "But... but you're supposed to be dead!"

CHAPTER FORTY-ONE

Tooms held on for dear life in the front seat of the Mustang. McCall was driving as if she was in the Indie 500. The busy streets gave way to the weaving GT 500 as if she had dynamite strapped to the sides. The hidden police lights in the grill flashed to give a warning, and the horn did the rest. Over the roar of the engine, the sound of the car's media system kicked it. The Bluetooth feature on the system had picked up an incoming call. McCall looked down quickly at the caller's ID. It was Tina's work number.

"Hi, Tina, sorry I didn't make it down. What you got?" McCall said as she forced the Mustang past two other cars.

"Well, I just finished doing a DNA check on your Mr Crispy to see if it is John Doe, or whatever his name is now," the ME told her.

"Nice. And is it him?"

"I found skin fibres on a piece of rope that had been used to bind the hands. Somehow the body had prevented it from catching fire and preserved it. We tested this, and it was a match to your John Doe." Even over the phone, Tina could almost sense McCall's look of disappointment. A witness had been kidnapped and killed on her watch, and Tina knew McCall wouldn't take that well.

"So, it was him. Oh shit."

"Uhm, well..." A note of uncertainty was in Tina's voice.

"What...*uhm?*" McCall asked impatiently, swerving fast, and thereby forcing Tooms's face against the door's window.

"I found a piece of undamaged flesh at the back of the throat; this, however, didn't match. In fact, he hasn't matched to anything yet," Tina said gingerly.

McCall suddenly felt as if she'd been fooled. Was John Doe alive and part of this? Or was someone playing games? Either way, they were going to confront Adams because she was sure he was behind all of it. Tina had hung up after getting another call, and this suited her friend fine. She wasn't in a talking mood.

"What the hell is going on, McCall?" Tooms screamed, more at the near crash with the VW Golf in front of them than anything else.

"You can ask Adams when we get there, preferably while hanging him out of his office window," Sam snapped back. Tooms shot her a look, but she didn't register it. She knew where Tara was going, and she hoped she was wrong. All roads led to Trent Shipping.

"Do you think he had Steel killed?" Tooms asked his boss.

"Probably. Who knows? I can't see him doing it himself though, more likely he'd contract out a hit on him or get one of his goons to do it. Adams is a businessman, not a mobster."

"So, do you think John Doe is still alive or is someone just messing with us?"

McCall shrugged at the question. Then after a short while shook her head. "I honestly don't know, Joshua. One thing is certain, we've got a corpse in the morgue that someone has gone to a lot of trouble to disguise." Suddenly she thought back to the conversation with Williams. He had warned her about the threat. But she still didn't know why he had done so.

"But there's one thing for sure. I know who *isn't* in the morgue," McCall said confidently.

———

"Hello, Tara, you're looking ... different," said Amber as she stepped out of the shadows. Tara could feel her legs begin to buckle under the stress of the situation. Amber was the last person she had expected to see there.

Distant sirens made Amber look over towards the cluster of buildings. She smiled and walked back down the walkway as though nothing was wrong.

Tara was still frozen to the spot. A mixture of fear and anger washed over her. She screamed loudly and rushed forward, chasing after the disappearing shadow of Amber.

Steel had made it to the roof's edge just in time to see Tara standing there like a statue. She appeared to be talking to someone, but part of the roof hid the other person from view. A sudden burst of sirens made him turn and look towards the gated entrance. Six black-and-whites and an SRU van were being led into the premises by a blue Mustang. He smiled as he watched the metallic beast skid to a halt, kicking up a cloud of dust and loose gravel.

The van emptied, as did the patrol vehicles. The SRU teams got into formation as they prepared to take the main building. They formed up in single file with the point man carrying a ballistic shield. The man behind him held his FN SCAR-L high, the barrel held above the shield for covering fire. They moved as one, each arc of fire covered, including the rear.

Simultaneously, the uniformed cops got out of their

vehicles. Black Kevlar vests covered their torsos, and they were armed with M4A1 assault rifles and Mossberg 590 shotguns. As the SRU entered the main building, the uniforms split off in pairs and made for the warehouses. Steel knew he had to leave. The sight of an armed man on a roof would only add to the stress of the situation, and most probably get him shot.

Steel knelt quickly as he saw McCall head for the corner of the main building. She wasn't going in. He probably thought she would leave the chaos to everyone else. As she grew near, he could see the look on her face, that 'something's not right' look.

As she got to the corner, she began to run. Steel looked down to see she was heading for the covered walkway. He figured she had seen Tara and was now heading after her. He got up quickly and headed forward, towards McCall, using the containers as if they were steppingstones. He had seen how everything was laid out, and it screamed set-up.

McCall got to the start of the walkway. She held her custom Glock tight in a double grip and pointed at the ground in front of her, a standard safety precaution. It meant that if Tara were to come around the corner suddenly, McCall wouldn't blow her head off by accident: better a bullet in the ground than an innocent life taken. That was something she had experienced long ago, and she had no intention of making the same mistake twice.

As she got to the first set of arranged boxes, two men appeared from nowhere and opened on her. The few seconds she needed to raise and fire the weapon were not enough — a hail of 5.56 impacted with the boxes, turning them into matchsticks. Something hit McCall hard, throwing her to the ground just as a volley came her way. Stunned, she checked herself over. Confused, she looked down, finding that her hands were covered in blood. She checked herself again, but she found no wound.

"I am not hit, thank God, I am not hit," she thought out loud, then her eyes moved from her bloodied hands to where she had been standing. Her mouth fell open in surprise. There, leaning against another set of boxes, was Steel. He was busy inspecting a nasty looking wound on his left shoulder. She didn't know whether to be angry, happy or just plain astonished. Her thoughts and emotions were being tossed around like rocks in a concrete mixer.

"Steel?" she said, stunned. "But you're – !"

" – bleeding. Yeah, just a little but don't worry, it's nothing."

"What...?" McCall shot him a confused look. After all this time letting her think he'd died, and that's all he could come out with?

Another spray of loose gunfire shredded the box above McCall's head, causing her to keep low. She returned fire but was quickly made to dive to cover. Steel pulled out the 9mm Glock that the sniper had been carrying and dropped the magazine from its housing. There was a full clip. He slid the magazine back into the housing, leaned out and opened fire on his attackers. He caught one of them in the shoulder, which sent him spinning. The other one concentrated his shooting on Steel's position, which gave McCall a chance to open fire. Four of her rounds impacted with the man's cover and the other two caught him full in the chest. The man stumbled back and swore loudly.

"Shit, they've got vests on!" she growled with disappointment.

"I do love well-trained bad guys, don't you?" Steel said as he found shelter behind a group of large crates.

"Why's that?" McCall yelled out, annoyed at his childish grin. Three bursts of single-shot tore into the wood above them.

"Because they use the same weapons and they only fire the necessary number of rounds," Steel said, getting comfortable.

"And that helps us how?" screamed McCall as she slapped in her final magazine into the Custom Glock 17.

"It means more guns and ammo for us when we take them down," Steel said before disappearing behind some crates. Sam McCall shook her head in amazement. She had forgotten how she had missed him, yet right now, she wanted to shoot him herself.

There was a mass of gunfire. Stray rounds went wide and impacted with the stacks of crates and cargo storage on the outside of the walkway. McCall sat with her back against the cover and waited. In the distance Tooms and Tony ran towards her, using as much cover as possible on the way. Tony dived for cover where Steel had been sitting, while Tooms's massive form joined McCall.

"Well, I see you found the bad guys," Tooms joked as the whistle of stray 5.56 bullets made them lean away from the noise. McCall could see the shapes of the SRU teams heading towards them. Rounds impacted with their ballistic shields, forcing them to move slowly.

"McCall, are you hit?" Tony asked, looking at the blood on his hand.

"No. It's Steel's blood. He got hit when he rescued me." She smiled awkwardly, knowing exactly how it sounded.

"So, Steel rose from the dead to save you. Did you hit your head or something?" Tooms asked, checking her head for wounds.

McCall slapped his massive shoulder playfully. "No. It appears our Mr Steel didn't die after all, well not yet anyway," she said angrily. She opened her mouth to speak again, but the sudden silence stopped her. All three detectives slowly stood up, their weapons trained forward, ready to take down anyone with a gun. McCall and Tooms looked at each other, both utterly confused.

"Do you think we scared them off?" Tooms asked jokingly as the SRU teams rushed forward to meet them.

The three detectives took up the rear as the tactical teams swept past them. Slowly they moved as one, each covering the other. There was a strong smell of freshly fired weapons which hung in the back of their throats.

Next, the point man threw up a clenched fist, signalling everyone to stop. He turned to the man behind him and pointed to one of the men who was lying on the ground. The third man moved forward while everyone covered him. The SRU man checked for a pulse then gave the thumbs up. Quickly, he zip-tied the injured man and checked him for hidden weapons and knives.

As he rejoined the group, they swept forward until they got to the next man. He, too, was searched and restrained.

"Where are we going, Detective?" asked the SRU team leader.

"Follow the bodies." She shrugged.

"Sounds like a plan," he answered, shrugging back as they all set off down the walkway.

———

Steel had used the cargo containers as cover as well as a walkway. He was positioned too high up for the enemy to see him, and what's more, they were fully occupied by laughing and shooting. They weren't guns for hire or a couple of mercenaries. They were just two guys that probably worked at the company driving forklifts or vans. Either way, they had been given a couple of extra bucks and were enjoying the chance of shooting at some cops.

Both men were in their late thirties, with bulky figures and shaven heads. The guy on the left had a black goatee, and both his arms were covered with tattoos. The other was a no-neck with a nice big scar on his left cheek. They both wore body armour and used M4 assault rifles. The belts around their waists were full of magazines for both the rifle and the 9mm Glocks they were packing.

Steel sprang from one stack to the other. His long coat carried up by his movement. The loud clatter from the unsuppressed gun barrels drowned out any noise. He stopped and crouched down to get a better view. He judged that these weren't bad men, just idiots having some fun. Steel headed for a stack that was close to them and hurried over. It would have to be quick, for he couldn't risk the other guy getting the drop on him. Steel felt the adrenaline course through his veins. He took a deep breath and made his move.

In one swift movement, he had dashed across the stacked cargo and jumped for the roof. Like an athlete, he leapt up and caught the roof's edge, his legs swinging up, and at that moment he released his grip and double-kicked one of the men in the side. His victim was thrust into the crates behind him, impacting hard onto the wood, knocking him out cold.

The second man turned, a look of utter surprise on his scarred face. This expression was wiped away by a blow from his fallen comrade's Glock.

In one fluid movement, Steel had kicked the first man. As he rolled, he'd picked up the loose 9mm pistol from the ground and tossed it at the second man. The top slide of the weapon met the man's skull on the bridge of his nose and above his left eye. The stricken man saw stars for about a second as he stumbled about, then he crashed to the ground unconscious.

The first guy was out cold as he lay in a pile of splintered wood. Steel didn't know whether his comatose condition had been caused by his kick, or from the apparent masses of alcohol that was probably oozing out of the man's bones. The spent roll-ups, and empty beer cans on the ground next to his firing position spoke volumes. These guys were so high they probably thought zombie hordes were coming, not cops.

Steel looked down towards where Tara had made off too. There were six more possible firing positions, which was five too many. Steel headed out and back to the tops of the containers. He had been lucky this time. Next time he might be up against mercenaries.

The next two guards turned out to be more of a challenge. These were weekend warriors: the guys who had all their combat gear. The first guy was in his forties, stocky, with a camouflaged baseball cap. The tattoo on his right arm said *Ranger*, but Steel figured he had failed to get into decent military units, let alone Special Forces. He had probably used his apparent 'Ranger' status several times in the past to get laid.

Since this man was bulky, a kick wouldn't work, not a kick in the chest anyway. However, he screamed in pain as Steel's double kick landed perfectly on his left knee. His gun hand gripped the pistol grip tightly as he fell, letting loose rounds cascade down the walkway and towards McCall. Steel quickly stood on the man's wrist, forcing his hand to open. The detective then quickly kicked the weapon up towards the second, skinnier man, who dropped his weapon to catch the empty M4. Shocked at what he had done, the second man looked down at the weapon and then at Steel. Those few seconds cost the man the contest. He was not Ranger material: A Ranger would have never dropped his weapon, and even if he had, he would never have taken his eyes off the enemy.

The second man dropped to the floor. His nose was

bleeding from where Steel had roundhouse his head straight into the nearby boxes. The first man got a pinch to the neck just to stop him screaming.

Then it was back to the silence. Back to the shadows.

The walkway led out into another open area. Three large warehouses stood lengthways, and behind them was the train yard. This area was predominantly for the loading of large goods for rail travel. There was a massive fifty-foot gap between the walkway and the warehouses: a perfect kill zone.

Steel looked up at the warehouses, taking note of their apexes. These would provide perfect cover for even an average sniper. However, Steel knew that this was where Adams's best men would be. Taking the sniper rifle from his back, he used the scope to search the rooftops. The meshed lens cover Killflash extension would hide the scope flash when the sun hit it. The gauze construction had saved his ass many times in the past. The whole point of being a sniper is not to be seen, and it isn't solely to kill. It was something his employers had spent a great deal of money on training him to do.

The Englishman spotted six men, two on each rooftop, each one spaced out at either end of each building. It made firing back and hitting them almost impossible. Or almost impossible. Steel got himself into a comfortable position before firing. The shot was complicated, as all he had was the weapon sights and not much of a view of the men's heads.

They were good. Now it was time to see if he was better. Steel knew he would only have a couple of seconds before they registered his muzzle flash and returned fire. Even with a suppressed weapon, the flash is visible, denoting the small explosion when the bullet leaves the gun's barrel when all those burning gases that force the bullet out are suddenly released.

Steel knew he would be able to get at least two, maybe three, of them before he was spotted. The distance between each man was large, making moving the weapon and staying on target a bitch, especially with the cover he had. The best thing about this shoot was the lack of wind. Just a sudden breeze could make all the difference between a hit and a miss. Millimetres on the scope was inches on the ground. Add a gust of wind, and it could be feet.

The marksman lined up his first shot. He adjusted the sight. He had a good line on the top of the man's head, but he chose the scope instead. If it went high, he would get him either way. Steel's breathing became shallow, almost non-existent. He would have to fire between breaths, for each inward breath would make the weapon rise. Breathe in ... Hold ... Fire ... Breathe out.

Steel rechecked his first target. Everything was perfect. His finger paused on the trigger, ready to take the slack, waiting for that first click before pulling and holding. Everything was ideal.

Suddenly there was an ungodly scream and Steel suddenly felt himself being picked up and thrown. As he hit the warm concrete of the open area, he rolled on his side to allow himself more breathing space. He looked up to see the thing that had crashed through the warehouse roof. The beast of a man was blooded and scratched. Bits of broken metal stuck out of his body, but he seemed unaffected by them. There was a loud crack as one of the snipers open fire, but Steel had moved just as the beast had brought down a massive boot where his head had been. The sniper's round hit the beast in the left shoulder. He screamed in pain and looked up at the shooter.

Then the beast's attention rested on the men on the roof. The sniper went pale as the beast began to climb the side of the building as if it was a child's climbing frame. Steel saw the opportunity and took it. He didn't have time to play. Tara was in danger. He had lost sight of her at the walkway, but there was only one place she was heading, and that was the train.

So, Steel rushed for the gap between two of the furthest warehouses. Above him shots rang out, followed by deathly screams. But he didn't stop to look. If he was right, whoever she was meeting wanted her on that train. If that happened, she would never be seen again, and Amber's killer would also be long gone.

As Steel made it to the corner of the building, more shots rang out. Two men stood by a carriage doorway, and their MP7 machine pistols sang a deadly tune. Streams of automatic 4.6 x 30mm rounds shattered the wall next to him, causing Steel to dive for cover behind a steel cargo container. The sound of hollow banging filled the air, like a wild beast trying to get out of the metal box. Steel waited until they had stopped firing. A few seconds was all he had before they could reload, depending on how good they were. Quickly he leant out and shot both men in the left kneecaps and fired another into their right shoulders. The men dropped, screaming in pain just as the train's whistle blew.

Steel's eyes searched the carriage windows and found Tara walking with two other people. The glare from the sun on the windows made the view to the interior almost impossible. However, one thing was sure: he had to get onto that train.

The monstrous EMD GP50 locomotive began to move. Its blue painted sides sported the Trent Shipping logo and a sign he had seen somewhere before: a red horse's head on a white background. There was a loud bang, and a screech of metal as the haul was suddenly being heaved forward. The snaking line of carriages and flatbeds began to move slowly, but they were picking up speed. Steel grabbed onto one of the railings and pulled himself up before the whole thing lumbered down the track.

CHAPTER FORTY-TWO

THE ENGINE MADE A SLOW START, WHICH WAS ALL THAT Steel needed as he pulled himself to the top of a baggage car. He needed to get to the car where he had seen Tara. The gunmen had slowed his boarding but had not prevented it. However, there was a problem, a big one. Between him and Tara, there were ten carriages. Two carried steel ISO containers, and three were baggage cars. To the centre were two long oval fuel containers, and their polished outer casings glinted in the midday sun. In front of those were three more passenger carriages. Steel knew that these would be filled with Adams's men.

The wind began to pick up, as did the speed. The monstrous locomotive was underway. The blast of oncoming gusts dulled the clitter clatter of metal on metal. Steel knew he had to get inside, out of the blasts of wind somehow. Being outside was going to slow him down. Also, the threat of been blown off was increasing all the time. If he lost his footing, Steel would be blown back several feet – or worse.

Steel moved to the back of the carriage and climbed down.

There was a small window in the door. Carefully he peered in. The car was full of armed men. He counted at least twenty before giving up. There were too many for close-quarters combat. Even if he disarmed one and took his weapon, getting all of them without injury was highly unlikely. Unlikely but not impossible.

He took out the 9mm pistol he had taken from one of the guards. Releasing the clip, he checked it: a full magazine of fifteen hollow points. He pressed down on the top round with his thumb. The spring was forced back on his pressure. He took another quick look, marking where everyone was. Most of the men were sitting down, chatting away. Others were rechecking their equipment. Seven men were standing up. One of the men was hanging off the baggage rail talking to two others. Two were standing next to the end doorway to the next car, making hand gestures as they talked. Another man was a monster who was probably standing because there was no room for him to sit. Even the momentum of the train failed to move him.

Three others stood and chatted with a group that was seated. But the one Steel was interested in, was the one who had just gone to the small toilet. As the man came out, Steel tapped on the window. The guy stopped and turned but didn't move forward. Steel tapped again. The man covered the pistol grip on his Glock with an open palm. Slowly, he moved forward. Looking out, he saw nothing, only the sight of the tracks they had left behind. He turned and began to walk back to his seat. Suddenly the door swung open, and Steel grabbed him and held him in front of him as a human shield.

Some of the men reacted instantaneously and opened fire. Losing a volley of 9mm bullets that ripped into the man's body and his body armour. Fountains of blood tossed into the air as the hot copper-jacketed bullets met flesh. Steel held the dead man and pushed him forward. As he grew near, he quickly put a round into each of the first two groups' kneecaps. Tossing the empty weapon aside, he grabbed the man's Glock from his holster. The pistol barked, and ten more men screamed in pain. There were five rounds left, but he knew it wasn't enough. On one of the seats, a guard's Heckler and Koch 45ACP UMP machine pistol sat ready. As he reached for it, a huge man, who appeared to be larger than a bear, suddenly ripped the blooded human shield from Steel's grasp.

What was left of the man smashed against the back wall, leaving a red stain on the window and wall. Steel fell to the ground before he could grab the weapon. A thick beard and facial tattoos covered the monster's massive, leering face. His grin revealed yellow, badly fitted teeth. His brown eyes that appeared to be almost black were wide with bloodlust. The man leapt towards Steel with malicious intent. Steel managed to roll backwards in time to avoid the giant's grasp. As he landed on his knees, Steel picked up one of the weapons that lay on the ground and fired into his shoulder. Steel's face dropped as the bear of a man bellowed and powered forward. The 9mm rounds just had the effect of pissing the man off. Steel looked at the pistol and then at his attacker before groaning with disappointment.

The man swung a massive open palmed hand, hoping to either catch or smash Steel in a sideward blow. Steel dropped to the ground barely in time, as the massive paw sailed over his head, and he felt the breeze scrape his scalp as he fell. Steel lay on his back and elbows for a second, looking up at the giant, wondering how he was going to get out of this one. The giant lunged again. Shocked at the man's speed, Steel double kicked upwards, hoping to catch him in the crotch. But the man was too quick and grabbed Steel's legs and swung him towards the windows.

Steel impacted with the large window and cracked the

glass. As he fell, the remaining two guards ran for him. Steel reached over to a pistol that lay next to one of the injured men. He grabbed it and put one round into each of the men's right knees. Screaming, they hit the ground and cradled their wounds. The giant ran for Steel, his hands raised, and fingers extended, looking like a monster from the old black-and-white movies. Steel spun round on his back and let off two rounds into the man's right foot. There was an explosion of red, and the man screamed and fell hard, nursing his foot, and his missing toes.

The detective jumped to his feet and grabbed one of the assault rifles from a bench. He smashed the butt of the weapon into his enemy's face several times. Blood flowed freely from his mouth and nose, but he kept coming. But his movements seemed laboured, as though he was trying to grab Steel by instinct rather than rational thought. Steel landed another blow, splintering the plastic grips of the rifle. This time the giant fell to the floor, spark out. The weapon was twisted and bent from the impact, and he tossed it away and picked up another that was lying next to one of the unconscious mercenaries.

Pulling off the double magazine, he checked that both were full, then slid it back on until it clicked home. Steel headed out of the railway car, leaving the injured men to their wounds.

The next car wasn't as full, but they were ready for him. As he opened the door, he dived inside. Automatic gunfire ripped into the door and surrounding walls. The men were in two groups and two ranks, each of which was using the seats as cover. Steel fired back but was quickly edged back by the onslaught of bullets. The first rank would fire, followed by the second as the first row reloaded.

Bits of timber from the bench flew up in the air. There were flashes of light as metal on metal gave short flaming sparks as the bullets hit railings and parts of the structure. Steel fired a quick burst from his FN SCAR, and five men were pulled down with shoulder wounds, while the others dived for cover, their ranks were broken. It allowed him enough time to move forward. As he went, he picked off any unlucky soul who was too quick to return to his post. The weapon was held high, and the butt fully pressed into his shoulder, his cheek resting on the guard, his eye trained on the red dot sight.

Four more of the enemy stood up. Steel fired only single shots, each one aiming for a hit in the shoulder. Another four stood up, but this time they were firing. Windows shattered, but each shot was a miss. Steel returned fire. Sparks flew as rounds impacted with the metal posts as the men took cover. They fired back, hoping to pin Steel down.

Their ears rang with proximity gunfire, and the overpowering stench of spent black powder hung in the air. Steel fired again, first towards the men on the right. The rounds missed. But he knew the men on the left would be breaking cover, and his weapon was already pointing in their direction. Each of them was too slow to fire, a single shot to their shoulders putting them down screaming, with blood oozing through their fingers as they held their wounds. Steel re-aimed his weapon just in time to catch the men on the right. Steel's gun roared, and the men fell with wounded shoulders.

Satisfied that the train carriage was secure, Steel knelt and relieved the men of their weapons and magazines, tossing what he didn't need under the wheels of the train.

The next carriage was empty, apart from the piles of military equipment boxes. Weapons, ammo and explosives were arranged in three different stacks. Steel opened the door he had just come from and took several shots at the carriage link. Sparks flew and a there was a scraping sound as the carriages separated. He didn't need soldiers coming up behind him, injured or not. He would have enough to contend with as he moved forward, so he didn't want to have to watch his back as well. Steel slipped in another double magazine into the weapon, cocked it and moved forward.

The next two cars were fuel containers, each one around twenty feet long and made of oval steel. Steel couldn't go over them. At the speed they were moving it would be like walking on ice in a wind tunnel. He would have to go alongside or underneath. Moving along the side would be slow and leave him vulnerable while clinging on underneath would mean he'd be hanging on for dear life. One slip and it would be game over: hitting the tracks at high speed would grind him into the unforgiving steel, where he would be chopped to pieces.

All his options had risks, and all were as crazy as his being on the train in the first place. He looked at his choices again, standing with a foot on each carriage, weighing up the pros and cons.

Suddenly the window behind him shattered and he looked up at the guards on the far fuel carrier. Steel dropped between the carriages and grabbed hold of whatever he could, clinging on underneath the train's chassis, just as a barrage of bullets came down from the two men above. As he held on to his assault rifle, he felt it begin to drag as it became caught on the tracks slipping past him at speed below.

Steel managed to hold on as the weapon began to pull him from his handhold. With all his strength, he managed to pull himself up, hoping to create some more distance between his body and the ground beneath. He knew he wouldn't have a chance with the weapon on his back, so he unclipped it and watched it disappear under the train. Sparks flew up as the heavy wheels gnawed at the rifle. Breathing a sigh of relief, he looked towards where he had to go. Underneath the train, all the undercarriage looked identical, making it hard to see which direction he was moving in. There were no slivers of daylight from above to set a marker as to where the next break in the carriages was. All he could do was gaze forward and begin moving.

Steel dragged himself along the undercarriage of the train, easing himself along the grease and grime-covered underbody. Stones shot up like bullets, thrown up by the wind and wheels. The stench of fuel and hot metal nearly choked him, making him look down at his feet to gasp for air because it was clearer than the oncoming gust. The clatter of the wheels on the track was deafening, but he knew he had to carry on. Tara was in danger – they all were. Steel dragged himself along to the next car. He had no idea what was there, who was waiting for him – possibly no one, or a boxcar full of mercenaries. Either way, he had to get from under the train and detach the cars – separate Adam's from his men. As Steel came up to the edge of the carriage, he waited to ensure his enemies weren't waiting for him. Steel held on as the train snaked its way along the miles of track. As quickly as he dared, he moved under the next carriage and headed onwards, using the underside as cover, hiding his approach. A risky manoeuvre for sure, but less dangerous than staying above, and visible.

The next car was a fuel carriage. It was a large cylindrical container held in an open metal construction. On each upper corner of the open crate knelt four guards. They waited for their prey to make a move. They waited for the first sign of Steel, anticipating his movements, waiting for him to move along the carriages. There were two of them on either side, each guarding a corner. They were well placed; each man had an arc of fire that would cover the front or rear of the container. Each man had a throat microphone and headset so that they could talk over the din, as well as ski goggles and a face mask against the wind and dust. They figured that Steel wouldn't be foolish enough to go over the top of the boxcars and wasn't crazy enough to try going underneath. They hoped he would go through the cars, using up his ammunition as he went. As they waited, they never noticed a figure emerge from between the carriages. They weren't aware of Steel removing the securing pin that held the carriages together. The men thought that the judder of the car was just the track. As they held on, they swore at the driver because of the rough ride.

"Shit...tunnel," screamed one of the men. All four guards made themselves small as not to slam into the oncoming stone construction. They laughed as the darkness passed, and they were once more in the open.

"That was fuckin close," laughed the man on the rear right.

"You got that right, look out next time you bastards," yelled the man on the rear left to his colleagues at the front using the small communications set they had to talk over the noise of the train.

"Maybe next time we'll just let the fuckin bridge smash you off ya perch, might improve ya looks," laughed the man on the front left. The man on the rear left replied with a sharp upper thrust with his middle finger.

"Hey...?" asked the man on the rear right, looking around puzzled. "are we slowing down?"

"Nah, it's just your brain," laughed one of the men. They all laughed. Suddenly their laughter stopped; they all started looking around. Something was wrong.

"Shit...we are," yelled the man on the front left, confused. The men looked over at the car in front, just in time to see the train disappearing into the distance. The men at the rear guard opened fire at the last car indiscriminately. Hot copper impacted with the sides of the far fuel tank.

"Ceasefire, you idiots!" yelled the men at the front as they dove for cover. The men at the rear guard stopped firing and let out a cry in anger.

"Are you trying to blow us to kingdom come, you bunch of dumb asses?" he screamed. One of the men stood up and ran over to the man at the front right, squaring the man off. "Who you callin' dumbass?" the big man said before spitting a gob of saliva onto his boss's boot. There was a hiss as one of the control panels on the carriage began to spark. Their eyes widened with horror.

"Oh, shi..."

The shockwave from the explosion downed some of the trees and ripped up the track. Loose stones were hurled in every direction, impacting against the cart above him. Steel smiled to himself as he watched the red-and-black plume of fire and smoke. He turned and climbed up the cargo containers. The roof of the containers was flat with hook holes for the cranes, which he gladly realised he could use to crawl along the top of the container. Steel's body was flat against the cold metal as he dragged himself along, the gusting wind doing its utmost to rip him from the surface.

Steel reached the end and peered over the top. The area below the freight cars seemed unguarded. Slowly he climbed down, fighting against the torrent of wind. The carriages had no windows, only a pair of heavy steel doors on the sides for loading and smaller doors for access from one car to the other. The walls had a strange patterned surface, with one-foot-square sheeting. To most people, it would just look like an elaborate pattern, like some type of old Japanese armour.

He tried pulling at the handle as slowly as possible. It turned easily, making no noise. All the while, Steel had a bad feeling about what was going to happen. So far, the operation had been too easy. Finally, there was a click, and the latch was released. Steel carefully opened the door and peered in. His mouth fell open at what was in front of him.

"Well that could certainly be a problem," he said almost casually, before closing the door again, equally as carefully.

———

Amber walked through the carriages with purpose, her head high. Her back was straight, and her long legs strode out as if she was a model on a catwalk. She wore a black business suit with only a waistcoat but no blouse to cover her bare chest.

Tara followed the other woman until they reached the furthest carriage. Inside it was set out like a modern office, and ceiling lights brightly lit the interior. It was a long room filled with a wall cabinet on the right-hand side and a couch on the left next to a long cabinet. All the furnishings were of black hard plastic that glistened with an unnatural glossy finish. Two leather armchairs with stainless steel legs sat side by side, and a huge black desk made from the same material was at the end of the room.

Behind the desk sat Adams. His face was emotionless and cold.

"Thank you for joining us, my dear," he said graciously. "Please sit down." He ushered Tara towards the seat opposite him. Carefully, Tara moved over to the high-backed leather chair and sat. The leather creaked under the sudden pressure. Amber moved away to the side of the room.

Two medium-built men dressed in black suits with black, high-necked T-shirts, stood either side of Adams's chair: bodyguards with short-cropped hair. Two other men of the same build stood guarding the door, their hands crossed in front of them, like bouncers at a club.

The long cabinet held a silver ice bucket and five champagne flutes. Large cubes of ice surrounded a bottle of Bollinger Special Cuvée. Amber picked up an already half-filled glass from the tray. Moving to the long black leather couch, she slowly eased herself down and relaxed. Adams smiled as if everything had gone according to some strange plan. Tara suddenly had a bad feeling, a feeling she couldn't explain, almost as if the situation was about to get worse. She could feel the beads of sweat beginning to form at the back of her neck and brow. She was glad she was sitting, for her knees had lost their strength out of pure fear.

"So, do you have it?" Adams asked before taking a sip from his champagne flute.

She said nothing, just nodded quickly.

He smiled and eased back into his chair. "Do you know what you've got there, young lady?" His words were soft and calm. Tara shivered at the question and the tone he was using. She would have preferred it if he had yelled at her. In her experience, good news was never given in such a deadly calm tone.

"It's just some bank accounts or something," she suddenly bit back, feeling a sudden rush of adrenaline. The more she looked at Adams, the more she felt anger swallowing up her fear. She began to loathe him as he sat in his fancy chair, behind his fancy desk, wearing his expensive clothes.

"You have no idea, do you?" Adams said smugly but also sounding curious. "Why on earth would you steal something if you did not know what was on it? What were you hoping to achieve?" His voice held an undertone of mockery. Tara watched as he took another sip from his glass.

"Maybe because she wanted to get back at you?"

A familiar voice rang out. Slowly from the shadows, stepped Jake Harding.

Tara's eyes widened at the sight of him, but not with joy. Her expression was one of disdain.

"You shit!" Tara growled. "I thought I'd killed you back at the apartment. I should have finished the job!"

Adams looked at her and then at Harding, who was moving towards the glasses of champagne.

"So, what connection do you have with her?" Adams asked, clearly confused.

"I was her boyfriend, I helped her to steal the stick," Jake Harding went on. "It was simple, really. She makes food delivery and grabs the stick. If she's caught, it doesn't come back on me, and if something was to happen to her afterwards—"

"—There's nothing to tie her to you. I get it." Adams's voice grew deep with disappointment.

"And why did you want the information? To blackmail me?" Adams gripped the desk with both hands to stop himself leaping forward to attack the smug Harding.

"Don't be stupid, Mr Adams, blackmail really! My sister asked me to get it. Personally, I don't even know what's on the damn thing, nor do I care." Harding smiled and looked over Adams's shoulder. There was a loud thumping sound followed by a piercing scream from Adams. Behind him stood Helen Adler holding a builder's industrial nail gun.

Harding paused before taking a sip from the champagne. "You didn't bring that with you, did you?" Harding asked her, almost afraid of the answer.

Helen looked at the gun and then back at her brother. "No, I found it at the yard, thought it would come in handy." She laughed, throwing it to the floor.

Tara had stood up, shocked at these revelations. Adams was still screaming in pain. Blood flowed freely from his hands, which Helen had nailed to the table, palms downwards.

"What are you doing, your crazy bitch?" screamed Adams, tears of pain gushing down his red face. Tara just stood and looked around at the people before her. She watched Helen as she walked past the desk and headed for the champagne.

"Don't worry, Mr Adams; I'm just finishing what we started. There's nothing for you to worry about ..." Helen paused, then shot Adams an apologetic look. "Although actually, that's not true. You have a lot to worry about, you see, Adams, you're getting blamed for everything. Amber's murder, the kidnapping of dear Tara here ... and, Oh yes, the SANTINI organisation wants its disk back. Apparently, you stole that as well. You naughty boy."

Adams scowled at Helen, who just smiled and blew him a kiss. He stood up suddenly in anger, but screamed in pain, momentarily forgetting about the nails embedded in his hands.

"You'll never get away with this!" he yelled at her. "The organisation will learn the truth, and they'll come for you." Adams spat his words as if they were venom.

Helen laughed out loud, clearly uninterested in his threats. "My dear Mr Adams, by the time they work out what's going on we'll be out of the country and far away." Her smug smile almost made him flare up again, but the bite of the metal in his hands soon stopped him.

Tara turned to Amber, frowning. "I...I don't get it, you...I saw your body at the apartment...you're dead?" Tara said, her words broken out of confusion. Amber looked shocked at first, almost as if she had no idea what Tara was talking about.

"Just a nobody we found in the street one day," Harding supplied the answer with a grin. "Her resemblance to Amber was almost uncanny Amber here was meant to watch you, that's why she moved in."

Helen took up the story. "It was all part of the plan, you see. I was to make sure you went through with picking up the disk and handing it over. Gaining your trust was easy. You are a sucker for a sad, hard times story. My dear brother, here was just another part of the plan, get you off balance. At first, I didn't think you would go for it, with your trust issues and whatnots, but well fuck me, if you didn't fall for him,"

Tara looked from Helen to Amber, who just shrugged and took a sip from her champagne.

"I thought you were going to kill me, that's why I hit you," Tara said, looking at Harding.

"Knocked me the hell out, more like it," Harding groaned, rubbing his head, remembering the pain from the blow from the heavy lamp.

"Yes, Tara, he was supposed to kill you," Helen continued. "It was one of the reasons we staged dear Amber's death, to make it look like a homicide robbery, then we planned to hack into medical records and swap them so that the 'Jane Doe' – the nobody whose body we left in the apartment – would come up as Amber Taylor. Unfortunately, you were quicker than he was. But all things considered, it worked out nicely." Helen chuckled callously.

"And the body at the park?" Tara asked Jake Harding. "The police said they'd found your body at the park, burnt and unrecognisable?"

"That was another unfortunate soul," Helen replied. "He had crossed the wrong person and got himself torched. Jake lent a bit of his skin and so, hey presto, we had the corpse of Jake Harding." Helen's words danced out of her mouth as if she was enjoying explaining the details of their devious scheme.

Tara felt confused and lost. She had been set up to take the fall when they hadn't succeeded in murdering her. Tara thought she had all the cards, but she soon realised she had none. They had played her like a fiddle, and she had let them.

"So, where's the disk?" Helen asked, sitting on the edge of the desk in front of Tara.

Tara's hand reached into her jacket pocket and felt the USB stick there, tucked into a corner.

"I don't suppose you're going to let me off the train if I give it to you?" she asked.

"I promise you'll leave the train at the next station," Helen said with a broad grin. Her eyes were open wide at first and then closed slightly in a snake-like manner.

Suddenly Tara knew that her enemy was lying. She had the feeling that the train would still be moving when they passed the station and threw her off.

She had the feeling that this was the end of the line.

CHAPTER FORTY-THREE

Steel moved slowly over the top of the carriage. Inside were ten large canisters, each of which had a biohazard warning sticker. Red blasting cable stretched between each barrel like a spider's web. Several large, green wooden crates sat in the middle of the room. The boxes had military markings and the words C4 marked in thin black stencilling.

There was no way through it, and he had no intention of going underneath the train again. He didn't know where they were all heading, but he knew one thing – *Terminus* was going to have a new meaning. The sound of the wheels clattering on the tracks was rhythmic, mixed with a whooshing noise as the train hurtled along, completing the concerto of deadly speed. Steel looked up at the roof of the carriage and knew what he had to do. Slowly he began to climb. Using the small maintenance ladder on the side, he ventured up. At the top, he slowly peered over the edge of the roof to ensure that he was alone. The curved metallic surface was empty. Along the top, Steel noticed several hatches that stuck out in a zigzag form. He smiled at his good fortune, for these would be good as both foot and handholds, making his crawl across that much easier.

As he ventured over the top of the carriage, the wind blew hard into his face. Steel felt the skin being forced away from his features, practically baring his skull. He slammed himself flat against the rough hard metal surface, hoping the hatches would cancel some of the drag. His movements were slow and deliberate. Using the top rail of the ladder as a foothold, he edged forward towards the first hatch.

The wind was deafening as it howled in his ears. Steel winced in pain, feeling that crawling over this roof was like dragging himself over a badly repaired road. The non-slip paint seemed to have small rocks in it, which dug into his hands and knees as he relentlessly dragged himself along. As he reached the middle, he stopped and looked over towards the edge, which seemed miles away from his position. He rested he head on his right hand for a moment, gathering his breath. While in training for the army, he and the other new recruits were forced to leopard-crawl under barbed wire obstacles in deep mud. But compared to what he was doing now, it had been a walk in the park.

As Steel continued his slow crawl across the rail car, he was unaware of a helicopter approach. The blades of the Airbus H145M cut through the air, making a heavy thumping sound. The gloss black finish of its hull contrasted nicely with the tinted windows. On one side was the side spur: a 12.7 mm machine-gun pod. On the other side was a 20mm cannon pod. The helicopter was no ordinary bird: this was one of the organisation's 'attack' helicopters.

The wind blast and *clickety-clack* from the speeding train dulled the noise from the rotor blades. Steel lay on the roof, oblivious to the bird's approach. Suddenly the side door of the helicopter opened, and a beast of a man edged out. The machine was about twelve feet from the rooftop when Steel felt its downdraught. The sudden blast sent him sliding towards the edge. His hands grasped at nothing until he managed to grab onto one of the hatches.

The giant of a man jumped down and landed hard onto the roof, leaving a dent from his impact. Steel looked over, noticing that the giant was so big and heavy, he seemed almost unaffected by the wind. Each step the huge man took was slow and deliberate – it was almost as if the man had a pair of diving boots on. Steel fought to pull himself up and tried diving for the next hatch. As he did so, the giant brought down a mighty boot where Steel's head had been moments before. The wind carried Steel far from where he wanted to be, but he didn't care, for at least he wasn't anywhere near the giant.

As Steel watched the man's movements, he tried to formulate a plan. If he was to defeat the man, he couldn't do it by using his usual tactics. This character was solid, almost as if he were made of iron. No, he would have to find a way to tackle him and fast. The man came forward again, slow and deliberate, but moving quicker than Steel was able to because the wind was virtually pushing him down onto the roof. Steel was too far from the end of the carriage to climb down. His only option would be to go over the side and climb along the walls.

Steel started to jump again, but the giant grabbed him in mid-air. The big man pulled Steel up to eye level. The man snorted, like a bull in an arena. Steel felt the massive hand gripped around his throat begin to tighten. Steel kicked out as he felt his air was being cut off. The giant smiled as he watched Steel squirm in his death throes. Steel couldn't figure out how this giant was staying upright against the wind. Sure he was big and heavy, but it didn't explain how he wasn't blown off the roof despite his size.

As Steel kicked, he felt his foot impact against something

had, not the man's midsection. It was more metallic. Steel kicked again, this time harder. The man suddenly began to slip and lost grip in his left leg. There was a loud thud as they both hit the metal surface. The man gave a panicked look as he pushed some buttons on a small control pad on his belt. A sudden look of terror filled the man's face as both his feet locked down onto the metal surface, followed by a puff of smoke from the pad. Steel's would-be killer looked up from the pad and just started forward. Steel followed the man's gaze just in time to see the low tunnel ahead.

Steel immediately hunkered down and spread himself low and waited until he saw daylight. The tunnel lasted only a few minutes before the bright sunshine replaced the darkness. Steel looked over to see a pair of massive black boots and a blood trail leading from them. Pieces of shinbone protruded from the footwear. The small control unit was waving around, tethered by a six-foot cable.

Steel rolled over to the boots and grabbed the control unit. Using the control buttons, he pushed one of the boots forward and then tried the other. Using them as an anchor, Steel pulled himself over the edge of the roof and slipped down onto the small gantry over the couplings. Steel took a moment to get his breath back, Smiling to himself.

He had one carriage to go, and then he would arrive at the one that held Tara. The carriage behind him had no windows, only a heavy door like the other one. Steel knelt and got to work on the couplings, hoping to split the train from one of its carriages, as he'd done before. As he was working to free up the connection mechanism, the door opened behind him, and a man's voice bellowed out. The man was looking back into the carriage, yelling obscenities to the other guards who he'd been playing cards with inside. The man was smaller than Steel but stocky, his red hair almost hidden by a black skullcap. The man walked forward, unzipping the flies on his trousers as he went. Steel turned slightly just in time to see him.

"Thanks for the offer, but sorry, I'm not that sort of passenger I am afraid," Steel joked with a shrug. The man spun round in shock and went for his 9mm Glock, but he wasn't quick enough. Steel grabbed the man and spun him around and shoved him off the train. The man's pistol clattered onto the deck in front of Steel. Four of the other men inside the carriage had watched Steel throw their comrade from the train, and they raced forward. Steel picked up the abandoned Glock and put a round into each men's right kneecap.

Screams and blood filled the carriage. Gunfire ripped at the doorway, forcing Steel to the side. Bright yellow ricochet sparks lit up the doorway, as the men's Heckler and Koch UMP's opened. The tinkling of spent .45 ACP ammo chimed out as the spent cases hit the hard metal floor. Steel slid out the clip from the magazine housing of the pistol grip. The small holes at the back showed that he had half a magazine left. Steel cursed he had been forced to ditch the assault rifle because of his ride under the train. He waited for his attackers to stop firing, knowing that they wouldn't waste ammo on something they couldn't see. Taking out his cell phone, he took a quick photograph of the carriage's interior.

The photo showed six men, each of them packing a .45 machine pistol. They were spaced out at different firing positions, making returning fire difficult but not impossible. Steel checked the photograph for anything else that may help him, but he had taken it too quickly, the background was blurred. Quickly he reset the camera and took another. This time it showed three of the men approaching slowly.

Steel quickly knelt and instinctively punched at the door. There was a sudden groan of pain as Steel realised that he had unwittingly rearranged a man's groin. In the blink of an eye,

Steel had the man held in front of him as a shield. The man jolted as his comrades opened fire at Steel. The guard twitched as bullets impacted against the human shield's body armour, absorbing most of the impact. Steel had also managed to grab the man's weapon that hung by his side and was firing back, firstly at the two who had followed. The men yelled out as they were hit in the back before they could dive for cover. One of the men flew forward, hitting his head on a handrail. The other was pushed in front of another man's gunfire, the bullets ripping into him like a knife through butter. Steel fired at a fire extinguisher that hung on the left-hand wall. A sudden blast of a white cloud of foam covered the remaining men. Grunts of pain followed coughing as Steel took them out by hand. Swift kicks to the knees brought them down, followed by uppercuts and blows from the butt of his weapon. Steel took another Glock pistol and tucked it away and found two magazines for the UMP from pouches on a fallen man's belt. *No point turning up empty*, he thought to himself.

Moving out of the carriage, Steel used the .45 to blow apart the cup links. A full magazine of thirty rounds ripped into the metal until it broke free. Jumping over, Steel looked back as the carriages began to slow down. He slid out the gun's empty magazine and replaced it with a fresh one, tucking the half-full Glock into his belt at the small of his back. Taking off his trench coat, he rammed it into one of the storage bins for safekeeping. He took a deep breath and waited for a moment, pausing so that his heartbeat could settle. This next part of the operation wasn't going to be about blazing guns: what he had to deal with next was ultimately a hostage situation.

He was going in blind. Not just because he had no idea how many people were in the room, but because he had no idea who was friend and who was foe.

———

Still pinned by industrial nails to his desk in the train carriage, Adams groaned in pain, and the sweat poured down his pale face. Helen smiled as she walked past Tara, her long fingers glide over Tara's shoulders. Tara shuddered but didn't dare move or push her away.

"So, tell me, Tara," Helen spoke as if to taunt her. "When did you learn that Mr Adams here was your father?" Adams looked over at Tara with wide eyes. He tried for a smile, but the pain was too much.

"My mom kept a picture of him in her dresser. He was just some man in a photo until I saw him in the paper a couple of years ago." Anger filled Tara's words. Her hatred for the man who had left her alone with a brutal, abusive mother. Anger at the man who had everything while she had nothing. The man who had tossed his family aside.

"So, you wanted to make him pay, make him suffer? I can understand that," Helen said as she refilled her glass and then took a sip from it.

"Is that why you used me to get the disk for you, or rather get *him* for you?" Tara's words were cold and angry as she turned towards Harding.

"The plan was simple, really. The file goes missing, and I recover it along with the opposition's disk. Adams is disgraced, and I get his job." Helen grinned wildly at the thought of it all.

"I guess I messed that up for you, didn't I? Sorry about that," Tara sneered. She smiled at the thought of causing so much trouble. After all, they had tried to kill her.

"Actually, plan B is much more ... let's say *delicious*." Helen's smiled.

Tara felt a sudden shiver down her spine as she looked around at the people in the room. Something wasn't right.

Helen could have killed Adams, but she was keeping him alive for some reason. Tara looked back at Amber, who was still sitting on the couch. She was quiet and still, but still alive.

"What's plan B?" Tara asked.

"Where's the disk?" Helen parried with her question.

"It's somewhere safe," Tara lied, hoping Helen would buy it.

"So, you didn't bring it?" Helen asked.

"Do you think I am stupid? Yeah, right. Someone tells you: 'come alone and bring the disk'. I ask you! Who would fall for that?"

Helen smiled at Tara's grit.

"It's a pity we have to kill you. I could certainly have used someone like you in my team." Helen sighed and pulled out a nickel-plated Walther PPKS.

"Helen, it's almost time," Harding said, walking up behind Helen, his hand resting affectionately on her shoulder. Helen closed her eyes and raised the shoulder, pulling his hand towards her face.

Tara wanted to be sick at the unnatural display: this was *much, much* more than brotherly love.

"So why keep us alive?" Tara asked, trying to take Helen's mind off her schedule.

"Let's just say that when they find your bodies, they need to be intact. A good ME can tell if you were alive or dead at the time of the crash, and a bullet to the head would sort of put a hole in that plan, wouldn't you say? I need people to think you have set off the bomb and not just become victims of it." Helen smiled and took another sip from the flute of champagne.

"What bomb?" Adams yelled in a rage of pain and anger.

"Why, the bomb that you two are going to deliver to Washington of course. Why else do you think you're in an armoured carriage? Live or die; you'll be classed as guilty. Oh, and yes, the District Attorney is on our payroll." Helen was so exhilarated that she almost sang the words. Tara's head began to spin wildly at the very idea of what was being planned.

"OK, so let's get down to it," Helen went on, all business now. "Where is the disk? And don't say you didn't bring it. Just remember it's easier to search a dead body than a live one." Helen raised the gun and pointed it towards Tara's head.

"You can't kill me. You need me alive, remember?" Tara's voice rang with panic.

"Don't worry, sweetie, I am not going to kill you now. Maybe I'll shoot you in the stomach. After all, some type of wounds would be expected when a bomb goes off. But don't worry, we know how to cover things up." Helen smiled wickedly.

Tara reached into her pocket and pulled out a data stick. Helen's eyes widened. She reached out to grab it.

Suddenly there was a bright flash of light as the door was opened, and it blinded everyone inside the room. It was quickly followed by two shots, each of which hit the guards at the back of the room. The guards at the door raced forward, and their pistols held ready. The bright sunlight behind Steel blinded the men for a second, making them shield their eyes with pain. Steel fired again, putting a bullet into each of the guards' knees. They hit the solid flooring with screams of pain. Then there were two more shots, one of which hit Harding in the right shoulder, while the second hit the ground in front of Helen. The bullet ricocheted off and smashed the bottle of champagne. Glass and sparkling wine ran across the floor near the desk. Helen quickly grabbed Tara and pulled her in front as a shield. Steel had Helen dead in his gun's sights.

"Drop the gun, Helen," Steel ordered. "It's over." His gaze switched from her to Harding.

"No, Mr Steel, *you* drop it!" said a voice from behind him.

Amber had leapt behind the door as he came in, and she had been on his blind side. Now she had stolen the Glock he had placed in the small of his back and was pointing it at the back of his head.

"Oops!" Helen laughed, pushing Tara to one side and walking up to Steel. He dropped the gun and raised his hands just above his head.

"Well, this will look good!" Helen announced cheerfully. "The missing cop is also found. I can't wait to see the headlines on this one." Helen howled with laughter as she picked up the data stick from the floor.

"At last, we've got it!" Helen said exultantly, raising the tiny item as if it was a mighty trophy.

"Uhm ... Not quite," Amber said, now pointing the Glock at Helen.

Helen's smile melted into an expression of confusion, then to anger as she realised, she'd been played all along. Steel just smiled and shook his head.

"Take the data stick from her, Mr Steel, if you'd be so kind," Amber ordered.

John Steel walked forward and stretched out an open hand. Helen slapped the stick into his palm, her face distorted with anger and disgust. Steel turned and walked towards Amber, the smile still on his face.

"I would love to know what you are smiling about, Mr Steel?" Amber asked him curiously. "After all, I have the disk, and you have nothing."

Steel handed over the stick, noticing that her hands were clammy and warm. He could see in her eyes that she was nervous, her act of being hard and ruthless betrayed by her large trusting blue eyes.

"Turn around, Mr Steel," she ordered. Amber knew that he

had seen something. Steel turned around; his hands still raised in the air.

"I am afraid, my dear Amber, that unless you are jumping off the train soon, you will die with the rest of us," Helen said, laughing nervously as she looked at the wall clock.

"What do you mean?" Amber asked, clearly confused.

Helen put her hands down and sat on the edge of the desk, all the while gazing at the other woman with mild amusement.

"She has put a bomb on the train next to some fuel containers," Steel explained. "I figure that it's not fuel in those containers but combustible aerosol or something else that's quite nasty." He looked directly at Helen, who just shrugged and smiled as if she was perfectly relaxed.

"Once we reach the Capitol, it will go off," Helen went on. "It'll be a large explosion, and the fallout should cover most of the area. Once that is done, our 'gang' friends – several lawless groups of people whom we've supplied with plenty of arms – will begin to cause havoc with their new weapons. New York will fall, L. A. will burn, and five other major cities will erupt in chaos." Helen laughed, still confident that she'd be able to get off the train before it reached its destination.

"But why?" Amber asked, almost numb with horror. "Why would your organisation want to do such a thing?"

Steel slowly put his hands down and moved to the side of the room, where the champagne had been. He picked up a full bottle and checked the label before opening it.

"Because they are probably getting a lot of money from a foreign government to do so," Steel told her, pouring himself a glass and taking a sip.

"Not quite, Mr Steel," Helen told him calmly. "Actually, the money is going to be coming from our government. Do you realise the vast amount of money that will have to be spent on contractors, improvements to the police forces and the military? This will see all our armed services boosted no end, equipped with better equipment to tackle possible future problems. What's more, our people will make sure that terrorists will be blamed for the bombs, and then of course plans for retaliation will begin. Do you realise the money involved when there are wars?" Helen's heartfelt words sounded as though they were part of a speech she was delivering to Congress or some other important world forum.

"And of course, your organisation will be right there ready and willing, with all the necessary aid and equipment to rescue the country from its crisis." Steel's words were delivered sarcastically, but all he was saying was nevertheless obviously true.

"How perspicacious you are, Mr Steel," Helen commented, smiling as she pushed herself off the desk and strolled over to a large map of the United States that hung on the right-hand wall.

"All this will soon be ours," she explained, waving her hand across the map. "We don't want to be in the hot seat, that's not where the power is. The power really comes from the biggest companies who have the biggest wealth. The companies that can make or break a nation. Let some well-meaning idiot be president, that's just some public relations guy sitting in a big house who makes speeches to pacify the masses. We hide in the shadows and control everything. We will be unstoppable. We will be—"

There was a massive explosion that pushed the remaining carriages off the rails. The armoured carriage bounced from one set of wheels to the other, almost as if it was trying to right itself. Then there was another explosion, and this was larger, more powerful. The blast heaved the armoured carriage right from the track and set it tumbling down a grassed embankment.

Inside the carriage, Steel tried to find a handhold as

furniture smashed against the sides of the interior. Broken glass and wood flew past them. The heavy desk splinted into deadly pieces of debris. The others screamed as they were tossed about like shoes in a tumble drier, somehow missing the flying broken furniture. Adams screamed as he was ripped from the desktop that he'd been nailed to, his hands virtually torn to pieces. The carriage rocked as it finally came to rest in a stream below them. The box of steel lay on its side and water was beginning to seep in from broken seams. Its interior was partially bathed in darkness, broken only by tiny pockets of cool orange illumination, some of which came from small ambient ceiling lights that were now under the water.

Helen pulled herself up. Small cuts on her face and arms were her only visible wounds, but a sudden wince of pain warned her of possible broken ribs. She looked around and saw Amber slumped over one of the armchairs. Was she unconscious or dead, Helen wondered? Not that she cared, for her, Amber should have died in the crash. Only the data stick in Amber's pocket was of importance. Helen searched wildly to try and find the small device.

When she couldn't locate it, she splashed about in the ankle-high water that was rising all the time. She turned suddenly at the sound of someone's slow approach. It was Harding, who was also visibly wounded. His hand pressed tightly to his left side, and blood oozed through his fingers. She looked at him for a moment, tears in her eyes, upset that her beloved brother was hurt. But then her expression changed as some dark and selfish driving force came over her. She turned back to her search and left her brother as he stumbled forward, using whatever he could find as support.

"Helen, help me... I need a doctor," her brother gasped.

"Shut the fuck up whining and help me look for that data

stick. It's in here somewhere," Helen said, her efforts focused solely on the location of the item she was so desperate to find.

"Sis, *please*, I need help! I ... I think I am dying."

There was a series loud explosion, which caused Helen's ears to ring. She looked over to see that her brother been ripped from the ground into the air. As he hit the water, the dim orange light turned the colour of red wine.

Helen looked over to the side and saw Adams, somehow managing to hold the Glock in his bloodied fingers. His face was twisted by pain, anger and satisfaction. He turned the weapon on Helen. Her face went pale, and her body froze with terror as she stared down the pistol's barrel.

Adams moved around slowly, high on adrenaline which seemed to anaesthetise his agony to some extent so that he appeared oddly unhurt by the tumble. Of course, blood was pouring from the mangled mess that his hands had become, but he didn't care. The adrenaline was doing its job, and his pure unadulterated hatred of the woman in front of him was giving him the strength to wield the weapon.

"Move over there!" he ordered, pointing his gun at the door they had all come through. The water was now up to their mid ankles and pouring in slowly.

Helen raised her hands and looked up at him, bewildered. "But what about the data stick?"

"Don't worry. My salvage crew will find it. In case you haven't noticed, no water is running out of here, it's only coming in. Now ... Move!" He spat the words between his bared teeth.

Helen obeyed, turning and heading towards the door, and clambering over the furnishings that now lay smashed and piled up. The large cabinet lay in a hundred pieces, and the two guards who had been stationed at the door now lay impaled on debris.

As Adams and Helen neared the door, they stopped. Light poured through the open hatch. They looked around in the dimly lit room.

"Where the hell is Tara?" demanded Adams.

"Screw that, where the fuck is Steel?" Helen exclaimed.

They both froze for a moment. Fear ran through their bodies like a rush of ice-cold mercury. Adams pushed the weapon into Helen's side, ushering her out first. She shot him a look of panic, but Adams just grinned and pointed.

"Get your treacherous ass out that door," he growled, almost hoping Steel had a 'shoot the first person he saw' policy.

Helen struggled out of the door, while Adams waited as she walked out into the daylight. He almost seemed disappointed at the silence. Slowly and painfully he then made his way out, pulling on the tilted doorframe to haul himself up.

The air outside was heavy with the stench of hot metal. The warm sun seemed so much brighter after spending so long in the dimly lit carriage. He closed his eyes for a moment, then gradually opened them, allowing them to adjust to the bright light.

Slowly, he clambered up the embankment. His body ached in pain from the tumble. Adams looked around at the burning carriages that lay on the side on the grass. Thick black smoke billowed from the twisted metal. Smouldering pieces of metal and shattered trees littered the landscape. Thick plumes of blackened smoke could be seen around a hundred feet from him as another carriage lay halfway across the tracks. The side panels were gone, blown away, leaving a burning shell.

The train's engine lay down the other side of the embankment. On its side, the wheels were still turning, spitting up grass and dirt as it continued to slide downwards. Adams looked both ways along the tracks. Helen lay on her back, holding her ribs on her right side, a look of agony on her face.

However, Steel and Tara were gone. Adams walked over to Helen and stood over her, his weapon still pointed at her.

"You're finished Miss Adler," Adams told her. "When the council hear of this, they will hunt you down." He took great pleasure in watching her face twist with a mixture of emotions. Adams turned when he heard the subtle thump of a helicopter's rotor blades in the distance.

"It appears my ride is here," he said, smiling and looking away for a second.

"You mean, my ride," Helen said, picking up a razor-sharp shard of metal and embedding it into Adams's stomach.

His eyes bulged, and he bent forward and spat thick dark-red blood. Helen stood up and laughed as the black war bird approached.

"So long, old man, don't worry, I'll take care of your company and your seat on the board of directors!" She laughed out loud until the broken ribs made it too painful. Helen left Adams to bleed out as she limped her way to the helicopter as it touched down. As the wheels hit the deck, the side gunner lept out and helped Helen aboard.

"Any more survivors ma;am?" he yelled. Helen shook her head. As she took her seat, Helen smiled. She had made it. They hadn't. She could tell whatever tale she wanted, and there was no one left to dispute the facts. The downwash pushed the smoke all over the area, creating the perfect smokescreen for her. Just as they began to climb, the machine rocked suddenly.

"What was that?" Helen asked, looking out into the black fog.

"Could have been a sudden crosswind," the pilot told her. "Nothing to worry about."

As they climbed out of the smoke, Helen looked down at the burning debris from the crash. For her, the hellish scenario was a thing of beauty: a wonderful medley of nature and chaos. Helen reached into her pocket and pulled out a data stick. The small aluminium case just looked like nothing at all. However, she knew that this tiny object would change everything.

She smiled wickedly.

She had done it.

She had won.

CHAPTER FORTY-FOUR

"Bitch!" Adams said, watching the black warbird fly away, but he was smiling. From the carriage they had just come from, Tara was helping Amber out of the doorway. The two women walked over to where Adams lay, watching the helicopter disappear into the distance.

"Father!" Tara screamed, running over to Adams, leaving Amber to fall onto the grass from exhaustion. Tara hugged Adams, and he hugged her back. Amber smiled at the touching scene. She stood up and walked slowly towards them.

"Are you OK, Mr A?" Amber asked. He nodded as best he could, with Tara's shoulder in the way. Tara quickly released him after feeling a sharp object pressed against her. She looked down in horror at the sight of the metal shard sticking out from his stomach.

"You're hurt!" Tara protested.

"Only a little, and it's all thanks to your friend Mr Steel," Adams said, successfully managing to pull the vicious-looking shard of metal from his mid-section.

Tara looked confused for a moment. Adams took his shirt off to reveal a thin vest of black weaved material.

"John Steel told me that I might need some security." Adams laughed at his narrow escape while Tara looked confused. "a present from Mr Steel, some kind of bulletproof weave," Adams admitted, punching his midsection in some kind of a display.

"But you're the bad guy! You work for the organisation, why would he – ?"

" – for you, my dear, for you. He figured I was been set up. Yes, he could have let me die, probably would have enjoyed doing it as well. But he said you'd suffered enough. He made me promise to look after you." Adams's voice and eyes boiled over with emotion.

"But you tried to kill her! You ordered her to be captured?" Amber said as she walked towards them. She was still confused by the events.

"The thing is, Amber, everything changed when I found out she was my child," Adams explained. "I may be a bad man, but I am not a monster." Adams stroked Tara's face with a bloodied hand, tears streaming from his eyes.

Amber nodded as she too shed a tear.

"And you, Miss Taylor, a government agent, and quite the role you played. You had me fooled, who were you looking into, the organisation or me?" Adams said with a courteous smile.

"You at first, we didn't know about the organisation or SANTINI until later, Mr Steel filled me in on the details later," Amber admitted.

"So this whole thing on the train...?" he asked.

"Steel's plan, he knew there was someone playing both sides, he just had to be sure his hunch was correct, as it was, he was right," Amber shrugged.

"What about Helen, she got away, and she has the data stick," Tara yelled, looking at the sky where the helicopter was disappearing. From a distance came another thumping of rotors. Another helicopter was on approach. The three people covered their eyes as a black Osprey landed. Its rear ramp began to lower, and from the darkness of the interior, someone stood there ready. There was a whoosh of the downdraft, and then the military craft touched down. As they watched, the figure began to approach the tailgate. There were gasps of surprise from the survivours, less for one. Amber Taylor. Shew stood up and waited for the man to come closer.

"Hello, Father, it's been a long time," Amber said to the man with a dull smile, brushing the dust from her clothes.

———

The black warbird flew to Adams's home in the country, a large estate in Rye. Rye was a quiet place on the East Coast that is an offcut from Harrison, New York. The place is full of tall trees and lawns that are so green you would think they had been painted. It was a sliver of land that was chock full of large estates and the stench of money.

The house was modest compared to some of them in Rye. It had beige coloured wooden walls and a stone-and-mortar chimney stack. A large outdoor pool fitted in well with the lush garden. Flowerbeds burst with colour, and tall oaks lined the borders. It was a modest place in which Adams had spent a lot of time alone since the death of his wife some years ago.

Now a new owner strutted into the house; her head held high as she paraded about, heading for Adams's study. She swung the door open and walked towards a large oak desk that sat next to a set of large windows: windows from which Adams had spent many a morning watching the sunrise, turning his garden into a blazing orange. Helen sat in the high-backed red-leather chair and rocked, taking in the splendour of the room. The walls were half wood and half white-plastered brick. Heavy oak bookshelves held leather-bound encyclopaedias, and volumes from literary giants, such as Dickens and Shakespeare. The heavy desk was clear apart from a computer monitor and keyboard. A brass captain's lamp sat at a corner, under which there was a picture of Adams's late wife.

A portrait in oils hung over the fireplace. It was of an older man, who was perhaps in his mid-seventies. But he had a strength about him: broad shoulders and high cheekbones.

Helen figured it was probably Adams's father or perhaps his grandfather. It didn't matter, for soon it would be put on a large bonfire and burnt, along with the rest of his stuff. She looked around until she spied a wooden globe of substantial size. She smiled and stood up and crossed the thick red shag pile carpet.

Finding the catch on the globe, she slid the top half down, to reveal the hidden drinks cabinet. She smiled and picked out a bottle of Jack Daniels and poured herself a glass.

Helen returned to the chair and sat, wincing with pain from her side. She raised the glass to the portrait and drank. The booze was a good painkiller, but she knew she needed to go to a hospital. She sat for a moment, her eyes closed, feeling the adrenaline fade, but the alcohol was beginning to kick in. She put down the glass and reached into her pocket, feeling inside until she found the data stick. She took it out and held it up at eye level.

It's amazing, how such a small thing could cause so much trouble, she thought as she smiled and placed it down on the desk. She was tired, weary from the day's excitement. But she had work to do.

Helen tapped the space bar on the keyboard, and the

monitor activated immediately. She knew Adams's password was *Victoria*, after his dead wife. She typed with her left hand, to avoid using her right arm, which was giving her pain.

She clicked on an icon of a horse's head. The screen quickly went onto another, presumably secret, site, which also required a password. Helen thought for a moment and then typed in *Faith and Honour*. She knew that this was something Adams strongly believed in. She smiled as the page opened and revealed an online conference mode. Eleven people, men and women, sat around a table, and the empty place there was reserved for Mr Adams. All the other conference members looked shocked to see Helen's face appear at the conference mode.

"Ladies and gentlemen of the board, I have grave news," she started to say. She bowed her head as if to show sorrow. "I have uncovered a plan by Mr Adams to give a copy of our accounts to our enemies. He also constructed a plan to set off an explosive device in Washington. An ex-soldier, Mr John Steel, currently working for the NYPD, was also an accomplice to the plan." She listened to the murmur of voices as the board began to chatter until there was a loud hammering on the long table.

"How do you know all this?" asked the chairman, who was a thin man in his early sixties.

"They kidnapped me and forced me onto the train," Helen replied. "Fortunately, there was an accident. The train was derailed, that's how I managed to escape." Helen made her voice tremble, injecting a false tone of fear.

"Miss Adler, how do we know you are speaking the truth?" came the chairman's voice. "What proof do you have?"

Helen lifted the data stick with a trembling hand. She watched the nodding heads of the board, their faces full of sympathy for her. She felt warm inside, *wanted*. She felt the need to smile, but she knew she couldn't, not yet.

"How do we know you have, what you say you have?" asked the chairman, his voice deep and serious.

"I shall prove it to you," she announced confidently, and then placed the stick into an empty USB port on her computer.

The file started to download. But suddenly the screen started to flash red, and a virus warning came up. Screens containing images of people's bank statements began to appear, and words saying *Data deletion* came on screen too, along with images of files were deleted and, huge amounts of money were transferred into another account.

The members of the board at the conference began to panic, as did Helen. She ripped out the data stick and hit every key on the keyboard, trying to terminate the programme.

Suddenly on the monitor, she saw a man walk up to the chairman and give him a piece of paper.

"What have you done, Miss Adler?" yelled the chairman. "Do you dare to steal from us?"

Helen shook her head frantically, confused and scared by what had happened.

"No!" she screamed desperately. "No, it wasn't me, I swear!" She was still tapping the keys, hoping her actions might bring everything back as before.

"Miss Adler," the chairman's voice growled. "The money had been transferred into an account – your account!"

Helen stood up suddenly, knocking the chair to the ground, her face ashen.

"Oh, and by the way, we know what happened on the train," the chairman continued. "Our late friend Mr Adams was more cautious than you thought. He had an emergency camera installed for such – unexpectant eventualities. We saw and heard everything."

Two men appeared in the doorway to the room where she stood trembling, with 9mm silenced Berretta 9's in their hands.

"We await your arrival, Miss Adler," the chairman concluded.

Helen began to tremble, and sweat began to pour from her forehead. She wanted to run, but she knew that would be futile.

As she to stepped out of the front door, she stopped suddenly. Adams stood there at the rear of a large black Mercedes. As she approached, he opened the door for her and smiled.

They gave each other a silent venomous glare as they passed one another. One of the armed men forced her into the back of the car and then followed her in. Adams closed the door, his grinning face reflected in the car's tinted glass windows.

There was a spit of gravel as the car accelerated away. As Adams watched the car disappear, Tara joined him, holding onto his arm for comfort. Amber and Steel walked up slowly and watched with them.

"Tell me, Mr Steel, how did you know it was her?" Adams asked.

"There was a picture of a staff party at the diner, and something bugged me about it," Steel explained. "Harding was in the background, almost as if he was trying not to be part of the group. Then I saw a picture of Helen at a fundraiser you'd had – for a children's care unit or something I believe."

Adams thought for a moment before nodding as the memory of that day came back to him.

"She was part of the group who helped arrange it all, or so the internet said," John Steel continued. "Anyway, that's when I saw the resemblance: how alike Helen and Harding looked. I mean, they seemed to be far too similar for some random coincidence: these were almost identical twins. I did some digging on Helen and Harding and found that they had been separated as kids and sent to different homes when their parents died. They must have met up years later and re-bonded. She must have seen you, and wanted revenge. After all, it was your family that was to blame for their family's death."

Adams looked confused for a moment, not knowing how he was at fault.

"Their father worked for your father, both employed at a coal mine," Steel continued. "One day there was a cave-in, and most of the miners were killed, including their father. When their mother asked for help, your family brushed them off, denying any responsibility for the aftermath of the accident, saying they were not liable or something. Because she was desperate for money, the mother tried to find work at a factory owned by your family. Two years later the factory burnt down because of faulty wiring. Their mother, along with twelve others, burnt to death in the fire. Having no other family, the kids were taken into care. That's when the siblings were separated."

Adams's gaze fell to where the vehicle had disappeared. A look of shame crossed his face.

"As I looked harder at the photograph, I noticed something about you two," Steel said, smiling at Adams and Tara. "It wasn't something as obvious as Helen and Harding's facial similarity, but you two were alike too. The eyes, the mouth, just little things like that. I also checked on you, Mr Adams. You went to Princeton with Tara's mother. In fact, you dated her for a while. I guess you had a great time, and emotions ran wild?"

Adams nodded with a sense of sadness as he thought back on his previous life, the life he left behind.

"It was a love that wasn't meant to be," he told Steel. "Our parents never approved of it, especially my father. One night after a party we ended up making love at a small hotel. It was the best night of my life. We made plans to run away together, elope to another state. But that evening when I returned home, I was told I was going to be studying business with one of my uncles in London for a year. I met her the next day to explain. She said she understood and that she would wait for me. But when I returned, your mother had gone. Years later I tracked her down, hoping we could start anew, but unfortunately, she was married to the man you knew as your father. It wasn't until yesterday that I found out about you from Mr Steel." Adams hugged Tara, holding her tight, and she hugged him in return.

"But everything else?" Adams asked Steel. "How on earth did you know about it?"

"I bugged your office and Helen's. Luckily she does a lot of business at work." Steel shrugged. "It loses the magic when you know how's it's done, doesn't it?" Steel joked.

"Oh, don't put yourself down, Jonny, I thought you did splendidly," came a voice from behind them. The four of them turned to see Mr Williams standing in the doorway.

"You know this will take some explaining with my superiors. How our enemy saved my life?" Adams joked.

Williams shrugged and smiled. Next to him was a young man holding a silver tray of champagne glasses.

"Oh, I wouldn't worry about that," Williams assured him. "They already know. We struck a truce while things got sorted out. She was doing the same to us. She was the one who hired the taxi driver and poisoned you, John. She put a bottle of poisoned water on the back seat. Apparently, it was laced quite nicely. The driver had no idea, of course, the poor man." Williams handed out the glasses.

"What about Brooke? Is she still alive?" Steel asked.

Williams shot him a dirty look before smiling. "Please, John, don't remind me, that hurts." He put a gloved hand over his heart. "I was asked to keep her safe, and I did so. The trouble is I don't think she wants to leave." His face crumpled with annoyance. "She's so bossy, and eat ... my God, for such a slim woman, she can eat so much!"

Everyone laughed as they headed inside the mansion. Steel stood outside with Amber, waiting for the others to close the door.

"So, what now?" Steel asked.

"Go back to the agency, I guess. My mission is over," Amber said, but she knew exactly what Steel meant.

"You hurt Tony; do you realise that?" Steel said, looking down at Amber.

She nodded, a tear trickling down her face.

Steel smiled softly. He could see she had feelings for him also.

"Well," he said to her, "it may take some explaining, but I am sure he'll understand."

"Do you think so?"

"Are you kidding? Tony is half Irish and half Italian. One half will try and kill you and the other half will try and romance you to death!"

They both laughed. Amber wiped away her tears and nodded.

"I will have a word with him, see if I can get you pair back together," John Steel promised.

Amber smiled and nodded in approval. "I'd like that. Thank you, Mr Steel. Thank you for everything." Amber kissed him on the cheek.

Steel smiled and handed over the champagne glass and breathed in a lungful of air. "I'll see you around, Amber. Keep out of trouble if you can," Steel said as he turned and started walking down the gravel driveway. The door behind her opened, and Williams walked out to join Amber, champagne bottle in one hand and a full glass in the other.

"A remarkable man, that," Williams said, downing the champagne in one. "Pity he's on the wrong side."

"Oh, really? And which side is that?"

"The most dangerous side. His own," Williams said, refilling his glass. "Come on, drink up," he said.

"Yes, Daddy," she said, smiling and watching the man in black disappear into the distance.

———

Streaks of lightning illuminated the night sky. Black billowing clouds approached across the water, bringing with them the storm. It was around seven in the evening by the time McCall had got back to her apartment. CSU was still at the shipping yard, and the derailed train.

It had been a hell of a day. Probably too much for her head to take in all at once. Tooms and Tony had been at the precinct for an hour or so. They had taken the train wreck. But as far as CSU was concerned, it was an accident. The explosion had pretty much evaporated any evidence of foul play, or at least that's what they had been told to say. Sure, it was a cover-up. The news of a faction war in New York would have caused all sorts of panic if it had been made public.

McCall sat on her couch with a glass full of red wine and just sat and stared into nothingness. Steel was alive. She didn't know whether to be angry or happy. Both emotions were erupting through her at the same time. She leant over and grabbed the remote for her stereo and turned it on. The silence was starting to become annoying; She needed something loud – she needed music.

The CD began, a mixed artist album was full of eighties music. McCall stood up and headed for the bathroom. She had good music, great wine and all she needed now was a deep bath, candles and lots of bubbles. She stripped down to her underwear and ran the water into the cast-iron tub, then poured in a mixed concoction of several different bath oils. McCall danced around with the wine glass in her hand while she waited for the water to foam up.

There was a rumble outside, and then the rain started. Suddenly one of her large windows blew open, and the lights went off as a clap of lightning brought everything into brightness for a second before the darkness became almost complete. Several candles around the room gave enough light to move by as she rushed to close the window.

McCall stood half soaked, watching the flash of lightning reflected off the buildings. It was a terrifying yet beautiful sight. She turned and headed back to her bath. Since the power had gone down, the sound of running water was the only noise. Ten large candles burnt brightly in the bathroom, creating shadows and an eerie reflection in the bathroom mirror, sliding a toe into the water she tested it for temperature. It was the right depth and warmth.

She slid out of her damp underwear and into the steaming bath. Her eyes rolled back as she felt the soothing water caress her body. All her troubles began to slip to the back of her mind. The scent of the bath oils and the warmth of the water was making her relax. She tilted her head back onto the bath pillow and closed her eyes.

McCall didn't know how long she had been in the bath, nor did she care. All she knew was that the water was now cold, and her wine was getting warm. Bubbles clung to her body like a strange bodysuit. She towelled off and headed for the living room. The place was still in darkness, which she found strange, as everything outside her window had power. She stared out of the window for a while. The storm had left lakes of water in the street, and several loose items lay there. She smiled at the beauty of the city at night. She sighed and turned. She let out a little yelp of fright as Steel stood behind her. She slammed a fist into his chest.

"Steel, you scared the shit out of me!" she said, trying not to seem glad to see him.

"Sorry. I did knock, but you were asleep in the bath." He smiled.

McCall suddenly blushed.

"I was not. And why were you watching me bathe? And how much of me did you see?" she asked, pulling the towel tighter. Steel stood closer and looked down on her. She could feel his warm breath on her wet skin, and it sent a shiver down her spine. As he moved closer, she could feel her knees begin to buckle with anticipation. He smiled gently. No words were spoken at first. She just wanted him to grab her and kiss her. Suddenly all those dreams she had ever had of this moment were coming true. She closed her eyes and angled her mouth upwards towards his. The feeling of electricity and tension was thick enough to cut with a knife. Suddenly there was a loud banging on her front door. McCall rushed over to the door to see who was there.

"Who is it?" she yelled in annoyance behind the closed door, not wanting to open it because she was still half-naked.

"Miss McCall? Hi, ma'am, it's the building superintendent. Just to let you know that the power will be back on in a minute," the man yelled through the closed door.

"Great, thanks." She tried to stop the anger in her voice because of the timing of the interruption.

She looked over to where Steel had been standing a moment before, only to find the window open and a blue rose on the table next to the wine glass.

McCall sat and picked up the rose and brought it to her nose. The flower's perfume was rich. She looked out into the night and promised:

One day, Mr Steel. One day...

Dear reader,

We hope you enjoyed reading *Blood and Steel*. Please take a moment to leave a review, even if it's a short one. Your opinion is important to us.

Discover more books by Stuart Field at https://www.nextchapter.pub/authors/stuart-field

Want to know when one of our books is free or discounted? Join the newsletter at http://eepurl.com/bqqB3H

Best regards,

Stuart Field and the Next Chapter Team

Printed in Great Britain
by Amazon

44365548R00284